"*Day of the Jumping Sun* does just that. It jumps into the readers' thoughts and takes hold of their attention and doesn't let go until the last page. For the human in us, all will feel the ink bubbling like lava."

—Martin Shone, poet and author

Day of the Jumping Sun

Margaret Panofsky

Day of the Jumping Sun

ISBN: 9781737767183

Library of Congress Control Number: 2022937205

Cover art: Margaret Panofsky
Inset cover photo: David Underwood, fire image from Pixabay

Cover Design by All Things that Matter Press

Published in 2022 by All Things that Matter Press

To my father, Wolfgang Panofsky,
who understood the consequences of nuclear war,
and my mother, Adele DuMond Panofsky,
who worships nature in all its diversity.

"Never forget what I said to Earth, the Queen of us all:
'I shall never own you, and I shall never knowingly hurt you.'"
—Sequoyah

Acknowledgments

Special thanks to my twin brother, Richard Panofsky, for his editing. Without his invaluable suggestions, corrections, and encouragement, there would be no *Day of the Jumping Sun*.

My thanks go to poet and author Martin Shone for writing a prepublication review, and to Steven Freygood who offered the helpful advice I needed to prod me along.

I am eternally grateful to Deb and Phil Harris of All Things That Matter Press for including me among their family of authors once again. Phil remained ever cool and collected as he prepared *Day of the Jumping Sun* for publication.

And I thank my husband, Kent Underwood, for being my sounding board as I weighed this or that storyline.

Huge thanks go to readers of *The Last Shade Tree* who persuaded me that the characters in the first novel still had a lot more to say.

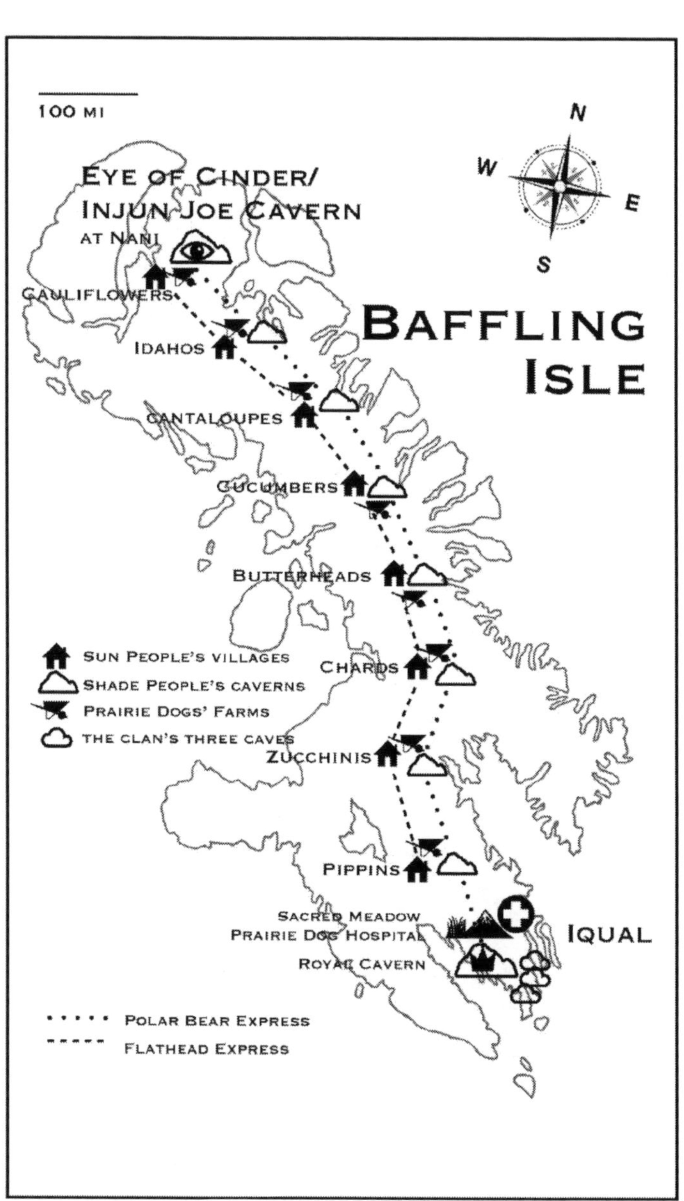
100 MI
N
W
E
S
EYE OF CINDER/
INJUN JOE CAVERN
AT NANI
BAFFLING
ISLE
CAULIFLOWERS
IDAHOS
CANTALOUPES
CUCUMBERS
BUTTERHEADS
CHARDS
ZUCCHINIS
PIPPINS
SACRED MEADOW
PRAIRIE DOG HOSPITAL
ROYAL CAVERN
IQUAL
SUN PEOPLE'S VILLAGES
SHADE PEOPLE'S CAVERNS
PRAIRIE DOGS' FARMS
THE CLAN'S THREE CAVES
POLAR BEAR EXPRESS
FLATHEAD EXPRESS

List of Characters

2050 AD - The Cavern Dwellers

Corpus Lazarus: Reverend of the Holy Cavern of Lazarus Storefront Tabernacle

Cyndi: Corpus Lazarus's wife; later, leader of the congregation

Corpus Lazarus Jr.: Corpus Lazarus and Cyndi's son, blinded by the nuclear blast

Merlin, aka **Mary Lynne**: Teenager adopted into the Tabernacle; a storyteller and seer

Rufus: Cyndi's second husband and lover of Violet; a scientist, botanist, inventor

Violet: Parishioner and artist, lover of Rufus

Lunk: Prairie Dog slave to Cyndi; later, the Prairie Dogs' first queen

A Million Years Later - The Time Travelers

Sequoyah: Adored leader of the three time-traveler families; Aleta's husband

Aleta: Sequoyah's wife, a sensitive and aggrieved soul

Ethan: Luz's husband; physicist/engineer who invented the ship's time-drive

Luz: Ethan's wife; one-time ROTC instructor and Sequoyah's advisor

Jaroslav: Anichka's husband; one-time forester from the Slovakian Alps

Anichka: Jaroslav's wife; a practitioner of Gypsy medicine

Svnoyi: Sequoyah's outspoken teenaged daughter from his first marriage

Kuaray: Sequoyah and Aleta's hotheaded teenaged son, a twin to Yacy

Yacy: Sequoyah and Aleta's artistic teenaged daughter, a twin to Kuaray

Oscar: Luz's teenaged son with spiritual insight

Phoenix: Aleta's younger teenaged son, a botanical expert

Lucy: Ethan and Luz's younger teenaged daughter, liaison to the Prairie Dogs

Agali: Sequoyah and Aleta's adventurous young daughter; Alexej's companion

Alexej: Jaroslav and Anichka's fair-minded young son; Agali's companion

Lucian: Ethan and Luz's one-year-old son, and Arielle Luz's playmate

Arielle Luz: Yacy's one-year-old daughter, Lucian's playmate

A Million Years Later - Inhabitants of Baffling Isle

Queen Gitli: Formidable queen of the Prairie Dogs

Tlke: Queen Gitli's teenaged courtier, who serves with Lucy as Prairie Dog translator

Captain Kirk: Queen Gitli's first husband; the high priest

Neshek: Queen Gitli's second husband; the palace chef

Saint George: Queen Gitli's third husband; the chief warrior

Sanctissima: Young Prairie Dog from the eighth cavern, the Eye of Cinder

Laz-Merlin the Fifteen-Thousandth: Leader and high priest of the Shade People

Corlion: Leader and high priest of the Pippin group of Sun People

Corlinia: Corlion's sister, a bowhunter for the Pippin group of Sun People

Arbel and **Arbeline:** Bear runners for the Prairie Dogs' Polar Bear Express

Ernie and **Bertha:** Bear runners for the Sun People's Flathead Express

Petey: A cloned giant centipede

BOOK ONE

2050 AD

1 ~ Day of the Jumping Sun

Cyndi Grabenstein Lazarus was not a patient mother. She stood inside the cavern mouth, huffing audibly, hands on hips. She scuffed the sand into little geysers with her glitter-painted toenails that stuck over the ends of her flip-flops. With growing exasperation, she used the Lord's name in vain for the fiftieth time that morning.

"*Goddammit,* how long has it been? Half an hour? Only my son, Corpus Lazarus Jr., could get lost walking in a straight line to fill a water jug."

Immediately she felt ashamed. *Jesus Christ, I'm such a bitch. Can't I ever cut my poor kid some slack? He's only seven.*

Cyndi, the least enthusiastic, most conflicted member of the Edgewater, Maryland, Holy Cavern of Lazarus Storefront Tabernacle, suffered another stab of self-recrimination. She hated to admit it, but if she put her mind to it, she could benefit from this annual summer retreat specifically designed for Soul-Cleansing and Self-Improvement. Her face turned red every time she recalled last month's *Hey, Sister! Share-Your-Feelings Seminar* in the Tabernacle's parish hall. The other ladies had voted her "most cynical," "most argumentative," and "least pleasant person to be around," too stinging an assessment to simply shrug off.

She could never quite process the ludicrousness of it all, transporting a hundred people to some cavern. This one was in the upper reaches of Baffin Island, almost at the North Pole. *Why hold the retreat in the goddam wilderness as far away from civilization as anyone could get? We're so close to the North Pole I'll be surprised if Santa Claus doesn't come knocking, asking to borrow a cup of sugar.*

She knew the answer perfectly well. She was married to the man who'd come up with the idea, the Reverend Corpus Lazarus. Personally, she thought it was kind of sick, his Freudian fixation on gigantic holes in the ground. In fact, her husband had built his entire ministry from Storefront to Megachurch on Jesus' miraculous raising of Lazarus from a rock burial chamber. As the Reverend put it every Sunday, "My Brothers and Sisters, tremble not. That ye may believe, our Lord Jesus, in 33 AD, wrested Lazarus from the Plutonian clutches of Death Eternal." Sometimes he substituted "Death Infernal." He wasn't the first man of the cloth to realize that juggling normal word order was a tried and true shortcut to powerful oratory.

There were a few other good reasons to be out of town for at least three months. The United States was a mess. Miami had fallen into the ocean, the president had water-boarded his Secretary of Labor for insubordination, and California and Texas had declared civil war on each other. The world was in even worse shape. Last fall after the UN had been abolished and South Korea had pulverized a sizable chunk of North Korea, the hands of the Doomsday Clock, possibly the scariest prognosticator ever devised, had been moved forward. The desperate scientists whom no one listened to anymore had reset it to a half second to midnight. *A half second.* Then there was the Foxy-Loxy Tru-News to drive you crazy because you weren't allowed to turn off your video screen.

Cyndi bowed her head to have a one-way chat with Jesus, her Lord and Personal Savior. "Jesus, are you even listening? For six months now, I've been reminding you, over and over. *It's 2050 and you've been gone too damn long.* The world sucks. If you're ever coming back to fix things, now would be a good time."

She started to pace up and down the long antechamber with the glittering ceiling but came to a sudden halt in front of the cavern's purple ombre guest placard in English and Inuit, strategically placed above an elaborate, multi-tiered coat rack and storage unit that resembled a piece of playground equipment. The sign was a pleasant distraction.

"Typical," she murmured. "Would you just look at that? Rules first. Hardly the warmest of welcomes, and geriatric font-size, too."

You are at "The Mark Twain," our largest luxury cavern.

—Injun Joe Cavern Rental

Attention: Even cavemen gotta follow Rules, and these are NON-NEGOTIABLE, straight from the mouths of Tom Sawyer, Becky Thatcher, and Injun Joe, himself!

No carving or writing on the walls.

No campfires except in rooms with natural chimneys (wood supplied).

No swimming in our underground Lake Spooky.

No spelunking past the red DANGER!!!! signs.

No peeing anywhere except at the comfort stations.

Cyndi rolled her eyes. "And get this. Fucking awful accommodations, although a vast improvement over last year's pick."

Amenities include:

9 natural rooms.

100 comfy metal cots in private hand-hewn alcoves (bring your own bedding).

100 curtain rods with six hooks above the alcove for bedtime privacy (bring your own curtain).

100 folding chairs in the VIP Room.

1 coat and storage rack for all your gear (bring your own hangers).

1 kitchen fire-pit and **2** kettles (bring your own dishes).

And in the outside courtyard:

18 deluxe BBQ pits with racks.

6 deep-dug comfort stations with 3-mo supply of TP and Purell, provided free!

Water spigot (non-potable, boil it!!!) straight from our very own melting glacier.

An elaborately detailed floor plan that nonetheless simplified the cavern's slants, twists, and irregularities hung below the sign, with each cluster of rooms displayed in a different neon color.

"Hmm," murmured Cyndi, fumbling in the pocket of a stylishly cut cowboy shirt for her reading glasses. "Did we really see all these rooms on the welcome tour, yesterday? I didn't realize the place was so gigantic."

The common rooms, numbered 1, 2, and 3, were outlined in lime-green magic marker. Room 1, the largest with a great hunk of stone at one end, was named the VIP Room by Injun Joe Cavern Rental. Room 2, the kitchen, had silver kettles hanging over an open fire pit beneath a twisting natural chimney, and Cyndi remembered massive stacks of firewood stored behind a porous stone wall. Room 3, with a chimney revealing the stars, was reserved for keg parties that the church group would never hold. There were five rooms numbered 4 through 8 with carved-out nooks big enough to fit a cot and little else, delineated on the floor plan in watermelon-red. Room 9, in burnt orange, was the smallest and good only for storage. Cyndi recalled its cramped five-foot ceilings and a sandy floor punctuated by slender rock formations.

In Cyndi's mind, the crown jewel of the place was a formidably sized underground reservoir, Lake Spooky, that lay a half mile away through claustrophobic corridors that slanted downhill. The entire congregation had warily descended the final narrow steps, slippery with condensation, that met its rocky shores. She was sure that they had been hewn into the steep and winding incline many centuries before Injun Joe Cavern Rental had assumed ownership.

"Wow," Cyndi whistled under her breath. "Some lucky bastard is making a pile of money with relatively low upkeep." She snapped her glasses case shut and slid it back into her shirt pocket.

***

Seconds later, in full view of his gaping mother, Corpus Lazarus Jr. burst through the entrance, zigzagging toward her. As each step narrowed the distance between them, he continued to clench his eyes tight shut and drop his jaw in what looked like a silent scream. The polyethylene water jug he carried clutched to his chest slipped from his grasp in slow motion as his knees began to buckle. Just as his Mommy had asked him to, the tenacious child had protected the water as long as he could, but now that he had completed his mission and made it home, he lost consciousness, falling flat on his face. The jug's neck croaked and gurgled as the water streamed out, emitting clouds of vapor. She had no idea why, but it must have been boiling inside the container.

Cyndi sank down on the sandy cavern floor, reaching for her son with that instinctive desire to protect that affects even mediocre parents. Shocked, she drew back, not daring to touch his tender face and arms that flamed with a blistery orange sunburn.

No, oh, no. What's happened to my little boy?

Sensing her beside him, Corpus Lazarus Jr. recovered consciousness. He blinked his teary eyes in a rapid staccato, waving his hands to palpate the air and anything else they happened to meet.

He choked through his singed throat, "Are you really Mommy? You're the right shape, you feel like Mommy, but I can't *see* you."

He tried to pull in closer, digging his nails into her neck and shoulders.

Only a half hour ago, her son's eyes had been a dark chocolate brown and adorably fringed with long lashes. Now they looked empty, the irises blasted to white, the lashes gone.

A particularly graphic picture of gory-eyed Oedipus from her high school textbook, *The Greco-Roman World, Cartoon Edition,* popped into Cyndi's distracted mind.

Weeping from terror, she blurted out something both cruel and inappropriate. "I've said it *a hundred times,* Corpus Lazarus Jr., a hundred times, at least. Never, *never* look at the sun, not even the setting sun. Did you stare into it? Did you look?"

"I didn't, Mommy, I didn't look."

His voice rose to a shriek, "The sun, *the whole big sun, jumped at me,* right out of the sky. And it made all these big crashes and bangs, way high up before it blew me sideways. Then fire started to fall down, and broken rocks, and dead birds."

He added in a whisper, "After that, I couldn't see any more."

***

The congregation, minus Corpus Lazarus Jr. and Cyndi Grabenstein Lazarus, filled the VIP Room to capacity. Sitting uneasily on the squeaky metal folding chairs so thoughtfully supplied by Injun Joe Cavern Rental, everyone stared ahead in shocked silence. Even the babes-in-arms and the youngest children huddling at their feet made hardly a peep.

At last the Reverend Corpus Lazarus shambled in to face his parishioners, drawing himself up with an effort to his full height of six feet, four inches. The less distracted among them noticed that the crisp hibiscus-print shirt with just the right number of buttons left undone to reveal his sculpted chest, and his sunshine yellow Bermuda shorts that showed off his manly knees and calves, looked uncharacteristically rumpled. And even though he bowed his head submissively and then rolled his eyes as he always did when starting a sermon, this time he skipped his usual elocutionary excesses.

In fact, he barely managed to choke out, "Today's sermon is about ... well, it's about the Unthinkable. It's about nuclear weapons, the whole shebang, all of 'em, *because they've been set off.*

"You've all peeked outside by now. Even here, way up north in the middle of nowhere, the horizon's on fire. And the rest of the world's gone totally silent. I tried all night to rouse someone on the Internet, and guess what? There's no Internet. No email, no iPhones, no CBC, no Inuit Broadcasting Corp., no Foxy-Loxy, no Voice of America, no Sputnik News, no Al Jazeera, no nothing."

Hoping to arouse sympathy, he added a gratuitous remark. "I'd like you to know I got no sleep. Not a wink."

There were no tears, cries, or gasps from his parishioners because they had already come to the same conclusion. They continued to sit in terrified silence, mouths agape.

"Okay, then," a deep voice boomed from the center row of chairs, the words echoing all over the cavern. "What do you intend to do about it? Because I have some great ideas. First, hydroponic gardening. So let's root our best-looking potatoes and carrots. Feed the bats irradiated mosquitos so they'll glow in the dark and light up the ceilings. And breed the creatures that keep rustling around in the shafts—rabbits, rats, or whatever. Grow 'em plump and tasty, bigger than Butterball turkeys."

"Oh for Pete's sake, Rufus Grabenstein," Reverend Lazarus thundered, "Not now. No one wants to eat turkey-sized rats. Save it for later."

He mumbled under his breath, "I loathe that man, smart-ass Jew, Cyndi's fucking ex-husband who converted to win her back. And a brilliant scientist, a regular Einstein. No doubt he's the congregation's gift-package in a time of crisis."

Shaken by the male competition when he had no ideas of his own to offer his congregation, the Reverend announced petulantly, "I was going to wrap up by offering a humble prayer of thanks to Jesus for saving us, but just forget it. You're free to leave. Remember, I want all of you back here this evening with your hymnals and tom-toms for Drum Circle."

"Wait."

Everyone turned en masse toward a wizened elf of a girl about fifteen years old, who sat perched on the edge of her chair, way at the back of the room.

The recently maligned Rufus Grabenstein bellowed again, this time with a hint of admiration, "Hallelujah, my friends, it's *Merlin.* Prepare for some words of *real* wisdom and compassion."

Merlin rose with grace even though her body barely topped four-and-a-half feet. The entire congregation knew her story, but as usual, a buzz of excitement ignited them all. Merlin was different and therefore exotic, the only Black face in a sea of white ones.

Eight years before, she had been abandoned on the stoop of the Holy Cavern of Lazarus Storefront Tabernacle with a short, apologetic note pinned to the lacy pinafore of her starched Sunday dress. The note's contents were sadly familiar, scrawled by a mother facing overwhelming medical bills for her daughter's hospitalization with smallpox, and ruinous expenses for her own mother's funeral and burial plot. A postscript describing the child's sudden blindness added poignancy to an already tragic tale.

Merlin spoke with clipped elegance, moving her sightless eyes around the entire room to graciously include everyone. "It's Mary Lynne here, and I want to inform you all that someone very dear to me suffered the brunt of the blast. That would be Corpus Lazarus Jr., my best friend. I *foresee* that he won't die, but please stop by his alcove to pay him a visit in Children's Room 4. He'd appreciate it *so much* because he gets lonely."

She stopped abruptly, tears running down her cheeks.

The Reverend Corpus Lazarus felt his mouth grow dry. *How did I forget to mention my own son at the beginning of the service? They'll think I'm an unfeeling s.o.b.*

He tried to call them back. "Of course I love my son, but I happen to love all of you, too, and—"

Everyone had turned away, murmuring Amens and dutifully folding their chairs to stack them against the wall.

"Goddam Cumaean Sibyl," he hissed to himself. "*Jesus,* Merlin gives me the heebie-geebies with all that visionary bullshit softened up with a Mother Teresa act."

He added spitefully, "Why the fuck did I take her in, anyway? I should've shipped her off to live with her own kind at our sister mission in Haiti."

Thoroughly riled up, he began to pace in tight circles, hitting a clenched fist into his open palm. "Runty as she is, I bet she and that Grabenstein are already putting their heads together. They're plotting and planning to steal my ministry, I can *feel* it."

Corpus Lazarus faced the cavern wall, falling dutifully to his knees. With hands clasped and eyes cast heavenward, he tried earnestly to pray for the strength to lead his flock through The Vale of Tears, The Valley of Death. His orisons went up, only to fall back to earth with a thud, and all that came out were waves of self-pity and excoriation.

Help me Jesus, because no one loves me, not Cyndi, not Corpus Lazarus Jr., not my congregation, and it's no fucking wonder. I'm impatient, intolerant, jealous, vain, a clotheshorse, a potty mouth, a jackass, not a good man. If I walked out of here this minute into that killer nuclear sun, no one would even notice that I'd left.

2 ~ Death Comes for Magnolia

"Tell me a story, Merlin, so I can go to sleep."

"You mean the same one I tell you every night?"

"Yes, that one. The one your grandmother told *you* every night about her great, great, great, great, great grandmother, Magnolia. There are lots of greats because she was great."

Merlin helped Corpus Lazarus Jr. reach his arms through the sleeves of a grimy nightshirt with fire engines on it. "You always make that silly joke. You know all those greats really mean that she was my ancestor from a long time ago. Grammy told me the story every night before the smallpox came along and killed her. It was the same smallpox that made me blind and shrunken—"

"Hurry up, Merlin, just tell the story, not the sad part about you and her."

Slanting mid-summer beams thick with motes of atomic dust passed all the way through the cavern's anteroom and into the big children's sleeping chamber, Room 4. They stabbed grey fingers straight into Corpus Lazarus Jr.'s face. The boy who would never again shut his eyes against an intrusive light turned toward the girl, his best friend, his second mother, his idol. Leaning forward expectantly, he balanced his narrow frame on the very edge of the cot.

Merlin sat down on the cavern floor, tucking her legs under her and wrapping her bony arms tightly across her diminutive body. She looked for all the world like a thoughtful praying mantis sunning on a green leaf. Thrilling with anticipation, she coughed to clear her throat of the stinging dust. She loved telling the story of her ancestor and was quite sure that a thousand repetitions would never bore her.

"Magnolia was a slave a long time ago when there were slaves down South. Her master was a Cherokee copying white men's ways, and when the government forced him to leave his plantation and move to Oklahoma, he gave her the gift of freedom. But she went along with him anyway because he had always been good to her. It was way back in the 1830s. She rode in a steamboat and walked along the Trail of Tears, that fearsome road where everybody cried—"

Corpus Lazarus Jr. always interrupted at this spot, "Why did they cry?" Merlin would push on without answering because she could never find the right words to describe the desolate picture she kept locked inside her head. What she saw was mile upon mile of exhausted people dressed in rags, torn from their homes and forced to walk toward a fate they could not imagine.

"The first day out on the Trail, the Angel of Death came for Magnolia. He was dressed in sweeping red robes with a black hood covering his face. Magnolia wasn't frightened because she'd gotten very strong working in the corn and cotton fields. So she choked him with her bare hands. He turned to run away, clutching his sore neck. But first he said, 'Magnolia, your number is up. I'm coming back for you tomorrow.'"

Every time Corpus Lazarus Jr. heard Merlin say, "Your number is up," he would puzzle over the meaning. But he never asked her to explain because this was the point where the story started to make his flesh crawl. He sat absolutely still to savor every word.

"On the second day, Magnolia tricked Death by covering herself with an ox hide. She bent her head low and gored him with both horns. Again he turned to run away, this time clutching his wounded chest. But first he said, 'Magnolia, good try. But only the Lord Jesus ever escaped from Death.'"

For the denouement, Corpus Lazarus Jr. always sat up straight, gripping his fingers in a knot and holding his breath.

"On the third day, Magnolia prepared herself for the final fight by hiding a bow and three sharp arrows in the folds of her long calico skirt. The first arrow struck Death near his left eye. The second arrow went through his right shoulder. She shot the third arrow at his heart, but clever Death caught the shaft in mid-air and broke it in two with his fists, *snap.* He turned to Magnolia and said sadly, 'My good lady, no mortal has ever won a battle with Death. Where you're going won't be so bad, really. It will be much better than here.' Then he swept her into his strong arms, and they flew high above the clouds to Abraham's Bosom."

"Merlin, how can anybody fly to a bosom, 'specially Abraham's?"

Even this very intelligent girl was stymied. "Really, I've never understood that part, but I think the bosom is what you call a *symbol.* A symbol for a very calm place."

***

Corpus Lazarus Jr. was getting sleepy, his lids drooping a little over his empty eyes that gleamed like iridescent mother-of-pearl. But he still had one more question to ask, and no matter how many times he'd repeated it, a wave of apprehension crossed his damaged face.

He scrabbled awkwardly to find his friend's hand. "Merlin, do you promise, cross your heart, that you didn't make up Magnolia's story to keep me from being afraid? Because Mommy and everybody else, I hear them say it all the time. That I'm going to die soon."

Merlin pulled herself up with a groan because her folded legs had never regained their resilience since her illness. They had fallen asleep and fighting the pins and needles, she gently prepared Corpus Lazarus Jr. for bed. She pushed him deep into his private alcove and pulled up his red Bay Point blanket with the black stripes. Then she slid his red inflatable camp pillow under his head.

Throughout her short life, she had seldom lied about anything. It was not her way, not even to soothe a child.

She lowered her voice to a murmur. "Sweetie, I've told you this so often, and you must try to believe me. They're wrong, plain and simple. They're just scared, like you and me. And you know what else? All of us are sick from the radiation, not just you. We get a little bit worse every time we leave the cavern to use the comfort stations."

Merlin sat back down on the cavern floor in her praying mantis position, but this time she rocked back and forth as if under a spell. She intoned, "On the night after the bombs went off, I had a dream that was so real I woke up shaking all over like a frightened rabbit. And this is what I saw."

She spread her arms wide to impress her sightless audience of one. "The descendants of the people in this cavern are going to go on and on for a million years, but they'll get sicker and sicker with every generation. And thinner and thinner. After a while they won't have eyes, just a thick layer of skin over the sockets."

Merlin leapt up, her lips quivering and her words tumbling out, *"Now hear this,* Corpus Lazarus Jr., hear our future! They will never, *ever,* leave these caverns. Because if you go past the DANGER!!!! signs, *all the caverns are attached together.* They will move into them, and they will be called the *Shade People.* Their dark realm will stretch from Iqaluit to Nanisivik, that is, from one end of Baffin Island to the other."

The little boy had heard her vision often enough that he was close to knowing it by heart. His words faded as his head nodded toward his chest. "Merlin, we'll ... get ... married."

"Yes, we'll get married, and we'll have children, too, years from now when you get old enough. But they won't be strong. Their hair will be white, and it will float about their heads like a nimbus."

Corpus Lazarus Jr. was snoring softly, so she stopped talking to pull the blanket up to his chin and give him a brush of a kiss on his forehead. She pulled his red and white striped alcove curtain shut and turned to leave. It was pointless for her to finish now that he couldn't hear her. Besides, the end of her vision had been so hazy that she could hardly make a good story out of it, although she had certainly tried the few times he'd managed to stay awake.

It had something to do with hundreds upon hundreds of Prairie Dogs and a handsome giant, tragically slain by his own son. But dreams being what they are, it could mean almost anything.

3 ~ Picking Up the Pieces

The entire congregation of the Lazarus Storefront Tabernacle slumped miserably into the folding chairs in the VIP Room waiting for someone to tell them what to do. At least half of them wept aloud, the sound resembling the pitiful baaing of lost sheep. They had looked everywhere, turning everything upside-down in the nine rooms. And they'd scoured the shores of Lake Spooky.

They'd come to a sad conclusion: Reverend Corpus Lazarus had simply vanished. They weren't sure when he'd left them, but no one had seen him for about half a day. Even a glimpse of his flashy hibiscus shirt could renew their flagging spirits; that's how dependent they had become upon him, the symbol of optimistic well-being. Never mind that he had been losing his grip quite noticeably since the Day of the Jumping Sun, as everyone called the Armageddon that had happened about two weeks ago.

The three individuals best known to the congregation gathered beside the Tabernacle's natural stone altar at the front of the VIP Room. Everyone knew Cyndi, Corpus Lazarus's wife. She looked teary, although the more observant members questioned the sincerity of her grief. During the past few weeks, she'd been caught exchanging amorous glances with her ex-husband, Rufus Grabenstein, who stood beside her now. Tall, rumpled Rufus, sloppy of dress, who had always interrupted Reverend Corpus Lazarus at Disciples' Daily Discourse with a superior thought or idea, was undeniably brilliant and the most outspoken member of the congregation.

The third was little Merlin, who stood out simply because she was so small and at the same time perfectly poised, her tiny feet turned outward in her Sunday-best Mary Janes. Certainly the most likable member of the disparate trio, she stepped forward now and raised her hand. Miraculously, the weeping ceased.

Rufus whispered into Cyndi's ear, "Unreal performance. Do you think she has extra-sensory powers we don't know about?"

"Yes, maybe ... I mean no, she probably doesn't. But she sure has charm. And don't knock it, Rufie; she has a lot more of it than we do."

Merlin cleared her throat. "Mary Lynne, here. First, I'd like to say that Corpus Lazarus Jr. is feeling much better, and thank you all for stopping by and for remembering him in your prayers."

She paused, clapping her dainty hands to make sure everyone was listening. "But now we have to be brave because I'm pretty sure Reverend Corpus Lazarus won't be back to take care of us anymore."

At the sound of renewed sobs, Merlin raised her arms. "Save your grief for later, dear friends. We have a lot to do, and I'm about to introduce your new leaders. They're standing right beside me: Cyndi and Rufus. And I'm always here if you need me."

There was faint applause from the gathering, certainly nothing approaching a unanimous proclamation. Nonetheless Cyndi and Rufus felt their jaws drop. Without discussion or argument, they had been handed the keys to the caverns, so to speak, by a fifteen-year-old gnome in ruffles and patent-leather shoes. They knew that they were hardly favorites. But Rufus, at least, was more than capable, and Cyndi had shown a level head now and then in the past. Why else would Merlin have picked them?

Rufus spent little time basking in the warm rays of a newly bestowed honor. Cyndi stood by as he blurted out an idea that he'd obviously analyzed carefully in his head as soon as they'd found themselves in such a daunting predicament.

"First off, we have to eat. And folks, we are going to be here for a very long while. That scorching heat and killer radiation isn't going away any time soon. And I bet nothing's left out there, no cities, no towns, no farms—"

A question from the back of the VIP Room broke through Rufus's monologue. "What if Jesus has returned to earth, and the Kingdom of God has—"

Rufus interrupted angrily, "Edwin, don't tell me about Jesus. He had his chance to come back and clean things up. But did he? Now we're on our own—"

Cyndi poked him in the ribs and hissed, "Watch it, Rufie."

Rufus took a moment to tuck in a loose shirttail and began anew, wearing an ingratiating smile. He'd used it occasionally in past years to impress the deans when chasing down grant money at the University of Maryland, his former place of employment.

"As you know, ladies and gentlemen, I have an extensive background in engineering and biology with a side interest in botany, and, to be specific, a lasting interest in hydroponic gardening."

***

Rufus and Cyndi made a formidable team. Rufus stuck to his many branches of science and to engineering—including his uncanny ability to create new objects seemingly out of nothing. Cyndi took over Sunday sermons, drum circle, and almost all the other tasks expected of a minister. Even though she didn't have half the charisma that had inspired Corpus Lazarus's pastoring, she had an equally valuable gift. She loved to fight against all odds. She took her new job seriously, working long hours far into the night. Many people forgot that they had ever disliked this indomitable woman. She retired long after snores echoed from the rocky ceilings of every sleeping chamber and then showed up revitalized the next morning to lead Pray 'n Chat.

Although Rufus had never attended Pray 'n Chat before, on this particular morning he stood dutifully beside Cyndi and Merlin by the altar. Everyone bowed their heads as Cyndi offered the wake-up invocation, this one with an added last line geared to Rufus's solicitation for gardening volunteers.

"Thank you for the world so sweet, thank you for the food we eat.

Thank you for the birds that sing, thank you God, for everything.

If you help the garden grow, health and blessings will you sow."

Rufus caught sight of a buxom, dimple-faced young woman with curly red-gold hair hiding shyly behind the others. She was still wearing the name tag that she'd made for herself on the first day, her curlicued name, *Violet,* entwined with flowers in purple ink.

Putting on his most appealing smile that showed a hint of vampire-like canines, he enthused, "We'll be starting a hydroponic garden in Room 3 by rooting most of the vegetables we brought. I'm thinking, carrots, beans, and potatoes, maybe lentils. Who wants to volunteer? Young lady in the back?"

Twenty women and a few men, all middle-aged with faces leathered by sunny outdoor gardening, raised their hands. Most of them remembered Rufus's intriguing introduction to hydroponics when he'd rudely interrupted Corpus Lazarus's first sermon following the Day of the Jumping Sun. Rufus led them to an empty room with a gritty floor and a natural chimney at one end that would let in a circle of sunlight as well as the inevitable atomic fallout.

Even though the cherubic girl with an angel's hair who had caught his fancy was not there, he cheerfully gave out instructions. "I had a great idea for the containers, but you'll have to collect them this afternoon. Ask folks for their traveling trunks and convince them to give them up by saying they can't ever use them again. We'll need about thirty. Gather up all the mirrors, every single one, to help angle the sun. Tell them the mirrors mean life or death for our garden. Some sand, water from our own underground Lake Spooky, a little bat guano, and lots of luck—"

"We have bats?"

"Yes, ma'am, they're flying high up next to the ceilings in three of the rooms. I think they're eating mosquitos that hatch on Lake Spooky. Don't any of you have bites?" He smiled, flashing his vampire teeth and waving an arm to show off the telltale welts.

"What about animal protein?"

"We'll wait on that."

A few days later, Merlin found an apple seed stuck in the lining of Corpus Lazarus Jr.'s backpack. When it sprouted, the entire congregation prayed nightly for its survival. It became such a symbol of hope that Merlin choreographed a dance in its honor, a pavane for slow-stepping couples who walked in lines like the spokes of a wheel, waving their arms to imitate the leafy branches promised by the seedling's first two cotyledons.

***

Cyndi managed the chores list with fairness and efficiency—something her sexist husband had never been able to do—rotating among the entire flock the cooking, dishwashing, sweeping and dusting, and myriad other cavern-keeping tasks. Resentful arguments over who would do what almost disappeared, and when particularly abhorrent chores such as scrubbing soot off the stalactites didn't get finished, Cyndi rolled up her sleeves and did them herself.

However, Cyndi's remarkable transformation did not erase overnight the flaws in her character that had earned her the negative votes at the *Hey, Sister! Share-Your-Feelings Seminar.* The parishioners learned early on not to cross her, adopting the self-protective dictum that Cyndi "is always right."

Cyndi had another weak link in her social outreach, a point beyond which she would not go. And who could blame her? She hated the female acolytes impregnated by Corpus Lazarus, both the ones expecting, and the ones with babes-in-arms. These women needed a lot of comforting in order to survive motherhood in the new Pleistocene Age, and Merlin was the only one able to do it, holding their hands and telling them soothing stories from her childhood, although she did not share the myth of Magnolia because that story was too personal and for Corpus Lazarus Jr., alone.

Even Rufus felt protective towards the mothers and mothers-to-be. He explained over-and-over to Cyndi that the congregation needed the healthy babies because they had been conceived before lethal radiation had swept across the earth, and, as far as any of them knew, these few babies would possibly be the key to preserving humanity.

Cyndi's retort was always the same. "Who says the human race is worth saving since it's so damn destructive? What makes you think we'll do any better the second time around?"

Rufus tended to agree, although he felt that her cynicism was self-defeating. Her rhetoric might have been cute in an adolescent sort of way if she'd said it *before* the Day of the Jumping Sun.

4 ~ Violet Ascends

Violet of the red-gold hair, the young woman who had charmed Rufus at Pray 'n Chat, sat bolt upright with a start, the frame of her metal cot grating against the cavern wall. A noise had jarred her awake, ruining the first real sleep she'd gotten during the short darkness of the arctic summer night. Even these hours were marred by the eerie light of a world on fire that penetrated all the way from the cavern's mouth to her sleeping alcove in Room 6 for Young Single Women.

Back in Maryland she'd been a craftsperson, and she was proud of her specialty: big metal coptic crosses on heavy round bases. They were encrusted on both sides with circular swirls of rhinestones and ice blue and ruby-red glass beads that formed a dove at the center. What she wouldn't give to copy onto her crosses the glittering designs of the stalactite-covered ceilings lit up by the unnatural sun.

What an idiot I am. I brought my tools but not the metal sheets for the crosses and all my pretty beads.

There was that noise again, the same one she'd been hearing every night. Or was it more than one noise, maybe two or three? Sure enough, it was a chorus of noises coming from behind the wall right by her bed, tip-tap-tipping just like that suave gentleman and his lady from the old musicals, Fred Astaire and Ginger Rogers. She made an identification: *animal feet.* She felt like jumping up and screaming, "Hey everybody, we aren't alone. Things are back there, alive, creepy things."

But she was not the screaming type, and the feet sounded more trapped than creepy. Besides, she happened to recall something that one of their new leaders, the real smart Rufus Grabenstein, had said on the Day of the Jumping Sun. He'd talked about rabbits or rats living in the shafts that he wanted to make as fat as Butterball turkeys. And she'd noticed that his cocksure attitude had made Corpus Lazarus angry.

But why, she asked herself, *was Rufus waiting so long to get rid of them?* Then she reconsidered. *Well, not so long, really, it's been just a few days since he and Cyndi took over, and when Corpus Lazarus was still here, he wasn't doing much of anything besides—*

She bounced up, suddenly. *A family of timid rabbits could be back there, too frightened to come out of hiding. And poor things, by now they must be starving and dying of thirst.*

Violet made up her mind: she had to *do* something right away. If the animals were starving, the leaders had to be notified. With a determination unusual for her, she hastily threw a cerise-colored shawl around her shoulders, the one with a border of paisley designs and long fringes in black that she'd created herself. Guided only by the gleam of the nuclear halo that shone in from outside, she marched to Cyndi's sleeping alcove, Room 5 for Senior Single Women.

She didn't intentionally peek behind Cyndi's sequined alcove curtain. The gaudy drape gaped at the sides, and she got a glimpse of both Cyndi and Rufus occupying the same short and narrow cot. She was ever so relieved that the pair was not up to something. They lay awkwardly sandwiched together in sleep, their forms outlined underneath an unusually loud Bay Point blanket with bold multi-colored stripes.

Violet considered waiting for Rufus to leave Cyndi's bed, but she realized the impropriety of lurking in the corridor as if stalking him. Nor could she loiter by the Single Men's quarters in Room 7. As she shuffled aimlessly along the sandy stone corridors trying to make up her mind, she considered Rufus and Cyndi.

It's kind of a farce staying separated into different sleeping rooms until you're married if the leaders don't follow their own rules. We hear the same thing every summer: no cohabiting. Why keep up the charade?

Her mind returned to that silly playboy, Corpus Lazarus. He made the rules for everybody else but could enter any alcove he chose—not that it mattered anymore now that he was gone. She felt a stab of jealousy thinking about the unfairness of it all. She hated the slender girls with vacuous eyes, high breasts and tiny bottoms, the ones Corpus Lazarus always chose.

He had never eyed *her* with that certain look. She would have *loved* his attention in spite of the disapproving glances some of the senior parishioners would have given her. When she'd joined the Storefront Temple two years ago and noticed how well-proportioned Corpus Lazarus was, she permitted herself an occasional illicit daydream. In a state of religious fervor, she would run her hands up those tanned limbs, way above the hems of his crisply ironed shorts.

A year ago she'd presented him with the most beautiful coptic cross she'd ever made. It had two doves with entwined necks at the center and a swirl of Swarovski crystals circling their feet. He'd admired it, twisting it to catch the sun, and then announced too jovially, "Fine work, um, Lavender." And then he'd kissed her, but not on the lips. For a fleeting moment he lightly brushed his face against her fly-away hair and put a hand on her shoulder. And tragically, this was the sum total of Violet's romantic contact with the opposite sex.

***

Violet had reached her own alcove before deciding that she simply couldn't face the distressing animal noises by her bed that would surely keep her awake, so she tiptoed back to the VIP Room to wait out the night. She planned to snuggle in the capacious cerise and black knit and lean her back against the stalagmite formation at the rear of the VIP Room where she'd try to catch a few winks before the rest of the congregation began stirring.

But she froze in the corridor as the sound of angry voices bounced off the VIP Room's rock ceiling, which projected the unruly discourse with the precision of a complex fugue heard in a Gothic cathedral. The content was hardly music although she recognized Merlin's sweet reasonable alto. She was obviously there to placate the others. But she was having a hard time competing with four yelling parishioners who filled in the gamut from bass to treble.

A booming bass voice barked, "What is going on around here? First we get marooned forever in Purgatory by a nuclear blast and then our pastor disappears in front of one hundred people—"

An angry tenor interrupted, "And I can hear animals walking around in the walls. What the hell is back there? They sound like a herd of elephants. And what the f—"

A soprano trilled, "Edwin, darling, there's no need to curse. You know you have better ways to express your feelings, and we've talked about that over and over. The real question is, exactly what, if anything, are Cyndi and Rufus doing about them?"

The soprano whispered to herself in a voice that nonetheless carried into the hall, "Woe is me that our beloved Corpus Lazarus walked into the nuclear sun. I'll follow him in my heart until the day I die. Cyndi and Rufus are imposters. Imposters, I tell you!"

Edwin, obviously married to the soprano, remarked in an undertone, "Betty Anne, if you don't stop criticizing me in front of other people, I'll—"

Another tenor broke in: "I went to find Rufus and his alcove was empty. Is he already bedding the pubescent girls, just like Corpy used to do? 'Cause my ten-year-old daughter is here, and I won't stand for it—"

The one named Betty Anne interrupted in her cutting soprano. "How dare you call him Corpy. You're insulting a godlike man, recently deceased. You should be ashamed of yourself."

Throughout this fretful chorus, Merlin tried unsuccessfully to shout above them, "Rufus knows about the animals, he knows about the animals. Would one of you volunteer to help lure them into traps? Rufus knows about the animals, he knows about the animals. Would one of you volunteer to help—"

Violet sprang into the room, inspired suddenly to act, to make a real difference, perhaps for the first time in her life. She stood staunchly by Merlin, and the entire crowd fell silent, surprised by her precipitous entrance and the startling swirl of her boldly colored cape.

"Oh, Merlin, I'd love to help Rufus. I'm good with animals, and I've always had an affinity for taming squirrels and pigeons. I could invent the traps, too—"

Merlin reached up to hug Violet through the wooly fuzziness that engulfed her body. "You're hired."

Then she whispered, "And yes, I know where Rufus is. He's with Cyndi. When he gets up, you two can get started."

There was only one blot staining Violet's perfect moment. She overheard Betty Anne whisper to Edwin, "Oh, look ... isn't she the fat one who makes those metal crosses? Some nerve butting in like that."

5 ~ Animals in the Shafts

Rufus couldn't quite believe the allure of this rubenesque young woman sitting beside him on the convenient ledge jutting from the cavern wall. He was sure that she was the same beauty who had resisted his invitation to join the gardening committee, and to verify his assumption, she still wore her flowery *Violet* name tag. Their *tête-à-tête* took place a few hours after the late-night citizens' revolt that Violet had stumbled upon in the VIP room. As soon as the mob had scattered, an agitated Merlin roused Rufus from Cyndi's bed about 4:00 a.m.

Rufus and Violet's bench was in a very public place by the coat rack in the passageway leading to the irradiated cavern's entrance. Nonetheless, his most private thoughts got the better of him as his heart made an unaccustomed adrenaline-fueled lurch.

Rufus gave himself a stern lecture: *No, don't even think about it. Cyndi's been the one-and-only ever since sixth grade at Edgewater Central, although sleeping with her last night was not that great. First time since the divorce, too ....* He declared aloud, "Let's concentrate on traps, the subject at hand is traps."

Violet, the object of such precipitous passion, remained at least partially oblivious to her new inventing partner's ardor. With knit brows and hands tightly clasped together in her lap, she tried to think. I will *solve this problem. We have to make traps that can double as cages. Lure the animals in with food that we don't have much of, only our hydroponic vegetables and canned beans. Vegetables are good if they're rabbits. We're out of luck if they're carnivores.*

Her mind took a momentary detour. *Rufus isn't all that intimidating, really ... not like everyone keeps saying. And he's not acting conceited just because he's smart. At least he isn't with me.*

Now thoroughly distracted from her task, Violet gazed out the entrance. She could barely make out some bulky shapes through the fiery haze. *Aren't those the row of barbecue pits, eighteen of them, that we never had a chance to use?*

She sprang up suddenly, clapping her hands. Her voice squeaked from a jolt of stage-fright, unexpected after last night's boldness coming to Merlin's aid. "I have it, Dr. Grabenstein. Every time someone goes to the comfort station, which everyone has to do, they could bring back a barbecue rack for making cages. That way no one person gets extra exposure making eighteen trips."

Rufus jumped up, too, stuttering with excitement, his mind racing. "V-Violet, y-you are going to tie the corners of the racks with some kind of string and make three cube-shaped cages, six sides each. Brilliant—"

"We'll tie the corners with shoelaces—"

"And the cages only need five racks for sides, bottom and top, with one extra rack to close 'em up later. Because we'll put the open ends facing the shafts—"

"We'll put carrots and beans inside to lure the animals out of the shafts. And we'll put something comfortable on the bottom like old dish towels. We'll sing soothing rabbit songs ... and in they'll go."

As Rufus tried to fathom her last remark about rabbit songs, Violet's voice tightened with anxiety as she sank back down on the ledge. "But Dr. Grabenstein, what if they're carnivorous, like bobcats? What if the heat has ruined the racks?"

Rufus announced cheerfully, "It'll be fine, I know it. The animals aren't as big as bobcats, or they wouldn't fit in the shafts. As for the condition of the racks, we'll have to see, won't we?"

He sat back down beside her, even daring to pat her hand. "You and me, we're the star inventors, now. Just the two us, we'll think up everything together from this moment on."

As Violet's naturally pale complexion turned a deep crimson from the unexpected compliment, Rufus refrained from kissing her or even putting his arms around her lovely smooth shoulders with the stunning bosom down below that positively beckoned to him.

***

In spite of the perpetual half-light from the fires outside, the congregation could distinguish night from day, and they had long since fallen asleep, leaving the six designated cage watchers to lure the animals out of the shafts. Joining Rufus and Violet, who couldn't wait to see if their cages would work, were the four people chosen from a sea of waving hands during the afternoon meeting. Here, at last, was a job people actually wanted to do.

Rufus gave last-minute instructions on how to stand silently on either side of the cages and shut the doors as soon as the animals had entered, lured by the fresh produce and a big bowl of slightly brackish water from Lake Spooky. "Your cages are set close to the shaft openings and the doors slide down from above on rollers that Violet invented from luggage wheels." He sent her a radiant smile, which she intercepted with a blush.

"If more animals show up, open the door a crack to let them in." He added with a sympathetic smile, "You might get sleepy, but resist the temptation to nod off."

Buoyed by optimism, the excited volunteers felt a thrill of camaraderie and at the same time wondered what had gotten into Rufus, who was being much nicer than usual.

Surveying the volunteers, Violet recognized the henpecked Edwin from the previous evening. He grinned continuously, perhaps relishing his evening of freedom away from Betty Anne. He was paired with a droopy-eyed teenager named Sylvie, one of the impregnated nymphettes in about her sixth month. Violet instantly felt sorry for her and could hardly believe that less than twenty-four hours earlier she'd been jealous of Corpus Lazarus's "chosen ones."

Neither Violet nor Rufus recognized the second pair, who may have been late converts to the Storefront Tabernacle. A septuagenarian with an unruly head of silver-grey hair announced in a grating bass, "Call me Burt, Political Science, University of Delaware. I advised the politicians in DC, so now I want to work extra hard to atone for the fix we're in."

If appearances meant anything, the tall, blond woman paired with Burt easily rivaled Cyndi's fashion style and haughty temperament. But when she opened her mouth a tiny peep of a voice emerged, indicating a medical condition. "I'm Arachne, my stage name, if you're wondering. And yes, I do love to knit. Nodes on my vocal cords, so destructive. I was an opera singer, but now I lead a life of misery working in a shop. Can you imagine, a common clothing shop?" The others couldn't imagine such a thing because no shops were left.

Hours passed. As the watchers had promised at Rufus's orientation, they did not break the silence or leave their posts at either side of their respective cages—except Rufus and Violet, who broke both rules immediately.

"Psst, Violet."

Violet, who had found out the night before how unpredictable the cavern's echoes could be, tiptoed around to his side. She spoke as softly as she could, "Rufus, even though the other cages are beyond the bend in the corridor, the people might hear you. Besides, we vowed to keep silent. The animals won't come out if—"

"I know we did, but I have to talk to you."

Although Violet was inexperienced in the ways of love, she couldn't deny the mutual attraction that had been simmering between them all day as they worked on the cages in a rare meeting of minds. She had already rehearsed a number of possible responses if the romance went further. Her heart was beating so fast that she was sure he could see it pounding beneath her prettiest blouse, the only one that wasn't grimy with dust. As usual, his eyes were lowered in a downward direction, toward her chest.

Rufus took Violet's hand and spoke as softly as he knew how, "Uh, Violet, you know how I feel about you, and I can't explain it. It just happened, out of the blue. I love you."

As Violet tried to come up with an answer from a brain that had slowed to a crawl, Rufus went on, "But my heart belongs to Cyndi, even if she doesn't like me very much, never has. We were married for five years, and it was awful; she's a conceited bitch. I joined this stupid church to win her back after she left me to marry Corpy, that pompous clotheshorse and child rapist. You wanna know what his real name was before he took a new one? Delphinius Trittlebone—"

Violet yanked her hand from his and sputtered, fists clenched on her round hips, "Spare me the story of your life, Rufus. I'll see you in my alcove as soon as this is over because you owe me a better explanation."

She wasn't entirely sure what she intended to do besides come up with some kind of retaliation against the man who'd gotten her hopes up and then dashed them. As she stomped around to the other side of the cage, she felt her face grow hot from a mixture of embarrassment and fury for having been wooed and then rejected, turned into a mere sounding board.

Unshed tears stung her eyes. *God, how I hate Cyndi. How come she gets all the men, and I don't get any?*

An idea struck. *Hey, if I make Rufus sleep with me, I'll hurt both of them at the same time.*

***

When the action started about a half hour later, it began and ended all in a rush. About fifty animals, approximately a foot long with light brown fur and white bibs at their throats, rushed inside the three cages almost simultaneously as if they had communicated to one another from the different shafts. They gobbled the carrots and beans and slurped up the water, then looked around expectantly for more.

As Arachne hastened off to the storage bags to fetch more vegetables, Rufus identified them. "Prairie Dog, *Cynomys ludovicianus,* order *Rodentia.* Damned cute if you ask me."

Sylvie spoke for the first time. "I bet they had to leave their burrows after the nuclear blast heated up the passageways. They ran into the cavern's ducts and were too scared to come out with all the people making noise."

Everyone noticed that Edwin had an arm on her shoulder. Violet thought snidely, Comfort in her time of need, perhaps? But she had to admit that Sylvie was no dummy.

Burt added in his ancient rasp, "I'm glad they're vegetarians, too. Now the politicians in DC, they were carnivores. Yup, saber-toothed tigers, vampires, and leeches, every last one."

The Prairie Dogs didn't seem to mind being caged. After a second feast, they bedded down, cuddling together to sleep. "How sweet," whispered Arachne. "Let's retire, too." Everyone nodded as Violet threw an angry "don't forget" look at Rufus.

He announced with a hearty swagger to cover his unease over the upcoming rendezvous, "Goodnight, all, good work."

***

Rufus arrived at Violet's alcove a discreet five minutes later than she. Once he'd slipped inside her rose-patterned chintz curtain, he could swear that he smelled perfume, but assumed that it was her own sweet, natural scent. His nose had not lied, although his intellect had failed him. She had smuggled into her luggage a tiny vial of Chanel No 5 for just such an occasion, although at the time she was sure it would never happen. A hasty dab on each side of her neck, and she was all set.

It didn't take long for Rufus to succumb to Violet, his ideal woman, the one who had always inhabited his daydreams. She smelled of jasmine and lilies-of-the-valley, not patchouli and lemongrass. Her curly red-gold hair shimmered loose about her shoulders rather than spiking and sparkling with neon braids and sequined baubles. She was seductively round and plushy in all the right places with no hipbones jutting out or calf muscles artificially honed at the gym. She could be both demure and passionate at the same time, not a perpetual she-devil playing hard-to-get. After they made love, she kissed his ears and neck affectionately rather than complaining about his performance.

Violet had unsheathed a double-edged sword with her plan to bring down Rufus and Cyndi. She fell in love with him, too, madly in love. She loved his six-foot-three frame with legs too short and arms too long. She loved his slightly crooked half-smile and his vampire teeth, his bushy black eyebrows and thick black hair, his recently acquired middle-aged paunch. The affair continued, and she became the "other woman," doomed to keep a secret that she wanted to yell from the rooftops.

She also became pregnant.

6 ~ Sentient Beings

Six months had passed since the Day of the Jumping Sun, and Merlin insisted that Corpus Lazarus Jr. leave his bed. As she had promised, he did survive the radiation burns, although they took a toll on both his body and spirit. He left his alcove a little taller and much thinner, with hair that had grown back stark white and spiderweb-thin. Scars laced his face and neck in irregular blotches, leaving a complexion that resembled an unfinished jigsaw puzzle. And once his lids had healed, he kept them closed to hide his blanked-out Orphan Annie eyes.

The first trip out did not go well. Corpus Lazarus Jr. gripped Merlin's hand tighter in both of his. He yanked at her arm, "Merl, please, please ... let's go back. I feel everyone looking at me, but I can't see them—"

"I can't see them either, Corpus Lazarus Jr., not really. But if you concentrate hard, you can feel where their bodies are and read their expressions."

He whined, "I don't know what you mean, Merl. That you can feel them and not see them?" He tried to hide behind Merlin but stumbled on the uneven stones. Tears rolled down his cheeks. "I'm scared. Take me back to bed."

"Give it time. I learned to do it, and so will you."

She guided him around a corner into an empty corridor and put her hands on his trembling shoulders. "Corpus Lazarus Jr., what did Magnolia do the first time she saw Death?"

"She ... I forget."

"Of course you remember, it's your bedtime story, the same every night. She was *very brave.* She choked Death, and he ran away." Merlin would never lose her patience. A long time ago, she'd been the same way.

***

Two days later when Merlin asked Corpus Lazarus Jr. to get up, he refused, turning his face to the wall.

"Corpus Lazarus Jr.," she cooed, tapping his shoulder. "I have a treat for you this time. We'll visit the Prairie Dogs. They live in Room 9 now, because they outgrew their cages."

He perked up. "Okay, I'd like that, but I don't want to visit any people."

Then he asked a question that no one had answered yet. "But how'd they grow big so fast?"

Merlin remained silent and shook her head even though he couldn't see it. She had her theories, but she knew as little as everyone else. Even Rufus didn't know for sure. Perhaps the radiation had worked in their favor, or perhaps the vegetables were fattening them up. People talked about little else. The Prairie Dogs had doubled in plumpness in less than six months, and they'd had dozens of cute new babies that grew larger than their parents in only a few weeks.

Violet and Rufus, called the Star Inventors by everyone, had converted the three cages into a single screen to keep the Prairie Dogs from leaving Room 9. The doorway, a squat arch five feet high, opened into a low-ceilinged room with narrow pillars every few yards. It was illuminated by a red glow from the poisoned outside atmosphere that entered through a natural chimney.

Luckily the room had a sandy floor. It wasn't deep enough for burrowing, but still reminded them of their old homes above ground. The Prairie Dogs had made a sleeping nest in one corner out of the ragged dishtowels, and during their waking hours, they sculpted the sand, fashioning and refashioning it into eerily beautiful concentric circles.

Corpus Lazarus Jr.'s face lit up, breaking into a broad smile. "I can hear them running over to see me, and they're talking. I can almost understand them!"

He gripped the barrier with his fingers and shook it. "I think it slides on wheels. I'm going in."

Before Merlin could say yes or no, Corpus Lazarus Jr. opened it far enough for them to slip through. He did not hesitate but marched around the pillars to the center of the room, quite a feat for someone newly sightless. He sat down cross-legged at the center of the concentric rings, surrounded by a crowd of Prairie Dogs who apparently approved his presence. Positioned on their haunches, they clasped their paws together in silence, hiding their formidable digging claws.

Soon yips and barks, loud and soft and in ordered sequences, filled the air. Corpus Lazarus Jr. bent his head low, listening carefully for a long time. He whispered softly to Merlin, "I really can understand them."

Merlin, who had been standing by the wall, sat down beside him, and he took her hand. "Do you hear what they're saying, Merl? They want to sleep here at night but come out during the day. They want to join us in the other rooms."

Then he laughed for the first time in six months, the sweetest of sounds to Merlin's ears. "They say they'll be good and can help with the chores. They'll sweep, and they'll lick the dishes clean so we won't have to wash them in Lake Spooky."

Merlin shook her head. "I can't understand them at all. How do you do it, Corpus Lazarus Jr.?"

Corpus Lazarus Jr. considered the question thoughtfully. "I don't know. I guess losing my sight made me special in another way.

"But Merlin, you have the greatest gifts anyone could wish for. You can tell stories and you can see into the future. No one else here can do that."

"What are they saying now?"

"They're bored, and they can't clean their nest properly when they're all cooped up."

Corpus Lazarus Jr. laughed at the Prairie Dogs' sudden burst of cacophony. "They're so excited, all of them are talking at once, and I can't understand them anymore. And I can tell they're all standing up tall, now, like little people.

"Oh, I *do* get it, or rather ... I don't. They say they want to 'dance in circles with colors and gods.'"

Merlin grew serious, pulling him to his feet. "What's 'dancing in circles with colors and gods' mean? It's a strange thing to say. We better talk to Cyndi and Rufus right away."

Corpus Lazarus Jr.'s good mood evaporated. "You mean Mommy and her ex-husband. After the first few days of my sickness, they didn't visit me hardly at all. Just because they're the leaders now doesn't mean they should've forgotten me. My *real* daddy didn't remember me either. He just walked outside into the fires, and he didn't even visit me in bed to say goodbye."

"You have *me,*" Merlin offered.

"Yes, Merl, thank goodness for that."

***

Merlin and Corpus Lazarus Jr. found Cyndi in the gigantic crystal-coated VIP Room. She was pacing in circles at its center, under the wavy shadows of the stalactites. She orated rather than spoke, "Thou hast beautified us, blessed us, we thank thee ... we thank thee for thy.... Oh, *dammit,* Corpus Lazarus was so *good* at this. What's wrong with me?"

Hearing footsteps behind her, she turned her head and snapped, "What are you two doing here? Sabbath's tomorrow. Can't you tell I'm preparing a sermon?"

Seconds later she scolded herself, *My very own child, blinded and just out of bed, and I yell at him. And Merlin, too. She looks after him much better than I do.*

Merlin hurried to Cyndi's side, gesticulating as words poured out, "You wouldn't believe it unless you saw it with your own eyes and heard it with your own ears, Cyndi. Corpus Lazarus Jr. understands every word the Prairie Dogs say. Every word! It's amazing. I don't understand them, but he does, it's his sightless gift."

She added, "We thought you should know that the Prairie Dogs are saying something we don't quite *get,* but it sounds really different. They want to 'dance in circles with colors and gods.' They all said it, over and over again—"

Cyndi interrupted, "'Dance in circles with colors and gods.' Well, obviously they want to come to the church services. And isn't it simply wonderful? We're converting the heathen. I know they're listening from Room 9 because when I stand at the altar, I can hear them barking rhythmically during the hymns—"

"They want more than that, Mommy." Irritated that she hadn't acknowledged his newly discovered ability to understand the creatures, Corpus Lazarus Jr. cut her short. "They hate being cooped up. They want to live with us all day long."

He paused for effect before declaring, "And *I'm* gonna let 'em out!"

Cyndi's admiration for their religious fervor vanished. She grabbed her son by the shoulder and shook him, her voice cutting and cruel: "The hell you will, Corpus Lazarus Jr. Are you kidding? *Live* with us? I hate the furry little buggers, eating all our vegetables, dropping litters like they're gonna take over the world, each generation bigger and fatter."

Corpus Lazarus Jr. twisted out of her grip, his face ashen and scowling.

Predictably, she apologized for her nastiness and attempted to rephrase. "I'm sorry, Corpus Lazarus Jr., I'm so mean, such a bitch. They can come to church, of course.

"But really, think about it for a minute." She was backtracking, her lip curled with disdain. "Should we let them crawl underfoot all day, *insinuating* themselves into our lives?"

Then she recalled her shared power, or rather the man who could help her out of her current fix. "I don't know, I'll talk to Rufus ... *if* he can tear himself away from that chubby inventing partner of his, what's her name, Lilac, Wisteria?"

Cyndi turned vicious: "What's she got that I don't?"

Both children reacted with disgust and reached for each other's hands. Corpus Lazarus Jr., especially, had heard that last comment all too often.

"I'm the pastor, dammit!" Another wave of resentment swept across Cyndi's features, denting her brow with two unattractive vertical lines above her nose.

"No more Wisterias. I can marry myself to Rufus, any time—*today, if I want to*—at the same time as I marry those others who fell in love catching Prairie Dogs, Burt the political advisor and that spider-woman. She's always knitting something from the lifetime supply of wool she must've brought. I remember, Arachne with the screwed-up vocal cords."

She rolled her eyes: "And one of the chosen maidens impregnated by my dead husband. You'd never guess that henpecked Edwin would dare divorce Betty Anne. But he did—to tie the knot with Sylvie, the doe-eyed nymphet about a month away from delivery."

She hissed in fury, "What's Sylvie got that I don't?"

Corpus Lazarus Jr. had had it "up to here" with his mother. As soon as he and Merlin had fled beyond the bend in the corridor, he stopped short, whispering under his breath, "That's it, Merl, I'm letting out the Prairie Dogs during the wedding ceremony. I don't care if I get into trouble."

Mary Lynne wasn't always as grown up as she appeared. She snickered and poked Corpus Lazarus Jr. in the ribs. "Great idea. Let's do it just before the vows."

***

Their hastily arranged meeting held in the pitch-black corridor beyond the DANGER!!!! sign at the narrow end of Lake Spooky confirmed the fate that Violet had been dreading for the past four months. Rufus held her tenderly, stroked her hair and kissed her, all the while promising her that nothing would change.

But Violet couldn't stop crying. *I knew this would happen someday, that Rufus would marry Cyndi. And, no warning, the ceremony's this afternoon. Lord help me, the baby's just starting to kick. Since that first night I always figured I'd be first in his heart and last in his life.*

7 ~ Cyndi and Lunk

It was early morning, and Rufus was off somewhere; Cyndi could never keep track of his comings and goings. In Married Couples' Room 8, she sat slumped on the cot that was slightly wider and much saggier than her old one in Room 5. She trailed her fingers along the garish stripes of her Bay Point blanket. *I'm glad I picked the brightest one from the* Lady Hotshot *hunting catalog. If not for this, my whole life would be one dull wash of brown and grey, a slow death by radiation trapped in these nine rooms.*

As she always did, Cyndi snapped her body upright, scolding herself. *What's wrong with me? I'm so ungrateful, I should be counting my blessings. It's been one year, three months, and we're still here, most of us, anyway—weak, yes, but far from dead, unlike the rest of the human race all destroyed in one day.*

Cyndi slumped again, running a comb through her mouse-brown hair that was straight as a pin and split on the ends. She sighed, remembering the old days back home at the Goldie-Lox Hair and Deli just around the corner from the Holy Cavern of Lazarus Storefront Tabernacle. Every month she'd step out of the place clutching a paper bag containing a supersized bagel with a cream cheese schmear, her reward for sticking to her low-carb diet. Her heart had thrilled as she felt all eyes turning to admire her spiky coif, suddenly a florescent pink-blond and glittering with interwoven sparkle-tresses that matched her toenails.

Frowning, Cyndi stretched out a handful of hair and whispered to no one in particular, "Aren't these grey streaks more obvious today than a week ago? I wonder if nature has been equally unkind to my face. It's sad, but without a mirror, I'll never know."

The Prairie Dog who helped every day to sweep the sand off the floor of her bedroom alcove looked up from puttering and snuffling behind Cyndi's cot.

"Damn beasts," Cyndi muttered. "They're everywhere, and they've gotten so freakin' big you can't help tripping on 'em. But just look at those intelligent eyes. I think she understood every word I said."

Cyndi addressed the creature directly, whom she'd rather cruelly named Lunk. She had a way of chattering on and on to the Prairie Dog, airing all her problems.

"If you're so damned smart, Lunk, and I know all of you have been spying on us since Day One, what ever happened to my first husband, Reverend Corpus Lazarus? Did he simply walk out of here, smiling as usual and prancing about in those absurd shorts?"

The way the Prairie Dog returned her gaze, Cyndi was pretty sure Lunk would have answered if she'd had the right-shaped mouth to form human words.

"Funny," Cyndi continued. "Why am I still hung up on that man? Rufus makes a pretty good husband, even if he doesn't know up from down in the sack. And it's too bad he's so infatuated with that fat girl he's taken under his wing.

"I bet she called him Dr. Genius and swung her chubby hips, and poof. Violet became a new Thomas Edison."

Anger flicked across Cyndi's face. "If I ever find out he's the father of her baby girl, I'll kill him. Her, too. What's Violet got that I don't?"

Then she berated herself, *Everything I say is so mean, I'm such a bitch.*

***

Cyndi rested her elbows on her knees and her face in her hands. *It's been more than a year since Corpus Lazarus disappeared. How I miss that man, even with all his irritating faults. We both did horrible things to each other, but for him to simply leave like that, what was he thinking?*

She remarked to Lunk, "I just know how awful it must've been, Corpus Lazarus walking out the front entrance into the world's nuclear bake-oven. How long before he suffocated in the heat? Maybe a half hour?"

Lunk was in apparent agreement, nodding sagely and sympathetically. To distract Cyndi from her woes, the obliging creature began braiding the mouse-brown hair, a relatively recent, and distinctly servile, ritual that the Prairie Dog had introduced about a month ago.

Cyndi closed her eyes, lulled by Lunk's gentle ministration. She recalled every moment following the Day of the Jumping Sun in detail, trying to think of a way to exonerate herself. *I'm not a bad person, I know I'm not. But when the whole congregation walked out on his lousy sermon that first day after the blast, I left my poor hurt son. I hid behind the stalagmites in the VIP Room, and I heard Corpus Lazarus say some shocking things, like accusing Rufus and Merlin of stealing his ministry. But it wasn't them at all, they couldn't care less.*

It was me, *Cyndi, the most glamorous and smartest woman that Edgewater, Maryland, has ever known. I wanted his ministry so bad I could taste it.*

She shifted uneasily, yanking the braid loose from Lunk's paws. With one shake of her head, it began to unfurl on its own, strand by strand. *I had good reasons, too. I deserved to have it after the way he treated me, ordering me around and sleeping with anything cute in a skirt. He said it was his "God-given prerogative" from that stupid book he wrote,* The Holy Book of Lazarus. *He carried that book around everywhere with him, even on the day he died walking into the fiery furnace.*

***

Cyndi left the cot and began pacing, voicing her frustration too loudly for a hole-in-the-wall without privacy. "So now I have his ministry and I'm lousy at everything I do. I open my mouth and they all fall asleep, even on those medieval torture racks, aka folding chairs, wheezing and snoring right in the front row. How do you make a congregation happy? No one's listening anymore, they're sick of remembering some rotting guy in a winding sheet. And Jesus never came back in their time of need. Where was he when the bombs fell?"

She twisted around, suddenly, to look Lunk in the eye. "I get it! They want the sermons to be about *them,* and the ones I give aren't about *any* of us, anymore. They want something to relate to because they'll never leave the cavern. What's in my old textbook, *The Greco-Roman World, Cartoon Edition?* There's Hades, where you go after you die: it's underground. There's the River Styx, kind of like Lake Spooky. There's the Elysian Fields, a place of rest that's no longer just somewhere vague, like Abraham's Bosom."

Cyndi talked on and on, thinking out loud, even if the recipient wasn't human. Some ideas made sense, some didn't. At last she said, "You've always lived in dark tunnels, Lunk. And you would love sermons that are about you. Right?"

Lunk clasped her paws together and bowed in silent acknowledgement.

8 ~ Self-Sacrifice

Cyndi was lost. She cried out, "The VIP Room, where the hell is it?" Her voice was swallowed by silence because no sound rebounded to reassure her that she was anywhere.

Caught in a jumble of tunnels, she nearly fell face-down when they widened without warning. She found herself inside the Colosseum in Rome. She saw a great circle of winking stars above the wall's broken crest, and at her feet a quarter-moon splayed its beams across the pebbled sod.

She pinched her nose. "I smell yesteryear's blood and old bones from sacrifices past because I'm inside my history book, Graeco-Roman World, Cartoon Edition. *But look at the stuff around me. No swords and battered helmets lie here; rather I see folding chairs and the big altar. And isn't this my own Bible with my Sunday sermon tucked inside?"*

Cyndi turned, and at the far end she noticed a gigantic handstitched banner stretched between two columns. She read the foot-high words over and over again, trying to make sense of them.

FROM SELF-SACRIFICE SPRINGS LIFE

She stared hard at the appliqued Prairie Dog beneath the maxim, and the word "life" seemed contradictory. It lay on its back with exes replacing the eyes. Without a doubt it was dead; embroidered blood coursed from a red rickrack wound that ran from neck to abdomen.

She heard a commotion and whirled around to see her Sunday congregation jumping up and down on the VIP Room's rickety chairs. In the front row a band of rowdy ringleaders brandished knives and forks. The others waggled their fingers or waved their arms, all the while snuffling and snorting like pigs.

"No," Cyndi yelled above the din. "Don't get any ideas from that banner." She set her mouth in a straight line, her jaw jutting forth, hands on hips. "No animal sacrifice, no Prairie Dog steaks, and no fur coats."

She chanced to turn toward the holy altar. She gasped, her hands flying to her mouth. It was too late. A plump corpse already lay outstretched, slit from neck to abdomen. Gobs of blood ran over the stone to pool and percolated into the sod.

"Lunk! Oh, my darling, not you—"

Cyndi wrenched herself awake and sat up abruptly, her whole body trembling. She cried out, "What a terrible, terrible dream. Oh, Lunk!" Rufus, who had performed his weekly conjugal duty ten minutes before, was jarred from deep slumber.

He propped himself up on an elbow. "Uh, Cyndi, *what the hell?* The neighbors will hear you."

In a voice choked and shaking, Cyndi dropped to a whisper, "Rufus, I had a horrible dream. The Prairie Dogs were killing themselves so we could eat them, and they were making it into a church ritual. In my dream, Lunk—"

"It's a good idea, honey, and it's what they want. I know that for a fact." He rolled over, as far as such a move were possible on the sagging cot, and in seconds, went back to sleep.

Cyndi shook his shoulder, demanding, "*Dammit,* Rufus, who told you that?"

"Hmm, what? Oh, Lunk told Corpus Lazarus Jr., who told Merlin and me. We're supposed to convince you to listen to what they have to say. Tomorrow when I'm awake, okay? You think having sex isn't exhausting on a lettuce and cucumber diet?"

With sleep an impossibility, Cyndi spent the rest of the night walking around in circles throughout the VIP Room's vast chamber, crisscrossing, circling the perimeter, and marching along the center isle that terminated at the bulky stone altar. To avoid the sacrifice issue, first she considered the pig-people of her dream. They bothered her immensely, because one of her recurring fears was an out-of-control congregation bent on destroying the fragile steps everyone had taken so far.

But a little voice deep down inside her began nagging: *Stick to the point, Cyndi. It's animal sacrifice and it isn't just about you. You like staying rail thin on a diet of tomatoes even though your hair is starting to fall out. Think of the nursing mothers with their milk drying up and those old folks, all weak and shaky. And the kids. They're too tired to swim in Lake Spooky anymore. Some of it's the radiation, of course, but a lot of babies are dying before birth.*

Cyndi came to a complete halt. To no one in particular, she announced, "It's malnutrition that's getting to us. No doubt about it, we need help from somewhere."

On her sixty-fifth rotation around the room, she began to consider the Prairie Dogs themselves, and she recalled that for three weeks now, her son had been relaying their complaints to her almost every day.

What was he saying? The population's too large. With all the new babies getting bigger with each generation, Room 9's gotten so small that they're walking all over each other, and they can't sleep. They're fighting more, snarling, pushing, biting, barking, bullying—

"This is terrible," Cyndi announced to the stalactites. "They're turning into humans." Then she remembered that only yesterday Lunk had arrived for her dusting chores with a twisted leg and an angry red claw-mark under her eye.

"My goodness," she said out loud, this time to the folding chairs. "Poor Lunk. I had no idea I cared so much for her until I had that dream."

Cyndi collapsed onto one of the chairs, her first rest since she'd started her frantic walking. But then she bounced up, yelling loud enough to fill the entire cavernous space, "From self-sacrifice springs life. From self-sacrifice *springs life!"*

"Life-ife-fff-ff-f," went the echo.

Cyndi sighed aloud, the sound of her unhappiness bouncing about the chamber in mournful ululations. "If that's the way the Prairie Dogs want it, okay, as long as they don't offer up Lunk.

"And I hope they won't do that hateful little circle dance every time, the one that looks like the spokes of a wheel. They already perform it with the eucharist."

***

Violet and Rufus tiptoed around the shore of Lake Spooky, trying to avoid the glances of late-night romantics obsessed by the bat-moon. The cheaters' usual rendezvous spot deep in the corridor at the narrow end was no longer a secret, and it was only a matter of time before other people would start walking past the DANGER!!!! sign.

Violet jumped when Rufus let out a gasp of dismay. He hissed *sotto voce,* "Violet, look. My best invention, the bat-moon. It's fading. Sure, the bats are irradiated and trapped in a salad-spinner, but they shouldn't be dying so fast."

Now that they had a legitimate reason for being at the lake, Rufus and Violet felt free to bellow as they ran for the ladder that had once been the coat rack by the entrance. "Vi, this place is like an old apartment building with failing plumbing. We're no better than superintendents."

"Speaking of which. The so-called comfort stations—"

Rufus grabbed Violet's arm. "Oh, no. The mosquito farm has shrunk. No wonder the bats are dying, they're starving." He frowned. "Where the hell is the children's Bat Committee? I should've gotten a report."

"Well, where's your gardening committee, Rufus? Last week I had to water the lah-di-dah apple tree that looks like a bonsai with a growth defect—"

"Eureka, Violet, I've just figured out what to do. We'll *clone* more mosquitos. They're not that complex, they're insects, *Diptera,* family, *Culcidae,* and I'm a pretty spectacular biologist."

"Oh my *Lord,* Rufus, don't be a fool. We're living in a replay of the Pleistocene Age; I turned my alcove curtain into diapers and the hooks into safety pins. We're one step away from wearing pelts. And you're gonna set up a cloning lab?"

Rufus plopped down on a convenient stone, his eyes shining with excitement. "Yes, and I don't need you, Vi, to make this happen, so shut up. Besides, you're not as nice as you were when I first met you.

"I'll train some Prairie Dogs. They'll make perfect lab assistants—patient, obedient, worshipful with big adoring eyes, and, best of all, they're *silent.*"

9 ~ Where No One Has Gone Before

Several months after Cyndi had acquiesced to sacrificing Prairie Dogs during Sunday services, she disappeared in the night. Rumors began to fly early the next day. She hadn't drowned in Lake Spooky because no body was found bobbing on its obsidian surface. Only two options remained: either she'd walked past the red DANGER!!!! signs into the cave's unexplored regions, or, like Corpus Lazarus, she'd committed suicide in the fiery world outside.

There was another possibility that appealed to sensation-seekers and caught on immediately, spreading like wildfire. She'd been murdered with a sharpened Prairie Dog femur taken from the trash after a Sacrifice Sunday, and the perpetrator had dragged her mutilated corpse outside by the ankles for a hasty, evidence-destroying cremation. That gruesome theory sprang from the cave's incredibly efficient gossip mill. Those closest to Cyndi—Rufus, Violet, Corpus Lazarus Jr., and Merlin—were doubly affected, becoming most-likely suspects even as they absorbed the horror of it. To the conspiracy-minded, the murder weapon also implicated the Prairie Dogs.

The whispering had started early when Cyndi didn't show up to lead Pray 'n Chat, the 6:30 a.m. service that had suffered a dwindling attendance as time passed. As happened every day, these words would emerge in a sing-song unison from a circle of bowed heads, the volume amplified many times by the convoluted crystalline ceiling. The prayer served as an alarm clock to wake the entire congregation:

"Thank you for the food we grow, thank you for the world below.

Thank you for the bat-moon's light, thank you for eternal night."

With a few notable exceptions, nobody considered Cyndi's alteration of the tried-and-true original sacrilegious. They accepted the reality of the lines, an evolution of thought for a people slowly growing accustomed to living underground where they would undoubtedly remain for a very long time.

As Merlin bowed her head to lead the congregants, Betty Anne whispered, "Where's Cyndi? She hasn't ever missed Pray 'n Chat, not one time since Corpus Lazarus died."

Her voice turned nasty, and she began a shockingly rebellious rant: "I bet Cyndi got murdered. Mark my words, that family is pure evil, through and through. Women of the night standing beside a bunch of Prairie Dog traps luring away my Edwin.

"I'm planning my *own* congregation, and any one of you is *free to join.* We'll be praying to Corpus Lazarus who walked into the sun, not to some devilish bat-moon inventor and his floozies. I have a name for us, too: the *Sun People.*"

***

Rufus, Violet, Corpus Lazarus Jr., and Merlin planned an emergency meeting to take place a half mile inside the corridor that opened at the narrow end of Lake Spooky. Rufus and Violet arrived first. The Prairie Dog Nebuchadnezzar, Merlin's personal alcove duster, helped her and Corpus Lazarus Jr. down the slippery stairs before standing sentinel at the corridor's entrance. Feeling like conspirators, they kept their voices low, remembering the cavern's propensity for making echoes.

Since the Prairie Dogs had also been accused of the alleged murder, Lunk, their new queen recently appointed democratically by a majority of raised paws, shambled in a few minutes after the human quartet had gathered. The picture of misery, she wrung her paws, her head and shoulders draped in a tatty dishtowel.

Rufus sat cross legged, groaning as his knees creaked, and the others sank down beside him to form a tight circle. They leaned their backs against the clammy walls that smelled of damp stone and bat guano, their brows knit as they tried to collect their thoughts. Lunk stood at Corpus Lazarus Jr.'s elbow in case she would be asked to join the conversation.

Rufus cleared his throat in preparation for whispering, a skill that he wasn't particularly good at. "Oh my God, how did this happen?" His eyes were dry, although he looked pale and disheveled, his hair rising in unruly peaks as he combed his fingers through it.

Violet, the "other woman," averted her eyes from his, while Merlin twisted sideways to put her arms around Corpus Lazarus Jr. who burst into tears, weeping into her shoulder. Lunk hid her visage deep within the dishtowel, whimpering in tiny yips that eventually annoyed everyone except Corpus Lazarus Jr.

Violet recovered her composure, folding her arms across her Mae West bosom. "Move this discussion along, people, I'm paying the babysitter three tomatoes an hour."

Rufus threw her a warning glance. "Vi, this doesn't sound like you." He turned to the others, his tone more of a plea than a factual statement: "We're sure we all trust each other. That none of us did it, right?"

He added an amendment that convinced no one, "I loved my wife, of course, but she could never be Violet ... oh hell, all of you know that."

After a considerable pause he gave a eulogy of sorts: "By the way, I thought she was a genius, much more than me." He added, "But that wouldn't be a reason to kill her." Frowning, Rufus turned his head away, disgusted by the weakness of his presentation.

The gnomelike Merlin stood up. "Mary Lynne, here." Rufus and Violet cringed at her formality. Even for this urgent meeting to contain the rumor-fed parishioners awaiting them in the VIP Room, she'd put on a ruffled dress and Mary Janes.

Merlin's uncharacteristically acerbic words set them aback: "Rufus and Violet, you make me sick, but I know you didn't do it because you had no cause. Okay, Cyndi did throw a fit when she found out about you two and the baby, but she got over it at least six months ago. She didn't even act mad after that because she had a lot of governing to do. And she preferred not having you underfoot, Rufus."

Then, oddly, Merlin puffed out her chest as she readjusted her features from angry to proud. "Don't you get it? She was really mad at *me,* not you. Mad because I hated her so-called reforms, and I fought her every inch of the way, like when she introduced Sisyphus with that stupid half-Christian name, Sisychrist. I prefer the ones that she took directly from her Graeco-Roman comic book, like baptizing the whole congregation as Shades into the Kingdom of Hades. That little whirlpool near the shore of Lake Spooky is just beautiful, the perfect place."

She flung her head defiantly. "And she didn't want me and Corpus Lazarus Jr. to get married until he turns twenty-one. Really, I think eighteen or even sixteen is more reasonable in times like these, but there was no budging her after she got something stuck in her head."

Merlin sat back down again, folding her hands primly in her ruffled lap. Elevating her nose haughtily, she proclaimed, "But I have plenty of ethics that my mother and grandmother taught me from about age one, so I didn't kill her, not even because of that."

As most of them began commenting on Merlin's lengthy and self-incriminating outburst, Corpus Lazarus Jr. wiped the tears from his sightless eyes on his shirtsleeve and stood up. He tried the impossible, yelling in an undertone to get everyone's attention.

At last he grabbed Lunk around her substantial middle and thrust her into the air. "Hey, everyone, Lunk has something to say."

After a few minutes of listening to Lunk's barks and yips, Corpus Lazarus Jr. translated, his voice squeaking with excitement: "My mother wasn't murdered, and she didn't kill herself, either."

"What?" This, a communal chorus of three voices.

"She walked past the DANGER!!!! sign at the front of this very passage to go exploring. She took Neshek, Hyperion, and Archbishop with her, also Captain Kirk, Lunk's boy and the bravest Prairie Dog in the whole cavern. No humans volunteered to go when she asked us last night at Drum Circle—"

Violet interrupted, "Then why was Lunk sobbing into a dishtowel and carrying on like a jilted bride?"

"That's easy, Violet," Corpus Lazarus Jr. replied. "And I don't even have to ask Lunk for the answer. She's devoted. She misses my mom like crazy ... unlike the rest of you."

Before they adjourned the clandestine meeting to take on the mutinous congregation, Rufus dropped the last puzzle piece into place. "Of course! Yesterday morning I was the one who worked out the statistics for Cyndi. In less than a year if you combine our lousy birthrate with the Prairie Dogs' exploding one, we'll outgrow the nine rooms and need more space—much more space. Cyndi's a hero on a mission."

He thought for a minute before adding an apt cliché: "'A mission to go where no one has gone before.' And I'll bet she'll look for veins of coal while she's at it. We're running out of wood."

Merlin nodded wisely, turning toward Corpus Lazarus Jr. "Isn't that exactly what I saw in my vision just after the Day of the Jumping Sun? 'If you go past the DANGER!!!! signs, all the caverns are attached together. Our descendants will be called the *Shade People,* and their dark realm will stretch from Iqaluit to Nanisivik.'"

***

That night after Merlin had pulled the red Bay Point blanket up to Corpus Lazarus Jr.'s chin and tucked him in, he freed his narrow arm from the warm cocoon and waved it about, searching for his best friend's hand. She sat down beside him on the metal cot, and their fingers interlaced.

He whispered words he'd been hesitant to say in front of everybody else. "I'm scared, Merl. Nobody's supposed to walk past Injun Joe's DANGER!!!! signs for a good reason. There are miles and miles *and miles* of twisting tunnels. And there are huge caverns and deep pits, and it's all very, very dark. Mommy's brave and strong, but ... but maybe she'll never come back."

Merlin nodded her head, even though the little boy couldn't see her. "Dearest Corpus Lazarus Jr., I will not lie to you, not now or ever. It's likely she's not going to—"

"But Merl, she *has* to. She's my *mommy."*

Mary Lynne smoothed his hair. Although she spoke kindly, her words had a grown-up conviction. "Corpus Lazarus Jr., *do* listen to what I'm saying. Your mommy was never like you and me—or anybody else in this cavern. She wasn't always nice to people around her, but she had a *fire* burning inside her, *a divine energy*. She wanted to save *many, many people way off in the future,* not just us."

As tears began coursing down the sides of the little boy's cheeks, Merlin helped him sit up, and she wiped his face on his big red bandana that he kept folded on his night table next to his drinking cup, toothbrush, and comb.

"Dear one, it's time for me to tell you about a new vision I had a few weeks ago. I thought I'd save it until I understood it better. And now I *do* understand it after what happened today."

Corpus Lazarus Jr. nodded. "Okay, I want to hear it, Merl, especially if you didn't dream it up just now to make me feel better."

Mary Lynne cleared her throat of the nasty radioactive dust. "Then here it is. We'll never learn how to read and write again because we don't have books, pencils and paper. But we'll pass on our stories out loud to our children and children's children, just like the story of Magnolia got passed on to me.

"And a million years from now, the *handsome giant*—remember, the one who gets murdered by his son—will write down our stories so we won't vanish from the earth without a trace, because the radiation will keep making us sicker and sicker.

"But his *real reason* for coming will be very much like your mother's. He, too, will be full to the brim with a divine energy. He'll arrive to find a world that's *wounded,* and he'll try to make it a better place. Because if he doesn't, *people will stop existing."*

Corpus Lazarus Jr. interrupted by grabbing her shoulders with both hands. "Merlin, Merlin, you don't mean he's a giant like the one who says 'fee fi fo fum' in 'Jack and the Beanstalk'—because that's make-believe. He's really a very, very tall *human being."*

After his outburst, the little boy felt smug because every once in a while, he had the courage to make a comment on his own. He was getting sleepy, too, lulled by the sweet sound of his dearest friend's voice. Merlin tucked him in again and kissed his cheek.

Corpus Lazarus Jr. had one more question to ask as he began to drift off. "Last time, you said ... you saw ... hundreds of Prairie Dogs ... in your vision. Are ... they ... still there?"

As Mary Lynne pulled his red and white striped curtain closed, she said, "I certainly *did* see them, big as life."

BOOK TWO

A Million Years Later

10 ~ My Daddy, Always a Giant to Me

How'd it come to this? —Svnoyi

"Sequoyah, my daddy, always a giant to me, don't die. Sequoyah, my daddy, always a giant to me, don't die."

Svnoyi mumbled the mantra over and over as she sat perched on a big flat boulder high up on a rock-strewn slope sparsely dotted with dwarf pines. It wasn't too far away from the cave where her father lay dying, stabbed in the stomach by his son. She was holding her own private vigil for him on that boulder, and her particular ritual required the mantra. She would never stop repeating it, not for a moment.

Saying the mantra didn't keep her mind from lurching forward on its own. Mantra and full orchestral accompaniment plus percussion, too many words that wouldn't stop, a sad tune wailing above violins, oboes, cellos, and all the rest, and the drums pounding and lacerating the delicate membranes inside her head—

I'm getting a terrible headache, and it's no ordinary one. A four-year-old's feet are the drums, running and jumping inside my brain. This is definitely not good. Not good at all, I have responsibilities now that Daddy's dying. I'm fifteen, going on sixteen. He didn't say it in so many words, but he would've wanted me to take over for him.

***

"Sequoyah, my daddy, always a giant to me, don't die. Sequoyah, my daddy, always a giant to me, don't die."

My daddy lies in Aleta's arms, stabbed by Kuaray. Aleta, darling Aleta, my stepmother. How will she bear it when he dies? And it's not just Aleta. It's his other children, including me. Especially me, because we were so close, Daddy and I. He's leaving everyone else, too, three whole families. He was our glue, our soul, our strength, our collective heart—I don't know how else to say it.

He was our leader, even though he wasn't great at leading. But what matters more is he was a great person, a giant to us all.

***

"Sequoyah, my daddy, always a giant to me, don't die. Sequoyah, my daddy, always a giant to me, don't die."

We got here last spring. We couldn't have done it without Ethan, our physicist and engineer, who can build just about anything. He designed our time machine and put it inside a Greyhound bus. The bus is still sitting up on a hill not too far from here. We left in 1976, and we moved forward in time. I do believe we're the only human survivors a million years beyond World War III. We knew in advance that the war would seriously mess up the planet by burning the outer surface right off, and that's why we jumped so far ahead.

How'd we know the war was going to happen in 2050 or thereabouts? That's a long story from the Time Before. I can't get into it right now. Besides, I couldn't stomach retelling the details because my head hurts too much.

***

"Sequoyah, my daddy, always a giant to me, don't die. Sequoyah, my daddy, always a giant to me, don't die."

We were hoping we'd find a place that was habitable, and we did. But it's kind of monotonous—all pines and no shade trees, not a single one. Why did Nature make such a narrow choice when she renewed the world?

I have to pinch myself sometimes, it's not a dream. We actually live in three caves, and Daddy's dying right now in the first one on the left because he's bleeding inside. The cave mouths are next to each other, in a cliff here on Baffin Island. They face the strait, overlooking the water. Quebec is to the south of us, somewhere. But that was the Time Before, a million years ago, when places had names. Now Quebec has no name and neither does Canada. Even Earth has no name.

Baffin Island does *have a name, though, and it's Baffling Isle. That's what the Prairie Dogs call it and believe me, they aren't those cute little things that pop out of burrows like during the Time Before. They're huge, they're brilliant, they're terrifying, and they run this place. Some of us call them Mafia, but not to their faces, of course. You look at them, and you want to laugh they're so freakish, especially their queen. But laugh at your peril.*

I can't stomach thinking about them right now.

"Sequoyah, my daddy, always a giant to me, don't die. Sequoyah, my daddy, always a giant to me, don't die."

I have to ask myself, how'd we get off to such a lousy start? Ever since we got here, we've made one mistake after another. We thought we knew a lot about survival, but somehow it wasn't quite enough. And we were fighting with each other, arguing all the time about this and that. For a while we seemed to be doing better because the Prairie Dogs helped us out with food and planting our crops, but they exacted a debt for their help. That's their way.

And then things got much worse. Our Luz, strong, competent, no-nonsense Luz ended up in a coma. She's still in a coma, and the Prairie Dogs have her. She's not dead, we know that much. But to us, she is *dead, because she's gone. Poor Ethan. He's trying to raise their newborn baby alone, and he's doing a pretty bad job.*

All that's another story for another day because I can't stomach it right now.

"Sequoyah, my daddy, always a giant to me, don't die. Sequoyah, my daddy, always a giant to me, don't die."

How'd it come to this? My daddy's wound was too deep, even my tears couldn't save him. We all watched our gypsy doctor Anichka try to sew shut that huge hole that was gaping and bleeding. There she was, operating right on the sandy floor of Sequoyah's cave where Jaroslav and Ethan had carried him after he got stabbed. She was using supple tendrils from the vines that grow here. And when she ran out, she sent Jaroslav to fetch more of them. He was driving her crazy, reciting a whole Latin Mass while sitting at Sequoyah's feet, but you'd think she must've been used to it after all those years of marriage.

Then Anichka sent everyone else away, too, especially Aleta because she was crying so loud. But I stayed. I watched the stitches rip out with every breath Daddy took until Anichka knew it was time to give up. Then all of the kids came back into the cave to say goodbye: Agali, Alexej, Phoenix, Oscar, and Lucy. Yacy brought Arielle Luz so Sequoyah could see his tiny granddaughter, but I don't think he was awake just then. Imagine having a granddaughter already at age thirty-six.

After that Aleta said she wanted to be alone with her husband until he died. Everyone went back to their own caves except me because I made a vow to stay and keep this vigil. That's why I'm sitting here on a freezing cold boulder. I made myself a promise to stay until the end.

"Sequoyah, my daddy, always a giant to me, don't die. Sequoyah, my daddy, always a giant to me, don't die."

I'm so cold. It's late October, and we had Indian Summer for a month with the sky a deep blue every day. And just this noon, the storm clouds came rolling over, socking in the pine forests. It's as if they knew this was going to be a very sad day—although, really, I know Mother Nature cares nothing about human affairs. But winter's coming early because we're so far north. Even though the weather's gotten much warmer on Baffin Island than it was during the Time Before, not even time's passage can alter the axis of the earth or its rotation around the sun. Soon the nights will get longer and longer until the sun doesn't rise at all during the day.

It's starting to snow already, big fat flakes. I hate this wind. I'm cold, even in my parka that I remembered to grab this morning before all this happened.

How can we bear winter without Daddy?

"Sequoyah, my daddy, always a—"

My mantra! Where'd it go? It stopped. I couldn't finish it just now. It's never good to break a mantra if you want it to work. It was the feet *that stopped it, the four-year-old's feet like drums, running and jumping inside my brain. They are my daddy's feet from when he was a little boy.*

Daddy gave me a vision of himself while he still could, a final gift from his dying brain. It's how he wanted me to remember him: four years old and running about free and happy before the big black government car came to take him away to the Indian boarding school. He runs in circles, his feet are pounding the earth, his tangled black hair flies behind him, and his head is thrown back because he's laughing.

At first, the vision made me so happy. Because we're all telepathic, all of us except Aleta and Ethan, we can do stuff like this. We have visions, we can talk without opening our mouths. But I was afraid, too, at first. I kept saying, "Daddy, don't let this circle be the last one because I know that when the footsteps stop, you'll be dead."

But they didn't stop. There's no pleasure anymore in having them running and pounding in circles through my brain. I feel sick, my head is bursting. Feet, going around and around too many times, I know you're still alive, Daddy, lying up there in Aleta's arms. But I can't stand the feet for even one more minute.

I can't say the mantra anymore, my head hurts too much. Because, Sequoyah, because, Daddy, I did something terrible, and I'm not sure you knew what I did even though you were right there, bent double and howling. I killed someone because of you. I killed Kuaray, my half brother—and your son. He was crazy when he stabbed you in the stomach. I saw the knife flash. I saw it go in. I watched you fall down. I couldn't save you from him, I reacted a few seconds too late.

So I broke his neck. Call it retribution, call it murder, call it what ever you like. Kuaray had to die, and I remember how it felt. I jumped on his back, I wrapped my fingers around his larynx, I tightened my grip with both hands, and I squeezed. The crunching sound his neck made is louder than my mantra, louder than all my stories ... but not as loud as your pounding four-year-old feet.

Oh, my head! It's splitting, shattering into a million, billion pieces.

"Sequoyah, my daddy, always a giant to me, perhaps you *won't die?"*

11 ~ Children in Mourning

Svnoyi felt delicate fingers brush her cheek, and her eyes sprang open. She hadn't meant to neglect her vigil for Sequoyah, but she'd fallen into a migraine-induced sleep. Momentarily disoriented, she teetered, nearly tumbling off her rocky perch into the scrub below.

The fingers belonged to her five-year-old half sister, Agali, who'd scrambled up beside her. Agali had always been Sequoyah and Aleta's most light-hearted child. But at the moment, there was nothing light-hearted about her.

With an effort, Svnoyi ignored the pounding in her head. She turned to look at the little girl, incongruously wrapped in a burlap bag. She scolded, "Agali, why are you dressed in a potato sack? You'll get *sick* in this cold. Go to your cave and get your parka."

Agali shook her head, her silver-haired pageboy flapping from side to side across her ears. Her huge grey eyes drooped like waning half moons. "I *can't,* Snail. Mama's in there with Daddy, and she sent all of us away so she could be alone with him. Don't you *remember?"*

To avoid looking foolish, Svnoyi didn't answer. She turned to Alexej, Agali's constant companion, who sat on her other side. Even though he was exactly Agali's age, he was a head taller and as muscular as a miniature prize fighter. He had a nervous habit of brushing aside a shock of black curls that continually fell in front of his eyes.

He was similarly covered in burlap, and before Svnoyi could ask him about his parka, he offered an explanation. "And my mama's in her cave crying because she couldn't sew up the place with vines where Sequoyah got stabbed. I was afraid I'd make her mad if I went in, so I couldn't get my parka, either."

Anichka's still *crying? This is awful: the adults are falling apart. It's so obvious that holding all of us together is up to me.*

The children announced in unison, "That's why we had to find *new* parkas in the tool shed."

Of course. Poor kids, how very resourceful of them. No one expected a winter storm to descend like this on the day Daddy was stabbed.

But she responded with unexpected irritation rather than sympathy, "So why didn't you go to *Ethan's* cave? It's only about fifteen feet away. He would've found *something* for you to wear, tarps or—"

"We tried, Snail, but he was in there having a big fight with Lucy about something."

"A fight with Lucy, his own *kid* at a time like this? Oh, god, what next."

The little girl tried reaching for the comfort of Svnoyi's hand, but it was hidden inside the parka's pouch. Agali settled on cupping her cold fingers around her big half sister's elbow.

"Snail," she whispered, "Daddy didn't die, I can feel it. That's why we came to see you—because I don't know ... is it good or bad?"

Alexej nodded. He'd felt it, too.

There's no hiding anything from these telepathic kids, and they're all that way, Agali and Alexej, Lucy, Phoenix, Oscar, and Yacy. So was Kuaray, except I just killed him.

If Svnoyi had been her usual self, she would have pulled the children close and hugged them, saying she agreed that Sequoyah hadn't died. She would have tried to answer Agali's wrenching question about their mortally wounded father.

But she couldn't do it, somehow. Remembering Kuaray, her aching brain suddenly expanded to the size of a jumbo pumpkin, hugely orange and stringy inside.

Instead, in a misbegotten attempt at leadership, she started barking orders. "Alexej, *go get your mama.* I don't care if Anichka thinks she's a failure, tell her Sequoyah needs medical help *right now.*

"Tell Jaroslav to come too."

"You mean my *daddy,* Snail."

"Yes, your daddy. Jaroslav is your daddy, Fer chrissake, Alexej, who else would I mean?"

Then Svnoyi turned to her half sister. "Agali, *find the other kids,* and get them up here, *fast."*

"But Snail, I don't know where they are."

Svnoyi burst out angrily, "That's why I said *find.*

"And stop calling me *Snail.* I hate it. My name is Svnoyi." She added condescendingly, "Three syllables, 'Su-noy-ye.' It's *Cherokee,* because Daddy named me."

Agali countered in a tiny voice, "My name's Cherokee, too, Snail. You *look* like a snail with your hood pulled over your head."

"I *do not.* I look like an intelligent person who remembered to grab a parka this morning."

Suddenly incensed by her fallen idol's inexplicable nastiness, Agali stuck out her tongue and jamming her thumbs in her ears, she waggled her fingers. She yelled, "Snail, Snail, Sna-il."

Svnoyi roared, "Good going, Agali. Since you did that, I'm gonna call you 'Algae' from now on. G*o away,* Algae, and do what I asked. You, too, Algae the Second."

The children slid to the ground and turned to leave. The picture of fury and dejection, they shivered in their wet burlap sacks.

Svnoyi bent double to lean her burning forehead against the boulder's blessedly cool surface. *How old was I acting just then? Four? This isn't me. My brain's been hijacked by a vision-gone-mad, by little running feet. And it's* no fair, *this handicap, when I'm supposed to be leading.*

***

In the first whiteout squall of the snowstorm, Agali and Alexej almost collided with Phoenix as he inched toward Svnoyi's rock. Alexej pointed in its direction, and Agali scowled and twirled a finger around her ear to imply that Svnoyi had a screw loose.

Phoenix approached the rock warily. He'd already sensed that something was wrong with Svnoyi beyond the lonely despair of keeping a deathwatch. When she came into view on her boulder looking like a curled-up lump with her head on the stone, he stopped short.

"Svnoyi," he called out tentatively, "Are you well enough to come down and talk?"

She roused herself and slid from her perch to stand beside him. They crept around to the sheltered side of the rock where the swirling wind couldn't reach them, and they didn't have to yell. In fact, the snow hadn't collected there yet, leaving a calm spot in the midst of the turmoil everywhere else.

It was hard to tell which of them was in worse shape. In a burst of compassion that she hadn't felt earlier, Svnoyi grasped Phoenix's hands, and his fingers were icy. He had been caught completely unprepared for the storm. As his whole body trembled inside his soaked chambray work shirt and blue jeans, she pulled off her parka lightning fast to give him the sweaters underneath. They were toasty warm from her own body heat.

"Thank you, Svnoyi, b-b-but I c-c-can't take these." His teeth were chattering. "You're the one who's sick."

What's he saying? Svnoyi couldn't concentrate.

Her headache had reached a new phase, and her thoughts ran wilder than before. *Phoenix isn't my brother at all, but he's part of my family because Sequoyah's his stepdad. Aleta never would tell him who his real father is, but I happen to know because I eavesdropped when she told Anichka.*

He's four years younger than me, but he was always a charmer with those big violet eyes and a tangle of dark ginger hair. He's cute, he's funny, what he knows about plants could fill an encyclopedia. God, I've treated him terribly, Yacy and me, how we ganged up on him when we were younger. One time we—

"Svnoyi, are you okay? You look like you're gonna pass out." His words came from far away, and he was supporting her under her armpits.

"What? No, I'm not okay. I mean yes, I'm okay, but let's sit down." They slid to their haunches because they didn't want to plant themselves on the freezing ground.

"I'm not really sick. It's a headache: I call it a *telepathic* headache, if there *is* such a thing. It was a last gift from Daddy, these Indian child's racing feet. But they were supposed to stop when he died. Or maybe my brain's gotten stuck, like when a song keeps repeating in your head.

"Do you think I'm crazy? I know the little kids think so, I was so *mean* to them a few minutes ago."

"Of course you're not crazy, Svnoyi. Anything that's telepathic is usually distorted and weird."

Phoenix bowed his head, mumbling, "How can I say this without pressuring you? But I *have* to. You're the oldest responsible kid, and we need you to lead us. Sequoyah's got to get medical help *right now* because like you said, he didn't die—"

Again, Svnoyi wasn't really listening. *Take over leading for Sequoyah? Of course. That's what I'm doing already 'cause he would've wanted me to—*

How I miss him. He didn't ever *want to lead, really. He made so many mistakes, and I kept getting mad at him. Once I yelled at him, "Do I always have to be your teacher, Daddy?"*

Svnoyi snapped out of her reverie. The whole time she'd been trapped inside her whirling brain, Phoenix's words had been tumbling out.

"Svnoyi, we can't leave Sequoyah lying there any longer. He's alive, I just know it. Let's all go into his cave and get him. We'll carry him really gently; we'll climb aboard the Greyhound bus and take him home as fast as we can. Home to 1976, the year when we left. There are real emergency rooms there with clean white sheets and doctors who don't have to sew up wounds with vines."

Svnoyi was suddenly alert. "Phoenix, no, that's nuts—"

"I think it's possible Ethan can reverse the Greyhound's drive. I know time travel is complicated, but I've been studying his physics books that he let me borrow. Maybe I can help him with the calculations now that Kuaray's dead. At least I could try."

He tugged insistently at her hands. "Svnoyi, please, please ... I want to go home."

To Svnoyi, the depth of his homesickness and sorrow came as a surprise. *But he's a middle child. Who would've cared what he thought?*

"Phoenix, it's impossible, just wishful thinking and a dead end." She tried not to look at his crumbling features.

"Even if we *could* go back, all the people would die a couple of generations after us, in 2050, World War III. You *knew* we had a big mission to fulfill when we left, jumping far into the future beyond all the terrible fires—

"Besides, we both know Ethan's been taking the Greyhound apart to make other things."

Phoenix made one last try, "Maybe the bus isn't too far gone, yet. We could go look at it."

He dropped his head into his hands. "Living here is just too hard. Kuaray's dead, the Prairie Dogs are huge and as smart as we are, Queen Gitli's an evil monster who keeps bred and cloned animals as slaves. Before all this happened, we were doing kind of okay, but only because they're helping us out. They give us those food rabbits every day to make us forever *beholden."*

"And the worst is, ever since they took Luz ... it's almost impossible to say it, I miss her so much. She was ... she was really like a mom to me—"

Just then, Agali and Alexej peered around the edge of the rock, not sure what to expect. They were still dripping wet in their potato sacks, although, ever resourceful, they'd found closely needled pine branches that they'd tied to their heads with the bandanas they always carried in their overall pockets.

Svnoyi twisted away from Phoenix to confront them, her voice tart. "Agali and Alexej, we don't have all night. You haven't brought a single person. Alexej, where are Anichka and Jaroslav? Agali, you were supposed to bring the other kids. Where are Yacy and Oscar? Where's Lucy?"

Svnoyi instantly berated herself. *A headache is no excuse. Go easy, they're only little kids. Maybe I shouldn't have sent them in the first place: they could've gotten lost out there in the squall.*

"Well," Agali crowed, as if she'd read Svnoyi's mind. "We could've gotten lost, but we didn't because we're good at knowing where we are, even in the snow.

"And we weren't hiding behind a rock like you and Phoenix."

Alexej added with less ferocity and a touch of pride, "We *did* bring two people, and they're coming right behind us. We couldn't find Lucy *anywhere,* and we didn't have time to go the long way around to the caves to get my mama and daddy."

***

By now the squall had become a serious blizzard that began obliterating the neighboring rocks and the smallest of the stunted pines at a record pace. The four of them chose a more visible spot to yell and wave at a stick figure emerging from the whiteness, and Oscar materialized. Tall and youthfully gawky, he wore a bright yellow slicker with the hood almost covering his dark skin and wide-open, friendly black eyes.

Oscar patted Phoenix's shoulder before embracing Svnoyi, kissing her on her aching forehead. "Sorry about your head, luv. When we get back, I'm sure Anichka will have something you can take."

Oscar is Luz's first-born son, and he's another one who doesn't know who his dad is. But I know because last year I simply asked Luz, and she told me. I adored Luz, and I think she was a great mom, but she was always kind of a warrior at heart. She never appreciated Oscar's gentleness—

Svnoyi stopped herself. *Where do all these strange, migrainous thoughts come from? My brain is still gushing uncontrollably.*

Anyway, I'm so glad he's here. Oscar and me, we just might be in love. And he has a strange way of sensing things about other people by connecting with their spirits. Won't he understand what's happened to Daddy better than anyone else?

Oscar grasped Agali's and Alexej's hands. "Hey, kids, you saved us, you know. After about a half hour of wandering in the snow, I said, 'Look at that fence. I think we've been here before. Aren't we walking in circles?'"

"Us?" Oh, that's right, he must've brought Yacy with him. A stab of jealousy swept over Svnoyi. *They seem to be together all the time these days.*

Yacy, rail-thin and barely five feet tall even though she was a few months older than Svnoyi, arrived a dozen steps behind Oscar, panting. She was so exhausted from the climb that she stumbled and fell at his feet. He picked her up gallantly and dusted off a navy-blue wool coat that was a few sizes too small for her.

Look at that coat. Well, it's way better than burlap bags or nothing at all the way Phoenix showed up. The coat's probably one Lucy outgrew that Yacy borrowed from Ethan's cave when she dropped her daughter off. And shame on me for being jealous. I didn't even say hello. She's my half sister, and today she lost her twin brother, thanks to me, and her father.

A more hapless person than Yacy never existed. Beautiful, blond-haired and pale, she's more artistic than any of us, but she's been almost crushed by life. Having your twin's kid at fourteen? I don't even want to think about it right now.

Yacy was crying, the tears freezing on her eyelashes. She managed to choke out, "I left my baby with Ethan so I could get here. Then Oscar and me, we got lost, and I was so scared."

Being Yacy, she articulated fears the others hadn't considered yet because they were still stuck pondering Sequoyah's medical condition.

"I just know something terrible's happened to Daddy, worse than we can imagine. And to Mama, too. Can't you just *feel* it?"

Oscar announced, "No one else is gonna show up. Let's get going—right now. Like Yacy said, whatever's happened feels so wrong."

"Yes, let's go," Svnoyi seconded.

Hey, I was supposed to say it, first. *I'm the one who's in charge. Dammit, leading is about split-second decisions. This headache ....*

***

On a sunny day, the four hundred yards from Svnoyi's rock to Sequoyah and Aleta's cave was a steep but bracing walk along a path that snaked upward between pines made picturesque by their wind-wizened deformities. But the blizzard had erased the entire landscape except for the trees' intimidating grey ghosts that pointed the children in the right direction.

Svnoyi insisted on taking the lead. Because the snow was already several feet deep in places, the climbers decided to walk single file holding hands so they could tread in her footsteps.

Every time she turned her head to look at the others, in her migrainous condition she saw the same thing. *We're doing a medieval dance of death, and I'm the one with the scythe. We're doing a medieval dance of death, and I'm the one—*

She staggered and almost fell.

"You okay?" Phoenix screamed above the wind.

"No," Svnoyi screamed back.

At last the cave mouth beckoned, heralded by a stream of lantern light across the snow that was bright enough to illuminate the remaining ten yards.

Oscar yelled out the unnerving thought that had occurred to all of them. "Careful, everybody. Aleta couldn't possibly have lit the lamp because she's alone in there, holding Sequoyah."

Svnoyi reached the cave first with the others a step behind her. They flocked to her side, and what they saw inside made no sense. Something about the warm ring of light illuminating the middle of the cave reminded them of a stage set. Aleta lay at the very center of the tableau flat on her back, her arms spread wide. Her ankles had been bound together with knotted vines.

Phoenix noticed first that his mama's face had a greenish tinge. "Emergency, everybody. I'm off to get Anichka and Jaroslav. 'Bye."

With their eyes riveted on Aleta, no one turned to watch Phoenix leave at a run.

Once inside, Svnoyi said matter-of-factly like a doctor in training, "We're supposed to raise her feet and check her throat. Let's cut off the vines around her ankles, first. Someone find a kitchen knife. And get a blanket to keep her warm."

Aleta, my Etsi, she begged silently. *I've always loved you like my own mama who died when I was born—even if you're* impossible *sometimes. Please wake up, not just for me, but for all of us.*

"Where's Sequoyah?" Agali asked in a tiny voice. "Where's Daddy?"

"Oh my god," Yacy cried out. "Only the Prairie Dogs could've done this. They took him! Daddy's gone."

12 ~ Saving Aleta

The shafts of snow-bright light that illuminated the cave began to fade as afternoon slid toward a too-early October evening. Aleta guessed that two hours had passed since the others had gone away to leave her alone with Sequoyah. She'd expected his death to be quick, but he hung on, hovering in a netherworld beyond consciousness. She held him close, rocking him ever so gently.

During a lucid moment when she wasn't weeping, she asked herself, *How did it come to this? We weren't doing too badly for the first year. We were treading water, at least.*

Then Luz left us, and now Sequoyah. They were our backbone and heart.

In six months, the rest of us will be gone, too. We'll all die like a flock of sparrows freezing to death and falling off a telephone wire, one by one.

She stared down at her husband's blue lips. *It has to be soon, now.* She clenched her eyes tight shut as fresh tears leaked out and fell on his neck. But Sequoyah didn't take a last breath, and his chest continued to rise and fall.

As her arms grew tired from holding up the weight of his limp torso and head, her thoughts became less coherent. Her eyes drooped and closed. *No, no, I mustn't sleep.*

Aleta jerked her head up, unsure what had startled her. Then she saw something move at the edge of her vision. She turned to look at the cave mouth: a willowy girl silhouetted against the opaque backdrop of falling snow tiptoed inside. It was Lucy, Ethan and Luz's child. Feeling like a sitting duck, Aleta watched her peer into the gloom, then creep inexorably closer with furtive steps as if she were hoping she wouldn't be noticed.

Amazed and alarmed by the girl's sneaky intrusion, Aleta burst out, "Lucy! I *told* everyone I wanted to be alone with my husband. As you can see, he's still breathing. Now, please go away."

Lucy sidled closer.

How odd *this child's behaving with her eyes shifting guiltily from side to side and that fixed grin.*

And what's she hiding behind her back? God, I wish I was telepathic like the others so I could see what she's up to.

Then Aleta saw it and cried out, "Oh my lord, Lucy, you have a thorn shot! Get that thing away from me—"

With the speed of a rattlesnake Lucy made her move, and Aleta felt a pinprick on her shoulder. The drug's effect was immediate: she gasped for breath. She cried for help with a tongue stuck to the roof of her mouth and lips clamped shut.

A thousand red, yellow, and blue concentric circles began waxing and waning, sighing as they died. The last circle was a blue glob. It came from blackness, smaller than a pinprick. It grew, all shiny-moist, pulsing and swelling until it swallowed her.

Through blue glue, slick and thick, my arms and legs move too slow to go anywhere but nowhere. I know where I'm going. To the redwoods to lie on needles and beetles to make love with you, my darling, like vines intertwined 'til death do us part. Twin babes born in June, hot mad sun and foolish moon.

Think'st thou we shall ever meet again, meet in Drancy where my violin played "After a Dream," meet on the Trail of Tears? Meet in the High Tatras where we made Agali, child of mirth? Frobisher Bay, land where the Moon People died, where a Greyhound flew to nowhere? I know where I am, but I know not where I am going.

They've come for you, Sequoyah, and I can't save you, my arms are stuck in blue glue. Drown, drown, the tears run down, they're taking my love to Prairie Dog Town.

They light the lamp, they bind my feet, they stretch my arms, scarecrow in snow.

***

When Aleta's eyes blinked and eventually opened, she found herself lying on a cushion of stacked quilts. Concerned faces greeted her from above, Anichka's and Jaroslav's upside-down, and Ethan's, right-side-up. She pulled herself to a sitting position, and even with three adults to help, the effort took most of her strength.

In her gentlest voice Anichka said what must have been foremost in Aleta's mind. "Aleta, dear, Sequoyah, he disappear, we do not know where. We think the Prairie Dogs take him."

"Yesh, I ...." Aleta's words slurred together even as her brain started to clear. "Lushy ga-me thorn shot. I had ba-a-ad dreams. But I ***saw*** them."

"He *is* alive, then," Jaroslav exclaimed eagerly. "Prairie Dogs not go to so much trouble to kidnap dead man."

Ethan frowned, and then nodded enthusiastically, for Aleta's sake. Jaroslav's logic escaped him.

He turned away to think. At least he knew now what Lucy had been up to, and he wasn't sure he liked it. On the other hand, if Sequoyah were indeed alive, she might have helped save him.

"Tch, tch, a disgrace," Anichka murmured, inspecting the injection site on Aleta's shoulder that had swollen up and turned plum-colored. "Prairie Dogs have no shame. They grow many poison plants, they make very clever drugs and put on blackberry thorn."

Suddenly, Aleta's head swam, and she cried out, "Oh, no, I'm falling back into that nightmare."

Jaroslav knelt down to steady her, wrapping strong arms about her shoulders. She recovered enough equilibrium to whisper, "Where am I? This isn't a place I know."

"You're in my cave," Ethan said.

After that, he hastened to explain her rescue, his excited words tumbling out. "Aleta, you wouldn't believe. Phoenix must've run faster than a frightened bunny rabbit across the top of the cliffs, and through all that snow, too. Then he ran downhill to Anichka and Jaroslav's cave, slipping and sliding, and screaming so loud I could hear him from next door: 'Anichka, save Mama, she's dying.'"

Ethan stopped short because he'd surprised himself. He hadn't said so many words to Aleta for years and only spoke to her when he had to. A severed college love affair had wounded him deeply, and he knew that by now, sixteen plus a million years later, it should be ancient history. Except it wasn't. Sequoyah had been the one to edge him out of her heart.

Jaroslav grew impatient. He demanded, "Ethan, tell to her more about the rescue. Tell Aleta about what *I* do."

"Okay, okay, I'm getting there.

"So next Jaroslav bolted out of his cave, putting on his parka as he ran. About ten minutes later, he came back with you slung over his shoulder like a rag doll. He brought you here because my cave's winterized, already."

Ethan nodded toward a boxy, spark-spewing stove that he'd obviously made out of corrugated metal from the sides of the Greyhound bus. Always the inventor *ne plus ultra,* he was thrilled to explain its inner workings.

"You can see it's an ordinary wood stove, but my own specialized air flow makes it burn slower and hotter. Look at the pipes underneath and the exhaust system that goes out the cave door."

Aleta would have been appalled at his bragging about an invention at a time like this, except she knew him too well. She graciously nodded her head in his direction. "Thank you for telling me, Ethan, especially about my rescue."

She stood up uncertainly, her knees feeling watery. She tried a few steps. When she focused her eyes on Ethan's piles of odds and ends for his inventing, she could walk more or less in a straight line. The cave was certainly warm enough and in addition to the stove, Ethan had built an elegant wooden door set on rollers that shut out the winter storm.

The families' two newest babies, Arielle Luz and Lucian, lay sleeping in an alcove at the back of the cave on more of Luz's quilts, a safe distance from the sparking stove. Looking down at them, Aleta's eyes filled with tears.

It still seems unbelievable, but tiny Arielle Luz is our granddaughter, *thanks to Yacy's and Kuaray's stupidity, at age fourteen, yet. It happened right under my nose a few months before we left, and it was all my fault because I wasn't a good mother when Yacy needed me. Sequoyah had been gone for months and months, and all I did was sulk in my bedroom. She turned to Kuaray for comfort: he was only too happy to oblige—*

Aleta interrupted herself as if she'd only just remembered. *A long time ago Kuaray was my darling baby-boy twin. I used to kiss his bellybutton. But now he's dead! Kuaray is dead.*

So much violence, and all in one day.

Aleta fell to her knees, and Anichka moved closer in case she needed help. *Should I weep? I can't. Look what he did to Yacy, and he always had hate in his heart. His crimes go on and on, and I know I should forgive him because Sequoyah did. Maybe I will, someday, because he was our son. But right now, I feel ... nothing at all.*

Aleta's eyes moved to the next child. *Just look at little Lucian, so rosy and plump compared to my delicate granddaughter who was born too early. I know Ethan's trying to help out caring for him, but Yacy has to nurse him along with Arielle Luz—like they're twins.*

She stole a glance at Ethan, his head already bent over the papers on his desk as he contemplated a new invention—even in the midst of the latest tragedy. *It's like an illness: he's been obsessed with his work ever since Luz got hurt in that terrible fall. No surprise, the Prairie Dogs have her.*

And you know what else I really *can't face?* Aleta turned away from the babies and let out a few sobs. She wrung her hands, Sequoyah's favorite gesture whenever life had overwhelmed him. *I haven't told anyone yet, but there are going to be more babies! I'm expecting Sequoyah's twins late next June.*

Anichka took Aleta by the elbows and lifted her to her feet. "Dear one, do not think only of the worst. Come to see your brave son: here is Phoenix where he sleeps."

Phoenix lay curled up bare-chested a few yards from the babies, snoring softly. Before giving in to exhaustion, he'd smoothed out his work shirt and Svnoyi's sweaters on a stone ledge where they dripped steadily, making puddles on the sandy floor.

Aleta bent to kiss his forehead, more affection than she'd given him in a long time. *My gentle boy-child, Phoenix, why can't I love him as much as Yacy and Agali, and my stepdaughter Svnoyi?*

Well, I know why. It's because he is the child who rose from the ashes of my shame, and he reminds me of the foul man who helped make him. To save my sanity, I mustn't remember.

She turned to Anichka, who hadn't left her side for a moment in case she grew faint once again. "Dear friend, how do you do it? How do you manage to stay so positive, even at a time like this?"

"Oh, but I do not! I grieve, too. And never again will I practice medicine after how I fail to save Sequoyah, today. Never."

She took a deep breath. "But the life, it must go on.

"And now I make dinner for all the families." She called to her husband, "Jaroslav, go back to Aleta's cave, find the other children and bring them here."

She peered doubtfully at the burners on Ethan's stove, mumbling to herself, "How works this—what are right words—this newfangled device?"

***

Svnoyi, Oscar, and Yacy sat huddled in Aleta's chilly cave, unsure what to do next. Predictably Yacy was most undone, still weeping over the latest revelations as the ever valiant Oscar tried to comfort her with little pats on the shoulder.

"So why are we hanging around here?" Svnoyi asked.

"And Oscar," she remarked snidely. "If you want to actually make Yacy feel better, put your arm on her shoulder." She ended with a snarl, "And stop pussyfooting around."

God, what a bitch I am. It's the headache. But maybe I'm jealous. He's in love with her and embarrassed to touch her in front of me. I swear I don't care all that much, except Oscar and me—we've been so close, ever since I was four. We've been kissing and fondling each other for two years now—

"Snail, Snail, Sna-il! You aren't listening." Agali and Alexej, who understood the art of keeping warm, were leaping up and down in excitement because they'd already come up with a plan.

"What?" Svnoyi snapped.

Clasping her hands in a position of prayer, Agali begged, "Alexej and me, we want to go through the secret tunnel to spy on the operating room at the Prairie Dog Hospital. 'Cause if they took him, I bet Daddy's in that place."

Both of them chimed in, "Snail, please, please, can we go? The tunnel entrance is just over there." They pointed into the darkness at the cave's back corner.

Actually, it's a great idea that would tell us a lot. They're just amazing, those two. By spying from the end of that tunnel, they were the ones who discovered Luz lying there in a coma. We all thought she was dead because the Prairie Dogs had already held a fake funeral for her.

"No, kids, you may not. It's disrespectful at a time like this. Aren't you even sad?"

Agali wailed, "Yes, but we're just trying to *help*—"

Oscar stood up abruptly. He was slow to anger, but Svnoyi had succeeded with her last comment about his ineffectual comforting technique.

He glared at her with his hands on his hips. "I don't care what you do, Svnoyi, although I suggest you take the others back to Ethan's cave before they freeze.

"I'm going to bury Kuaray. He's still lying in that house where *you* broke his neck this morning."

"I-I can help you," Svnoyi stammered.

"No, I'm doing it alone. I'm sick of being around you."

"Wait." Yacy's tearful howl spoke volumes about her feelings for the young man caught in the middle. "Don't go, Oscar. Wait for a grownup to help you."

Someone appeared at the entrance, and everybody jumped. It was Jaroslav completing his wife's errand to summon them to dinner.

He had overheard the latest exchange and announced with gravity, "It is done, children, it is done. All of you mourn for Sequoyah, I sneak away to bury Kuaray deep in forest. I feel the cold wind, I know soon the earth is too frozen.

"I finish, I build a little cairn, I say three Hail Marys. And that is the end."

He spread his arms in a gesture of welcome. "So children, come home to Ethan's cave. All is better, Anichka help Aleta wake up, Phoenix take nap of tired hero. Is warm from new stove Ethan invent, and Anichka say, 'Time for dinner!'"

Jaroslav walked over to Yacy who sat alone by the oil lamp that cast her elongated shadow against the cave wall. He pulled the weeping girl to her feet. "Come along, don't cry. Kuaray would hurt you by and by, and now he can't. Aleta waits for you. Sequoyah, I promise we will find."

Yacy resisted. "I want to stay here, where Daddy was ... at the very last."

"No, Little Mama. Think of the babies. They want you, too."

***

Svnoyi hung back, waiting for the others to leave. She hoped that a few minutes alone would give her the strength to act sociably once she got to Ethan's cave, especially with the headache throbbing inside her skull.

How'd I get so snappish and mean? All the kids must hate me now, except for Phoenix. And why'd I give the adults so little credit?

I really screwed up my first day as leader. In fact, I didn't lead at all.

Inexplicably, she wanted to say goodbye to Kuaray. She knelt and bent her body over her knees to rest her forehead on the cave floor. The humble position felt good, somehow: she was finally ready to level with herself.

Kuaray, poor dead Kuaray, why are some people born to nurture and others to destroy?

You were a destroyer, and for years I watched our precious families suffer because of you. Yacy, Aleta, Luz .... My god, Kuaray, you chased Luz through the forest with a new baby in her arms, and she fell into the skylight at the

Prairie Dog Hospital and most likely hit her head on a stone bed. You made Ethan miserable forever when she didn't come back. And you ruined the whole clan, in a way: she was so strong, she made up for Daddy's wishy-washy mistakes.

And why did you throw away the ashes of Daddy's father Mohe that he brought specially to bury in the new land? Did you know how much Mohe meant to him? Of course *you did, and that move tore Daddy to bits. But somehow, he found it in his heart to forgive you and love you afterwards. Your thanks was to stab him?*

But you were my own flesh and blood, my half brother. And now I'm not so different from you. We share a common bond because I'm a destroyer, too. I killed you. I broke your neck.

I'm sorry, so sorry. Goodbye, Kuaray, goodbye.

Suddenly, she missed her father so much she fell flat on her stomach, reaching out her arms to touch him, as if such a thing were possible.

Daddy, I'll never believe you died, never. I think you'll be back, someday. Even if I don't see you ever again, I know you're somewhere, making other people happy.

Svnoyi rose and clasping her hands tight, she closed her eyes to concentrate on sending Sequoyah a telepathic message.

Daddy, I love you so. If you can hear me at all, please, please ... can you take away the pain? Can you stop the running feet inside my head?

And the feet stopped.

13 ~ Lucy Outside the Door

An hour later, everyone except Yacy sat cross-legged on the cave floor around Ethan's large oval table, quietly eating stew. It was made of ingredients they'd begun to despise long ago: rabbit, beans, and a bitter-tasting wild root from the forest that looked like a sweet potato. Yacy had retreated to the back of the cave to try soothing her two-month-old daughter who had erupted in high-pitched wails.

The mood was bleak. Ordinarily they would have ribbed Anichka, who hated being teased, for scorching the dinner she'd cooked on the unfamiliar, ultra-efficient stove. And Lucy, the finicky one, wasn't there to offer imaginative complaints about the food that always made everyone laugh. To manage eating at all, they avoided looking at Sequoyah's empty place.

Breaking the silence, Svnoyi said, "First of all, I'd like to apologize to everybody for everything I said. I had a terrible headache. It turned me into someone I hardly recognized."

Agali pouted, "She was so mean. She called me 'Algae.'"

"But you kept calling her 'Snail,'" Alexej remarked. "Fair's fair."

Phoenix burst out laughing. "Algae and Snail?"

Aleta's earlier contemplative mood had vanished. She interjected tearfully, "I know some of you are immature enough to fight grief with merriment. But it's unfitting at a time like this. I don't think my Sequoyah's even alive—"

"Well, I *do* think so, Auntie Aleta." Oscar slipped beside her and put an arm around her shoulder. "I can feel his spirit."

"Oscar should know, Mama," Yacy called out. "I understand it's hard to feel good about anything right now but try listening to him. He can read souls, and the rest of us can't."

Genuinely curious, Phoenix asked, "What's it feel like, Oscar? Do they contact you like in seances where they knock on a table?" He tried out a few raps with his knuckles.

"It's hard to explain, and it's not like seances. Those are fake." Oscar sounded mildly miffed by the question. "Either someone's spirit is there in the back of my head, or it isn't. And if it isn't and the person's dead, I feel it in a different way, deeper down, more in my heart."

"Clear as mud and absolutely impossible," Ethan, ever the scientist, remarked. "But I'm still glad you're in touch with my Luzzie, what with her being in a coma, and all."

He added the conclusion everyone was expecting, "Even if I don't believe you."

The clan fell silent except for Aleta who dropped her face onto her folded arms and began sobbing. Even Anichka's comforting presence on one side with an arm around her waist and Oscar on the other side patting her shoulder didn't help.

Svnoyi and Phoenix stood up to clear the dishes and then helped Agali and Alexej fill the galvanized buckets from the big kettle that had stayed hot on the stove. The children labored quietly over their biggest chore of the day and for the first time, they had no desire to hold their customary water fight. In another first that would likely never happen again, Jaroslav stood by with a dishtowel over his arm, waiting to dry.

With dinner over, the three families huddled together for mutual warmth as the stove burned low. Ethan held his sleeping baby son Lucian on one arm and draped his other arm quite unconsciously across Oscar's shoulder. Oscar could tell from the faraway look in his stepfather's eyes that he was thinking about Luz. But a minute later, his forehead wrinkled with worry like a piece of corrugated cardboard.

Even the inseparable Agali and Alexej had gotten tired of each other. Aleta had recovered enough to hold her snoozing daughter in a loosening embrace as she herself began to nod. Alexej, who was big for his age, lay stretched across the laps of Jaroslav and Anichka. Even though attention from both parents was nice, he would have found more comfort sucking his thumb, which he wasn't allowed to do anymore.

Svnoyi slipped to the back of the cave and dropped down beside Yacy. First, she offered the new mother a bowl of stew that Anichka had saved for her on the stove, but Yacy shook her head.

After that, Svnoyi didn't know how to start the conversation that she felt had to happen sooner or later. "Yacy, I—"

Yacy, who usually deferred to her more forceful half sister, finished the sentence with a touch of impatience. "You're here to talk about Kuaray."

"Yes." Svnoyi sounded relieved. "What I did ...." She couldn't bring herself to say aloud that she'd broken her half brother's neck. "I'm really sorry, and I know that sounds pretty lame. But I'm hoping you can at least talk to me about it."

Yacy sounded short. "I've been crying about it all afternoon, and you've been pretty broken up, too. I know you didn't have to do it ... but you did. And like Jaroslav said, now it's over."

Her voice softened. "He was brilliant and wonderful to be around at least some of the time, but he was crazy and dangerous. He did terrible things to me, and I realize that now.

"You did us all a favor, as awful as that sounds." Yacy gripped Svnoyi's arm. "Now, please, never mention him again."

"But losing our Daddy Sequoyah, isn't that worse?"

"Yes, but how can you compare the two?"

Yacy turned her back and buried her head into her daughter Arielle Luz's wispy hair, clutching the sleeping infant as if she could gather comfort from the wee thing.

Svnoyi left her to drop down beside Phoenix, who was sitting by the door, half-heartedly pulling on his wet boots over damp socks. He had to shovel the snowdrifts from the mouth of his own cave before his extended family could pass the threshold.

"Dammit, Phoenix," she whispered. "That was awful."

"Yeah, I bet. I heard some of it." He gave her hand a quick squeeze. "Wanna come and help me dig us out?"

Ethan snapped out of his current mood and stood up. "Hey everyone, Luz made a whole stack of quilts before we left Frobisher Bay, maybe for a time just like this. Your caves aren't winterized yet, and mine already is. So how about all of you staying the night?"

***

When a sliver of light crawled under Ethan's winter door, Svnoyi woke up shivering. She tried to pull her quilt, a blue one with white and yellow birds on it, into a tighter cocoon around herself. Her whole body, especially her feet, had reached the point of iciness where getting up seemed even worse than staying put.

I have to get used to it. Winter's only just starting. Will a grownup please *wake up and get the stove going?*

She looked at the others all around her, rolled up in Luz's quilts like tightly packed rainbow-colored sardines in a can. Everyone lay still, some snoring lightly. *No help, there. I'll have to do it myself, and hope I get it right.*

Just two more minutes …

She let her eyes wander over the back wall's floor-to-ceiling frieze carved into the crystalline rock. The entire surface was densely covered with realistic sculptures of the plants and animals they'd known from the Time Before.

This is a creepy mystery we might never solve, even though we've talked about it often enough. All three caves have 'em. The question is, why are they here at all, and who could've made them with no models to copy? Almost everything was wiped out during World War III, and only pine forests grew back. In six months, we haven't seen many animals and no shade trees, anywhere.

Just look *at this one. Even in the dim light it's beautiful with the same plants and animals you could've seen in the country: weeping willow trees, eucalyptus, cows, sheep, pigs, horses, and even a dog. Our own cave has monkeys, birds and bats, and lots of tropical trees like coconut and banana trees.*

Svnoyi stood up and dressed in a hurry, throwing on her jeans and a flannel shirt, and on top of it, her warm wool sweater. Now that the new day had truly begun, yesterday's horrors suddenly bombarded her fully alert brain.

Oh, my god, how could I forget, even for a moment? I killed Kuaray. It was like I had some kind of fit when I saw him stab Daddy. She dropped her face into her hands.

Her next thought was hardly more comforting. *And my Daddy Sequoyah's gone. Everyone but Aleta thinks he's alive somewhere, and I could swear he sent me a telepathic message, yesterday. But what do I truly think way down deep inside my heart? I'm just not sure.*

She grimaced. *And what could've happened to Lucy? We have to get her back. Yesterday she was grieving like the rest of us, and suddenly she runs away and turns traitor. It's a puzzle that doesn't add up.*

Yeah, but it does! I remember Agali and Alexej saying she had a huge fight with her dad.

She found Ethan in the crowd of sleepers and poked him in the shoulder. She whispered, "Sorry, but you need to wake up and talk to me, it's really important.

"I know you and Lucy had a fight. Was it serious enough to make her run away?"

Ethan jerked to a sitting position, squinting at Svnoyi through nearsighted eyes still swollen with sleep. "Um, what? Fight with Lucy? I, uh, maybe." Guilt flicked across his face.

He pulled himself to his feet, fumbling for his glasses in the breast pocket of his tattered nightshirt. He adjusted them with care, fussing with the fit on the bridge of his nose. At last he beckoned Svnoyi to join him in front of the stove. He refused to look into her eyes but walked back and forth, adding wood from the stack by the door.

He murmured, "I built a winterized outhouse for everyone, y'know. Have you tried it? It's innovative and strategically located: the seat is warmed by the angle of the low winter sun bouncing off a seasonably adjustable reflective panel—"

Svnoyi hissed impatiently, "Enough, Ethan. You're a genius of course, and we all appreciate it. But you have to stop hiding behind your inventions."

She pivoted toward him, angry now. "You let your own child run away? What did you say to her?"

Ethan sat down on the woodpile and patted a spot on the split pine logs for Svnoyi to join him. He sighed before starting in. "I wish Luz had been here. She was always *so much better* at this kind of thing than me.

"Yesterday afternoon when I was trying to put Lucian to sleep and everyone was so sad with Sequoyah dying and all—"

Ethan stopped to inhale a shaky breath. "Lucy comes in. She asks me if Tlke, you know, her little friend the Prairie Dog translator, could stay the night."

He rose to light the wood inside the stove and returned reluctantly, shuffling along in his fleece-lined moccasins. "Well, Svnoyi, her timing was rotten, if you know what I mean.

"And I asked her, 'Then Tlke would be sleeping right in the same cave with you, me, and Oscar, and a brand-new baby?' And before Lucy said anything, I answered my own question: 'No, absolutely not. Tlke is an *animal*—'"

Svnoyi interrupted, "You actually said that? Did you mean that Tlke is dirty and would make the baby sick?"

She stood up, putting her hands on her hips. "That was totally dumb, Ethan. She loves animals, for one thing. For another, Tlke isn't an animal to her, she's her best friend.

"What happened next?"

After a long pause, Ethan mumbled, "So after I said no, Lucy said she'd run away with Tlke to join the Prairie Dogs. Then she just stomped out, all huffy ... you know how she gets."

"And you let her go? It's not what she wanted, Ethan. She wanted you to make a big fuss like you really cared about her."

"And another thing." Svnoyi's voice rose because she was about to make the kind of assertion she was so fond of. "You and everybody else have to stop thinking the Prairie Dogs are big animals who are dumber and less sophisticated than we are."

"We could think of them like they're intelligent aliens from another planet—except they happen to live right here," Ethan suggested timidly.

"Yes!" Svnoyi exclaimed. "Wonderful idea, Ethan. They're not animals, and we've been making a big mistake to think so. They're more like aliens who somehow learned to mimic the *worst* kinds of things humans do."

***

Fists pummeled the door. Svnoyi bolted toward the latch, almost certain that Lucy would be standing on the other side. At her touch, the door slid open a crack on its elegantly designed wooden rollers. Svnoyi poked her head out and just as she'd thought, Lucy stood opposite her.

She hoped her runaway friend was alone, attempting a clandestine return. But shadows moving behind four snow-laden dwarf pines revealed Prairie Dogs armed with *azvrkts,* a weapon that resembles humankind's bow and arrow.

Svnoyi took one look at the poor girl with her droopy blue eyes and delicate limbs shaking with cold. "Lucy, dear, you're turning to ice. Where's your coat?"

She turned toward a wooden rack, another of Ethan's creations, that stood by the door. "That's lucky. Here's your own red parka, and it has a hat and mittens in the pockets. Are these your boots? They have wooly red socks in them. Until you grow fur like Tlke—"

She tried handing them through the crack, but the guards raised their *azvrkts* and pulled the strings taut against the arrows.

"Jesus, Lucy, call off your goons. Why are they here, anyway?"

Lucy looked around nervously before answering in a tiny whisper, "They're here because I'm delivering a note. They're the usual palace guard."

"A note, Lucy? What sort of note? Can't you just tell me what it says? And when are you coming home?"

Lucy hissed in an undertone, "Shh, Svnoyi, keep your voice down. One of the palace guards is Tlke, and she can understand almost everything you're saying."

With something resembling a rehearsed flourish, the trembling girl handed Svnoyi a large envelope, obviously her own handiwork, that she'd been holding behind her back. It was fashioned out of paper from Sequoyah's precious supply that he'd brought along for worthy uses such as writing memoirs and poems. Her mission accomplished, she took the parka and boots from Svnoyi's outstretched arms.

Before Lucy turned to leave, she whispered so softly that Svnoyi had to read her lips, "Don't damage the flap."

***

By now everyone was up and dressed. And thanks to Ethan's new stove, the air had already reached an acceptable temperature. They pushed tightly around Svnoyi, who clutched the envelope to her bosom to protect it as a jumble of questions reverberated in the open space. Agali and Alexej, sensing a new adventure in the making, leapt up and down at the perimeter.

Jaroslav added to the din by crying out, "Order, order," in his deep bass, although no one heeded him.

Svnoyi pushed them aside and dropped to her knees at the big table where streams of light coming from slits cut high in the door illuminated the envelope. "Just sit down, everybody. Give me a chance to open it."

She was excited, too. Her hands trembled a little as she ran her fingers lightly over the triangular flap where she could feel tiny bumps made by penciled script on its underside.

So that's what Lucy meant by "Don't damage the flap." How very cloak-and-dagger: a secret message is under there.

When the flap's last bit of adhesive, a smear of pine pitch, gave way, Svnoyi pulled out the letter, another sheet from Sequoyah's paper stash. Eight people held their breaths, although she could hear Yacy, a few feet away, pant from anxiety as she sat nursing her daughter.

"Look," Svnoyi exclaimed. "It's an invitation from Queen Gitli. We're supposed to go to a dinner party at the palace at sundown." She passed the letter to Oscar because she wanted to get away from the crowd to decipher the hidden words on the envelope.

Oscar stood and began reading Lucy's ornate script in a voice laced with misgiving. "Dear Families, one and all, including the babies. You are invited to a banquet by order of the queen. The time: when the sun vanishes. Formal dress is required. To reach the palace, take the tunnel that starts in the back of Ethan's cave.

"It's signed, 'from Her Majesty, as dictated to Lucy and Tlke.'"

The first comment came from Phoenix, who groaned and rolled his eyes. "We're supposed to dress up in what, exactly? I forgot my tux at the cleaners."

Jaroslav leapt up, a clenched fist thrust on his hip. "Babies not go. Is too risky. I am a man of authority. I go alone!"

As the others shook their heads at Jaroslav's offer, Aleta suggested, "More than one person has to go, or the queen will be furious. Let's send Svnoyi, Oscar, and Phoenix with Jaroslav. I'd rather not go until we know more."

Then she brought her fingers to her temples. "Besides, I'm still dizzy from their poison."

Anichka took Aleta's hand and nodded in agreement.

"But *we* want to go," Agali and Alexej wheedled.

Agali stood up and waved her hands above her head to remind everyone, "We discovered the first tunnel."

"Yes," Ethan broke in, showing a forcefulness unusual for him. "We all have to go and find out how they tick. Besides, there's strength in numbers."

Svnoyi strode back into their midst. "Okay, enough, everybody, of course we're all going." She made a show of waving the envelope: "Listen, this is so exciting. We have a heroic mole in the enemy camp. Lucy wrote some messages for us under the flap."

She squinted and brought it up to her nose in order to read Lucy's minuscule script in the poor light. "Mama Luz is awake. Sequoyah is alive, but he's not here anymore."

Everyone jumped up, exclaiming at the same time in overlapping bursts of sound that shook the air in a complex fugue, "Awake? Alive? Oh, oh, oh, thank goodness." Jaroslav fell to his knees to mumble a prayer of thanksgiving.

Svnoyi called out, "Quiet down. There's more, and listen carefully." She spaced her words so that no one could misinterpret them. "Prairie Dogs have big trouble with the *Shade People.* Prairie Dogs have even *more* trouble with the *Sun People.*"

Suddenly, no one had a thing to say.

Yacy filled the void with an aghast whisper: "There are other people here ... besides us?"

Phoenix threw back his head, laughing. "So much for thinking we're so damned unique."

14 ~ Table Mannerisms

She always say one thing and mean two things. —**Anichka**

Aleta turned toward the others, and her words tumbled out. "I'm so relieved, I could just, I don't know what, laugh? Cry? Like Jaroslav said when I first woke up, he was sure my Sequoyah was alive because the Prairie Dogs made such an effort to snatch him away from me. And Oscar thought so, too. But now I'm absolutely certain of it.

"The question is, *where did they take him?"*

Ethan beamed down at his infant son, asleep in his lap. Patting the child through a rabbit skin bunting made by Luz, he slipped into parentese, "Hey, wittle guy, Wuzzie's getting well."

He looked up. "It's a miracle, everyone, that Luz woke up from her coma. I'd just about lost hope. I wonder, when do you think she'll be ready to come home?"

"Put we on our finery, now," Jaroslav announced. "Is time to discover tunnel, to go to the banquet. Only Her Majesty can answer our questions."

"Well, I doubt that she'll simply blurt out the information," Aleta said, returning to her previous funk.

To fulfill the queen's request for formalwear, the clan settled on Luz's quilts turned into sari-like drapes. Yacy performed her usual artistic magic stitching everyone into them, and as she worked, Oscar helped her by holding the heavy cloth in place, his eyes shining with admiration. Once Anichka had completed Yacy's attire, everyone agreed: the whole party looked as stunning as a flock of peafowl with open fans.

The entrance to the passageway lay almost in plain sight: all they had to do was walk a few feet down a short corridor to the right of Ethan's main room. No one had detected the opening because it was hidden behind a crystal-studded boulder large enough to sit on.

Before they squeezed through the low, mouse hole-shaped archway, Jaroslav, who had assumed the position of default leader, cleared his throat to give last-minute instructions. "Agali and Alexi, zip mouths! Children who are older, set good example by best behavior. To Aleta, may I say—"

"That I don't tangle with the queen? Jaroslav, give it a rest, you aren't in charge."

At Aleta's remark, Anichka hid a smile behind her hand. She whispered, "I wish I had this boldness."

Beyond the opening, the passage widened enough for them to stand upright. Everyone, including the seasoned Agali and Alexej, needed a minute to orient themselves. They had expected the passage to be pitch-dark. Instead, a surprise awaited them: a lighting system worthy of Dracula's castle. Live bats, undoubtedly one of the Prairie Dogs' enslaved animal populations, hung upside-down from the ceiling holding tiny torches in their teeth. There were hundreds of them spaced a few feet apart, illuminating a mile-long limestone shaft that made a slow ascent along shallow steps hewn into the rock.

About a minute into the trek, Svnoyi felt a gentle prod on the left side of her brain. It came from Phoenix who was near the front of the queue, directly behind Jaroslav. She was momentarily startled; she'd never talked mind-to-mind with him before.

Snail, we didn't even know about this second tunnel until today, and it's like a red carpet leading to Queen Gitli's palace. The first tunnel was totally dark and creepy and ended up at the Prairie Dog Hospital.

Aren't you curious to find the third tunnel with me? Is it a date?

Except for her Daddy Sequoyah and Oscar, her intended fiancé, she'd always communicated with everyone else by speaking aloud.

When she answered, she hedged a little on purpose. *You may be right that there's a third tunnel, and it would start in Jaroslav's cave. Yes, let's look for it sometime. A date? Well, maybe.*

To Svnoyi's surprise, her heart went pit-a-pat. She began wringing her hands, something she'd never done before, although she'd watched her Daddy Sequoyah do it often enough whenever he was unsure of himself.

First of all, he spoke to me telepathically, which was bold, but I really, really liked that. I think the way I answered was about right, because I just don't know if this flirting is a good idea, especially if it's going to lead somewhere. But he's so *good-looking.*

There's Oscar, although that's been cooling off for a while. I saw the way he was looking at Yacy when she sewed us into our costumes. And they're together at the back of the line right now, probably wishing they could hold hands if she wasn't carrying Arielle Luz.

And there's one thing I'm absolutely sure *of. Losing Sequoyah's been so, so awful, these last few days would've been unbearable for me without Phoenix.*

She halted suddenly, causing a minor collision with Aleta, who was directly behind her.

No, just plain no! *It's a bad idea because he's way younger than me.*

***

The corridor made a sharp turn before ending on a ledge elevated about a foot above the floor of a huge subterranean chamber.

"So this is how the royalty lives," Svnoyi whispered. "Not bad."

Everyone stared at the glittering expanse of a room that was easily three times the size of any of their own caves. It was lit as brightly as a stadium with floodlights: thousands of bats, big brown ones larger than their cousins in the corridor, clung to the stalactites holding thick wax tapers.

The clan stood still, not daring to venture down to the cavern floor without an invitation. But not a single Prairie Dog was in sight.

Phoenix called out, "Yoo-hoo, anybody home?"

His ludicrous question set off a wave of giggles that bounced off the crystal-studded ceiling, the sound transformed to a hundred hens cackling. Even Aleta snickered as she imagined the spectacle that the queen would put on in that gargantuan space to show off her mightiness.

With a little laugh, Svnoyi reminisced, "Do you remember the show Queen Gitli held for Luz's sham funeral? Hundreds of circling Prairie Dogs like spokes of a wheel all beating their breasts, the pine branches wrapped with roses—"

"No, I don't remember," Ethan replied curtly. "I couldn't watch, I was too sad."

Realizing her insensitivity toward the man whose wife still hadn't returned, Svnoyi opened her mouth to apologize. But just then, at least two hundred Prairie Dogs flooded the center of the chamber. They emerged from the shadows and advancing with mincing steps, they waddled from side to side in order to walk on their hind legs. They didn't need clothes for any season: they were elegantly attired in their own sleek brown coats with white ruffs at their necks.

Yacy whispered in wonder, "I'll never get over just how huge they are, four feet tall, at least. What did Daddy Sequoyah say they looked like when he first saw them? I remember, 'The circus freaks of the rodent world.'"

In a repeat of the funeral's entertainment, the Prairie Dogs began with their signature moves, first swishing the pine branches entwined with wild roses from side to side in stately arcs. Then they began marching, slowly at first, their formation resembling the spokes of a giant wheel. But soon they deviated from the staid choreography of the funeral: the wheel accelerated and at the same time, each Prairie Dog pirouetted in place, faster and faster, the branches a mere smudge of green against a mass of fur.

For the terpsichorean climax, they fell to the ground all together in a heap, revealing at the wheel's hub their own Queen Gitli. She was attired in a magnificent dress made entirely of pearly clamshells, stitched to hang in overlapping rows. With every twitch of her hips, the shells emitted a strident clatter.

Queen Gitli, with Tlke and Lucy following in her wake, strode through the crowd, her shaking shells accompanied by a sea of her subjects' waving claws. She stopped, clacking her own claws for attention so all could appreciate the speech of welcome she was about to bestow in the Prairie Dogs' rococo, adjective-laden tongue.

The queen would communicate telepathically: some time during the last million years while the creatures had evolved, they'd given up their ancestors' yips and barks for more artful, silent discourse. The exception was laughter that they could never render except out loud.

Lucy and Tlke no longer needed to prepare their translations by touching each others' temples with hands and paws. Instead, they conferred rapidly mind-to-mind to come up with the best translations for Lucy to recite aloud to the humans, and for Tlke to relate back silently to Queen Gitli. During the past six months Lucy had perfected the alien syntax and could now speak colloquially with ease.

The queen began, but her welcome was more of a rebuke. "Dearest visitors to my palace, I heard not a single round of applause for the newly choreographed *tour de force* that I had prepared for you, alone. Was this a willful, or an unintended, *slap in my face?"*

An embarrassing pause stretched to eternity as the clan realized they should have cheered for the dance rather than waiting for the end of the queen's presentation.

Their faux pas grew worse with each passing second. But they were in luck because their own youngsters saved them. Agali and Alexej—who at Jaroslav's request had zipped their own mouths shut by passing pinched fingers across their compressed lips—began leaping up and down, clapping wildly. "Yay, yay, yay, Queen Gitli, your Prairie Dogs looked so-o-o-o marvelous. And we love your shell dre-e-e-ess!"

At that, the entire clan applauded. Queen Gitli nodded her satisfaction and gestured for the troupe to leave. She, too, departed with a clatter of shells along with Lucy and Tlke, leaving the room empty.

Everyone relaxed with a unison sigh of relief, and Aleta, Jaroslav, and Anichka gave their clever children quick hugs. Then all of them maintained an uneasy silence as they waited at the entrance to the chamber. They had not yet been invited in. They tried to dispel the tension by shuffling from one foot to the other and walking in small circles. They had no idea what to think as a few minutes lengthened into a half hour.

At last Svnoyi asked in a whisper, "Is she making us wait on purpose to send our anxiety level through the roof?"

***

Oscar, standing at the front, whispered abruptly, "Hold on, everybody, something's happening."

They followed his gaze to take in a squat archway no one had noticed earlier. Dangling shells on strings that curtained the entrance to another room began to undulate before parting with a melodious tinkling. The dining table, laden with wooden serving bowls and tureens, floated into the room like a magic carpet.

The illusion of self-locomotion was short-lived. Four polar bears, oddly shrunken in size from their heyday in the Arctic a million years previously, bore the entire weight of the huge wooden slab on their heads, each one of them holding up a corner. They panted, and their oversized feet scraped against the stone at every labored step. The table came to a standstill in the middle of the chamber as the bears crouched down. And so they remained, supporting the lavish spread for the entire length of the meal, like ursine caryatids.

Svnoyi whispered, "Okay, everyone, I know what you're thinking, but save it for when we get home."

A long silence followed, equivalent to the break after Queen Gitli's opener.

"Now what does she want?" Ethan asked in disgust.

"Praise," said Svnoyi. "Isn't it obvious?"

Jaroslav stepped into the breach. He yelled, "Bravo, bravo, bravo, Queen, is first time I see walking table."

All of them took his cue, yelling lusty compliments—with a few rebel remarks camouflaged by the din. Svnoyi was pretty sure she heard Phoenix say, "Bravo, bravo, is first time I see something so disgusting."

Aleta went off on a different tangent. "What could Lucy, our most devoted animal lover, be thinking right now? And she still works for that monster?"

Queen Gitli seemed satisfied. She bustled forth from the back room, the shells on her dress and the shells on the curtain uniting in a brief seaside duet. This time no hordes accompanied her, and only a reduced retinue of three Prairie Dogs wearing medals proclaiming their status followed her, their eyes cast down to show their deference. Lucy and Tlke drew up the rear.

Queen Gitli took her place, standing at the head of the table while the others gathered along one of the sides. Lucy, who was too tall to stand, sat cross-legged on the stone floor.

The queen commanded, "Enter, all, and sit. Queen Gitli wishes highest person to face me at my royal table."

The families were unprepared to rank themselves. After some jostling, Jaroslav, Anichka, and Ethan, holding Lucian, sat cross-legged and jammed together at the table's end. Aleta, visibly miffed by the slight, sat beside the children: Phoenix, Svnoyi, Oscar, and Yacy with Arielle Luz in her lap. Like the Prairie Dogs, Alexej and Agali had to stand to see over the top.

The queen waved her claws to gain everyone's attention. She announced, "Eat, eat! Let not the babble of statesmanship detract from the pleasure of filling the stomach."

She and her companions tucked into two great bowls of scrumptious salad greens garnished with plump tomatoes and wild mushrooms as if they'd been fasting for a week, their cheeks puffing with every chew. The humans found steaming rabbit stew, delectably prepared, waiting for them beneath the lids of the tureens. They tried their best to eat with dignity, dipping into the communal pots with their fingers and sipping the gravy from the individual mussel shells set at each place.

When Queen Gitli grew tired of eating, she clapped her paws together three times and the table rose up and walked off through the curtain of jingling shells. As the strings parted, the children glimpsed a pair of bobcats teetering on their hind legs to scrub out the cooking pots in deep wooden tubs, their whiskers dragging in the soapsuds.

Sentinel owls stood by with little packets of narcotics in their beaks, waiting to reward the beasts once they'd finished their duties. Undoubtedly, the bats holding tapers would be paid in powders at the end of the evening, and the polar bears could expect their rewards at the termination of the meal. None of this was new to the clan. Phoenix had seen addicted and enslaved animals last summer when he'd spied on them cultivating the Prairie Dogs' fields.

Only Agali dared to speak up during the silence that followed. She nudged Alexej and announced, "I don't like this. Alexej and me, after dinner we want to help the bobcats with the dishes."

Anichka laughed behind her hand and remarked in a stage whisper, "Well, that is new, and very sweet. They offer to wash dishes."

Soon the table re-emerged with the dessert, floating back into the center of the room and sinking to resume its two-foot height. The clan took one look and groaned inwardly. It was the dessert they'd all feared, a twin of the delicate confection Anichka had made from whipped sweet potatoes and the opium-tainted honey the Prairie Dogs had given her. Few memories from their early days in the forest could equal this one for quirkiness: accidental or not, the innocent-appearing treat had poisoned the entire clan except Jaroslav, sending them instantly into opium-induced stupors that lasted for hours.

Another pause seemed to stretch out for an eternity. Svnoyi agonized, *What should we do now? We don't want to insult her, but we can't eat it.*

Yacy's voice rang out suddenly, shattering the silence that Queen Gitli had imposed earlier. "Don't you see, everyone? It's a test about if we trust her or not."

She scooped a spoonful from the side of the pudding with her mussel shell and slurped it down, spilling some of it on her infant daughter's lightly fuzzed head. Yacy waited a full two minutes to diagnose any change to her health as everyone held their breaths.

She grinned. "See, I was right. I'm still sitting here, and I'm feeling ... just fine."

***

After everyone at the table had eaten every bite of the pudding, Queen Gitli spoke her first words since the meal had begun. "Dear friends, I appreciate your trust. Now we can plan for the future and may our meeting-of-the-minds prove fruitful."

She held up a paw, "But attend! Your Queen Gitli is ever thoughtful. For you, I now conjure up a comfortable place for what you've all been waiting for—our discussion."

She clapped four times. The first table left, and a second table, petite and circular, made its entry. The top was small enough for one polar bear to balance on its flattened head, and a pot of aromatic coffee, freshly brewed, sat at the center, surrounded by stacks of cups.

At five claps, the chamber filled with eleven white rabbits, their coats so abundant that they appeared larger than the polar bears and as spherical as beachballs. With only a hint of eyes and ears beneath the fur, they rolled rather than hopped from their hiding places behind grey boulders that lined the wall opposite the curtained archway. The queen nudged them into a cozy circle near the table: the rabbits had been bred to serve as overstuffed chairs.

Momentarily freed from her translating duties, Lucy edged toward the families where they stood in a clump, not sure what to do with themselves during Queen Gitli's entr'acte. They watched as the wayward daughter hesitated, then rushed past her father even though he looked truly contrite, stretching toward her imploringly the arm that wasn't holding his son.

Ethan was hurt. He let the arm fall to his side with a slap, murmuring, "Why'd my little girl do that? She pretended she didn't see me. If Luzzie was here, she would've had a cow."

Jaroslav put a hand on Ethan's shoulder and clucked his tongue. "So unkind, but this not always happen. Right now, no one act right."

Lucy's snub of her father was not entirely intentional; she had a more urgent problem to take care of and headed straight for Aleta. Grasping the overly emotional woman's hands, she whispered, "I'm so, so sorry, Auntie Aleta, but I had to do it, give you the thorn shot, I mean. I promise you'll know why in a minute, and you'll be really relieved."

Aleta's eyes filled with tears. "I wish there'd been another way, Lucy. The hallucinations were terrifying, and they're still haunting me more than a day later."

Her voice grew louder and more strident. "But that's not really what's bothering me right now. All this pomp is a distraction because

Queen Gitli's hiding my Sequoyah for some reason. Why doesn't she just get to the point?"

Anichka had a ready reply. "The queen, she cannot help it. She like to show off, she is Barnum and Bailey. But beware. I remember from Luz's fake funeral; she always say one thing and *mean two* things. She play many games at the same time."

At that moment, Queen Gitli clapped her paws in brisk repetitions, and Lucy had to hurry back to her place at the monarch's side opposite Tlke.

The queen smiled expansively toward her audience, raising her rubbery lips to reveal five-inch front teeth. "Dear friends, please be seated. I introduce to you not only the best coffee in the world. I also present the most comfortable chairs, another example of Prairie Dog breeding and cloning ingenuity."

15 ~ Three Missions

After some discussion, the clan agreed that the coffee's spectacular flavor had hints of peppermint, hibiscus, cinnamon, dark chocolate, and something musky.

Anichka, who considered herself a connoisseur of hot beverages, coveted it for her own collection. She inquired politely, "Queen Gitli, where comes this plant for the coffee?"

The queen's answer, even in translation, sounded like gibberish. "We gather the stone-fruit from bushes by a cavern door. It is the spot where the rebel Shade People first came above ground to seek the Sun. Its name is 'Corlaz One's Folly.'" She turned to the clan's horticultural expert. "Phoenix, you know this fruit?"

Phoenix said nothing. He, along with everyone except Agali and Alexej who didn't drink coffee, had a mere second to rue a repeat of last summer's opium pudding fiasco. Their fingers and toes grew icy, the backs of their brains tingled, and their tongues felt too large to fit in their mouths. If they hadn't been sitting within the embrace of the rabbit chairs, they would have fallen down.

As their brains cleared, they heard Queen Gitli's voice via Lucy, as if from miles away: "My dear friends, I give you this coffee with a special drug added so you understand my absolute power. No matter what I reveal to you this evening, you do not make a fuss. *I am in charge.*"

Aleta came to her senses, sputtering, "Queen Gitli, we already *know* you're in charge and we know we're supposed to trust you after you set us up with that stupid pudding test at dinner. So what kind of nonsense *is* all this? It's utterly childish. You didn't drug us before, so you couldn't resist doing it now?

"And you're holding us captive. These rabbits aren't chairs. They're part of the palace guard, holding us down with their claws—"

Before the queen had a chance to retort, Ethan interrupted, his voice shaking. "Queen Gitli, where are the babies? My son was in my arms a minute ago before the drug took hold. And Yacy's crying because her daughter is gone, too ... listen to the poor girl. She's hysterical."

The queen remained unruffled by the furor swirling around her. She gestured with a forepaw. "Look behind you, parents. They're being cared for by the same nursery rabbits we use for our own pups."

Everybody turned their heads. The cooing babies lay perfectly content on the furry white bellies of nursery rabbits, who rocked back and forth on their spines like hammocks on a rolling ship.

With the others' minds on the babies, only Svnoyi, Phoenix, and Oscar heard the queen's next comment. "I shall release you from the rabbit chairs only when I feel like it."

The three of them tried pulling free and concluded that she was right; it couldn't be done. Svnoyi and Phoenix pictured themselves trying to flee with the giant rabbits attached to their backsides. The corners of Svnoyi's mouth twitched, her eyes puckering at the corners, and soon, she and her co-conspirator were roaring with laughter. Oscar looked straight ahead as if he didn't know them.

Jaroslav shook his fist at the guffawing duo. He was about to erupt in patriarchal anger when Anichka patted his hand and whispered, "Say nothing, please. The queen must not see us lose our tempers." She added wisely, "Do not forget, everyone experience the grief differently. They laugh to keep from crying for Sequoyah."

Disgusted, Jaroslav snorted at his wife's reprimand as well as her peculiarly modern interpretation of their behavior that sounded to him like an excuse.

***

Queen Gitli began by introducing her three husbands, who stood one at a time and nodded their heads as each received his moment of praise.

"To my left is Captain Kirk, Twenty-One Thousand and Two of the Orator-Priest Caste. He holds our entire religion in his memory, which is like a vessel full to the brim with holy lore. He must pass down every word to a few chosen acolytes before his demise. Thus do our beliefs remain intact and unchanged from one generation to the next."

She moved on to the second Prairie Dog sitting to her right. "And here we have Neshek, the Master Chef who designs all the palace meals. You may not recognize him, but he attended the Event of the Opium Pudding last summer that left you all comatose. It was I, actually, who sent both the honey and my second and third husbands as ambassadors of good will.

"And here on his other side is my third husband, Saint George, who is First Warrior and an expert carver of the *azvrkt.* You will get to know him better, I assure you."

The adult members of the clan applauded politely, but Jaroslav mumbled under his breath, "Ptah, three husbands. Is not what God wanted."

The queen put her paw on her heart in order to introduce herself. "My Prairie Dog name is Majesty Lunk of the Twenty-Five Thousand and Third Election Cycle. Ever since our first Queen Lunk was chosen by a show of paws, all our monarchs have assumed the crown that way. But I prefer to be called Queen Gitli when I converse with you, the name you gave me last spring when we first met. That way, we keep our species at arm's length and do not intermingle our most sensitive traditions."

She puffed her chest. "My reign lasts a lifetime. A monarch's dethronement occurs only when she commits treason or breaks her vow of celibacy. I may have as many husbands as I like, but to prevent inherited dynasties, I remain a Virgin Queen."

Svnoyi and Phoenix still hadn't settled down from their previous outburst. They tittered behind their hands trying to picture the sex life—or lack of it in Queen Gitli's case—of creatures so unattractively alien.

The queen turned toward them abruptly and hissed, "Unruly children, if you two laugh a third time, I'll order your chairs to bite you."

After a pause, she made a grandiose statement that surprised them all. "You do realize that you are not ordinary humans. Quite the opposite, your arrival was predicted a million years ago by Goddess Merlin, also known as Mary Lynne. She's one of the Original Holy Six, and one of our most beloved deities."

Unexpectedly, she hit the table with her fist, and the polar bear beneath it groaned. "But we never imagined you'd show up in a giant pea pod all coated with ice and kiss the dirt, not plant your crops on time, and pass out from a taste of opium. You also yell far too much and recently you tried to kill each other. Such a lack of discipline, especially of the children. It has appalled us."

She shook her head and frowned. "And really, now. Only two of you come close to being giants.

"If we seemed hostile at first, it was from disbelief. And you were uncommonly rude as well. You trampled our Funeral Meadow, poached our breed rabbits and pheasants, and even spied on our pharmaceutical fields.

"I've only forgiven you because I need your help as much as you need mine."

Aleta bridled in alarm, "What's that supposed to mean?"

"Ah-h-h," replied the queen smoothly. "Well you might ask. Did you think I invited you here for an entire evening only to exchange pleasantries? But first, for your edification, my husband Captain Kirk, with Lucy's help, will explain in poetry just who our gods, the Original Holy Six, really are.

"So you may enjoy it fully, I release you from your chairs." She clapped her paws in a staccato tattoo, and the rabbits loosened their grips.

***

Lucy stood up, flushing crimson. She was especially nervous because she hadn't made up with her father since running away from home. Trembling, she announced in a barely audible voice, "I'm going to tell you about the six gods of the Prairie Dogs and the Shade People."

"Speak up," yelled Agali and Alexej in unison. "We love stories, especially yours."

Giving the children a grateful look, she began handing out to everyone sheets of paper covered in her minute writing. "Here's everything Captain Kirk said in my best poetic translation. These are your copies. I'm reading the words in printing, and you shout out the handwritten words, really loud. That's how it's supposed to work."

She cleared her throat and began. "'A Canticle to the Original Holy Six' as told by Captain Kirk of the Orator-Priest Caste, translated by Tlke, first courtier to the queen, and Lucy, scribe to the queen.

"The Jumping Sun spewed forth one fiery wave,
And all fair Earth's creation came undone.
The Original Holy Six fled to a cave,
And there they stayed to hide from deadly Sun.
"We worship ***Goddess Cinder***, holy priestess,
with eagle eye and ten-foot raptor's wings."
The clan answered hesitatingly,
"Savior of the Shade People,
ill for a million years.
Explorer of the caverns
from Nani to Iqual."

Jaroslav beamed with delight, exclaiming, "Is like church back home. But make it louder, everyone! Follow us." He took Anichka's hand and placed his arm on Alexej's shoulder.

Lucy went on with a new verse:
"We worship ***God Rough,*** supreme inventor,
with mighty voice and owner of two heads."
This time, everyone roared their response:
"Husband to our Cinder,
master of the cloning.
grower of the greens,
maker of the whirlpool."
"We worship ***Goddess Merlin,*** storyteller,
Body bent, soothsayer's eyes unseeing."
"Wife to Corlaz Two,
Bringer of Commandments.
Seer of the Future
who dreamt Sequoyah's coming."
"We worship ***Corlaz Two***, the hot Sun's victim,
cruelly singed, his eyes with fire blasted."
"Husband to blind Merlin.
Prairie Dogs' protector,

first to understand
the tk,tk Prairie Dog tongue."
"We worship ***Goddess Violent,*** muse of art,
her bosom round and red-gold tresses flying."
"Beautiful as Venus,
Beloved of God Rough,
Carver of Three Caves
that house a million seeds."
"Last comes ***Corlaz One,*** disgraceful sinner,
joining with the Sun to save himself."
"Living god of the Sun People
who plunder and steal in his name.
Deadly foe of the Shade People,
we ban him from our Pantheon!"

Lucy returned to Tlke's side as the entire clan sat still, stunned into silence. Only Ethan blurted out, "Lucy, my god, that was amazing, just amazing." He held out his arms to his daughter, and she blew him a kiss.

The others beamed. With any luck, their rift would be over soon, and she'd come home. Then the families stood and gathering together, all of them tried to talk at the same time.

Svnoyi, who had the gift of considerable vocal power, won out. "These Shade People survived World War III by hiding in a cavern way up north. I remember from when we lived in Frobisher Bay that there was a town of Nanisivik, except now it's called 'Nani' in Goddess Cinder's verse. I bet some Prairie Dogs got stuck with the Shade People in the same cavern. Can you believe? These people have survived a million years."

"It's funny, though," Phoenix added. "The Shade People have been sick the whole time, but meanwhile the Prairie Dogs got huge and super smart. Do you think it was the radiation that caused both things to happen?"

Ethan broke in, "That's junk science, Phoenix, comic-book stuff. I hate it. But look at the facts: these Prairie Dogs are almost as big, and certainly as intelligent as humans. In this particular case, the radiation theory sure makes sense."

Oscar added, "Their Goddess Merlin foresaw our arrival in a vision, so we've been expected for a million years." He laughed, "They looked forward to us for so long, no wonder they're disappointed.

"And what about Goddess Violent's carvings? Are they the same as the ones in our own caves?"

Alexej and Agali, who had been surprisingly patient, began jumping up and down to attract attention.

Alexej started out, "Ha, ha, everyone. There's one thing no one's said, not even Svnoyi who's always so smart."

"Right," Agali concluded. "This is really important. Don't forget there's a whole bunch of other guys who're still alive called the Sun People!"

She made a face. "But nobody likes 'em."

***

Queen Gitli sashayed forward, the shells on her dress clanking, and grabbed center-stage once more. "Now comes the moment when we need Truth. Remember from the coffee how powerful I am, and I would hope that you will behave with civility. I urge you to sit down for your comfort, and in good faith, I shall not relock the chairs."

Once everyone had returned to their rabbit chairs, Queen Gitli said simply, "Then let us begin." She clapped her paws three times, which sent the coffee table shuffling back to the kitchen.

But within seconds, Agali sprang up. She curtsied, pulling out the sides of her quilt as if it were a dress. "Mrs. Virgin Queen, Alexej and me, may we help the bobcats do the dishes?"

Queen Gitli nodded, returning the curtsy. "Of course Miss Agali, you and Alexej may enter the kitchen with my husband, Chef Neshek, as your escort. If you wouldn't mind, you might try to teach the bobcats not to throw so much water around."

The other two husbands, Saint George and Captain Kirk, took the opportunity to slip out at the same time. Queen Gitli sat down to the accompaniment of rattling shells, but her translators remained standing.

The queen did not mince her words. "My friends, as indeed you are, as I said before, the Prairie Dogs need your help as much as you need ours.

"As you undoubtedly have surmised by now, Sequoyah did not die."

She turned to Anichka. "Phoenix should have warned you, Doctor. However, he may have been ignorant about the plant we call the 'necros vine' that you used to close the wound. The tendrils ate at Sequoyah's flesh, causing the stitches to tear out."

Anichka gasped. Then she bent her head in shame and to capitalize on her humiliation, Queen Gitli flaunted her superior knowledge. "You should have tried cauterization."

She moved on. "So Aleta, you do understand why we had to snatch Sequoyah from your loving arms. We saved his life, really just in time."

Aleta nodded reverently, saying, "Queen Gitli, in all sincerity, I thank you. But please tell me, where is he now? Oscar says he isn't here because his spirit's gone somewhere else—"

"No, he is not." Queen Gitli replied. "And it's time to level with you. We gave him to the Shade People."

As everyone began shouting, she raised a paw. "Friends, I don't accept your sudden agitation! He never lacked for care. He will be at the Shade People's northernmost cavern, the Eye of Cinder, at Nani. He's being transported to the finest medical facility in my entire kingdom, the Cinder Reconstructive Center.

"Please listen, now. We've been the Shade People's *slaves* for the last million years, so there are plenty of our nursemaids running around serving those good-for-nothing hypochondriacs. They will undoubtedly care for Sequoyah during his rehabilitation. It may be lengthy, considering his almost-mortal wound."

With the queen's remarks, two questions popped into Svnoyi's head. *The prairie dogs were slaves to the Shade People? And they still are ... after a million years? Something's wrong with this picture.*

Jaroslav shouted above the rest, "What relief is it that our Queen Gitli puts Sequoyah in good hands. But why these Shade People want him? What do you receive in exchange?" He shook a big fist. "I know this is not God's way. You make a Devil's bargain."

Queen Gitli eyed the large mountaineer with a new respect for his canny thinking. "You speak with conviction, and I quite agree, Jaroslav. It is not a holy bargain. But more I will not say until we discuss our options. And it grows late. The babies are asleep, rocking in the rabbits' arms.

"I add but one comment. I am sending some of you to bring Sequoyah home, but only when we are done with him. You may choose who will go. Consider it your First Mission."

Ethan yelled, "What about my Luz?"

The queen's answer was smooth. "Calm yourself, Ethan Marcus, this will be your easiest task and also your Second Mission. All you need to do is restore our most holy site, the broken waterworks at the Sacred Meadow—our whirlpool and the ten rivers designed by God Rough—and you can have her back."

"What happened to them? They were fine a few months ago when you put on my wife's sham funeral—"

"Things change, Ethan. Since then, the waterworks were sabotaged by the Sun People. The damage is extreme. We don't even know how the whole thing was laid out to begin with, and the accursed heretics stole all of the gears and tubing in the middle of the night."

Svnoyi had been mulling over the mysterious Sun People so astutely mentioned by Alexej and Agali. "Your Majesty, about these Sun People. They were once Shade People who got tired of the caves and came above ground, right?"

"Yes, Svnoyi, you think with clarity. But now the two peoples are as different as night and day. The Sun People follow the evil god, Corlaz One, agent of the Sun, the god we threw out of our holy Pantheon. They're savages. They survive by pillaging, not by farming. And long, long ago, they stole the design of our *azvrkt*—"

"This is getting bad. What about the *azvrkt?"* Oscar asked.

"They've become champion archers. What with raiding my farms and ruining my Sacred Meadow, which I consider an act of provocation, I'd say they're asking for trouble!"

"And what else, Queen Gitli?" Ethan hissed, his brows twitching. "I can smell deception. You are still hiding something huge."

Queen Gitli rose, surprised by Ethan's insight, not one of his usual fortes. She began walking in circles. "I don't think all of you will appreciate what I'm going to say next."

Abruptly, she offered two superfluous pieces of information, "Death isn't final until *rigor mortis* sets in—at least for those of us who practice truly advanced medicine. And no offense, but you left him under a pitiful stack of river stones without a proper funeral."

She let her bemused audience absorb her non sequiturs before going on. "We needed a superb marksman to teach our own army how to shoot as brilliantly as the Sun People. And therein lies the seed of your Third Mission that I'll let you figure out for yourselves—"

"No," wailed Yacy, "you didn't dig up Kuaray, say you didn't. He was better off dead. Believe me, for all our sakes, he was."

"That may be since he lost the use of his legs when Svnoyi broke his neck. There was only so much my genius physicians could do, but don't worry. We have an unusual solution for his legs, and the rest of him works just fine." Queen Gitli looked smug.

Phoenix stole a look at Svnoyi. Her tawny complexion had turned a ghastly white, and he interpreted her shocked expression as a cross between horror and relief. Next, he turned to his mother, but her reaction was unreadable. She'd buried her face in her hands.

Anichka found her voice, although it squeaked with nervousness. "Please Queen Gitli, you'll regret it if you don't put him out of—"

The queen interrupted, "Doctors should never say awful things like that, especially when little children might hear."

On cue, Alexej and Agali popped through the shell curtain carrying muffins in a string bag, a gift from Chef Neshek. They asked in unison, "We heard you yelling from the kitchen. Do we get to go on an adventure?"

Aleta stood up and took Agali's hand. "Apparently, but more like *three* adventures, or call them missions, if you like. Two of them make sense because we're going to find Sequoyah and Luz, too, but the third one's a mystery."

She added loudly enough for the entire group and Queen Gitli to hear, "We're leaving, now. Naturally I'm grateful that you saved my husband's life, and I'm sure Ethan feels the same about Luz. But this is hardly comforting. You clear up one or two fears and create ten more."

Queen Gitli had the last word. "Do not fret unnecessarily, my friends. Take your Lucy and go home.

"Pray don't bother me again until the snow melts. Most of us Prairie Dogs hibernate for the winter, except for the caretakers of those incessantly demanding Shade People, of course.

"And you owe me thanks. While you were here, my best workers swept the snow from two of your caves and installed replicas of Ethan's stove and the cave doors on rollers. Your homes should be warm and cozy on your arrival."

She drew up the corners of her flexible rodent lips into a patronizing smile.

16 ~ The Third Tunnel

Svnoyi's eyes popped open when a beam of sunlight slid beneath the cave's winter door and hit her squarely in the face. She sat up abruptly, letting her quilt fall from her shoulders.

The sun shouldn't be this high yet. We're still waking up in the dark, even though I'm pretty sure spring is just around the corner. How could I sleep so long?

Yacy was kneeling on a rabbit skin rug playing with Arielle Luz. But Aleta, Phoenix, and Agali had left long ago.

"Yacy, what time is it? Why didn't you wake me up?"

Yacy set her daughter on her lap. "It's pretty late. But Mama said you were overtired and to let you sleep in because you had a terrible dream last night. You were thrashing around and yelling—"

"I was? Yelling? How embarrassing, I wonder what it was about."

She lowered her head, frowning in concentration. She turned to Yacy and said, "Wait, I do remember. It was really intense, but somehow stupid, kind of a copy of a fairy tale from Brothers Grimm. Yes, it was 'Snow White.'"

"It couldn't have been that stupid, Svnoyi. Three of us had to hold down your arms and legs, Agali, Mama, and me. Phoenix pulled his quilt over his head and pretended to be asleep."

Oh my god, it's all coming back. It was a vision, and so hideous I made myself forget it.

Svnoyi closed her eyes to recall it for Yacy.

"Our Daddy Sequoyah was in an ice cave that must've been way up north. The ceiling was covered with frozen stalactites that ran with blood, and each drop oozed down slowly, making a great plop and splash when it landed. The dark red pools had gotten deep, and they swirled around a glass casket with the lid on. He lay sleeping inside, kind of like Snow White with the poison apple stuck in her throat.

"I could see Daddy's breath condensing on the glass and he said something to me even though his lips didn't move. 'Daughter of my heart, walk with Phoenix through the third tunnel. Where it ends is horrible beyond imagination, but don't kill the centipedes.'"

Yacy reached over to caress Svnoyi's arm. "Oh my god, that's awful, and so scary. I'm glad you could remember it for me. But maybe you should tell Phoenix, too, because the vision had him in it."

***

Svnoyi found Phoenix inside the greenhouse in the forest clearing above the three caves. The clan had built it the previous summer from one of Ethan's cleverest designs that utilized the Greyhound's windows. Still shaking from her recollection, she pushed through the tarp covering the door frame.

Without even a hello, Svnoyi asked, "Remember that date we made mind-to-mind when we were walking through the second tunnel to Queen Gitli's soirée?"

Phoenix smiled up at her from the row of half-grown winter squashes he was covering with wood chips. "Sure I remember. Does going on a date with you have something to do with the bad dream you had last night, Snail?"

"That's what I came to tell you. I'm embarrassed that I woke everybody up, but I actually saw Sequoyah in my dream, and he *talked* to me. From what he said, I know there's something strange happening at the end of the third tunnel. So let's check it out."

"It's fine with me ... if there even *is* a third tunnel. What did Sequoyah say?"

"He said something about centipedes."

Then feeling foolish, she murmured, "Do you ever see things in dreams? Anyway, this one was more intense. I think it was a vision."

Phoenix nodded. "Of course I see things in visions and dreams. In visions it's mainly ugly premonitions. But no centipedes so far."

He finished the row and stood up, brushing the chips off his knees. He winked at her. "You ask Anichka if we can snoop around in the back of her cave to find this tunnel."

He headed for the door while putting his arms through his parka sleeves.

***

Anichka sat at the front of her cave darning Alexej's socks. A weak light that held the promise of spring crept through the half-open winter door, illuminating her work. After she'd exchanged greetings with the pair who could barely mask their excitement, she bent her head to her task once more.

Soon she looked up with a sly smile. "Go on, find it, Phoenix and Svnoyi, I know is why you are here. You not able to hide search for third tunnel from me. But from Alexej and Agali *please* keep a secret. Every day they wander too far."

The adventurers had no trouble locating the third passageway at the end of a short ell at the rear of the cave. Like the others, this entrance was camouflaged behind a boulder large enough for three people to sit on. But once they'd wriggled through, no bats greeted them with glowing tapers. In a draft that suggested open air at the other end, Phoenix barely managed to light the oil lamp that Anichka had lent them. They walked cautiously along a path as it wound around heaps of stones and over protruding tree roots, and even through the occasional underground stream that soaked their jeans above their boots.

Phoenix whispered, "The path's a mess. I guess this tunnel isn't used much." His voice didn't reverberate against the muddy walls.

They continued in silence, concentrating on the rock-strewn ground that appeared to shift and heave in the lamp's unsteady light.

Svnoyi touched his shoulder. "Are you nervous?"

"I won't lie. A little, I guess." He took her hand.

A sudden realization shot through Svnoyi's head. *This is not a kid's hand. And he's taller than I am.*

They followed the trail ever upward for about two miles until light gradually filtered through the passage, and the lamp lost its gleam. To save oil, Phoenix blew it out, hoping he had enough matches to relight it for the return journey.

Soon silhouettes of branches danced along the sides of the tunnel as if they were being wafted by a breeze, and the path made a gentle turn. It came to an abrupt halt behind a wall of brambles.

Phoenix spat out his next words, "Damn it all, blackberry bushes are blocking the exit."

A diamond-slatted wooden lattice supported the thicket that presently bore a crop of ripe berries. The vines stood ten feet tall, reminding Svnoyi of the impenetrable forest in "Sleeping Beauty" of Grimm's *Fairy Tales.* She'd left that beloved volume behind a million years in the past, standing beside Hans Andersen's *Fairy Tales.*

She wished she'd brought them both. *Such great books. I keep running into the stories, "Snow White" this morning and "Sleeping Beauty" now.*

She and Phoenix bent forward to peer through the thorny branches but kept their hands safely at their sides.

Svnoyi sighed, "Look, a meadow's in there. And I can make out a vertical stone canyon surrounding it and a bit of blue sky up above."

She attempted a laugh to mask her disappointment, "We've been denied entry into Paradise."

Phoenix bent closer. "It's possible to get a glimpse, but we could always go back and get clippers. Hey, there's actually a two-foot door at the bottom we could crawl through, over here on the left."

He began reaching a hand down carefully through the briars for the knob but caught his breath first. "What the hell?"

Two polar bears, larger than the ones that had carried the banquet tables, sniffed the air, then peered in their direction through rolling eyes set too high in abnormally small heads. They lumbered towards the bushes, clacking their teeth in fright. They made mindless slashes at the thorns, but all they got for their efforts were bleeding paws. After a brief rest, they renewed their attack with twice the fury. Eventually one bear fell to the ground howling in pain, but the other, smelling blood on his own foot, tried to chew it off.

"Oh, no, poor things," Svnoyi whispered. "They're acting demented because they can't possibly get to us through a wall of brambles. I bet the Prairie Dogs bred them for carrying tables but made their skulls so flat there wasn't enough room left for a full set of brains."

A herd of rabbits sat blinking at the commotion the polar bears made, the vestiges of their front legs no more than toes protruding from their shoulders. When a sudden rustling disturbed them, they ran for cover as best they could, leaping like frogs but falling flat on their faces at every landing.

Svnoyi and Phoenix turned their heads toward the swish and crackle of separating grass blades. Something large and long with an armor-plated back seemed to float rather than walk into view.

Svnoyi, standing a little way in front, instinctively thrust out her arms and fingers, palms facing back, as if to protect Phoenix. He put both his hands on her shoulders and whispered into her ear, "Oh, my god, there's your centipede, Svnoyi. No, wait, there are more of 'em, and they're easily twenty feet long. They're after the rabbits."

The rabbits, even without front legs, had escaped this time. The centipedes turned their heads as something more interesting attracted them: the smell of blood. And the polar bears didn't have the presence of mind to run away on feet that hurt with every step they took. The two lead centipedes coordinated the attack by touching antennae. Then, out of a primitive kindness, they numbed the woofing bears with their venomous front pinchers before snapping mandibles as large as lions' jaws around their victims' fleshy necks.

Phoenix and Svnoyi didn't wait around to watch the bears' final moments. They turned and left at a run, not slowing until they could no longer see in the blackness of the corridor.

Panting, Phoenix crouched down to light the lamp. He succeeded in one try even with shaking fingers, as Svnoyi cheered him on with encouraging pats on the shoulder. They watched in silence as the blue flame climbed along the wick.

When she finally spoke, her voice sounded hoarse after their frightened scramble. "The Prairie Dogs have tampered with so many creatures, and those rabbits and bears must've been just a few of their genetic mistakes. They stuck the poor things out there where no one could see them."

Phoenix added, "But the centipedes look just fine, and I'm sure they're in the process of becoming the Prairie Dogs' trendiest slaves. Dammit, Svnoyi, they're just so huge."

Svnoyi grimaced. "It's awful, but it's nature—the centipedes were hungry. How convenient for the Prairie Dogs to have their other errors disappear. Resourceful, too."

"I'm guessing, Svnoyi, but I think the bears weren't interested in us. They wanted to escape into the corridor and that's why they were slashing at the bushes. They weren't so dumb after all, just ... too ugly for the Prairie Dogs to look at."

Svnoyi added, "Yes, it's terribly sad, and that's not the whole picture. Everywhere else outside it's still cold, so why did we see a green meadow and blackberry bushes with summer fruit? The whole place can't be in a natural canyon. Those grey walls must be buildings that hold in the heat."

***

The pair continued home at a slower pace. They weren't scared anymore, but every few minutes Phoenix shined the lamp behind them to reassure himself that a centipede hadn't broken through the hedge. At about the halfway mark, he stopped abruptly in the middle of the path. He took Svnoyi's hand and pulled her down beside him where they both leaned their backs against the moist mud and stone of the corridor wall.

Even though Svnoyi had slid to the ground willingly, she pulled her hand away, whispering, "No, Phoenix, this isn't right. You're years younger than me, and even though we're not related, we've seen the worst in each other, already. Besides, we just witnessed something horrible."

Phoenix responded oddly by pulling closer to her and putting one arm around her shoulder. "No, Snail, I didn't mean *that,* but thanks for thinking I did."

"If it isn't about you and me, then what's it about? The existential awfulness of life?" She smiled, and Phoenix laughed.

"Well put, Snail. Yes, something like that. But I had a more specific topic in mind."

He was no longer laughing. By the paltry beam of the lamp Svnoyi could see him frowning and chewing his lip.

He burst out, "What do you know about my father?"

His question was so unexpected that Svnoyi went silent trying to figure out a reply. Eventually she stuttered, "Your father? I-I do know about him, but I'm not the one—I'll ask Aleta to talk to you."

"I've already asked her, dozens of times. She said she won't ever tell me, not even when I'm older. She said it's a secret she'll carry to her grave. And believe me, that hurts, I'm her own kid—"

"I'll try to reason with her—"

"No, please, Svnoyi, if you like me even a little—*please* tell me. It's killing me not to know, because it's about me ... who I am."

Svnoyi knew her answer was evasive. "Three of us kids don't know very much about one of our parents. My mother died just after I was born and Daddy jumped off a cliff in the High Tatras mountains, he was so sad. Jaroslav and Anichka saved him.

"Oscar's father was a handsome foreign student from the Congo who was in Luz's ROTC class, so it's the same for him. Luz was so lonely back in those days. And luckily, she and Ethan got together just after Oscar was born—"

"Stop it, Svnoyi. Tell me who he is."

Svnoyi took Phoenix's hand absent-mindedly, and let her mind wander a long way back to when she was four.

"Okay, I will. When you were born, we were living in the High Tatras in Jaroslav and Anichka's cabin. Your mama—I called her Etsi back then and I still do, sometimes—well, she didn't get along with anybody because of what had happened to her. She was especially mean to Sequoyah. And she wouldn't take care of you. You were cute, too, with violet eyes about as big as silver dollars."

"And?"

"And one afternoon when I wasn't supposed to be listening, I heard her tell Anichka about it."

Phoenix fidgeted uneasily even though he'd been longing for this moment.

Svnoyi began whispering as if hidden microphones would pick up her voice. "When time travel was still part of our lives, your mama was pushed backward to a concentration camp in France for Jews. She had Yacy and Kuaray with her, and they were only three years old. She tried to protect them by getting help from the police captain. He's your father, Phoenix, and it was rape, I mean, over and over for as long as she was there."

Phoenix sat perfectly still, trying to pull himself together. But when Svnoyi twisted to put comforting arms around him, he turned away from her, whispering to the wall, "Poor Mama. I knew it must've been something really awful like that."

He kept his face averted so she couldn't see him. "No wonder she's so far away half the time and doesn't always like me much. It's a good thing Sequoyah was an amazing stepdad ... before he was taken away, I mean."

Svnoyi grabbed him by the shoulders and stared directly at him. "Phoenix, don't keep looking away from me. You're stalling, there's something more worrying you, isn't there?"

He stared back and his voice came out in a croak. "Yes, much more. So my Nazi father must've been telepathic—because *I* am. Do you think he was cruel?"

Svnoyi didn't hesitate. "Of course he was cruel, a real sadist. Yacy told me he hurt her with his mind, and it really terrified her. She was only a tiny kid.

"Why are you asking this? You don't think you're like him, do you?"

"Yes, *I am* like him. I-I'm pretty sure I inherited the same sadism. I think I could hurt people with my *mind*, I mean, really hurt them."

"The same as I did to Kuaray?"

Phoenix pulled away. When he finally spoke, he choked on the words. "But you ... I thought you did it with your hands."

"No, only partly with my hands but mostly with my mind."

"Listen to me, Phoenix." Svnoyi gripped her fingers together in her lap. "When I had my awful headache, I couldn't control my thoughts, and all I could do was let them race. And I couldn't get past the terrible thing I'd just done. I'd killed my half brother."

"My god, Svnoyi. He'd stabbed your father just before—"

"Let me finish."

She'd been considering it ever since in detail, and now she stood up to explain. "This is the conclusion I've come to. All of us who are telepathic, adults and kids, we have more power than just that. And we all use it differently. You could call it heightened feelings with physical force to back it up.

"But it's all about death."

Phoenix nodded as if he already knew she'd say that.

"My Daddy Sequoyah turned it on himself, and Yacy's like that, too. Suicidal. Oscar's empathic. He uses his power to see past death, right into people's spirits. Then there's Anichka and Jaroslav who want to save people from death, no matter what."

Her voice rose. "Luz hides behind that blustery exterior, but she's all about love, even if she has to die for it. It seems strange to me, anyway, but she joined the Air Force in the Time Before because she loved her country. Lucy's the same way, only she would die for animals. I'm sure she'll get around to people before long.

"And Kuaray isn't different from me, really. He's a killer and I am, too."

Phoenix stood up. "Then there's me. I'm like you and Kuaray. I'm capable of killing, too. I was that close," he made a gesture with his fingers, "to zapping those centipedes by thinking them dead. Except I didn't forget what Sequoyah said in your vision."

He took her hand. "I swear I don't want to kill anything or anyone, and I know you don't want to, ever again. We have to be vigilant, help each other—"

Svnoyi interrupted enthusiastically, "You and me, do you think we could do it together? I mean, I love being with you. It's more than that. For weeks, now, I've wanted to be with you all the time—"

She couldn't believe what she'd said. Her outburst had sounded like a clumsy proposition. She clapped her hand over her mouth and turned her back to hide her face that had flushed hot from embarrassment.

All at once they were both laughing, and embracing, too.

Phoenix asked cautiously, "You know I feel the same about you. But what about Oscar?"

Svnoyi said simply, "He'll be relieved. He's in love with Yacy, and she feels the same about him. I mean, they're deeply in love. You can see it in their eyes. After Kuaray died, he was the only one who comforted her.

"Yacy really needs his empathy, and I ... I never did."

She reflected, her eyes looking inward. "Oscar and I go way back, you know. During the Time Before, we talked every day across continents, starting when I was four years old. I guess the romance happened when we got older because everybody expected it to."

They pulled close and Svnoyi slipped her hand around the back of Phoenix's neck. The first kiss was a bit of a fumble on Phoenix's part, and the second held promise. The third lasted a long time.

Phoenix broke free to pick up the lamp, and his tone was light. "Anyway, the minute we get home, all the others except Aleta and Ethan are gonna know."

***

By the time Svnoyi and Phoenix had wriggled through the cramped archway opening on the cul-de-sac in Anichka and Jaroslav's cave, they were already late for dinner. Prominently displayed at eye-level was a rolled-up note from Anichka that she'd pushed into a crack in the big boulder by the entrance.

They flattened it out and read aloud: "Dinner at Ethan's, be on time. Do NOT tell Alexej and Agali about THIRD TUNNEL!!" The capital letters and exclamation marks served as an emphatic reminder that the anxious mother would like to curb the children's increasingly risky adventures. Svnoyi and Phoenix looked at each other and nodded. Both of them still felt queasy from seeing the meadow.

When the tardy pair slipped into their places around Ethan's oval table, they felt Agali and Alexej surveying them and for one uneasy minute, they tried to bury their thoughts. But soon the children launched into an annoying couplet as old as the hills:

"Snail and Phoenix, sitting in a tree,

K-I-S-S-I-N-G!"

Jaroslav gave the red-faced recipients a gimlet-eyed appraisal. "What Alexej and Agali say, I do not understand. Here is no tree."

"Is very old *teasing poem* children repeat," said Anichka, laughing.

After a moment's thought, Jaroslav snapped back, "Ah, wife, now I get it, and is not good."

He announced for the benefit of all, "Our many teenagers need father figure to give advice, and I say, stop right now. Svnoyi is too old, Phoenix is too young. Is not God's—"

Ethan, like everyone else, was sick of Jaroslav's patriarchal rants. He slammed down his mug, splashing tea on the table. "Jaroslav, fer chrissake, I don't see anything wrong with it. It's not like there's a big choice of dating partners around here."

But then he scratched his head. "Wow. It beats me how the little kids could've figured out something like that so fast, in under a minute."

"How many years have you been hanging out with telepaths, Dad?" Oscar asked him, grinning from ear to ear. "It's high time you got used to it."

Svnoyi turned her head to glance at the speaker, who sounded a little too ecstatic. She noticed that he'd already edged closer to Yacy and slipped his arm around her slender waist.

That was quick, and probably the simplest break-up in history. At least now I don't have to write him a Dear John letter.

She added ruefully to herself, *Maybe we weren't very much in love after all. So am I feeling jealous? Hmm, not at all: how many men do I need? And I feel totally happy for Yacy.*

Lucy, too, noticed the second pair of lovebirds because she happened to be sitting next to Yacy. She called across the table, "Hey, Agali and Alexej, we need another round of your witty poem. 'Oscar and Yacy, sitting in a—'"

"Nah," Agali shot back. "They're no fun to tease like Snail is."

Aleta wiped her mouth delicately on her napkin and clapped her hands to capture everyone's attention. "Now that spring is almost here and love is in the air, this is the perfect time for me to make an announcement." She waited until everyone had put down their spoons and turned her way.

Patting her belly through her thick wool sweater, she uttered what sounded like a prepared speech. "I'm not just getting fat as you might have thought. I'm happy to say that my darling Sequoyah gave me a 'parting gift' a few weeks before the Prairie Dogs took him. Twins will be arriving in late June. It's been four months, now, and everything's going as well as can be expected under the circumstances."

Yacy reached across the table to take Aleta's hand. She gave it a quick squeeze accompanied by a dazzling smile quite unusual for her. "Mama, dear, all of us already knew about it ages ago. Well, maybe not Ethan because he can't read minds.

"We've been waiting for you to tell us."

"Congratulations, Mama," Phoenix whispered. "I guess you might say light springs from darkness, at least some of the time."

17 ~ What Sequoyah Would Do

Wildflowers had appeared seemingly overnight in last summer's vegetable patch, filling in the flattened furrows with splotches of yellow and blue. Alexej and Agali skipped along the rows until Agali fell on her knees and put her ear to the ground.

"I can hear what they're saying," she announced.

"Who?"

"The flowers, of course, down at the roots."

Both of them tried another spot, then a third and fourth. After sampling the entire plot, they sprang up and chased each other through the chilly morning air toward Jaroslav and Anichka's cave for breakfast.

A few minutes short of their destination, Agali sat down in the middle of the path that ran along the crest of the cliff above the three caves. She gave her folded arms a defiant pump across her stomach and frowned up at Alexej. "I hate breakfast."

"Me, too."

Agali elaborated. "Every morning, all they do is argue and complain. My mama is the worst." The little girl commenced whining to imitate Aleta, "I'm expecting my darling Sequoyah's twins at the end of June. Does anybody even ... care?"

Alexej dropped down on the path across from her assuming the same position, arms crossed. "No, my daddy's the worst, 'cause he bosses everyone around." He offered an impersonation of Jaroslav in his deepest voice: "Order, order!"

"No, Snail's the worst, 'cause she yells twice as loud as the grown-ups, like she knows everything." Agali took in a great breath before bellowing, "Shu-ut uppp!"

"But she does know everything," Alexej remarked thoughtfully.

***

Once the children had squeezed through the winter door's narrow opening to Anichka and Jaroslav's cave, they burst into song, their poetry set to the opening notes of "Frère Jacques." "We heard the wee-eds, we heard the flowers. What did they say, this fine day?" And a repetition: "We heard the wee-eds, we heard the flowers. What did they say—"

"Well, *what?"* Aleta snapped.

"Nothing." With wounded feelings, they pouted down at the pine-nut porridge that Anichka had already put at their places on the low table of Ethan's design.

Everyone was still sitting cross-legged around it even though they'd finished breakfast except for drinking the last of Anichka's tea. No one was smiling.

Agali remarked, "What a bunch of grouches."

Phoenix pulled his half sister onto his folded knees. "I bet I know what the weeds and flowers said. They whispered right in your ear, 'Yank me up, right away; don't delay, don't say nay. And plant those seeds, today, today. It's springtime!'"

The children answered in unison, "They did say it was springtime. They didn't say 'yank me up.'"

Ever since Queen Gitli's memorable banquet, Jaroslav had taken up his old position as director of house meetings from the days in the High Tatras. He rapped on the table with his knuckles and raised a hand. "Okay, is enough. Order, order, I say this for third time this morning."

Hearing the words they'd predicted, Agali's and Alexej's eyes met, and they nudged each other under the table. "First one," they whispered.

Jaroslav stood up. "Today we must figure out. We do our spring work; we repair, we build, we till, we plant the crops. Then what we do? We go on missions we do not understand, yet."

"Why do you keep saying that, over and over?" Ethan made yet another grab for seven-month-old Lucian's arm before a half-full porridge bowl could crash to the floor. His son's experiment with gravity thwarted, the irritated father continued, "We knew we had three missions to go on as soon as we left the Prairie Dogs' freakin' do last October. Gitli said as much. The only problem is, one of the missions isn't at all clear—"

Aleta interrupted in a teary voice, "We've been worrying all winter long and right into spring. And we still have no idea what we're facing, even for the missions we do understand.

"I'm expecting my darling Sequoyah's twins at the end of June. Does anybody even care?"

Agali whispered to Alexej, "She said it. Second one." They smirked and punched each other.

Aleta twisted around to catch Anichka's usual glance of sympathy, but the Roma was up to her elbows in dish suds at the other side of the cave and did not turn her head. She was fed up: her tense shoulders and arrow-straight back above her billowy red skirt spoke volumes.

"Aleta." Ethan turned to face her head-on. "All you do is complain, complain, complain, and I'm damned sick of it. My Luzzie simply disappeared into a black hole somewhere in that horrible kingdom, and nobody cares about that."

Svnoyi got to her feet, livid, shaking a fist for emphasis. "Everyone, just shut up. We have the same petty sniping and the same stupid discussion every morning."

"That's the third one, Svnoyi said it!" The children burst into laughter they smothered with their hands so that it came out more like spitting.

Svnoyi glared at them before asking with a tinge of sarcasm, "Remind me again, everyone, what are the two missions we actually understand? And what do we *think* the third one is?"

"Order, order!" Jaroslav shook his fist at Svnoyi. "I say sit down. Every day you steal my meeting. So rude, this 'shut up' coming from young girl's mouth."

Yacy, who almost never offered a comment, deposited Arielle Luz in Oscar's arms before standing up beside Svnoyi. Her unusually pale features flushed crimson as all eyes turned toward her. "Of course the first two missions are getting Luz back and finding Daddy Sequoyah. It'll be harder than we think, because we don't know exactly how, yet. But at least we already know what our goal is."

"Go on," Svnoyi said, sensing Yacy veering away from the usual platitudes. She put an encouraging arm around her friend's spare shoulders.

Yacy spoke so softly that everyone had to strain to hear her. "For the third mission the queen wants us to help the Prairie Dogs fight a war against the Sun People. We know that because she revived Kuaray to have him train her army to shoot with *azvrkts.*"

Unexpectedly, her voice soared with faith in her conviction: "But if we're going on a real mission, it won't be to fight a war. It'll be to stop it before it starts—if we can. *'Cause that's what Daddy Sequoyah would do.*"

"Yes," said Svnoyi, her eyes shining. "The third mission will be to head off the war, somehow. We could find the Sun People and ask them to behave—"

"You think is what Queen Gitli wants?" asked Jaroslav.

Phoenix quipped without effort, "You mean peace between the Prairie Dogs and the Sun People? No, of course not, and she's manipulating us, somehow. Just wait, none of the missions will go the way we expect, anyway.

"What matters is, we have three missions. It's the higher purpose we've been looking for."

All at once, adults and children alike were laughing. Anichka left her dishpan to clasp Jaroslav around the waist, her hands still dripping suds. Svnoyi, Lucy, and Phoenix hopped onto the table, kicking aside bowls and mugs. The others sprang up to dance on either side, bouncing the babies and hugging.

Phoenix thrust his arms in the air and cried out, "Freeze!" Like the children's game, Statues, the spontaneous celebrating ceased, and no one moved a muscle.

In the sudden silence, he laughed from the pleasure of making his own discovery. "Look around you. It's either a miracle or pure chance, but our three mission teams are in front of our eyes, left, right, and standing on the table." He threw his arms around Svnoyi while grinning at Lucy. "Most likely when people are happy, they just naturally gravitate toward the ones they want to be with."

***

When the glaringly bright sun reached its zenith, most of the clan left their hoes and rakes beside the vegetable patch to break for lunch. Anichka had packed sliced rabbit and watercress sandwiches into three baskets woven last summer by Yacy, one for each of the teams so propitiously chosen that morning by Phoenix. The thoughtful chef had also tucked in surprises to heighten the already boisterous mood from the morning: chewy balls she'd made out of ground pine-nuts, raisins, and honey that everyone agreed later had tasted delicious.

The Sequoyah Search Team settled down among the pines by a sheered boulder, its flat side coated with a pale green lichen flecked with mustard-yellow dots. They sat on the jackets they'd spread out on the sun-dappled forest floor, and everybody except Aleta took off mud-encrusted boots and damp socks to wiggle their toes.

Jaroslav mumbled the same hurried grace he'd said at every meal since the Prairie Dogs had set up daily deliveries of fresh-killed rabbits. "Thank God and Queen Gitli for the food we eat. Amen."

He passed around the thick sandwiches, one each for Agali, Alexej, Anichka, and himself, and two for Aleta because she was pregnant. As he always did, he commented on the excellence of his wife's wholesome bread that she called "Gypsy *zdravý chléb."*

Aleta sipped from her metal cup, relishing water from the snow-fed brook bubbling over nearby rocks. She offered an apology, her head bowed. "I've been so difficult and short with everybody all winter long. It's because I've been ever so worried about my Sequoyah, and I do apologize. That and the morning sickness ...."

She glanced lovingly at her friends before biting into her second sandwich and chewing thoughtfully. "With Jaroslav, the best mountain guide for traveling north, and Anichka, the best doctor for my delivery, what can go wrong?"

"Nothing, because you have us, too," Agali announced brightly.

She and Alexej leapt up to make a mock bow. "Alexej and me, we're the best cavers, we'll bring him back all by ourselves."

Aleta smiled wistfully at the children's naïveté, then sighed, signaling an end to her brief burst of optimism.

Distressed about the task ahead of them, Jaroslav lowered his voice to a conspiratorial whisper. "But this I do not understand, and I have much worry, all day, all night. Why the Prairie Dogs help us find Sequoyah *now?* Last October they give him away to Shade People."

"I know why," Agali offered, brightly. "Svnoyi says all the time that the Prairie Dogs don't know what the hell they're doing."

Jaroslav glowered at the little girl beneath his brows, but Anichka laughed, her eyes crinkling at the corners. "What language. How learn these children so fast?"

***

Ethan, leader of the team to recover Luz because of his all-around knowledge of engineering, set out for lunch walking backward. Clutching roly-poly and squirming Lucian around the middle, he fixed his gaze on the half-dug garden plot.

He grumbled, "We came here in a time machine last spring, and this spring we're hacking at the dirt with primitive slabs of bent metal." He tripped on a tree root, hardly noticing. "I call that regression. How difficult is it to make a plow? An angled blade, two handles—"

He tripped on a second root, almost dropping Lucian. "And why are we hauling around these *tubs* when they could be riding in a wagon? A lightweight rolling frame's enough. You know, the wheel transformed mankind."

Oscar steered his stepfather by the elbow toward a ring of young pines that had sprung up around the decayed stump of their parent, the tips of their boughs showing brushy new growth. "Here's a good spot for lunch, Dad."

Ethan handed his howling, hungry son to Yacy who already had her hands full with her own child. Then he sat down carefully on the pine-needle carpet, groaning in accompaniment to his creaking knees. Oscar knelt to fill the team's three cups with the cold tea Ethan preferred over water, carefully aiming the gurgling mouth of their army-surplus canteen. That done, he pulled the sandwiches from their basket: one each for Ethan and himself, and two for Yacy because she was breastfeeding.

He cleared his throat to preface a remark he didn't want to make. "Listen Dad, you gotta stop inventing all the time. You get preoccupied and don't concentrate." He forged on reluctantly, swirling the tea around in his cup. "You could've hurt Lucian just now when you tripped on that root. And yourself."

Ethan slapped a solid hand on Oscar's shoulder. "I'm sorry, Oscar. But y'know, if I don't keep inventing, I feel like I'll go crazy thinking about Luz." His mouth turned down at the corners, and he fell silent.

But not for long: he suddenly exploded like a pent-up volcano. "I'm worried sick about this herculean labor that most likely can't be done. Twelve rivers to go every which way and a whirlpool that sounds like a flushing toilet? And you turn the whole fuckin' thing off every night? Have any of us even seen the damn water source?"

"Ten rivers, not twelve," Oscar prompted.

Ethan waved his arms, dropping his half-eaten sandwich. "Ten, twelve, what's the difference? I'm pretty sure the Prairie Dogs don't have blueprints lying around for the million-year-old Charybdis Aquatic Funeral Park, or what ever it's called, most likely kept in repair by drug-addicted sewer rats. And those manic Sun People stole all the pipes and gears—"

A ringing soprano voice cut through his monologue. Yacy, supporting a plump baby in the crook of each fine-boned elbow, stared Ethan down without mercy: "As of this morning, we're all happy, remember?" Her eyes flashed fire. "Toughen up, Ethan. There's no room on this team for depressed old men."

Then clapping both hands over her mouth, she bent double in an agony of guilt. Losing their support, the babies teetered but remained upright on their sturdy behinds, their eyes round with surprise. "Oh, my *god,*" she whispered. "Did I say that?"

Ethan blinked a few times; he was hurt. He tried out a few appeasing chuckles although his heart wasn't in it.

Oscar started laughing so hard the tea he'd been drinking came out his nostrils. Choking, he barely managed to say. "How I love you guys. We'll make the best team ever, you'll see. And when we get Mama Luz back, we'll be unbeatable."

He rose to his knees to fish out the bandana that he kept in his front jeans pocket and blew his nose. His next remarks turned sober: "Okay, there're a few more things. We're the home team, so to speak, and responsible for the vegetable garden. And everything else around here."

Ethan nodded and then frowned, trying to articulate an unwelcome thought. "Hmm. You could say we'll be damned busy doing everything *but* engineering."

***

At noon Phoenix stubbornly refused to leave the garden patch, even though blisters had started filling with water on his palms from his relentless turning of the heavy soil. He called after Lucy's and Svnoyi's receding backs, "I think it's gonna drizzle tonight, perfect for softening the seeds, and they won't be in the ground on time."

Svnoyi called over her shoulder, "I remember something Kuaray said once. That you'd marry a stick of bamboo."

"Okay, okay, I'm coming." He hurried to catch up, mopping his neck with a big red bandana as he ran.

The trio sat under an ancient Douglas fir that still dropped an occasional seed from the cones that had matured last September. "Hmm, sexy," Phoenix remarked, running his fingers along the tight-bound needles. "Male and female in the same plant."

Lucy unpacked the sandwiches, rabbit for Svnoyi and Phoenix, and dried fruit and butternut squash for her. "Are you sure this is the man you want, Svnoyi? He's obsessed."

"And you're not?" Svnoyi asked innocently.

"Y'know," said Phoenix, finishing off the last bite of his pine-nut confection and peeking wistfully inside the empty basket. "Our new quest should be called the 'Mission of High Ideals and No Facts.'"

Svnoyi clapped her hands rhythmically in agreement. "You got that right. Should we go searching for these Sun People? Or wait for them to plunder something to reveal their location? Queen Gitli said—"

Lucy jumped up with terror in her face. "Queen Gitli? Lord love a duck, I forgot. There's something I promised her I'd do, and I'm late." She left without a goodbye, her long blond hair streaming behind her.

"Lord love a *what*?" Svnoyi stopped putting away their cups and the empty canteen in the basket.

Phoenix stared into space. "Yeah, Luz used to say that all the time. 'Lord love a duck.' No wonder Lucy's picked it up."

"But did you see the look on Lucy's face just now?" Svnoyi asked. "She was scared."

Phoenix scratched his head. "Scared of Queen Gitli? Maybe, I don't really know." He added thoughtfully, "Putting up with the Prairie Dogs and us, too, can't be easy."

***

By late afternoon, the clan had sown all of the early spring vegetables: carrots, peas, potatoes, and radishes. Svnoyi and Phoenix walked in silence along the crest of the cliff above the caves. They scrambled down a little way to sit together on the broad, flat rock that everyone called "Snail's Place" ever since she'd kept vigil there for Sequoyah last October. It was twilight, and they could feel the gritty surface cooling beneath them. Their shoulders touched, he held her hand in his lap, she tightened her fingers around his. *I could kiss his neck. Or put my hand on his thigh.* She momentarily considered searching beneath the surface of his mind to see if he had similar notions but rejected the idea.

She closed her eyes and emptied her own mind to let his thoughts flow in. They did, filling the grey spaces behind her temples with the scent of fresh-cut grass and daisies. She took a deep breath and held it. *It's perfect. I mustn't think, I'll ruin it for us both ....*

Two distant voices began to pick at the edges of their idyll. The high-pitched twittering drew closer, and Agali and Alexej rounded the rock, slipping on the sand-covered incline. Something about the children's nervous haste put Svnoyi and Phoenix on alert; they broke apart and slid from their perch to the ground, anticipating the usual breathy presentation.

"We just saw something *so weird,* and please don't get mad," Agali begged. Both of them clasped their hands in attitudes of beseeching prayer.

Alexej explained: "We went someplace we promised my mama and daddy we'd never go by ourselves."

"Where?" Svnoyi asked in alarm.

"Queen Gitli's palace. Agali and me, we saw Lucy running and running from lunch, and suddenly we were following her. She ran through the tunnel in Ethan's cave to the palace. Then she ran through a big, wide tunnel that started by the kitchen, and we followed her some more.

"The bobcats weren't there. Maybe they went home for lunch."

"Maybe," Svnoyi said crisply. She restrained herself from scolding the children because she was relieved they hadn't discovered the third tunnel. But this adventure had so many possibilities for disaster, it took her breath away.

"Go on."

Agali took over. "At the end of the big, wide tunnel was a funny, long grey room made of rock, and guess who was in it?"

"I can't. You tell me."

She nodded. "Well, Alexej and me, we thought we were seeing a room in the Prairie Dog Hospital because *Kuaray* was in there. The queen told you she brought him back to life, so we thought he'd still be kinda sick and in the hospital."

Alexej filled in more details. "He was wearing a hospital dress and his legs wouldn't work. They're floppy like Raggedy Andy's."

Together they said, "He was with Lucy."

Phoenix whispered to Svnoyi behind his hand, "I still can't believe the Prairie Dogs could've revived him, even if his legs didn't make it."

Svnoyi whispered back, "Right. I'm not used to it yet, either. And they performed an absolute miracle on Sequoyah, and who knows what they're doing for Luz. And, my god, they knew how to *create* those centipedes—"

She clapped her hands over her mouth. So much for keeping their secret.

The children piped in an excited unison, "But that's exactly what we came to tell you about."

"We saw a giant creepy thing with hundreds of legs bigger than a crocodile—"

"And with wavy antennas on his head and an icky mouth."

"Of course he must be a centipede because Lucy calls him Petey," Agali added thoughtfully. "Get it? 'Pede,' 'Petey.'"

Svnoyi shot Phoenix a telepathic message. *These kids. Can you believe? Nothing fazes them. They weren't horrified by any of it.*

The children giggled and punched each other. Alexej said, "You should'a been there, Phoenix and Snail. They looked so silly. She was teaching him how to *ride* on Petey's back, and he kept falling off."

Agali jumped up and down with pleasure. "And every time, yeah, every time, he said the same thing, 'Goddammit to hell, I *hate* this.'"

"Hey kids," Svnoyi remarked, grabbing their shoulders and looking deep into their eyes. "Keep this to yourselves. I'm sure you wouldn't want your parents to find out where you went."

Both children nodded decisively. They didn't need to be told.

18 ~ Coercion

Queen Gitli kept the Sequoyah Search Team waiting for a half hour at the end of the passageway leading to the banquet hall. Their eyes drifted upward to the ceiling where they observed the bats' tapers blinking out, one by one. They counted and recounted the stalactites that glistened above their heads, each fanciful cone distilling a solitary jewel drop at its tip.

Groaning, Aleta lowered herself to the moist stone, hoping to relieve her legs that ached from supporting the eighth-month bulge of her belly. Even with Agali and Alexej supporting her by the elbows, it was a long way down to the rock floor.

She said for the fourth time, "Her Royal Highness is rude making us wait, especially me. And I simply can't believe it. We're all packed and ready to leave, and so far, she hasn't told us why she sent away my husband to those Shade People."

"Shh, have patience, dear one. Maybe this time ...." Anichka bent down to put a hand on Aleta's shoulder, only to have it shaken off by a petulant shrug.

Jaroslav rolled his eyes and gave his wife a sideways glance. They recalled an entirely different person when she'd been carrying Agali, seemingly so long ago in the High Tatras. "Aleta, I repeat again—what is the word? We must learn to *appreciate* each other. Only together do we succeed."

A bobcat padded toward them, his nails clicking on the stone floor. He turned his head toward the vast, dimly lit chamber, a gesture meant to direct them into the queen's presence. Agali and Alexi giggled aloud. Obviously the cat had been ordered away from his usual task because his whiskers dripped soapsuds from the dishpan, and he'd left a wet trail behind him.

Aleta sniffed, "The queen couldn't come herself? This greeting is impolite to the extreme. And where's the usual bat brigade that gives this place some light?"

She whispered into Anichka's ear, "Something's going wrong at this court."

They focused through the gloom on the spine of a lone rabbit chair lit by a single bat globe. It was set dead center, dwarfed and solitary in the immense space. Lucy and Tlke stood on either side like statues, ready to translate.

Queen Gitli asked peevishly form the depths of the chair, "Why are you people still hanging around? What are you waiting for? Go find Sequoyah ... and leave me alone."

Her sour introduction made the visitors freeze, except for the children who were no longer there. They'd followed the bobcat into the kitchen.

Aleta was not intimidated. She remarked acidly, "Your Highness, you were the one who invited us yourself— "

"Well, come on in, then, and hurry up. I don't bite."

Baffled by the queen's inhospitality, they tiptoed closer. Then Anichka noticed a tray of powders and vials beside the chair. Disregarding the caustic remark, the doctor rushed to the monarch's side, red skirt billowing, and knelt to match her height. "Queen Gitli, I must inquire, you are not well?" She gently caressed the gnarled paw that extended from the sleeve of a loosely woven nightgown and palpated the furry wrist, searching for the pulse.

The queen let her paw remain in Anichka's sure hands. Her face twisted with misery. "It's old age, dear Doctor Anichka. I've lost count of the years, but I may be seventy, very ancient for our kind."

She heaved a sigh. "I am nearing the end of my reign because soon comes my death. There will be a paltry funeral in the shambles of that ransacked meadow, and my successor will be elected the same day. They will pull down my royal statue in the center of town—"

"No, surely, not," Anichka cried out. She calmed herself and put on a professional air. "Good Queen, tell me where it hurts ... exactly."

"It's my knees, Doctor. Also my elbows, my neck, and all my joints. They creak, and fiery pains torture me day and night. Not even marijuana helps, and I never sleep longer than five minutes at a stretch."

She grimaced. "I'm sure it comes from all those years I spent gyrating in that damn fifty-pound shell dress. And from walking everywhere on my hind legs."

Anichka nodded sagely. "Queen Gitli, how lucky are you to say something to me. From our time living in the past I bring powdered yucca for arthritis pain, and the seeds, too. Your gardeners can grow big plants. It is *the* recommended remedy for the arthritis of old age."

The queen withdrew her paw. "Hmm, none of my own specialists have said anything like this. Are you absolutely sure?"

Anichka nodded, and for a fleeting moment, Queen Gitli looked faintly contrite for her shoddy treatment of the gypsy doctor.

The arthritis expert said brightly, "Now I call Agali and Alexej from the kitchen. They are young, they run very fast to my cave and come back with the yucca powder. You take good-size dose, and what we all wait for, our meeting can start."

At the queen's commands, additional chairs hopped in, enough for everyone except her translators, who stood on constant alert to intercept her every rumination. The rabbits formed a circle and assumed their chair shapes, and a flathead bear shuffled into the center, balancing on his head a huge tray loaded with six cups of

Corlaz One's Folly. The aromatic brew sloshed in concentric circles as he lowered himself to his knees and commenced his stony pose.

Agali and Alexej arrived out of breath from running the length of the passage in both directions and plopped down in the waiting rabbit chairs—kits-in-training, miniature in size and silky-soft. The queen's pain must have been extreme. Without a thank you she grabbed the sack from Agali's hands and poured a stream of powdered yucca into her coffee. Not bothering to stir it in, she polished off the entire cup, and within minutes a beatific smile wreathed and smoothed her crabbed face. She extended her paws forward, wiggling them in wonder. Cautiously, she turned her neck from side to side.

"Oh, my, this is bliss ten times over, my dears. And please drink your own coffee. It is free of drugs, I promise."

She sat up straight. "Let's begin. I will tell you everything you need to know to depart on your journey."

***

"How can I adequately describe these disgusting Shade People to you?" Queen Gitli rolled her eyes aloft as she sorted out the details of her story inside her head.

"Early on they must've been nice enough when the Original Holy Six walked among them. You remember our gods from the liturgy: Goddess Cinder, God Rough, the gnome-girl Merlin who predicted that you giants would all show up in a million years, and sexy Violent. Young Corlaz Two learned our primitive language of yips and barks. It was Corlaz One who walked into the sun, and only those execrable Sun People, scum that they are, followed him."

The queen paused to rotate her back feet that splayed in front of her from the folds of the nightgown. She nodded with satisfaction and went on. "Since the beginning, both Prairie Dogs and Shade People worshiped the same gods, which is the only thing we have in common. And at first, we had no objection to being turned into slaves or even being sacrificed at the altar—by religious commandment, of course. After all, we were thankful the Shade People had saved us from starvation after the Day of the Jumping Sun."

Raising a front paw for emphasis, she concluded, "And please note, my friends. There's another reason why we didn't mind. We always knew we were superior to them. The fiery tongues from the Jumping Sun made the Prairie Dogs grow bigger and smarter with each generation while the Shade People got ever more pathetic and sickly."

The monarch nodded her head carefully, soon smiling at the smooth lateral action of her neck's seven vertebrae. "And from early on, everything we did was *extremely intelligent.* The mother cavern, the Eye of Cinder, got too small to hold all of us. The Shade People stayed underground, but many of them moved into seven caverns to the south joined by passageways the Prairie Dogs had dug with the help of Goddess Cinder. And above ground near each cavern we established eight farms, and we tried out the agriculture God Rough had taught us. But mind you, we saved the southernmost cavern where you sit at this moment for ourselves when we made Iqual our capital."

Anichka's eyes were shining as she imagined their ingenuity and industry. "You settle like *we* did during the Time Before. You clear the farmland, you plant the fields, you make the town."

"Not so fast, dear doctor, it's hardly remarkable. It's called *survival,* an instinct the Shade People happened to lose being waited on hand and foot all day by us. We carted food to them through the passageways in a continuous caravan: fresh carrots, apples, potatoes, everything we knew how to grow or learned how to clone from the seed closets.

"And we bred food-rabbits from the forest for their dinner tables and their altar. Soon dead rabbits took our places at Sunday services because they looked just as convincingly plump as Prairie Dogs—once we took their skins off."

"Ew," Agali commented.

The others thought she was referring to the queen's graphic description of the rabbits, but she had something else in mind.

"With so much to eat, I bet the Shade People got fat."

Queen Gitli rubbed her paws together to preface a particularly good part of her story. "Yes, dear Agali, fat, and so bloated they wouldn't even get up to use the comfort stations. We slaves cleaned up their poo and started to despise them."

There was a pause as everyone took in this unsavory revelation.

"And they made only a few babies a year because it was too much effort. And soon, all they did with their time was talk about genealogy."

"What?"

"Yes, which *gods* they'd descended from."

***

The queen clapped for refills of Corlaz One's Folly, and the polar bear groaned to a standing position, his knees cracking.

"My friends, no questions, if you please. The coffee I serve will explain all, and soon you will see for yourselves the place where the stone-fruit bushes grow. The grove stands by the cavern door where the rebel Shade People, followers of Corlaz One, departed the Eye of Cinder."

When the bear returned, Queen Gitli handed around the cups with her rejuvenated paws. The refreshment heralded a presentation by

Lucy, who stood to read "The Parable of Corlaz One's Folly." She and Tlke had spent the morning transcribing it straight from the memory and mouth of Captain Kirk, Twenty-One Thousand and Two of the Orator-Priest Caste.

Lucy unrolled her document and began. "Lo, I say unto you who gather here." Jaroslav perked up; this type of wording was familiar territory for him.

"Heed the Parable of the Stone-fruit Bushes that grow by the cave door, hereby named the 'Rear of Corlaz One'—for was that not the same Corlaz who condemned his flock to weep the brine of severance when he left them to join Sun? Now that I have your ears, I tell you Truth, for Lies issue not from the mouths of the pure."

The introduction completed, Lucy rustled her sheets of paper loudly, hoping to hide from the queen the titters of Agali and Alexej, who were overcome by the word "Rear." Then she took a deep breath.

"During the hours of daylight, the deep gorge by the Rear of Corlaz One lies half in the cool shade and half in hot sunshine. A grove of stone-fruit bushes grows on the steep incline, where, during certain favorable seasons, coffee beans cluster on their sturdy branches. A fair wind treats both alike, the pebbled hill shews the same red loam, the rain falls equally upon them. Oh fie, why drop off the shaded beans from their boughs whilst the beans of the sun grow thick and rank?"

Lucy sat down as Tlke beamed broadly. They glanced around at everyone's hanging mouths; their rendition had certainly made an impression.

"Is that all?"

"Who said that?" snapped the queen, suddenly less charitable in spite of her miraculous recovery.

When no one confessed, Alexej popped out of his chair. "I know what it means." His face reddening, he looked down at his feet because he seldom spoke without Agali's prompting.

"It's a riddle, not a parable, everyone knows that."

He launched in, "All the beans are like people who grow on the same kind of bushes. The beans in the sun are the Sun People, and they're doing fine. The beans in the shade are the Shade People. They're dying."

"Ah, wisdom springs from the mouths of babes." Queen Gitli tried to pat the boy's shoulder, but he'd already slipped past her to take his proud parents' hands.

Jaroslav scratched his head. "There's one thing that makes no sense, Queen. How grow the coffee bushes where only pine trees—"

"Oh, spare us, Jaroslav," Aleta snapped. "Save it for another time." Her patience had worn thin, and she'd already had to exit through the kitchen twice to use the prairie dogs' primitive facilities as her great belly pressed relentlessly on her bladder.

She turned to the queen, her voice laced with anger. "We sit here for an entire evening and there's not one word about my Sequoyah. You're hiding something: out with it!"

Queen Gitli looked momentarily offended, but then she nodded in agreement. "I knew this moment had to come, and I promised you I'd speak the truth, and so I will."

Again, she rolled her eyes upward to organize her thoughts.

"I don't know how the Shade People found out, but news has a way of getting around. The prophesy issuing from Goddess Merlin's very own lips a million years ago had finally come true. Yes, indeed, Sequoyah, the giant poet, really had shown up, even if he arrived without pomp or elegance."

The queen shifted in her chair to stretch out her newly aligned spine. "You have no idea how excited they all got, rolling around on their plump bottoms because they can't stand up anymore."

"And?" Aleta began tapping her foot.

"Their one and only High Priest, Mr. Laz-Merlin the Fifteen-Thousandth, also the fattest and smartest of the entire bunch, got this bright idea that he relayed to me by messenger. And really, you *do* have to understand just how sickened with life they've become after almost a million years of lying around letting their brains and bodies go to seed."

This time a little louder from Jaroslav, "Go on!"

With a frown, Queen Gitli held up her paw like a stop sign. "That's what I'm doing. Laz-Merlin promised that his followers would, en masse, exit this world by drinking poison after Sequoyah had finished writing up their genealogy in an epic poem."

"Come on," Aleta shouted. "You expect us to believe that? They'd trade their lives for a bunch of poetry?" She amended, "Even great poetry?"

"Tush," Queen Gitli replied soothingly. "It's perfectly easy to understand. They want a fitting memorial for a noble race that will soon be passing into history, no matter what. Because, you might say, they've just about bored themselves to death."

She described the more romantic aspects of the arrangement. "I think Laz-Merlin's idea is absolutely lovely. The exquisite manuscript Sequoyah creates will be preserved in amber and placed in the crystal vault beside the reliquary purported to hold Goddess Violent's remains."

"I not ever heard such a-a, how you say, disrespect for life," Jaroslav thundered, and for once, Anichka nodded her head vehemently in agreement.

Queen Gitli leapt up. "How could you blame me for saying yes to Laz-Merlin? Because then my subjects would be freed from their tyranny—forever. So when the opportunity arose for me to steal Sequoyah, I went ahead. I did save him, don't forget."

Aleta hoisted herself to her feet to stare threateningly downward into Queen Gitli's eyes. "Precisely *what* do you expect us to do, Queen? It seems like you've already set this plan in motion."

"Ah, now we're getting somewhere." She gestured for Aleta to sit down and returned to her own chair. "Laz-Merlin the Fifteen-Thousandth informs me that Sequoyah hasn't started his writing in spite of much prodding. A little persuasion from his family might help him begin, yes?

"I must warn you, however, the Eye of Cinder is rather a fortress to enter. You are certainly welcome to *abduct* Sequoyah before he finishes, but in that case, you have to figure out a way to kill all the Shade People, first.

"In other words, one way or the other, Sequoyah is not yours until the Shade People are no more."

Everyone began milling about, gesticulating.

Jaroslav roared above the rest, "Anyone who believe Laz-Merlin story buy Brooklyn Bridge."

"No killing! Do it, we won't," screeched Anichka, her voice bordering on the hysterical.

Aleta tried to have the last word. "Yes, that's absolutely final. We don't kill. I do believe the Laz-Merlin story; we get my husband to write."

The queen said calmly, both paws raised, "I swear, good people, the story is true down to the *last word* and not exaggerated one little bit."

"Oh, oh," Lucy whispered, dropping her translator role and reaching for the security of Tlke's paw. "Maybe I should've told 'em in advance they'd be in for a shock."

Under cover of the excitement, she slipped a rolled sheaf into Alexej's hands and spoke telepathically to the thrilled child who had never received a message from this awesome older girl before. *Queen Gitli doesn't know I wrote down an extra copy of these religious stories Captain Kirk told to me. Maybe they'll help you understand the Shade People better, 'cause their gods are just* so *weird.*

Oh, thank you. Alexej turned red with pleasure at being singled out for an important role. He slid the papers into his shirt.

Agali tried to cut through the adults' turmoil by yelling excitedly above the din. "Oh, Queen Gitli, is the train gonna leave tomorrow morning?"

"The what? Oh, yes, I almost forgot." Queen Gitli turned toward the young adventurers, deftly extricating herself from the messy adult emotions roiling behind her.

"You tell the grownups, once they've calmed down, to meet me tomorrow bright and early at 6:00 o'clock sharp, here in the banquet hall. I'll lead you down to the underground station where the Polar Bear Express will be waiting."

19 ~ Polar Bear Express

I think Daddy is still living inside the coffin. —**Agali**

As Queen Gitli had requested the night before, the bleary-eyed Sequoyah Search Team stumbled into the cavern's huge banquet hall at 6:00 a.m. on the dot, laden with baggage. The chamber was empty and almost completely dark at this hour. Apparently, the rabbits that had doubled as chairs spent their nights elsewhere. Only scattered beams of light came through the shell curtain leading to the kitchen, and the children heard the bobcats stirring behind it. Agali was sure one of them was humming a plaintive tune that sounded like a bamboo flute, although Alexej laughed at her when she mentioned it later.

The adults sagged with exhaustion from having been up all night doing last-minute packing, and even though they'd been preparing mentally for weeks, they didn't feel eager to leave when the moment arrived. They'd lugged from their own caves several months' worth of food and clothing as well as newborn supplies in anticipation of Aleta's twins. Alexej kept checking the front of his shirt to make certain Lucy's precious manuscript was safely hidden next to his chest.

Everyone was relieved when Lucy and Tlke showed up to translate any instructions that Queen Gitli might offer. But where was Her Majesty? Time passed, a half hour and then an hour. They fidgeted uneasily, hopping from one foot to the other. And would they miss the train? In fact, they had no idea what kind of vehicle they were waiting for.

When the queen finally appeared carrying her breakfast coffee that wafted the aroma of Corlaz One's Folly, the party sprang to attention. She gestured impatiently with her free paw as if they were the ones who had arrived late. "You'd better get going and make it snappy. Go straight through the passage to your right and down three flights of stairs. I've seen to your private carriage. It's traveling with a supply caravan bound for the Rear of Corlaz One."

She singled out Aleta. "Now Mama, don't get impatient. The entire trip takes ten days. There will be seven stops at stations along the way because the Shade People who live there are waiting for deliveries of fresh produce and slaves."

"Slaves?" Jaroslav asked incredulously. "Your own subjects are slaves?"

The queen glared. "Of course, Jaroslav. From everything I've been saying for the last six months, what did you expect?"

Turning to all of them, she offered final instructions. "I request that you stay inside your own carriage at the stations except to use the facilities. I don't need any troublemakers disrupting my schedule. Oh, and if you treat your polar-bear team with respect, they'll protect you."

***

The private carriage was little more than a wooden cart harnessed to a pair of huge polar bears with long muscular limbs. Aleta thought they faintly resembled chunkier versions of the families' previous vehicle's namesake, the greyhound. Their cart sat among a string of others, each pulled by its own team. Some carts were laden with bags of vegetables and apples. Others carried live rabbits in cages. At the front of the line, carts stood ready to transport hundreds of Prairie Dogs, the white-ruffed beasts sitting stiffly in rows and staring resolutely forward.

Alexej and Agali remembered the queen's words about being nice to the bears, and sidling close to the shaggy heads, they peered into the red-rimmed eyes.

The bear standing closest to Agali gave her a sideways glance, so she tried communicating mind-to-mind. *I'm Agali. I wish I could speak Bearish, but it's not my first language. Can you understand me, anyway?*

Anro. Bishwash Arbeline eset Arbel. Forenish! Wib toxach allo aiswinot.

Agali shook her head vigorously to clear her brain. She turned to Alexej. "I think I'm going crazy. That bear spoke to me, and I understood even though all of us know only Lucy does animal talk."

"What did it say?"

"I'm not sure of all of it. To begin with, it's a she, and I think she said hello. Her name is Arbeline, and her mate is Arbel. And I know she gave us a warning about something, maybe bad air in the tunnel, because she said *Forenish!*"

The entire line of bears began pawing the stone, ready to go, the thick pads on the bottoms of their feet making a whisk-whisk sound that reverberated through the tunnel. The children clambered aboard with barely time to settle down beside their parents when the entire line of carts lurched, two hundred wooden wheels creaking and groaning in a deafening chorus of multiple accelerations. The gloom in the tunnel would have been complete if not for the usual brigade of bats lining the ceiling, each holding a little torch.

Queen Gitli had made the cart comfortable. The built-in benches had enough rabbit skins for all of them to wrap around themselves. But even with these amenities, unnatural discord began to settle on the adults like a virulent fog.

Anichka and Jaroslav huddled at the front end, and when the devout man knelt to pray, he stretched a rabbit skin over his thick grey hair like a monk's hood. His booming voice bounced off the tunnel's walls, ringing out with sing-song regularity. "Yea, though I walk through the valley of the shadow of death, I will fear no evil: for thou art with me; thy rod and thy staff."

Even though produce carts were the only neighbors in earshot, Anichka glanced over her shoulder in embarrassment. She patted his arm to gain his attention. "Shh, Jaroslav. I'm sure all will be well. The queen would not send us to our deaths because she expects us to rescue Sequoyah and be the saviors of the Prairie Dogs—"

Jaroslav glared up at Anichka, offended. In a gesture worthy of Aleta, he shrugged off her hand. "Who is Savior of the Prairie Dogs? Is for God to do the saving, wife! We do not presume to take His place."

"Do not be so sure, *husband*. Here God's rules are not the same." Anichka twisted away from him, her mouth drawn down in disgust. *Always he call me "wife." Sometimes I hate that man.*

At the other end of the cart Aleta sat hunched over, her forehead clutched viselike between her fingers. She hid herself under a rabbit skin. Maybe now her daughter would stop pestering her.

"Read to Alexej and me, Mama," Agali wheedled. "We brought stories that Lucy wrote down. Captain Kirk told them to her—"

"I can't," Aleta murmured through her blanket.

"Why not? Lucy said there's things in them we need to know about the Shade People. Look, there's enough light, and right now it's not too bumpy."

"Leave me alone. I just can't."

Agali was about to ask why when she heard her mother sobbing.

The Trail of Tears. How'd I get here, and why am I pregnant? The air stinks. We're suffocating in the sick-wagon; we're choking on the trail dust. Unalii, Magnolia, both dead, and me, I'm not dead yet. But I might as well be. I itch all over, I wish I could swat the flies landing on my sores. Someone's putting wet leaves on my forehead and fanning my face. Please, please, nice Cherokee ladies, please carry me to that little copse by the riverbank so I can die in peace—

"Mama, read! You gotta stop thinking that way!"

Aleta jerked herself out of her reverie and let the blanket fall to the bottom of the cart. She raised her voice. "What way? Don't you start snooping in my head like the others."

"I didn't, Mama." Then Agali offered her own interpretation of the Bearish she'd heard before their departure: "Arbeline said we'd better watch out because the air is poisonous down here. She said soon we'd all get sad and start fighting with each other. First Jaroslav and Anichka did that stupid yelling, and now you."

"Who the hell's Arbeline?"

But Aleta seemed more curious than angered by Agali's analysis of her intractable moodiness. "You mean you talked to one of the bears? Queen Gitli did say we'd be wise to heed them."

She considered, then burst out, "Okay, then, give me the first story."

Aleta sat up straight and dried her face, pulling the children close to her on either side. She squinted to focus her eyes on Lucy's precise but tiny longhand, wondering if she would need reading glasses soon.

I'll ask Mother to make an appointment for me with Dr. Eisen because I hear he's the best there is, and isn't his ophthalmology clinic on Red Oak Avenue?

Aleta stopped herself. *No, no, no, it's not! I'm thinking of Albany where I grew up, and that was at least fifteen years ago plus a million.*

She shook her head to clear it. *If I'm not vigilant, I'll lose my mind.*

Aleta focused on the manuscript a second time and cleared her throat. Agali and Alexej rested their heads against her shoulders, amazed at their good fortune to have a real story read aloud to them. Anichka and Jaroslav drew near to hear Aleta better, clumsily negotiating the hazardous shaking of the cart.

***

"Myth the First: Jumping Sun and Corlaz One

"The day cruel Sun jumped, gentle Earth's outer skin was singed off down to bare rock. Sun and Earth had long been at war, and when Sun's rays grew hotter and the rain ceased to fall across the vast deserts of Us, As, and Af, Earth began to shrivel in some places and to drown in her own melted ice in others—but not fast enough to please Sun! He decided to jump from the sky, and in one blinding flash, Earth's trees and fields were burnt to ash, the animals incinerated, and the Lesser People cremated as they screamed in terror from inside their tall towers. The towers, too, fell down, and all that remained of them were mountains of shattered and melted stone.

"Earth cried out in pain, and her wailing summoned her own circle of gods, the Original Holy Five, to the only safe place left in the world—a dark cavern at Nani that lay beneath Baffling Isle near Norpole at the top of the earth. They fled their usual habitation far away to the south, a spacious god-dwelling at Water's Edge in the Land of Us.

"God Rough, Goddess Cinder, Goddess Merlin or Mary Lynne if you prefer her real name, Corlaz One, and Corlaz Two, son of Corlaz One, were blown by the hot breath of Sun into the cavern, where they arrived just in time to save themselves. Only Corlaz Two looked back at Sun's red and swollen face to have his eyes burnt out. Beautiful Goddess Violent, the youngest of the gods, increased their numbers to the Original Holy Six after they arrived in Nani. She was a near-equal deity made by Corlaz One, and she sprang full-grown from the depths of the cavern's Lake Spooky.

"At first, Corlaz One sat at the Head of the Table within their dark dwelling that he named the Eye of Cinder. All the gods lay on his breast, although Goddess Cinder was his favorite and his wife with whom he had begotten Corlaz Two. And he was The Bubbler, creator of the Lesser Men and Women, henceforth called the Shade People. He did this because he knew that not one Lesser Man or Woman was left on the face of Earth.

"This is how the Shade People, so called because they would soon dwell underground in caverns the length of Baffling Isle, came to be: Corlaz One stirred the Creation Pot in the middle of Lake Spooky, the great Pool of life-giving slime. And out stepped a woman with red-gold hair that cascaded in waves from the circlet of pearls atop her head down to her dainty seven-toed feet encased in clamshells. At first, she was ice-cold and naked, and without a name. Because she had shot from the obsidian depths of Lake Spooky with the force of a geyser, Corlaz One named her Goddess Violent. All five gods welcomed her and heated her up with their warmest smiles.

"The water that ran down from Violent's dripping hair and her fourteen fingers fell on the sands by the lake. Each holy drop swelled many times its size, and when Corlaz One blew his breath into the bubbles' pulsing bellybuttons, they came to life. The bubbles stretched this way and that, reshaping to form Shade People, male and female, young and old, fat and thin, comely and ugly, smart and stupid, tall and short. He made one hundred souls, *for what god or goddess can live without worshipers?*

"When Corlaz One's work of creation was done, he fell into a sadness. He drew his only comfort coupling with many of the most beautiful Shade Women whose luxuriant locks showed off their sweet faces to advantage. Soon they bulged with his offspring. Goddess Cinder tried in vain to discourage her husband's licentious behavior by recapturing his attention, even robing herself in little more than diaphanous wisps of white smoke that rose from the cooking fire. When her stratagem failed, she cursed his women by giving them wispy white hair that their descendants bear to this day.

"Corlaz One's despair only increased with time: his mind drifted, and he forgot his son Corlaz Two who lay ill, his young eyes burnt out by the Jumping Sun—for strange as it may sound, the Original Holy Six were subject to the might of Sun and Earth. But Corlaz One's most grievous error came when the one hundred Shade People clamored to be fed, and he didn't remember how to provide for them. Instead, his unusually resonant voice sputtered and spat words that meant nothing. Only useless platitudes and unworthy insults hurled at the other gods issued from his mouth. He seemed to have lost his mind.

"Corlaz One had fallen under the spell of that ferocious tyrant, Sun. The day of the Sputtering and Spatting, he decided to break away from the benign rule of gentle Earth to join victorious Sun, whose flames would lick Earth's skin for five hundred more years. He did not have the wisdom to realize that Sun would never win the war entirely, that Earth would always survive Sun's vicious attacks even if she emerged many years later wearing new raiment.

"No one saw it happen. The next day he walked out the cavern's front door to ride away in a chariot of fire. It bore him aloft along with his life's work, *The Book of Laz,* that he clutched to his chest with both arms. Its contents were known to no one except Goddess Cinder who never revealed them, although it is thought that Corlaz One expounded upon this belief: he was the Son of Sun and would rise to meet his Father who dwelt at the center of that great alien ball of fire that had shot its arms everywhere except into the depths of the Eye of Cinder.

"And tragic was that day many years later when a band of heretic Shade People proclaimed Corlaz One's defection to Sun as the Only Truth and followed his path out the door of the Eye of Cinder. Ever the lowliest of cowards, they left the cavern, not by the front door but by the back door, while the others slept.

"Once outside, they became Sun People, living like parasites by plundering the fields and game preserves of their good neighbors, the Prairie Dogs. At their Sunday worship, they curse five out of the Original Holy Six gods. They whirl about and throw themselves into their campfires, chanting, 'Afraid we're not, of fire so hot. We love Sun, and Corlaz One.' Their belief in Sun's power is so strong, they don't get burned.

"The Sun People are now, and always have been, abhorred by all decent folk.

"Note: I, Captain Kirk, Twenty-One Thousand and Two of the Orator-Priest Caste, have no respect for either Corlaz One or the Sun People.

"This was recorded by Lucy, Scribe to the Queen."

***

"Did you understand the myth?" asked Aleta, doubt creeping into her voice.

The children answered, "Of course we did, every word."

Agali added, "You remember the poem Lucy recited that evening when Queen Gitli asked us to come over. 'Last comes Corlaz One, disgraceful sinner, joining with the Sun to save himself. Deadly foe of the Shade People, we ban him from our Pantheon!'"

Jaroslav shook his head from side to side adamantly. "I do not like stories of many gods."

"Lighten up, husband," Anichka snapped.

Aleta looked up in surprise. *What's gotten into her? Those aren't even the words she'd use normally. She sounds like an obnoxious teenager. The bad air in the tunnel is making us all nuts.*

20 ~ Catatonia

During last December's stretch of unrelenting darkness, even from inside the caves the families had always managed to differentiate night from day and clearly understood the passage of time. They'd gotten up and dressed, eaten three meals, done their chores, prepared for bed, and even laughed sometimes. But in this new world of blatant sameness, the blur of bare walls and hanging bats, the whisk-whisk of polar-bear feet and two hundred scraping wheels, the adults fell into a trance and had no idea how to rouse themselves. Sometimes they slept sitting upright on their benches, but usually they stared straight ahead, glassy-eyed and slack-jawed.

Agali and Alexej realized that their newly acquired job was to jolt their parents awake by being pests. But soon they ran out of ideas, and they, too, were bored. All they really wanted was to have Aleta read the next myth to them.

"Look at 'em," whispered Alexej. "My mama and papa are catsonic."

"Are what? Oh, I know what you mean. Catatonic. So's my mama."

Agali summed up their dilemma: "We poked them, we shook them, we tickled them, we yelled in their ears. We even passed sandwiches under their noses at lunchtime. Now what?"

"At the next stop, ask Arbeline what to do."

The little girl nodded. She felt a rare twinge of self-doubt and reached for Alexej's hand. "I can try. I hope she understands me because I'm guessing at most of her words."

The stop was a brief one between stations, a pit stop for Prairie Dogs and polar bears. The bears lumbered off to a low shed and the children decided by default to use the Prairie Dogs' individual stalls. Their parents continued to sit, their catatonia unchanged by the cessation of the cart's wheels.

Agali got back barely in time to address Arbeline telepathically as two Prairie Dogs prepared to refasten the harnesses.

She bent close to the polar bear's ear. *Anro, bishwash Agali. My mama Aleta and Anichka and Jaroslav are fast asleep. We think it's toxach aiswinot. Forenish!*

Both Arbeline and Arbel took immediate action. With surprising agility, they scaled the sides of the cart. Without hesitating, the bears pushed the baggage aside and knocked the sleepers off the benches by delivering lightning-fast punches with their forepaws. When the parents struggled to sit up, the bears licked their faces in grand circular sweeps that left saliva pooling at the base of their necks. Three pairs of eyes opened simultaneously. Then Arbeline put an ear to Aleta's stomach to check on the babies *in utero* and nodding with apparent satisfaction, she leapt back to the ground to join Arbel.

Agali and Alexej looked on, trying not to laugh as their mortified elders mopped saliva from their faces and necks with the bandanas they'd pulled from their pockets.

Aleta was the first to speak. "Come on, kids, give me those myths. I'm not going back to sleep for the rest of this trip."

***

"Myth the Second: Goddess Cinder

"After Corlaz One's shameful defection to join Sun, his subjects the Shade People wrung their hands and tore their hair. They didn't know how to go on living without their creator, and they mourned him for three days and three nights. On the fourth day, their wailing began to worry the other gods. Without delay Goddess Cinder, who had been Corlaz One's wife, joined hands with God Rough in marriage. And it must be said that they did not mind at all: they had long felt the tug of desire forbidden to them. Then they ascended the throne to give the Shade People new gods to worship. Most of the Shade People were satisfied, but a few refused to extinguish Corlaz One from their hearts.

"A day of celebration was called to verify the ascension of Cinder and Rough, and Goddess Cinder's eyes swept over the hundred Shade People who sat patiently awaiting her words of greeting. All that issued from her throat was a bird's unpleasant screech. Was she a raptor or a goddess? Sometimes even she wasn't sure.

"Goddess Cinder was stately and tall with piercing eyes that reminded the other gods and even her own son Corlaz Two of a golden eagle perched high in her aerie. Indeed, she possessed a pair of sweeping wings that sprouted from her shoulders, the glossy tips sweeping the ground. She seldom flew but kept her wings tightly folded. Because she preferred that they not be seen, she hid them beneath a cloak of spun copper that her own coterie of Prairie Dogs had lovingly stitched for her. As she strode through the many chambers of the gigantic cavern with her cloak billowing behind her, the Shade People bowed their heads in awe, inspired more by fear than love.

"And yet, Goddess Cinder loved the Shade People. She ruled with a fair and even hand while her consort God Rough was busy in other parts of their realm. She taught the Shade People new ways to worship when the religion of Corlaz One began to fade along with their memory of him. And she initiated the seer Goddess Merlin, who also called herself Goddess Mary Lynne, into the new religion's mysteries. Cinder loved the Prairie Dogs, too, and invited them to church services. She gave her son Corlaz Two the wisdom to speak the tk,tk,tk Prairie Dog tongue so that he could relay to her all their woes.

"Goddess Cinder's undoing was not her fault. Her husband God Rough deserted her bed, preferring the embrace of the voluptuous Goddess Violent. When she discovered God Rough's betrayal, she realized that she could never compete with Violent's bountiful and perfectly rounded flesh. And she knew of no potion that could have rekindled Rough's almost extinguished love-flame.

"Goddess Cinder's wrath knew no bounds. She considered strangling Rough and Violent in front of their illegitimate infant or hurling the child outside the cave mouth to roast in Sun's fire. She even considered drowning herself in Lake Spooky to cause remorse in the errant pair's unfaithful hearts. In the end, she made up her mind to leave the tainted Eye of Cinder forever to explore every underground cavern from Nani to the other end of Baffling Isle. For hadn't Goddess Merlin, the seer, prophesied that the caves would be joined together?

"The goddess's dramatic departure is celebrated to this day in song and story. Throwing off her copper cloak to unfurl her wings, she circled the main cavern three times. During the first round she flew high, cursing Rough and Violent with a bird's ear-splitting screech. During the second round she swooped low, collecting fifty Prairie Dogs within the feathers of one wing to assist her on the journey. During the third round she flew through the kitchen, scooping up with the other wing enough provisions to feed herself and the Prairie Dogs for eleven years in the uncharted regions that lay before them. Thus she caused a near-famine within the cavern that lasted half a century. In time, the resourceful Prairie Dogs started farming above ground to stave off the starvation that would have killed them all.

"Ready to depart, Goddess Cinder paused a fraction of a second to bid her son Corlaz Two farewell. Then she shot a stream of fire from the black center of one round raptor's eye that blasted right through the back of her namesake cavern, enlarging the narrow passage that joined it to the next cavern. Unfortunately, eye-blasting takes practice, and her first effort caused a landslide that closed off the hole. She and the fifty Prairie Dogs made it through to the other side just in time with only a few bumps and scratches.

"They continued on. The goddess blasted her way from cavern to cavern, leaving tunnels wide enough to accommodate the future Polar Bear Express. At every newly discovered cavern, she and the Prairie Dogs would pause to survey the chambers for future settlers. Cinder left notes that can still be seen today, scratched in the stone. These had long been considered natural, if curiously looped, markings until God Rough interpreted them as the goddess's own hand. He read them aloud to assist those Shade People moving to new homes to the south of the Eye of Cinder.

"Goddess Cinder had almost reached her final destination, the great expanse of water at the other end of Baffling Isle, when she was struck down by Earth herself. The final eye-blast broke through Earth's skin and took down half of a mighty mountain. The stones plummeted with such force that they crushed her flat at the bottom of the great hole the mountain made when it split in two. As it happened, Earth had had enough. Using the broken mountain as a bludgeon, she took revenge upon the goddess for inflicting so many wounds within her virgin rock-beds. If Goddess Cinder had been less driven by fury and had asked humble permission accompanied by incantations, her punishment would not have been a mortal one.

"The fifty Prairie Dogs mourned her death with barking cries that made the remaining half of the mountain tremble. They vowed to settle there in order to turn the site into a funeral meadow honoring their mistress. They never returned home through the newly excavated tunnels, but stayed on, wearing mourning dishtowels on their heads and beating their breasts. Eventually, they founded a city not far from her memorial. It is built half above ground and has its own majestic cavern underneath. They named it Iqual.

"Five-hundred years later, God Rough visited the site. Feeling remorse for his shoddy treatment of the wife he'd once vowed to love and cherish, he designed a whirlpool above her flattened body that had long since turned into a sheet of glistening rose quartz. He also fashioned ten roaring rivers going every which way to dance through the vibrant green of her vast funeral meadow.

"After Goddess Cinder's precipitous departure eleven years before, the Prairie Dogs inside the Eye of Cinder tried to reopen the hole caused by the eye-blasted rockslide. They had to claw through muddy deposits and move heavy stones one by one, and somehow, they missed their mark, creating a back door to the cavern that opened on a narrow gorge. It was the same back door that those descendants of the Shade People who had never forgotten Corlaz One or accepted the union of Rough and Cinder would use to make their midnight escape. They would become the odious Sun People, hellbent on praising the ways of a heretic. The door was henceforth called the Rear of Corlaz One, an undignified slur upon his disgraced person.

"Note: I, Captain Kirk, Twenty-One Thousand and Two of the Orator-Priest Caste, attest that I saw many times the beauteous Funeral Meadow that God Rough created for Goddess Cinder until it was razed by the Sun People.

"This was recorded by Lucy, Scribe to the Queen."

***

"Oh, my." Aleta sucked in her breath. "This story wasn't edited for children. It's full of passion and anger. I wonder what Lucy was thinking when she wrote it down."

"Why don't you ask us what *we* thought?" Agali suggested. "Because we're sitting right here."

"Well then, what did you think—"

Alexej was too impatient to let her finish. "I loved the story, and the first one, too. But are they about real people and all the good and bad things they did a long time ago? Do you think the stories are true?"

"They have to be a little bit true," Agali remarked thoughtfully. "They talk about real places like the Funeral Meadow and the tunnel we're going through right now."

Aleta hedged about to complete her answer. "The stories are thousands of years old, and who knows how they began. But they're sacred to a lot of people and the Prairie Dogs, and we'd be wrong to close our minds."

"Stop this talk, Aleta, is not good for children," yelled Jaroslav, his jowls trembling with anger. "Is about many goddesses and gods, and all are lies. Because is not the way of One God."

"Husband," remarked Anichka, who had begun to enjoy the new form of address, "Why not try to see a bigger God? We left home more than a year ago and like it or not, we live now in a strange new land."

She grew bold and patted his arm, the same gesture that had infuriated him before. "Who is to make judgment that what others believe is lies? Surely not you."

After the passage of a few painful minutes, Jaroslav's shoulders slumped. He frowned, his eyebrows meeting over his nose. At last he murmured, "Is hard to give up old ways."

Even the children nodded in sympathy.

21 ~ Rough and Violent

During a particularly long stretch with no break, the children vowed to explore inside the next cavern they stopped at, no matter the risk.

They whispered like gleeful conspirators until Alexej had second thoughts. He fell silent, then blurted, "I changed my mind. We shouldn't try it because Queen Gitli said not to."

But Agali refused to give up on their escapade. "Don't you want to see a Shade Person before we get to the last stop? We need to be prepared. What if they are too roly-poly to walk and really wear diapers like the queen said? What if they have tiny pinpricks for eyes like mole rats from living in the dark for so long?"

"We could miss the carts when they start up again."

"No, Arbeline and Arbel won't let them leave without us."

"Oh, all right, but I don't like it. And if we get in trouble, don't forget I said it was a bad idea."

An hour later the carts pulled up at a cavern where two formidable wooden gates blocked the main entrance, the innermost pickets held shut by chains. Fifteen Prairie Dogs walked down the platform from the front cars to unload and then shoulder bags of apples from a cart not far from the children's own.

Delighted, Agali clapped her hands. The ideal opportunity to go on their spy mission had just presented itself. They climbed over the cart's side that faced the tunnel wall opposite the cavern and crept around the back wheels to avoid Arbeline's and Arbel's eyes. Their parents didn't notice them; in spite of Aleta's vow to stay awake for the rest of the trip, the adults sat nodding. The children edged toward the Prairie Dog workers, bending their knees a little to match the animals' height. They hoisted apples onto their shoulders and joined the end of the queue, hoping to blend in.

The Prairie Dogs seemed not to realize the children were behind them as each carried a heavy bag, their bodies robotically stiff with heads bent forward and eyes glued to the ground to keep from stumbling. They entered the cavern by a side door that led directly to a massive kitchen where long shelves stocked with piles of vegetables and grains lined an entire wall. They laid their bags in a row on the appropriate shelf, and the children did the same. Prairie Dog slaves were everywhere, tending pots, scrubbing dishes, and peeling vegetables. One lone Prairie Dog held down a screaming rabbit, and as the knife flashed, the children clenched their eyes tight shut.

Agali gave Alexej a poke. She whispered so softly that her message required some lip reading. "No Shade People are here, and we won't have time to go exploring."

"Good," Alexej mouthed back. "I'm scared, so let's leave ... right now."

But suddenly a commotion broke out. Two Prairie Dogs in doctors' long blue gowns rolled a genuine Shade Person through the kitchen's broad front door. He was also dressed in a gown, but it was striped black and white and had something resembling epaulettes on the shoulders. He reclined on a daybed, and his appearance alarmed the children and the Prairie Dogs alike—but for different reasons.

Agali and Alexej noticed right away that he wasn't fat or wearing diapers as they'd privately hoped he'd be. To children as young and robust as they were, his wispy white hair and ghastly pallor convinced them that he was dying before their eyes. Agali wondered if his last request had brought him here: to bite into one of the orchard-fresh apples from a farm in the provinces.

All the Prairie Dogs backed into corners, terrified of something quite different. His frailness was an illusion. He sat up with ease and brandished a folded whip that he held in his right hand, swatting the handle into the palm of his left hand, *thwack, thwack, thwack.* The Prairie Dogs were well acquainted with the ritual even if they had no idea what they'd done wrong. He would choose one at random for a beating, and then another and yet another until he had obtained a confession.

The Shade Person gestured for the fifteen Prairie Dogs who had carried the apples to come forward, and they fell to their knees in a half circle at his feet, bowing their heads. He slipped off his daybed in one smooth motion and stood solidly on the ground to announce their infraction: "Toi bagges afeli ro cartes misset!"

He did not delay the punishment, but selected the smallest Prairie Dog, who cringed at the edge of the pack. He threw her flat on the stone floor and raising a well-muscled arm, he inflicted seven lashes. Rivulets of blood ran down her back, staining her pretty, almost-pink fur in sticky patches.

"Oh, mercy, Alexej," Agali whispered. "I understood what he said, and I think I know what happened. Someone in charge counted the bags left in the cart, and the two we took were missing—"

"I'm going to say we did it." He took a step forward.

"No, Alexej, don't!" She grabbed him by the back of his shirt.

"But the Shade Person won't stop with just one Prairie Dog."

Arbeline and Arbel pushed their way through the crowd. The bears had understood all. They grasped in their jaws the extra bags they'd found on the supply shelf where the children had left them.

"Baeren tak bagges afeli?" asked the incredulous Shade Person.

Arbeline and Arbel nodded. They accepted silently the children's punishment without flinching: seventeen lashes each across their noses and ears. Afterwards, they bent their heads as blood from the oozing welts pooled at their feet.

The bears found the children hiding behind a stack of fire-blackened cauldrons and nudged them forward past the storage shelves and out the side door. Thus Queen Gitli's dutiful and competent polar bears managed to slip out as quietly as they'd arrived, successfully shielding the miscreants from the Shade Person's wrath.

***

Instead of his usual athletic leap, Alexej flopped clumsily over the side of the cart. Without a word of explanation, he curled up between his baffled parents and snuggled his face into his mother's shoulder. He began sucking his thumb, something he hadn't done since he was three.

Jaroslav seldom pried into Alexej's thoughts, but this time he did. As the father read his son's agonized mind, he shook his head slowly from side to side. When he finally spoke, his voice came out in a low rumble, "Alexej, usually you get old-fashioned spanking for very, very bad things you do."

He paused to lend weight to his next words. "But this time your mother and father think you already suffer very much and is enough punishment." He nodded in self-satisfaction over the fairness of his judgment and tousled the boy's hair.

"No," said Anichka. "Do not speak always for me, husband." She drew her mouth into a determined line and glared at him.

She turned to her son and yanked his thumb from his mouth. "I see your thoughts, too. There is more to do than 'forgive and forget' because your father says is enough punishment. Next time stop the carts, you and Agali find the poor little Prairie Dog, and I fix her wounds with my good salve of aloe. You say 'sorry' to Prairie Dogs. You say 'sorry' to bears, and I fix their ears and noses also."

During the next stop, Agali waited outside the cart almost until the bears were ready to leave. No matter how hard she tried to prepare her apology, she couldn't find a way to express her guilt and sorrow. At last she made a feeble telepathic effort: *Arbeline and Arbel, I am so, so sorry for what I did. Thank you for saving me, and I love you.* She added, *Maybe you can understand what I'm trying to say. I sure hope so.*

Neither of them nodded to acknowledge her words, but the little girl had a feeling that she had been at least partially forgiven.

When Agali sat down by her mother, two sparkling crystalline tears, the same kind that Svnoyi wept on rare occasions, rolled down her cheeks. Because of the peculiar physiology of these children's saucer-shaped eyes, they couldn't cry the salt tears that flowed from their parents' eyes. During Agali's entire childhood and even as an infant, Aleta couldn't remember her daughter shedding a single tear.

Aleta wiped her daughter's eyes with the corner of the much-used bandana. "Agali, you have always been my sunshine child and also the bravest and most adventurous of my children. But this time you got into serious trouble. Tell me, what were you and Alexej up to?"

Agali whispered huskily, "We wanted to see what Shade People looked like. Then a Prairie Dog and Arbeline and Arbel got whipped because of two bags of apples we took. We didn't really mean to steal them—"

"I know you didn't. I happened to wake up, and I watched you two sneaking off, hiding at the end of the Prairie Dogs' queue. You used the bags as props to get into the cavern's back door. Very clever."

"Mama, you don't sound all that mad."

"I know why you did it, so you're right, I'm not all that angry. First, some of the sillier things Queen Gitli told us about the Shade People sounded like lies. That's why you had to find out for yourself. And second, you were very, very bored."

Then she grew stern. "But you used others to get your own way, and they got hurt because of you. Don't let that happen again. Ever."

After Aleta had allowed a suitable amount of time to pass for her daughter to reflect, she pulled her close. "Listen to this, Agali. I peeked ahead, and our own families start to creep into the next myth. An explanation for our cave sculptures is in there. Even Marmalade—you remember Lucy's cat from the Time Before—is in this myth. The lab where Ethan worked is there. It's amazing, really, even before we got here, our lives were tied to theirs. We are as important to the Shade People and the Prairie Dogs as they are to us. I can't even guess how the Sun People fit in, but I'm sure they do."

Agali loved it when her usually silent mother grew impassioned enough to instruct her, and she snuggled closer. "Always look beneath the surface of the myths, Agali. We aren't spectators in this strange land, anymore. In fact, we never were. We are part of the grand story, and everything we do—even sneaking into the back door of a kitchen—could have consequences."

Aleta supported her belly with one hand and gripped Agali's shoulder with the other. For the first time, she made her way to the center of the vibrating cart, groaning as her overburdened joints protested her every step. The others helped lower her to the rabbit skins before sitting down themselves. Hearing Aleta read the myths had become the high point of their day, and they would not have missed the third installment for all the world.

***

"Myth the Third: God Rough and Goddess Violent

"Through no fault of her own, Goddess Violent would end up earning the tempestuous name that Corlaz One had given her on her birthday when she shot out of Lake Spooky. At that moment, even the extraordinary sight of one hundred newly created Shade People writhing on the beach did not interest the other gods. The reason was simple: they had seen the long lashes that shadowed Goddess Violent's chiseled cheeks, and they'd inhaled the scent wafting from her skin of the enchanted black lake from whence she'd come. The seven digits on each of her hands and feet seemed lovely, too, reminding them of a koi's undulating fins.

"Only Corlaz One, who was usually an aficionado of the female form, was unimpressed by his creation. As the others stood transfixed, he whispered to his wife, Goddess Cinder, 'What was I thinking when I made those horrible mitts? Do I get a second chance?'"

"Goddess Cinder snapped, 'Forget the hands. The feet, too. You goofed for a different reason: beauty like that spells trouble. Sooner or later she'll start busting up marriages.'

"'Well, she won't bust up mine,' said Corlaz One, unhooking the fingers of a Shade Person who was climbing up his leg. 'I'm too high-minded to be impressed by my own daughter.'

"And thus did Corlaz One unknowingly set the stage upon which Goddess Cinder, God Rough, and Goddess Violent would play out their lives—long after he himself had exited the scene to join Sun.

"Goddess Violent was shy. She hid among the Shade People to avoid the other gods' notice. She wrapped herself in one of the heavy cloaks the Shade People wore and went about her way humbly. But try as she might, she couldn't cover her seven-fingered hands when she performed the chores that all the mortals had to do. Nor could she disguise her glorious red-gold hair that cascaded down to brush the insteps of her seven-toed feet.

"Besides her beauty, this demure maiden had another gift that gave her away. At her birth, Corlaz One did not realize that he'd bestowed such power to her fin-like hands and feet: he had made her the quintessential God's Gift to the Arts, a muse, an inspiration, an aery beacon within the oppressive darkness of the Eye of Cinder. She could dance on the tips of her toes, twirling in the circles so loved by the Prairie Dogs. She could act, rolling her eyes and beating her breast, another art to which they aspired. She could sing, improvising tunes to fit any emotion. Her music was often so poignant that the cavern's floors and ceilings wept the tears that formed stalagmites and stalactites.

"But mainly, Goddess Violent could draw, paint, and sculpt, her speed enhanced by her multiple fingers and occasionally her toes for hard-to-reach places. Late at night when she thought no one was awake, she would dance through the empty passages, all the while singing in harmony to her voice's own echoes. Then she'd find a secluded spot to turn the rocks molten and shape them with her bare hands into fantastic images.

"But what of God Rough? He was far from handsome, although his brash enthusiasm and scintillating brilliance held attractions all their own. He'd spent his entire life on an insatiable quest for scientific knowledge. When his first head became full, he took it off and grew a second. He carried the old head under his arm and would exchange it for the new one, planting it firmly on his neck whenever he needed to recall the old information stored therein.

"Thus, doubly brilliant, he infuriated some of the gods and intrigued the others. No one hated God Rough more than Corlaz One. For years at Water's Edge in the Land of Us the two had competed for Goddess Cinder's affection. Then Corlaz One disappeared to join Sun. All could have gone well: she and God Rough were married under the light of a June bat-moon.

"But God Rough's eyes happened to stray, falling on the desirable Goddess Violent as she made her midnight sweep through the dark passages in a terpsichorean frenzy. Her eyes met his between pirouettes and in terror she threw off her cloak in order to run faster, her many toes skimming above the marbled stone. When he feared that he might lose her along the passageway that began to dip sharply, he applied science to his pursuit. He *rolled* his old head, which chased her to a stop a half mile further on by the shores of Lake Spooky. When he caught up with his old head, she prostrated herself upon the sand and kissed his feet. For who can resist a man so intriguing that his first head can run faster than his second?

"Mortal men and Prairie Dogs, heed these words: the joining of Art and Science causes a bond both harmonious and volatile. Put oil in water and the two can never mix although lovely rainbow patterns form on the surface. And so it was with Violent and Rough. For several centuries the couple worked together unceasingly to improve the lot of the Shade People and the Prairie Dogs, arguing over each new endeavor as passionately as they agreed. Although half their efforts ended in discord, the other half improved the cavern they called home.

"Once the pair reached their three-hundredth anniversary, they decided to take a honeymoon, long postponed by Violent's childbearing. They left unobtrusively before breakfast, taking the underground route blasted by Goddess Cinder's eagle eye. They emerged from the tunnel close to the spot where Cinder had died. A short walk brought them to a body of water so vast they couldn't see land on the other side—unlike Lake Spooky that lay enclosed within its moist chamber.

"There, in three modest caves that nature had carved into the cliffs above the water, they discovered the seed closets that looked remarkably like the metal file cabinets God Rough had used in his office before Sun jumped. They were coated with rust, but the drawers still slid open and shut on wheels. Apparently, the closets had been put there by an Ur-inhabitant who signed his name *Skidder, Geophysical Arctic Studies Project,* the looping letters etched onto three plaques, one in each cave. The closets contained many vials with messages attached: I am the DNA of an elephant, or I am the DNA of a Mojave Desert sidewinder. Only one vial had a picture with it and the words, I am the DNA of Marmalade.

"There were ten thousand vials in all.

"For once, the pair did not argue. They stared at each other in baffled silence.

"Eventually God Rough put on his other head. It cycled through its entire repertoire until it found the letters DNA. 'Ah,' said God Rough. 'Cloning! It all comes back to me now.'

"'So?' asked Goddess Violent. She felt an attack of belligerence coming on.

"But God Rough hadn't heard her. He murmured, 'This is unprecedented. The entire world could be put back to just the way it was. Elephants roaming through the pine forests with giant sloths riding on their backs. Toucans eating pecans—'

"'Oh, oh,' Goddess Violent broke in. 'I'm getting a bad feeling about this.'

"'Me, too.' God Rough thought a while longer before springing to his feet. 'I have it, I'll teach the *Prairie Dogs* how to do cloning, but I won't say a word to those vacuous Shade People.'

"'But will the Prairie Dogs make the wrong decisions, like putting desert animals into snow banks or waking up the poison ivy? Besides, they can't read the inscriptions.'

"'Of course they won't act *that* dumb, and reading the inscriptions is where you come in. Carve the picture of each animal and plant into the cave wall and we'll put the DNA behind it in a hidden niche. Use the Marmalade illustration as a template.'

"Goddess Violent wailed, 'But I was born too late to have ever seen an elephant or a pecan.'

"God Rough took her hand. 'Darling, that's what my two heads are for. We'll cycle through, and together I'm sure we'll find all the plants and animals, also with illustrations.'

"Unfortunately, Goddess Violent died violently several days after completing the three floor-to-ceiling friezes. During the entire operation she had balanced artfully on shaky ladders thrown together by God Rough. When she found herself walking on the ground, she was not prepared for its solidity. And so she stumbled from the top of a mountain cliff as she gazed far below at a sparkling sheet of rose quartz. Ordinarily such a fall wouldn't have killed an immortal. But there was vengeance behind gravity's work, instigated by the rock bed that had once been Goddess Cinder.

"God Rough carried his true love's ashes back to the mother cavern, the Eye of Cinder. He enclosed them in a bronze coffer and placed them inside a crystal vault awaiting the holy ashes of all Gods Deceased. The vault stood behind the stone altar that saw the sacrifice of a blessed and fatted Prairie Dog every Sunday, and he promised that a coffer with his own ashes would go beside hers one day. His brash enthusiasm much diminished, God Rough lived on to teach the Prairie Dogs how to clone and perform other extravagant medical tricks, and how to make many marvelous artifacts.

"Note: I, Captain Kirk, Twenty-One Thousand and Two of the Orator-Priest Caste, assume that God Rough lives still.

"This was recorded by Lucy, Scribe to the Queen."

22 ~ Six-Day Revolt

When Aleta put down Lucy's manuscript, the five of them sat silently, amazed how the myth had meshed with their own lives.

Agali spoke first, reminiscing. "It was The Skidder who put the DNA in the seed closets. He was the scientist from a long, long time ago, more than a whole year. He drove a taxi at that place where we lived ... I forget the name."

She drew figures in the air. "Anyway, he liked to skid in eights and circles when the roads were icy, which was all the time."

"You're so wrong, Agali," Alexej replied coolly. "He was a Skid Artist, *not* a scientist. And we were in Frobisher Bay, remember? Ethan worked at the same lab that's in the myth. It was called the Geophysical Arctic, something, something. I forget the rest."

Agali tried to recover her poise after forgetting where they'd lived. "No, Alexej. The Skidder was an Undercover Scientist at the Geophysical Arctic pretending to be a Skid Artist. The taxi was his disguise."

Alexej shook a fist. "There's no such thing as an Undercover Scientist—"

"Yes, there is! Who else put the DNA inside the seed closets?"

"Hold it," Aleta shouted in annoyance. "Let's not argue. Has anybody checked to see if hidden niches even exist behind the sculptures? With intact DNA, no less? That was a *myth* I just read, not a million-year history of Baffin Island."

"Well," said Agali, laughing. "We could ask Queen Gitli to clone Lucy's cat."

"You can't clone a cat!" Alexej announced with self-righteous passion, waving his arms. "It will eat all the birds and upset the Balance of Nature."

Jaroslav tried to soothe him, "No one's cloning a cat. Is not God's way."

Anichka glared at him. She tried to stand for emphasis but couldn't because the cart shook violently going over a sudden rough patch. "I thought we not talk any more about God's way. Remember, husband?" In her pique, she tried out a phrase she'd never used before. "From now on, we try to ... to enlarge our perspective, yes?"

"I have an idea," said Aleta cheerfully. "Naturally, we're all totally sick of each other, but look on the bright side. Things are gonna get a lot worse."

Jaroslav snubbed his wife by turning to Aleta. "What is your idea? I listen to wife's smart remarks no longer."

"I'm reading the next and final myth. Not tomorrow. Right now."

***

"Last Testament of Goddess Mary Lynne: From the Apocrypha

"Everyone calls me Merlin, but my real name is Mary Lynne. This will be my last testament, and as soon as our Orator-Priest, Hyperion the Prairie Dog, commits it to memory, I plan to end my life. I am the oldest of the Original Holy Six, and because I have lived the lives of many gods, I am more than a million years old.

"Corlaz Two was certainly not my first husband. But during all my reincarnations, he was the only one I ever loved. He died last year, three days after my 1,055,194th birthday. His death was tragic, and the world lost its most perfect god. He was more beautiful than Baldr, although I can only guess about that. You see, in my present body of Mary Lynne, I am blind and could never look at him. But I could touch him, and that's much the same thing to those of us who cannot see.

"He died during the Prairie Dogs' Six-Day Revolt of 523,072, AJS, and I know Mary Lynne will be my last reincarnation because his death was my fault. Please put my ashes in a box and lay them with reverence inside the crystal vault behind the great stone altar that is the center of the Eye of Cinder.

"I've always been a 'Ma,' as in Mary Lynne. If your name starts with those letters, you could have been me and not realized it.

"I am Mau. I am black and beautiful, short-haired and silky, and I have four legs. I was Egypt's Great Cat, personification of Ra. I killed the serpent Apophis who rose from the underworld over and over to devour souls. I crouched in the shade of the Tree of Life to protect its emerald crown and its two fat taproots that stretched beneath As and Af.

"I am Macaria, a daughter of Hades, and I am the goddess of blessed death. I stood on the welcome mat at the front door to Elysium on the western edge of earth. Elysium was the Dead Old Boys Club for the wealthy and the famous. The men treated me worse than the doormat where I dutifully stood, toes turned out and eyes cast down. So I begged my father, 'If you love me at all, free me from this servitude.' Perhaps he did free me, or it may have been the work of the Creator-Unknown. In any case, I moved on.

"I am Máni, Norse moon god. Every night I fled across the sky pursued by Hati the wolf, uglier than Grendel. The wolf had no choice: his job was to clear the way for my sister Sól's day-journey along the same path. Do you think I escaped Ragnarök? I did, barely, but it seems I keep moving from one hotspot to another. The Day of the Jumping Sun wasn't all that different.

"I am Mawu of Dahomey. Again, I am the moon, and a goddess this time. With my husband Lisa the sun, we created life on earth, beginning in Af. Soon we started to worry; all that extra baggage would surely weigh the crusty old girl down. I asked the serpent Aido Hwedo to wind itself beneath earth to help toss her heavenward.

"Being a god means lots of things can potentially go wrong. I was the moon twice, and both times it was an awesome responsibility getting across the sky every night, especially with the work of creation thrown in. I'll tell you this: I never want to be the moon again. I begged the Creator-Unknown to bring me back next time in a human body, how ever humble, and to throw in some human frailties.

"I got my wish. *I am Magnolia.* I was a slave, and I walked the Trail of Tears with my master, a Cherokee landowner. We walked from Lousy to Okly in Us, and everyone suffered just the same. How we suffered: death soon came for me, and I'd hoped that this time would be the last of my reincarnations.

"Now I am Goddess Mary Lynne, and I understand why I was given another life. I met a giant on the Trail of Tears, and I became Mary Lynne to prophesy his coming. On the Trail of Tears he was in his astral form and no bigger than a sigh. You may doubt me, but he will arrive in less than five hundred thousand years. He will appear on earth in his own flesh, his chariot grey and pockmarked from passing in the blink of an eye through the asteroid dust of a million years. He will alight from his chariot with all his family, and his shoulders will brush the sky. With tender humility, he will fall to kiss the ground.

"How well I remember the way things were before Jumping Sun. We call Before Jumping Sun BJS, and we call After Jumping Sun AJS. A long time ago in Water's Edge in the Land of Us, 10 BJS, Corlaz One taught all of us about Cris-god-son, who brought the old corpse Laz back from the dead. Even back then it was getting tiresome: every day and twice on Sundays old Laz did the same thing: woke up and rose up. So luckily after Corlaz One left to join Sun, Goddess Cinder gave us new things to believe that were more appropriate for people living in the dark. When she left us to blast her way to Iqual, I had no choice. I took over making the religion where she'd left off.

"Corlaz Two and I were very much in love, but we didn't always agree. How my husband adored those Prairie Dogs, sometimes more than he loved me! I'll explain: he understood them telepathically in the tk,tk,tk Prairie Dog tongue. So he alone could chat with them, leaving me out.

"And he didn't appreciate my work. He would say to me, 'If your religion can't include the Prairie Dogs fair and square, it's no better than the Dead Old Boys Club at Elysium.' Then he'd say, 'You gave everyone baptism in Lake Spooky's swiftest whirlpool. And you gave everyone circle dances for worship on Sundays. So why aren't the commandments also the same for everyone?' After that, he'd get angry. 'Merl, get rid of Commandments Six, Seven, and Eight!' I'd refuse, and he'd get really angry. 'Didn't your life as Magnolia the slave teach you anything?'

"But I couldn't make myself change the commandments because they were holy scripture, even though I happened to think them up myself. Naturally there's a big difference between Prairie Dogs and people. The Prairie Dogs just weren't as good because they hadn't been created in our own images. Even if The Word tells you the opposite, for example, 'In the Eyes of Gods, the poorest Creature is equal to the Mightiest amongst you,' it doesn't mean it literally. What's religion for? It's to sort out who's at the top of the heap and who's at the bottom.

"All of us know the Sixth, Seventh, and Eighth Commandments:

"*Commandment Six.* Lo, the Prairie Dogs shall henceforth be but humble slaves of the Shade People from the first bloom of youth until death.

"*Commandment Seven.* A chosen few well-fatted Prairie Dogs shall die in holy sacrifice every Sunday on the altar of the Eye of Cinder.

"*Commandment Eight.* No Prairie Dog shall injure or kill a Person, although a Person is not so bound.

"Then came the Prairie Dogs' Six-Day Revolt of 523,072, and my dearest's death.

"The revolt began simply enough. An angry Shade Person choked an adolescent Prairie Dog half to death because she always forgot to dust under the bed. She was a silly little thing named Acanthus and had fallen in love for the first time. But why should I make excuses for her? Scripture is scripture. Her friends carried her to the Prairie Dogs-Only infirmary where she died. Then all the other Prairie Dogs joined her friends to do something unheard-of. They marched out the Rear of Corlaz One and refused to come back until Commandments Six, Seven, and Eight had been revised. After three days, the Shade People started getting thinner. They hadn't had a bite to eat except for scraps they found in the garbage.

"Oh, how can I tell this part without weeping, even though my dearest was clearly in the wrong? He joined the Prairie Dogs in sympathy, but soon found that Sun, even in winter, was too strong for him. After all, he'd become a tender-skinned god from living in the dark for 523,072 years. As his body began to heat up painfully, he hammered on the Rear of Corlaz One's stout wooden door. How can I explain? My raging anger destroyed my reason, and I refused to let him back in.

"Corlaz Two died by Sun an hour later even though the Prairie Dogs tried to save him by plunging him into ice water to cool his burning flesh. They buried him in the gorge above the Rear of Corlaz One beneath the snow that covered the steep, pebbled earth. By spring Corlaz Two's body was gone, and a grove of coffee bushes had sprouted there—whether by a miraculous transformation or by the Prairie Dogs' raiding the DNA from one of the cave friezes, I do not know. A few days after my husband's death, they returned to work, beating their breasts with their paws. Their heads were wrapped in the dishtowels of mourning.

"Note from Captain Kirk, Twenty-One Thousand and Two of the Orator-Priest Caste: I gave Lucy, Scribe to the Queen, permission to write down this history even though it is apocryphal and an add-on to the myth treasury. Did Goddess Mary Lynne actually kill herself? Personally, I think she lives still, although mine is not the generally accepted belief.

"Goddess Mary Lynne's testimony was first memorized 476,829 years ago by Hyperion, Eight-Thousand and Thirty-Nine of the Orator-Priest Caste."

***

Aleta sighed as she rolled up the pages and slid them with care into one of the bundles stored on the floor of the cart. "So that's the last one. Thank you, dear Lucy, wherever you are back home, for giving us these." She blew a kiss into the tunnel from the direction they'd come.

She turned to the others. "I think this myth was the best. Sequoyah was in it. And the Trail of Tears was just like I knew it because Magnolia sat beside me in the sick-wagon before she died. The third myth's the same. I can't believe how closely we're tied to these Shade People and the Prairie Dogs."

"Of all the myths is this one saddest." Anichka took Jaroslav's hand and snuggled her face into his neck. "The Goddess Merlin-Mary Lynne. She get so angry, she kill own husband."

"Yes, very sad," said Jaroslav, patting his wife's hand in response. "But I think even more sad is unjust religion that allow slaves. Our little Prairie Dog ... her story not so different from Acanthus." He peeked at the children, who turned away their heads guiltily.

"Yes, you're right," said Aleta. "And there are plenty of horrible examples from our own past. But remember this: the Prairie Dogs enslave animals, themselves."

Her voice rose, "The sly queen cries slavery, but it's a double game called 'who's at the mercy of whom,' Prairie Dogs or Shade People? These Sun People, who ***are*** they, really? Do they deserve to die simply because they exist?"

Grasping the side of the shaking cart, she managed to pull herself upright. "Heed the myths, everyone, *heed the myths.* The Jumping Sun was World War III, and it wiped out the world's population in a single day except in a little corner at the top of Baffin Island.

"A new war is coming that'll be much worse than any Six-Day Revolt, and it is only weeks away." She theatrically flung out her arm.

"No one's learned a damned thing about war, not even with a million years to figure out a better way—"

"Mama," shrieked Agali in disbelief. "You're making a puddle all over the rabbit skins."

Aleta plumped down, her eyes wide with fear. Then she doubled up, rocked by her first contraction. "I was afraid of this, and it's too soon."

"No, no," Anichka murmured gently, embracing her. "Not for twins, not too early. All will be well—"

Groaning, Aleta interrupted, "Agali, ask the bears to pull out of the caravan. I can't have my babies in this cart. The air's poisonous."

Agali sent the bears a hasty message: *Arbeline eset Arbel, forenish, forenish, forenish! My mama is having her babies.*

Their response was immediate. They communicated directly with their fellow runners and as wooden wheels screeched against stone, the entire procession came to a halt from back to front.

The Prairie Dogs from the slave carts began swarming around the tunnel in confusion. Alexej said wistfully, "I wish Lucy and Tlke were here to explain."

Anichka whispered to Jaroslav. "Mercy, we have riot any minute."

"I try to fix things," declared Jaroslav.

He stood up in the cart. Showing some of the authority from the old days in the High Tatras and taking advantage of his towering height, he bellowed, "Do not worry, friends."

The entire animal population turned to him as he attempted what he hoped would be universal sign language. He arched his hands over his own flat belly to show the bulge of pregnancy and then rocked an imaginary baby in his arms. To complete his pantomime, he fell to his knees in the attitude of thankful prayer.

Apparently, Queen Gitli had forewarned several Prairie Dogs. Four of them in blue doctors' gowns broke away from the crowd to lead the bears, still hitched up, through a dank airshaft just high and wide enough to accommodate the cart and its passengers. It emerged five minutes later into the twilight of a late spring night. The low sun illuminated with clarity a verdant spot at the center of a thick pine grove with a brook nearby, the ideal location to set up their shelter.

The air was chilly with a gusty wind coming out of the North. With his usual expertise, Jaroslav rapidly dug a fire pit and lined it with stones. As the others constructed the tent from rabbit skins and poles, he and his son gathered wood at the forest's edge.

Putting a hand on the boy's shoulder, Jaroslav confided, "Alexej, I hope our journey bring us close to Rear of Corlaz One. We make the seven stops for all other caverns, but how many miles is still to go?"

He added offhandedly, "I do not yet smell the coffee beans."

Alexej realized that his father was making a joke. After a weak attempt at a chuckle, he asked all in one breath, "Dad, will it take a long time for the babies to come? Can we—I mean me and Agali—can we go on an adventure?"

"Of course, son. Waiting for babies can take many, many hours."

The father's communication was not a wise one to make to such a high-spirited child, and the consequences were all too obvious a few hours later. Jaroslav tore himself away from helping Aleta long enough to notice that both children, apparently accompanied by Arbeline, were not having their adventure nearby, but had left the camp.

23 ~ Do I Know You, Little Girl?

In the half light, Arbeline and the children cut over from their camp to the drainage ditch that ran alongside the Polar Bear Express route, intent upon following it to the final stop at the Rear of Corlaz One. In spite of the early hour, every hundred feet two Prairie Dogs were already hard at work maintaining the tunnel from the outside. They bent low, manually pumping water with a clanking gadget that spewed a torrent of rain runoff from its rusty spout into the ditch. Other Prairie Dogs stood waist-deep in the murky water to clean out rocks and broken branches. They knew what would happen if the air vents placed high along the ditch's steep sides were to become blocked. The workers didn't turn their heads as the trio passed.

After they'd walked for several hours, Agali whispered to her companion, "We've passed by hundreds of Prairie Dogs all doing the same awful work. I wonder if anyone loves them enough to say thank you."

Alexej didn't answer. He stopped in his tracks to squint at something to his right. Then he gripped Agali's elbow and pointed with his free hand. "Look, Agi, over there. I think I see the grove of coffee bushes on that steep hill. They're growing in rows, and they sure don't look like pine trees."

"We're here," Agali said, simply. "And I'm scared."

"Don't be. I'm going with you—"

"No, Alexej. I have to do this by myself. Don't worry, I know exactly what I'm doing."

"But it isn't safe for you to go alone—"

"It is. If two of us run around in there, we'll get spotted for sure."

She couldn't articulate even to her dearest friend the real reasons. *I've been dreaming about this for so long, and I want Mama to be proud of me and notice me, and Daddy, too. It's more'n that: I want to do things as good as Svnoyi does.*

Alexej knew she wouldn't change her mind. He hung back beside Arbeline as they watched the little girl vanish into a thicket of dense junipers, her pale hair catching on the needles. She reappeared at the top of the ridge looking barely bigger than a doll. And when she scrambled down the slope dodging coffee bush branches and slipping on the round pebbles, Alexej turned away, unable to watch her any longer. He had never felt lonelier in his entire life.

***

Agali slid the last fifteen feet to the valley floor, landing on her bottom among a swirl of furry limbs and bags of produce. Mercifully, she felt herself rise to her feet, buoyed by many little paws. She almost laughed out loud. Apparently, she'd arrived at the Rear of Corlaz One simultaneously with her own caravan.

Even in all the turmoil, she recognized by her shaved and bandaged back and pinkish fur the Prairie Dog who had been so viciously whipped. The little creature looked at her pleadingly.

Agali understood at once. *Of course! The poor thing can't carry the sack of apples on her hurt back.* She couldn't help adding, *And it's my fault.*

She shouldered the bag and again found herself entering a kitchen by the back door, shielded by the same Prairie Dogs as before. Her mother's words flashed through her mind: *Even sneaking into the back door of a kitchen could have lasting consequences.*

Agali and the other Prairie Dogs unloaded the bags on the shelves holding fruit: apples, summer grapes, and blackberries. As she turned to orient herself in the storeroom, she felt a gentle tug at the back of her plaid shirt. The injured Prairie Dog was at her elbow, urging her to duck behind a mountain of split firewood in the corner. It never occurred to Agali to distrust her, and she followed without question.

A delicate voice seemed to sound in Agali's head behind both ears. At first she wondered if the Prairie Dog had spoken telepathically, or if she'd made it up. But after a whole conversation, she decided she possessed more than a hint of Lucy's extraordinary gift.

Agali, I'm taking you to your daddy because I know that's why you're here.

Agali asked, *Is it safe? Do you know the way?*

If we stay low when we run and keep very quiet, we'll be safe. My masters don't see well. And I know the way because I live here.

You know my name, but what's yours? And what's your job?

It's Sanctissima. I do cooking and dusting for ten masters and mistresses when I'm not on caravan duty delivering produce from the farms. When I'm older, I'll get to be a breeder for six seasons.

Are you happy?

Of course not. None of us are. I'd like to work on a farm like the boys do.

Agali shivered. She remembered the *Last Testament of Goddess Mary Lynne* and the little Prairie Dog named Acanthus who had been choked to death.

Because the Eye of Cinder was the last cavern on the route, no produce bags needed to be counted. All the Prairie Dogs hastened through the kitchen's front door in a silent mob with eyes averted from one another. In their haste to reach their own quarters to rest before preparing a midday meal for the masters and mistresses, they didn't notice Agali and Sanctissima turning in the opposite direction.

The two bent low, scurrying down a long hallway. When Agali glanced upward, she saw glittering stalactites winking above their heads, lit by the ubiquitous bats that hung on the ceiling.

Agali asked, *Did you ever get to meet my daddy?*

Oh no, Sanctissima replied. *We're not allowed to go to Lake Spooky very often, and that's where he is. I know some things, though. At first the nurses stayed with him night and day. Now he just sits by himself except when that fat Mr. Laz-Merlin the Fifteen-Thousandth goes into his chamber to talk about religion and family trees.*

Suddenly she pulled Agali into a storeroom and put a paw over the girl's mouth. *Stay still. Two of them are coming.*

Agali's view was blocked by four hefty stalagmites that sprouted from the floor, but she heard the familiar squeak of daybed wheels and the wheezing of the human beings reclining on them. She couldn't help asking Sanctissima, *Are all of them awful?*

Not all of them. A few of mine are nice if I do my work properly. But they're always saying, "Do this, do that, don't forget to dust the knickknacks." Or, "Oh, mercy, I feel so unwell, today." Only they say it like this: "Ai, ai, moicet, Icta foile unwoidel."

Agali snickered aloud, and the paw tightened over her lips.

At the end of the hallway the pair made a left turn and began a steep descent on a path formed by a million years of footprints in wet sand. Agali said more to herself than to Sanctissima, *This is where Goddess Violent ran when God Rough chased her. She was born down there in the middle of the lake when Corlaz One stirred the creation pot.*

They stopped. Up ahead, a crudely carved flight of stone stairs threaded its way down a steep bank, terminating at the lake of legend. Agali turned toward Sanctissima, feeling for her paw in the gloom. She stared hard, trying to make out details, but all she could see was a foamy scum that lined the shore.

Sanctissima halted on the top step. *I can't go any further, Agali. The lake is a sacred place, and only your father's nurses are allowed down there. If I get caught, they'll choke me to death. But you're a human, and maybe you could get away with it if you get caught.* She sank to her haunches behind a mica-encrusted boulder on the other side of the narrow path. It hid her completely.

She offered last bits of advice from her sanctuary: *Go around the narrow end of the lake, and about a third of the way, you'll find a passage that leads to his chamber. I'll wait here, but hurry. My kitchen shift starts in an hour.*

***

The air by the lake was dank and cold as if a squall would brush past any minute, bringing sheets of rain. Wrapping her arms tightly around herself to keep from shaking, Agali walked as fast as she could in the dark.

"But it can't rain," she whispered aloud.

"Rain-nain-ain-n," the nearby wall replied.

"You're an echo, and I don't like you."

"Like you-ike you-you-ou."

I shouldn't be talking to a wall, but I'm really alone for the first time in my life. There's no Alexej, no Mama, no Svnoyi, no Phoenix, no Yacy, no Sanctissima. It's so dark, all I can see is the scum at the edge of the water and lights on the ceiling flashing a scary blue. Where are those bats with tapers when you need them?

Then she asked herself a truly dangerous question for a little girl in her situation.

What if ghosts live under the water? If this is Hades like it says in my daddy's books, they'll come out when they smell a live person. They'll make me dance myself to death, and then they'll tear me to bits. They'll all say together, "Fee, fi, fo, fum, whirl and twirl, naughty girl. You can't stop until you drop because you stole the—"

Before her horrified eyes the black lake turned transparent as every bubble on its surface emitted a sigh that rose to a shriek, making the blue lights on the ceiling tremble. Beneath the waves, long, floating hair wafted with the current, black, yellow, curly, straight. The hair was attached to the heads of girl-children big and small, who stared at her from empty eye sockets. Eels wriggled in their mouths, or were they tongues? A baby floated by on its stomach, its head beneath the surface and its naked bottom above the water ....

Before Agali could scream, an angel streaming orange fire flew past her, beating aqua wings that almost hit her in the face. "Run, run, little girl. Don't stop until you reach the tunnel where a light will beckon you to its end."

Agali ran. She remembered careening off the tunnel's clammy walls that smelled of bat guano. She fell twice, the second time scraping her knees through her overalls. But just as the angel had said, the light was there. And she never stopped following it.

***

Agali landed in an undignified heap in someone's room. There was a bed and a table, and a tall man was sitting across from her in a wooden chair. Even with her eyes half hidden behind her hands to protect them from the sudden glare, she recognized the voice. It was deep and warm, her very own daddy's voice before he'd almost died last October.

"Do I know you, little girl?"

Agali hadn't thought about the possible consequences of making a sudden appearance in her father's room. She had simply assumed that he'd be thrilled to see her after such a long absence—especially considering all she'd been through. His "Do I know you, little girl?" reverberated in her ears, then slid down her spine like ice water. For a solid minute she simply sat where she'd landed, mouth agape. Then she felt her face go hot and her hands clench as if they weren't a part of her own body.

She shot up, flailing her fists like an out-of-control pugilist. She found herself shouting, "I rode all day and all night by Polar Bear Express for *weeks* to come here. I left Mama alone in the woods having *your* babies. The ghosts in Lake Spooky almost chewed me to pieces."

She added emphasis to her fury by stomping a foot, "I'm your daughter Agali, and I *hate* you." She turned her back and hung her head. She wanted to cry, but her tear ducts wouldn't cooperate. In fact, they seldom did.

Sequoyah made no attempt to comfort her, but kept his big hands loosely folded in his lap. "Hmm," he commented, his voice cool and distant. "Agali, *agali.* I *know* that word. I believe it means 'sunshine' in Cherokee." He paused in thought, rolling his eyes toward the glinting rock ceiling. "How very strange that I should remember it."

Then he peered at her, fixing his eyes on her face. "You do resemble a daughter I had once, a long time ago, but your hair isn't black like hers. Her name was Svnoyi. And I talk to her mother Miriam every evening when I take my stroll because her shade lives in Lake Acheron. We *are* in Hades, you know."

Agali sat down on the lumpy stone of his chamber floor and crossed her arms peremptorily. "No, Daddy, no! I'm Agali, your sunshine child, and I'm your daughter, too. Svnoyi's my big sister. And this is a real place. It's called the Eye of Cinder, and it's a cavern where the real Shade People live. You're supposed to be writing their history—"

"Ah, yes, so Mr. Laz-Merlin the Fifteen-Thousandth keeps telling me." He raised his head to stare at his personal bat globe, a sphere containing a dozen bats that emitted a powerful glow in the small chamber. At the same time, he drummed his fingers on a ream of his own paper that sat on the table, quite unused.

Agali peeked at Sequoyah's mournful face with the high cheekbones and the aquiline nose. He frowned, suddenly, his long lashes opening and closing rapidly. His lips drooped at the corners as he tried to pull his thoughts together.

Her own mind raced. *He looks the same: he's handsome, he's nice, he's my daddy. But he's changed a lot. He talks funny like he's searching for the right words. And he acts kind of bogged down like he's living underwater. I wonder what's wrong with him.*

Sequoyah turned to his daughter in slow motion. "Little girl, about this place, the Eye of Cinder that I call Hades. Laz-Merlin tells me that more than one hundred people live in it, but I've never seen a single person besides him."

Then his eyes sparkled and for the first time, he bent toward her eagerly. "But there are these cunning little furry creatures about your height, with white ruffs around their necks and little black tails. They seem to run everything. They dart about, dusting, bringing my meals, plumping my pillows, fixing my lamp. They nursed me back to health with poultices and foul-tasting potions."

He turned his fingers into a bridge and contemplated the nails. "Believe me, I've thought hard about it, and this is what I conclude. They were once exquisite young maidens, but they were enchanted by Circe and turned into beasts for some offense long forgotten."

Agali's mouth dropped open, and then she snapped it shut, her face growing hot once again. She sprang to her feet, hands on her hips. "Daddy, you listen to me! Those are not enchanted maidens. You know who they are. They're big Prairie Dogs, and they hate the Shade People for turning them into slaves."

As her father's face registered surprise, then disappointment at his failure to identify his nurses, a sudden revelation hit Agali. *Poor Daddy. He can't help how he's acting. He got hurt really bad, and I bet after he woke up, he couldn't remember lots of things. So he makes stuff up to explain.*

She didn't get to analyze her new discovery further because annoying electric shocks began pricking the tender skin behind her ears. *Oh no, I almost forgot something really important. Sanctissima is waiting for me behind that rock. Her kitchen shift is starting in a few minutes, and I'll never forgive myself if she gets punished again.*

Agali still had so much to say, and already she regretted the tantrums that had wasted valuable time. Trying to keep her voice from trembling, she made the appeal she'd practiced all along the caravan route. "Daddy, please listen, it's very important. Mama's waiting for you with your two new babies. All your children and your friends are waiting for you to help fix things back home. That's why you have to finish writing your poem."

Sequoyah may not have heard her, and in any case, she didn't expect a reply. He'd turned toward his bat globe again, tilting his head to one side. A gentle smile lifted his lips, crinkling the corners of his sad black eyes.

This time two tears did trickle down her cheeks. As she turned to leave, she whispered more to herself than to him, "I'll never give up on you, Daddy. I'll be back tomorrow."

To her surprise, in a moment of mental clarity Sequoyah called after her as she started her rush through the passage toward the lake. "Little girl ... Agali's your name, isn't it? You may be right. Every once in a while, I do remember some terrible things that happened to me, but I don't like to think about it."

***

For every three feet Agali gained climbing the hill above the Rear of Corlaz One, she slid back two, grabbing for the coffee bush branches to stop herself. Meanwhile, her mind worked furiously as she tried to reinforce the good over the bad. *I got past the lake ghosts the second time by not looking at the water. Instead I looked at my feet and followed the scum. And I put my fingers in my ears. That was good. Sanctissima promised to help me every day, and I can understand everything she says. That was very good. I really saw my daddy, and that was very,* very *good.*

But by the time she reached the top and battled her way back through the low-hanging boughs to the spot where Alexej and Arbeline stood waiting, her courage collapsed. In her misery, Agali covered her eyes with her hands. She stumbled and fell, and when Alexej touched her shoulder, she refused to look at him.

She bowed her head to her knees and mumbled almost inaudibly between her fingers, "I saw Daddy, but he wasn't okay, not at all. He barely recognized me, and he had all these funny ideas. He's not ready to write. He hardly knows who he is."

She wailed through her hands, "What ever shall I tell Mama?"

Alexej knelt beside her and bent his head low to meet hers. "I don't know, Agali, really I don't. But my mama and papa always say telling the truth works best."

When Agali didn't respond, he thrust a handful of blackberries toward her averted face. "I went berry-picking with Arbeline when you were gone because I thought you'd ..."

When his voice trailed off, Agali sat up. "You thought I'd come back from the cavern feeling sad, and you knew I'd be hungry."

She took one of the berries from a hand stained purple-red by the juice. "Do you have a better one that isn't squished?"

He inspected the remaining berries and shook his head.

Agali burst out laughing. "Squished berries are as good as whole ones. They're all the same in your stomach."

After she'd eaten them, one-by-one, she grew serious.

"One night I did something bad. I looked into Svnoyi's head when she was having a nightmare. Or maybe it was a vision because the colors were much too real, even for a dream."

Alexej drew back. "Why'd you do that? Everyone knows it's wrong to spy on somebody else's dreams, or even their thoughts unless they want you to."

"I couldn't help it. Yacy and Mama and me—we were holding her arms and legs down because she was kicking and screaming in her sleep. I took a teeny, tiny peek. I didn't mean to."

Alexej couldn't contain his curiosity, and his voice dropped to a whisper. "Okay, tell me what you saw."

Agali lowered her voice too, as if she were telling a secret. "Her dream was about my daddy—well, her daddy, too. He was in the same place where he is right now, and it was pretty dark. He was lying in a coffin, but it was made of glass, not wood, so you could see him inside it."

She shivered even though the sun was beating down on her shoulders. "It was weird. His eyes were open, so he wasn't dead. And here's the horrible part. There was blood all over the place, dripping from the ceiling and lying in big puddles on the floor."

"Ugh," Alexej remarked. "That's a terrible dream. No wonder Svnoyi was acting crazy."

He asked hesitantly, "So what do you think it means?"

Agali closed her eyes and took a deep breath. "Here goes. In a way, I think Daddy is still living inside the coffin—like when he almost died. And he's not ready to come back. To live in the real world, I mean, where everything's scary."

"Then that's what you tell your mama."

Arbeline padded close and lay down beside them as if she agreed.

"But she doesn't understand us, she can't possibly." Alexej whispered.

"Don't be so sure. At least she understands when we get happier."

He took Agali's hand. "Come on, let's go see your mama and the new babies. We've been gone so long, I bet they're born."

24 ~ Mr. Tunnel

***Is Mama being used as some kind of pawn in the queen's game? And me, too, and all the rest of us? —*Lucy**

As soon as the Polar Bear Express carrying Sequoyah's search party had pulled away from the terminal, Queen Gitli turned toward Tlke, her face determined. "Hurry now, go fetch Svnoyi and Phoenix from their cave on the shore cliff. And don't forget my lazy slug-abed husbands, Captain Kirk and Saint George. I must discuss the next phase of my master plan."

Bursting with unusual energy for 7:00 a.m., she twirled on her heel, forgetting that she still held her morning cup of Corlaz One's Folly. It sloshed out, splashing on the stone at her feet. Half way up the stairs to the palace, she flung out a paw toward her retinue. "Don't just stand there. Someone mop that up."

An hour later in the great hall, a fresh cadre of morning bats twinkled overhead holding tapers in their teeth as they nestled among the stalactites hanging from the ceiling. If they had cared at all about the goings-on in the chamber below them, they would have noticed Queen Gitli's strategy session dissolving into chaos. Even the rabbit chairs, the most docile slaves in her retinue, wiggled and shifted nervously around the backsides of her cabinet members and guests.

The husbands—her religious advisor, Captain Kirk, and her war expert, Saint George— shook their heads while clacking their front claws and stomping their back feet in frustration over their queen's demands. Svnoyi and Phoenix smirked and giggled in amusement, sending Queen Gitli into a pet. Only Lucy and Tlke, translators *par excellence,* kept their professional cool as they stood at attention on either side of the queen.

The one person conspicuously absent from the session was Kuaray because the meeting was largely about him. Lucy had more than a translator's interest in any conversation about Kuaray because she was his personal trainer. Presently she was teaching the crippled youth who was still recuperating in the Prairie Dog Hospital how to ride Petey, the giant centipede. The queen hoped that Petey eventually would serve as transportation and warrior's steed.

Saint George, the master of the *azvrkt,* stood up so abruptly that his chair laid its ears back in fright. "With all due respect, Your Majesty, preparing for battle against the Sun People and promoting peace at the same time by sending Svnoyi and Phoenix to the provinces as envoys is crazy, and it won't accomplish anything except to confuse them. The Sun People aren't the brightest—"

The queen cut in. "Saint George, from now on, please drop 'with all due respect.' What you really mean by that is you have absolutely *no* respect for me, and you hate my guts."

She sweetened her tone. "Dearest husband, you challenge any policy of mine that's the least bit complex, you are so unimaginative. If Plan A fails, and I expect it will when Svnoyi and Phoenix can't either tame them or talk sense into them, Plan B kicks in. At that point we'll have a perfect right to expunge them for rejecting our heartfelt humanitarian efforts.

"Besides, the Sun People won't know that Kuaray will be training an army, teaching our Prairie Dog youth how to shoot with a bow and arrow."

The queen smirked. "Properly, I might add, rather than waving the *azvrkt* about for show like you do. The two of you will instruct them in the shambles of the Sacred Meadow."

The expert *azvrkt* carver and champion drill master bristled and sat down. He'd been at his queen's side a year ago when she'd confronted Kuaray for poaching her prize breeding rabbits and pheasants. He'd shot every single animal cleanly through the heart with a thrown-together excuse for a bow and arrow. There was no doubt about it: the kid was good, most likely worth the effort the queen had taken to revive him.

Saint George glowered nonetheless, murmuring to himself, "But can he teach little Prairie Dog recruits fresh off the farm? He's not even one of us."

Queen Gitli's Orator of the Priest Caste, Captain Kirk, took his turn by springing with equal drama from his uneasy chair. "So that's why you saved the rotter's life after sweet little Svnoyi, here, broke his neck. To teach your subjects how to aim the *azvrkt* to *kill,* even though you knew full well that we don't murder humans ... by *holy edict.*" He whispered an aside, "Not even useless leeches like the Sun People."

His voice rose a notch. "For your information, dear Queen, your rubes from the provinces won't do it, nor will anyone else. They're instilled with the commandments every Sunday from birth, on. If I might refresh your royal memory, here it is, Commandment Eight: 'No Prairie Dog shall injure or kill a Person, although a Person is not so bound.'"

"Then change their minds."

Queen Gitli turned away with her nose in the air, refusing to glance toward Captain Kirk, who slowly sank into his chair. She loved a good confrontation. Because she had never lost an argument, she had the perfect right to issue orders with absolute authority.

The queen's next move was brutal, even for her. She feigned a dignified rise from her own chair, her face wrapped in a disarming smile that stretched wide beneath her prominent cheek pouches—only to spin around and make a sudden lunge for Svnoyi and Phoenix. With brows bristling, she grabbed each of them by an ear, digging in her claws. She shook them hard where they sat, pinned within their rabbit chairs.

"Ye gods, how dare you smirk and laugh in my court while I'm talking, you miserable little delinquents. What's so damned funny, anyway?"

She gave Svnoyi another shake before releasing her. "Your boyfriend's younger, he almost has an excuse. But *you.* You used to be such a responsible girl, so mature, managing everything—even your father. What's gotten into you?"

Everyone else in the hall froze. Not even a bat rustled.

Svnoyi sat still, rubbing her painfully reddened ear. Stunned as she was by the cruelty of the attack, she knew she deserved it. She managed to whisper, "I-I don't know what to say, Queen Gitli. It's just been so hard for me since I lost my daddy ...."

She could go no further and changed tack, her voice raspy. "Believe me, we're prepared to follow your orders. But please tell us how to find these Sun People."

Ready to talk business, the queen relaxed her scowling features. "I suggest you take the Polar Bear Express to the first stop. They can't be far away. They tend to hang out near the farms where they can do the most pillaging.

"There are eight farms along the Polar Bear Express route about one hundred miles apart, and I expect you to cover one village per week, including transportation time—because you will report back to me in eight weeks, give or take a few days."

She turned to Phoenix. "Take along some seeds and farming tools. Try explaining to them how to plant their own apple trees and vegetable gardens.

"Oh, there's one more detail." Smiling unpleasantly to show off her oversized teeth, she clacked them for good measure. "You won't be finished until you get every last Sun Person to swear an Oath of Fealty to me."

She tipped her head back and closed her eyes to recite, '"I, blank, blank, do solemnly swear that Queen Gitli is my liege. She is henceforth the Sole Owner of my lands, and in return she will keep me from starving—'"

"Hold on a minute," Phoenix cried. "We can't agree to do that."

"I think you can, as long as I know where Sequoyah is, and you don't. And remember, an army is gathering to attack the barbarians within their own villages if you fail."

Queen Gitli dismissed them by flicking her claws in the direction of the exit tunnel.

"Now, go, you two, the sooner the better. I expect you'll ready yourselves to depart by tomorrow on my Polar Bear Express."

Done with Svnoyi and Phoenix, she gestured for the sulking husbands to rise. They stood before her with what dignity they could muster and bowed their heads, ready to accept her word.

"Saint George, you and Kuaray will train recruits, twenty soldiers to a class, how to kill. Youngsters from all over the land have been riding into town for several weeks, now, on the Polar Bear Express. They're bivouacked here in the forest. Neshek, who's presently in the kitchen preparing my lunch, is seeing to their accommodations and feeding them. Eventually the force will number one thousand, almost an entire generation of our darling adolescent pups.

"Captain Kirk, you will begin tomorrow indoctrinating them daily, teaching them to overlook the Eighth Commandment."

With her rodent lips pursed into a rosette, she gave each husband a token kiss on the cheek before waving them away.

***

Queen Gitli turned to her translators. "And now, my dear little Lucy whom I can't do without, please tell me, how is Kuaray getting along with his training?"

Lucy hadn't expected to be questioned during this session and stuttered at first. "W-what should I say? Petey's so great, for a centipede, I mean. He's kind of smelly the way bugs are, but in the end, he'll be much better than a fast horse. Because he'll be like a dog, too, a loyal friend. That's real important right now because Kuaray's kind of messed up."

When she saw the queen stiffen at her description of Kuaray, Lucy hastened to correct herself. "No, Queen, it's really nothing. Kuaray's short-tempered. He falls off Petey a lot, and then he swears. But he gets right back up to try again. You have to understand, he's still getting used to ... his new life."

Then she uttered a rather remarkable truth. "I think I can promise you that Kuaray will love Petey more than he's ever loved any of us."

Lucy bowed to the queen, her way of saying that she'd like to be dismissed. But then she changed her mind. "Queen Gitli, if I might ask, how did Petey, um, get made?"

"Ah," Queen Gitli replied. "He's a product of science. We made him and a few others like him in the operating theater of the hospital. A little cloning with larger arthropods, many injections of growth hormone, a lot of controlled breeding ... I can't explain it well because I'm hardly a specialist."

Lucy wrinkled her forehead in thought before rephrasing her question, "No, Queen, that's not quite what I meant. What I really want to know is, where did you get the raw materials to make him in the first place?"

"You don't know?" The queen raised her eyebrows in surprise.

"How could I know if no one's ever told me."

"My goodness child, you wrote it down yourself. All of it's right there in the myth of God Rough and Goddess Violent. And the niches are in your own caves behind the sculptures. There were seeds and ten thousand vials of DNA, even for a curious beast resembling a long-tailed bobcat called a 'marmalade.'"

"Oh," Lucy replied in a tiny voice. "The details were so precise I thought Captain Kirk had picked my mind and was fooling around to tease me. You see, I had a kind of daydream when we first got here where I imagined almost the exact same thing."

"And Marmalade was my pet cat from the Time Before."

"You mean your slave—"

Lucy shook her head emphatically. "No, there's a difference between a pet and a slave. May I inspect the niches when I get home?"

"Of course, dear. But you won't find much. Eons before my reign some overzealous house-cleaner of a queen destroyed all the vials that weren't useful to a Prairie Dog's or Shade Person's tastes. She kept all the vegetables and only some animals, flowers, and fruit bushes. She wisely saved the medicinal and hallucinogenic plants for health, religious trances, and entertainment. Also enslavement—you understand, addiction of my animals to keep them docile.

"But she tossed every single tree. Mercy, we didn't need any more of them. We have enough of those goddam pines of every variety and description. They just keep popping out of their cones and sweeping over the whole of Baffling Isle, and some of 'em are more than two hundred fifty feet tall. I'm a lover of grassy fields, myself, and I've long recommended that we cut the cursed things down—the whole lot."

"Thank you, Queen Gitli. I've heard enough. It was all very educational. May I go home, now?"

No wonder there aren't any shade trees. If The Skidder meant for us to recreate the world of the Time Before, it's far too late, now.

"Indeed, child. You're a credit to humankind." She bestowed on Lucy's cheek one of her patent rubbery kisses.

***

To leave Queen Gitli's meeting, the miscreants had to tiptoe in front of everyone, red-faced from the scolding. The moment Svnoyi rounded the bend in the passage that led to the comfort of Ethan's cave, she sat down on the ground. With a broken spirit and a smarting ear, she crooked her knees and lay her head down on her folded arms.

Even from this distance, she could hear Lucy translating, the individual words sounding like an incomprehensible blur. *But who's she translating for? Phoenix and I, we aren't even there. My god, Lucy's insufferable, blabbing on and on for the queen out of habit. She's such a palace stooge.*

In the midst of this unkind reflection, Phoenix touched her shoulder, and she started. "Svnoyi, darling, get up and let's go on home. Do you really care that much what the queen says? She's such an old bitch ...."

His voice died out when Svnoyi lurched to a standing position, her face flushing with rage, fists clenched. All sorts of retorts raced through her head, but what did burst out was a gem of irrationality that stunned her almost as much as it did him.

"Yes, I care, because I know what Queen Gitli was really saying. It's all your fault she got mad. You're such a baby, four years younger than me, you've dragged me down to your level."

Then, opening her fists and waving her hands about like undulating patches of seaweed, she delivered the *coup de grâce.* "Phoenix, just go. You and me, we're finished."

Phoenix sucked in his breath and backed off, so hurt he had no rebuttal. He smacked into the wall behind him, and the impact made something snap in his shoulder. Cradling the injury with his opposite hand, he limped away from her in a daze, his zigzagging path resembling the throes of a mortally wounded beast.

Svnoyi hurled out a last remark toward his retreating back: "Lucky thing we never had sex!"

"Sex, ex, x," replied the tunnel.

"Oh, shut up," Svnoyi snapped, much as her little sister Agali had replied to the cavern wall surrounding Lake Spooky.

But this particular formation was different. It answered Svnoyi quite coherently in a low rumble, "You live in a land where echoes come with the territory, a dime a dozen, so don't get mad at me."

As Svnoyi twisted from side to side looking for a prankster, the tunnel erupted in an onslaught of chastisement: "Echoes are a good thing, the sign of a clean conscience. I echo. You, on the other hand, have gotten so full of shit since your father disappeared, you'll never echo—not now, not ever."

In a terrifying basso, the tunnel summed up, "Go girl, and fetch a bar of yellow soap and a big bristled brush and pail. Start scrubbing from your frontal lobes on down, and don't stop until you reach your metatarsals."

Svnoyi plopped down hard on the tunnel floor, stunned by equal parts terror and curiosity because she didn't know what to expect.

"Ready, then?" asked the tunnel. "Let's start with Queen Gitli, and I know you think she's the equivalent of a clown from the Commedia dell'Arte. She's not. She's smart, she's lethal, and she's holding a disintegrating world together with sticky-tape. Not to mention, every word she uttered about you is true, and you twisted them, turning them against poor Phoenix."

The tunnel went on vengefully, "What did she say, exactly? Remind me, Svnoyi!"

"I don't remember," Svnoyi whispered, her head lowered.

"I'll refresh your memory then," roared the tunnel. "The queen said, 'Your boyfriend's younger, he almost has an excuse. But you. You used to be such a responsible girl, so mature, managing everything—even your father. What's gotten into you?'"

"Yes, I know what she said," the frightened girl whispered. "I didn't really forget."

"Okay, then, for starters, be nicer to Lucy. You might not like her attachment to the palace, but she's juggling two loyalties with the grace and wisdom of a seasoned diplomat."

The tunnel paused to let the reverberations die out before blasting with renewed vigor, "And lift a finger, now and then, to help Yacy and your old flame Oscar with housework and farming instead of lallygagging and giggling with Phoenix all day. That pair is beginning to chafe."

"I'll try, uh, Mr. Tunnel, although I don't plan to be around much longer. Can I go, now?" begged Svnoyi.

"Are you joking? We've barely touched the muck with that scrub-brush of yours. What the hell happened to you when your father was taken away?"

"I-I guess I didn't have anyone to care for, anymore. Maybe you don't know this, but I used to advise him about everything—"

"Wrong!" The tunnel shed a few stones with the vehemence of its reply. "Lord love a duck, girl, you can be so superficial. You lost the person who loved you best, the linchpin of your existence. He was advising you, not the other way around, teaching you how to become a loving, responsible grownup. Did none of it stick?"

"I guess not all of it, Mr. Tunnel. But he never talks to me anymore, not in my dreams or visions, not telepathically—"

"Oh, spare me the excuses, Svnoyi. You aren't even trying to reach him these days. He could be unconscious, or he's lost his memory. Don't you want to help him—wherever he is—to get well faster?"

"It's easier not to think about him at all when he's so sick."

"Say what?" exclaimed the tunnel, shaking like an earthquake. "You're appalling."

"Can we talk about Phoenix, instead? He was my boyfriend until a half hour ago."

To her surprise, the tunnel shifted topics easily, and she sensed a decline in the energy of its replies. Perhaps it was losing steam as fast as she was.

It grumbled rather than roared, "The two of you clung together like a sinking lifeboat. Foolish, very foolish. Not that I blame you, losing your dad was so traumatic. It didn't hurt that he'd grown up drop-dead gorgeous with those violet eyes and—"

Svnoyi interrupted the tunnel's wisdom rudely, "What the hell does it matter? I sure ruined that."

"Yes, you did, in the crudest, nastiest way possible. But you had to end it; he really was too young. Mark my reverberations, though, you may never meet his equal for kindness and beauty again."

The tunnel was reduced to whispering. "But there's a war coming. Keep that mind-killing that both of you can do under control ...."

Its echo had dwindled to nothing, and Svnoyi fell flat on her face on the gritty floor. She barely managed to pant, "That's over, thank goodness. Goodbye, Mr. Tunnel, it's been ... weird."

***

Exhausted, Svnoyi wriggled through the Prairie Dog-sized archway at the end of the tunnel, arriving in the dark cul-de-sac at the back of Ethan's cave. The monstrous crystal-studded boulder that was meant to hide the entrance was presently occupied by Phoenix, who sat on top of it. Svnoyi felt a stab of anger. *Why's my life have to be so complicated? He's the last person I want to see right now.*

"I was worried, but I didn't think I should go back into the tunnel," Phoenix ventured hesitantly, not sure if she wanted to talk to him. "Lucy passed you on her way home from the palace. She said you were on your knees in some kind of trance with your eyes rolled up, mumbling to yourself."

"Yeah, I was," said Svnoyi. "And I don't feel like chit-chatting, if you don't mind."

She pushed her way around the boulder, rudely leaving him behind, sitting on it. She hoped he hadn't seen her face that she was sure was streaked with tunnel dust. She patted her hair, and her braid had come totally undone.

Phoenix slid off the boulder. "Wait, Svnoyi. We can't leave it like this. Tomorrow morning we're taking the Polar Bear Express to see the Sun People, and we have to get ready—"

"That's what you think," Svnoyi snapped back. She berated herself, *What kind of idiot comment was that? Of course we're going. It's not like we have a choice.*

She noticed that he had suffered, too, which annoyed her rather than arousing her sympathy. His eyes were puffy even though he rarely cried, and she assumed he'd hurt himself on purpose because his fist was bleeding through the T-shirt clumsily wrapped around it.

"What stupid, immature thing did you do to your hand?"

Phoenix stalked away from her through the murk of Ethan's cave. He yelled over his shoulder, "Like you even give a damn?"

Good, at least Phoenix finally is acting as childish as I am. I'm sorry, Mr. Tunnel. My debut at reforming myself didn't go too well.

25 ~ Petey

Lucy arrived breathless and a little late for Kuaray's centipede-riding lesson at the Prairie Dog Hospital. To reach the long and narrow anteroom adjacent to the operating theater with the stone beds, she'd taken the two-mile secret passage that originated in a dark corner beside the palace kitchen. The lessons were always held here. Kuaray would be waiting for her with Petey standing somewhere nearby. She never asked, but she assumed that a few of the queen's slaves, most likely the flathead polar bears, would set up the scene, bringing Kuaray in on a gurney and Petey, on a leash.

"Look at this, Kuaray. I made a harness and reins for Petey."

Lucy's eyes shone with pride when she displayed her handiwork, a heavy pile of knotted ropes and buckles that she held cradled in her arms. She would try anything that might help him learn. Although Kuaray practiced dutifully between lessons, his progress was abysmal.

He snapped, "Can't you see I'm too busy to turn around?"

"Kneel, Petey, kneel, goddammit," he bellowed, grabbing the centipede's first segment behind the forcipules. He hung onto the apex of the joint and using his formidable upper-body strength, he almost managed to pull himself onto Petey's back.

But Petey didn't kneel. He bucked instead by neatly arching body segments two through five. Tipping sideways, he dumped Kuaray into a heap on the stone floor. Over Kuaray's swearing, Lucy heard Petey make a chirpy comment by scraping some of his limbs.

"Kuaray, did you hear that crickety sound? It's called a 'stridulation.' Petey is grinding his legs together because he's trying to talk to you. What he's saying is, 'Why should I be nice to you if you're not nice to me?'"

"You've got to be kidding, he can't say that."

"No, I'm *not* kidding. He said it, or something like it."

Lucy sat down beside Kuaray on the floor to match his height. She took his hand, which he tolerated better than she thought he would. Ever since the Prairie Dogs had restored his life, the surly youth had made a show of not wanting or needing her, even though she was his sole companion.

"Kuaray, it's all about love." A wizard with animals, Lucy stretched out her free hand to caress Petey's brow. The creature shuffled close to her and knelt down. Lying his spherical head in her lap, his nearly sightless eyes radiated contentment. He drooped his antennae, a sign that he wasn't afraid in her presence.

"Believe me, he's waiting to love you as soon as you reach out to him—literally, I mean."

"But he's dirty, and he smells." Kuaray pinched his nose childishly, making the words come out sounding nasal.

"He's not dirty, and that's his natural scent. Is it so bad? It's kind of like bitter almonds.

"He washes his legs one at a time, every day, as fastidiously as any cat. Come on, pet him. Try loving him for who he is and not for how he looks."

Kuaray shook his head. "I'll learn to ride him, but I can't love him."

"The two go hand in hand. Love him, and he'll let you stay on his back; don't love him, and he won't. It's that simple."

"No, he's disgusting." An obstinate frown distorted his ruggedly handsome face.

Lucy's patience began to fray. "Jeez, Kuaray, we have almost the exact same stupid conversation every day. Don't you realize he's your ticket to independence, to a new set of legs?"

Petey, who hated the arguments, turned skittish. He pulled away from her and made a beeline for the corner.

Lucy stood then, folding her arms peremptorily. "Okay then, Kuaray, listen. It's time to shape up because there's something else." Her voice sounded suddenly ominous. For the first time, he turned his eyes to look directly at her.

"What?"

"Petey's not just your transportation. He's your war steed. In a few days, you and Saint George will start teaching Queen Gitli's military recruits, the Prairie Dog pups, how to aim a bow and arrow. And how to shoot at targets—"

Kuaray didn't wait for her to finish. "You're not serious. I'll never work for that bitch, teaching her creepy, stubby-limbed army how to shoot with a bow and arrow. It can't be done; their arms are too short.

"Besides," he murmured softly. "I'm an invalid, and I don't want anyone to see me."

The admission startled Lucy, who had no idea how he felt about himself. But she did not relent an iota. "Yes, you will, Kuaray. You're gonna pull yourself together. The queen saved your life and nursed you back to health. Some of us, like me, happen to be thrilled because you're still here, even if you aren't."

She chirruped to Petey who came running, his legs swishing back and forth like the brushes in a car wash from the Time Before. "There's not much time. I'm telling you, not asking you: reach out your hand right now, and pat Petey's head."

Kuaray did, with only a slight grimace.

Lucy coached him, "Gently, gently. That's perfect."

Petey reciprocated by rubbing his head on Kuaray's shoulder and lowering his antennae. His legs vibrated, making a purring stridulation of contentment. Lucy pretended not to notice Kuaray's surprise and the sudden softening of his tense features. She knew the right time had arrived at last and attached the harness around the docile centipede's first two body segments.

"Now, pull yourself onto his back and say something sweet at the same time."

"I can't. I'm not sweet."

"Kuaray, I'm warning you, cut it out. Talk like you would to your girlfriend."

Lucy was hardly surprised when Kuaray rolled his eyes to the ceiling and spoke in a falsetto, "Oh darling, please let me climb on your back and kick you in your armor plates."

The wise teacher knew when to laugh instead of losing her temper. "Pretty good. Now say it like you mean it but pick better words."

Patting the beast gently, Kuaray lowered his voice and let it grow sweet and soft. "Petey, stand still, that's a good boy. I love you."

Petey liked what he heard and purred with his legs. Before Kuaray realized what he was doing, he'd pulled himself up by his arms and rolled onto the animal's back.

Lucy handed her human riding pupil the reins and a bag of four- and six-legged live treats that she'd bargained for and received from the bobcats in exchange for their Tuesday evening dishwashing shift.

"Good luck, dear. Reward him every time he lets you stay on his back—like right now, for example. You don't need me when you're working on a love match. Bye, I'll be back in an hour."

"No wait, Lucy, stay. You have to help me."

Lucy scooted out of earshot because she knew Kuaray would be better off forging the friendship without her. She hadn't expected her stomach to make a little adrenaline leap. *For the very first time, Kuaray asked me for help, and he asked me not to leave him.*

***

In truth, she had a mission of her own to accomplish. In addition to providing the treats, the bobcats had gone on a hasty reconnaissance. They assured her that the hospital was empty with no surgeries scheduled because the war effort had started. That serendipitous fact left her free to roam around and find her mother. After she'd asked offhandedly, Kuaray had described the hospital's simple T-shaped floor plan. Through the door in front of her was the operating theater, and on the far side of it, a long hallway that went both directions. One side had closets for supplies and the other, rooms for housing patients. Luz had to be living somewhere in the patients' wing where she'd been recuperating in total isolation from her family for almost a year.

Lucy had never understood it. *Her being away for so long doesn't make sense. Kuaray's almost cured, and his injury was much more serious. Mama's was still pretty bad, falling through the skylight and hitting her head on one of the stone beds in the operating theater. But what could they be keeping her for?*

She opened the anteroom's door to the theater and stopped in her tracks. *Oh, my, here they are. The beds.*

She hurried past maybe twenty of them, noticing that they were lined up in a long row the same distance apart. She glanced about hastily. This room lacked the glittering rock formations that brought magic to the palace: the walls of grey stone weren't ugly, exactly, although the evenly distributed tiny white pebbles imparted a gritty institutional sameness to the surface. Looking upward at the skylight, she noticed that the weather was fine. Shafts of sun filled with motes of pollen shone down, the light turning the room a delicate green as it filtered through the old-growth boughs that hung above.

Amazed by the size of the place, Lucy started running as she tried to tamp down her imagination. *It's not just about my mama lying here for so long. Such grisly things happened on these beds, and I hate that because I love animals so much. Petey was one of the lucky guys. The Prairie Dog doctors made him perfect—eventually, that is. I wonder how many failures came before him. And now I know what happened to them. They got dumped into the Valley of Rejects if they didn't die, first. The valley's somewhere nearby, probably attached to the hospital, and that's where Petey catches his breakfast, lunch, and dinner.*

Lucy turned right in the hallway, which turned out to be the wrong direction. Through the occasional open door she could see supplies, endless heaps of them: gowns, bedding, mops, buckets, crocks, sutures, needles, knives, vials, probes, balloons, bandages, trusses—all carefully stacked on wooden shelves.

In the opposite direction, only one door was open. Lucy ran toward it eagerly but slowed to a walk and approached on tiptoe for the last few feet, her heart knocking against her ribs. She craned her neck around the frame and peeked inside. *Oh, please, please, let Mama be in there!*

The room was unoccupied presently, but it obviously belonged to Kuaray. His clothes were strewn about in heaps, and his bed of quilts and pillows was in a swirl. Apparently, he had a roommate: mounds of straw that must be Petey's bed filled the length of an entire wall. Lucy noticed that any stray pieces had been neatly swept into place, undoubtedly by the centipede's efficient legs.

Wow, both in the same room. The Prairie Dogs are serious about getting those two to like each other.

She laughed to herself. *I have to wonder, though, what Petey thinks about Kuaray's housekeeping after all the mean things Kuaray said about Petey's hygiene.*

After that brief moment of levity, Lucy gave in to her fears. *What if Mama isn't here at all? She never answers me telepathically. It's probably not because she's too sick. Whenever I ask Queen Gitli, she tells me Mama's almost well and coming along just great.*

Lucy started. *But what's that?* Breaking the pin-drop silence in the empty hallway, muffled sounds erupted at its end. A woman's voice was singing loudly and hopelessly out of tune, but the words were decipherable:

Off we go into the wild blue yonder,
Climbing high into the sun.
Here they come zooming to meet our thunder,
At 'em boys, Give 'er the gun!
Blah, blah, blah, blah, blah, blah, blah.
Goddammit, what're the words?
We live in fame or go down in flame. Hey!
Nothing can stop the US Air Force!

Oh my god, it's Mama. She's singing the "Air Force Song," just like she used to. She'd sing it for fun, and she always forgot those very same words. That's how I know *it's* her *behind the last door.*

Lucy tore the length of the hall, crying out, "Mama, Mama, it's me, Lucy. I'm here, I'm here, I've found you at last!"

She had the flats of her palms on the panels of the door when it swung outward forcefully, almost hitting her in the face.

"Mama?"

Lucy received a telepathic answer from none other than Tlke, who stomped into the hall, sour-faced. *No, not Mama.* Tlke! *Why, exactly, are you here? No one gave you permission to leave the anteroom.*

Lucy stuttered illogically, *W-why are* you *here? This is my mama's room.*

Tlke advanced on Lucy, her teeth clacking and brows lowering, something Lucy had only seen Queen Gitli do. Her words were separated by menacing pauses. *Because I work for the* queen, *that's why. I obey her every wish, I serve where she asks me to, and I am in charge of your mother's rehabilitation.*

Lucy backed up, bumping into the wall. *I-I also work for the queen. She'd want what's best for me, too.*

No, Lucy, you're wrong. She wants what's best for her subjects, and that means she doesn't put people first. Do you think she'd betray her own kind?

Without warning, Lucy felt such fear for her mother and herself that her knees shook, and a notion flew through her head that she hoped Tlke hadn't caught. *Is Mama being used as some kind of pawn in the queen's game? And me too, and all the rest of us? We're so vulnerable.*

Lucy's courage left her. Her face puckered as if she wanted to cry. *I thought we were friends, Tlke.*

We are friends. Why would you think otherwise? But you know perfectly well you overstepped by snooping around. And right now you aren't obeying your orders to tutor Kuaray for the required two hours. His success means everything to the queen.

She gestured for Lucy to follow her back down the hall, and her usually limpid brown eyes had turned an uncompromising, steely gray. She set off at a rapid trot, forcing Lucy to scramble.

The girl arrived at the Prairie Dog's side, puffing. *Tlke, do you think the queen really wants war? I don't like killing at all, do you?*

Of course she doesn't want war! Her Majesty hasn't got an aggressive bone in her entire body.

Hearing this last piece of misinformation, Lucy stopped walking. She found herself in that uncomfortable place between howling with laughter and weeping bitter tears.

26 ~ The Sacred Meadow

For the past few weeks, hundreds of adolescent pups, Queen Gitli's army recruits, had been arriving in droves by Polar Bear Express. Their quarters in the forest that were basically dig-it-yourself with a commissary in the center, didn't dampen their spirits; they were on holiday. The base commanders escorted the excited youngsters in parties of twenty to tour Iqual, the capital they'd heard so much about but had never seen.

The Prairie Dogs hailed from the eight super-farms and the Shade People's eight caverns. With soil from the fields permanently caked under their claws or the lingering odor of cave-dust embedded in their nostrils, these Prairie Dog youth gasped at the sheer size and sights of Baffling Isle's one real above-ground city. They stared at the circular yellow brick avenue, all three thousand feet of it, that surrounded the imposing Prairie Dog Infirmary and medical school, and the communal children's nursery. They were less impressed by the rambling government building, even though it was rumored to have an abacus in every single one of its two hundred cubicles. Mansions buried half underground where the adults lived dotted the woods nearby. They couldn't see, but they could certainly smell, the pharmaceutical fields a half mile away that reeked of marijuana and hemp.

At the exact center of the yellow brick circle stood a twenty-foot statue of Queen Gitli made of marble. None of these dwellers from the provinces had met their queen, and some of them lay on their backs to experience the towering figure foreshortened, from the manicured toeclaws to the sweeping and curled eyebrows. She had posed for the rendering twenty-five years earlier during her second royal jubilee when she was still in her prime. Her plump figure, enlarged eight-fold and in full seashell regalia, delighted some of them and filled others with awe. Indeed, viewing Her Majesty in stone put everyone in a fine mood.

Obviously missing from Iqual's grounds were a temple to worship the gods, and the royal palace. As the base commanders explained, the palace was actually there, but not visible. It lay entirely beneath the city in the largest, most magnificent cavern of them all—with the exception of the Eye of Cinder. It had no main entrance, although a number of tactical secret passages led to the fabled royal chambers of the queen and her three consorts. The inner sanctum of the priesthood also lay at a lower level, its rooms reeking of trance-inducing vapors. In addition to her staff and slave animals, only a few select visitors were ever allowed to see her, and these fresh-faced youths of Her Majesty's army would never have that honor.

The Prairie Dog army would soon become acquainted with the Sacred Meadow, the once-magnificent outdoor park where their kind had worshipped the gods until the Sun People pillaged it a few months ago. Military exercises would be held there as a constant reminder of their enemy's sacrilegious deed.

At the end of the tour, the twenty Prairie Dogs stood in a circle around Queen Gitli's statue, touching claws. Because their communication was telepathic except for a few isolated yips and barks, and because they couldn't sing, they listened to Tlke's lusty recitation of Luz's "Air Force Song," the words altered to rouse an entirely different species of warrior. It left the tender recruits deeply moved.

Azvrkt raised, don't pause to ponder,
Aim it straight into their eyes.
Here they come to meet our thunder,
Let go the string and watch it fly!
Yip yip, yippity, yap, yap, yap,
Who needs words when you got ZAP?
We live to kill! The gods say, "Swell!" Hey!
Nothing stops Queen Gitli's Girls 'n Boys.

Never mentioned on the recruits' tour was the Prairie Dog Hospital and the Valley of Rejects that lay a few miles away, adjacent to the Sacred Meadow. Only top-secret work was performed there by the most brilliant physicians and scientists.

***

On the first day of the training sessions, Lucy decided to go early to the Sacred Meadow to make certain that everything was ready for the Prairie Dog recruits. She headed for the valley on an overland route through the forest marked by splotches of silver paint that had appeared overnight on the tree trunks. She assumed the base commanders had put the markers up to help the newcomers from farms and caverns find their way.

The consummate animal lover frowned, biting her lip. *With all those scraping feet there will soon be a path, then a rutted road, and finally a highway. The wild creatures I love so much will all go somewhere else.*

Lucy entered the Sacred Meadow's long valley at its open end by walking across a single slab of magnificent pink granite thirty feet wide. Someone had stacked up multi-hued boulders to form a pair of chunky cairns on either side. Had they been there last summer? She couldn't remember. She'd been too preoccupied to take in the details.

Even shorn of its luxuriant green grass and most of its trees, the topography of the place possessed a spooky grandeur. She turned her head slowly to take it all in. From where she stood, rocky ridges slanted up around the perimeter of the valley, emerging from level ground to rise ever higher and steeper. They culminated in a single peak at the opposite end, its almost sheer face studded with white stones and dangling roots. A handful of dwarfed pines that vied with wind, rain, and snow dotted the mountain's boulder-strewn slopes.

Leaping the empty riverbeds at their narrowest points and threading through piles of rocks and broken branches, Lucy crossed the length of the valley floor until she reached the base of the peak. When she leaned back to take in its height, she felt dizzy: the summit that scraped the sky appeared to move with the clouds. She lowered her head slowly to track the length of a black fissure with her eyes. It terminated fifteen feet below the ground in a perfectly rounded basin, the floor lined with rose quartz slabs. Even at that depth and in shadow, the shiny crystals on the surface winked coyly from time to time. *It's the fountain, but I hardly recognized it without the roaring of the water.*

Lucy lay down on the tufts of dry weeds, stretching out flat on her back in the mountain's shadow to keep the sun out of her eyes. She linked her fingers behind her head and gazed skyward in order to think. *I was so sad last summer at Mama's funeral—even if it turned out not to be real. The queen was prancing around in that clanking shell dress telling lies, saying Mama had drowned in the whirlpool trying to save Lucian. It's hard for me to remember much of anything except that the valley looked totally different when it was green.*

She tried to picture herself on the dais in the middle of the meadow with Tlke at her side. *I remember translating. And from where I was standing, I couldn't see the fountain and the ten rivers that ran in those trenches. But they made so much noise, I had to yell over them.*

Then she asked herself, ruefully, *What good did it do the Sun People to ruin it?*

The sun had rounded the peak, spreading its radiance across her body. Lucy tried hard to concentrate, but her eyes grew heavy as soon as she closed them against the glare. *What was it Sequoyah called the place when he discovered it? "Charybdis and Scylla." The name comes from one of Ulysses's adventures when his boats had to pass between a whirlpool on the one side and a dangerous cliff on the other.*

I'm so tired.

In her sleep, Lucy batted at her itchy nose and sneezed. Returning from somewhere far away, she managed to squint open one eye at the offending tickler, a white daisy on a long stem that inched across her cheek.

She sat up. "Kuaray, stop it. You woke me up."

"But I had to, silly girl. The first class is starting in ten minutes."

Twiddling the daisy between his thumb and forefinger, Kuaray sat proud and straight, mounted on Petey. He chirruped to his new steed and riding one-handed, he threw back his head and laughed from sheer pleasure. He raced Petey around Lucy three times in widening circles, hoping to impress her.

When she clapped her hands, Kuaray called out, "Hop on, let's take a ride to look at the targets."

But is Petey's back strong enough for two people? Lucy wondered.

Of course it is.

Lucy smiled to herself. *Hmm, this is new, a telepathic conversation with Kuaray. I better watch what I think.*

With her arms around his waist like a motorcycle passenger of a million years ago, Lucy rode behind Kuaray to the valley's center. Petey took off at a terrifying clip. Even though her heart pounded and she clenched her eyes shut for most of the journey, she noticed that Kuaray was already an expert at guiding Petey over the riverbeds' gullies.

They reached a grove of six lanky pine trees that stood in a row among dying juniper bushes. Someone had painted targets on the trunks, the bright red concentric circles about five feet above the ground, transforming them into an archery range.

"Well, Lucy, we better trot on over because Saint George is already lining up our first class of recruits. Ooh, they're getting their *azvrkts,* and look, they're so happy. They can't wait to kill someone."

Lucy replied, "Oh, for goodness sake, Kuaray, they're such pups, they don't even know why they were brought here."

He tried to make amends. "Okay, sorry I said that. I really *am* trying to be nicer."

He added, "But they'll never hit those targets, let alone kill someone. Like I said before, they're too small to use those huge, heavy *azvrkts*. Just wait, you'll see."

The pair made a dash for the valley's edge and pulled up next to Saint George. He was fussing over the recruits who stood in a ragged row, wiggling about, trying to control their excitement. The First Warrior and champion carver of the *azvrkt* criticized each one separately, prodding the pup to stand straight and hold the equipment in the correct paw—bow in the left, arrow in the right. Then he moved to the next until all twenty were aligned. Saint George nearly burst with pride at his accomplishment thus far. He puffed his chest, showing off his chunky military medal that glinted in the sunlight.

He and his assistants had worked furiously to finish *azvrkts* for an army of one thousand in time for the opening exercises. In spite of the rushed preparation, each bow was a masterpiece of fine workmanship, elaborately carved and shaped of composite wood and bone. The recruits also had slung over their shoulders quivers fashioned of stiffened rabbit skin filled with twenty arrows apiece made of Norway pine, the feathers obtained from diverse birds of the forest.

Saint George's egotistic moment was short-lived. As Kuaray had predicted, the Prairie Dog recruits' upper limbs proved too weak to budge the bowstring. When they got tired of fruitless pulling, they let the arrows drop to the ground. Their enthusiasm vanished, and most of them sank to their haunches. They refused to stand when Saint George ordered them to try again, which sent him into a frenzy.

Lucy whispered into Kuaray's ear, translating Saint George's meltdown. "Rise up, my hearties, muster your courage." Then, "Dammit, you're breaking ranks, soldiers."

After a pause he said more to himself than to them, "Goddam little squirts, why'd I agree to do this insulting job?"

Kuaray laughed so hard he almost fell off Petey's back.

Saint George snapped his head around, ready for a confrontation. "What's so funny, you centipede-riding half-man?"

Kuaray turned white with anger. "I may be half a man, but you're a third of a Prairie Dog's pecker in the good queen's bed—"

Lucy interrupted, "Your creativity slays me, Kuaray, and I'm not translating that. Just shut up and let me handle this."

After a brief telepathic exchange with Saint George, the First Warrior nodded his head in a reluctant assent. Then he strode stiffly toward Kuaray and extended a paw.

Kuaray whispered hastily, "And you said what exactly, Lucy?"

She whispered back, "I told him his reputation at the palace depends on the recruits' success, and that you, Kuaray, expect all thousand *azvrkts* to be made lighter and shorter by tomorrow morning."

"What am I supposed to do now?"

"Come on, Kuaray, you're acting like an idiot. Don't be obtuse on purpose. Shake Saint George's paw that he's been sticking in your face for the last five minutes—before he gets mad and changes his mind. And tell him it's an honor to work with him. Say you can't wait to see the remodeled *azvrkts.*"

"I hate this. Why don't you tell him?"

"No, I'm not covering for you again. As long as your father and my mother are Queen Gitli's hostages, we play their game."

Lucy knew the handshake was a big step forward for the socially stunted youth. After it was over, her voice softened. "Fantastic diplomacy, Kuaray."

Kuaray looked surprised and then blushed. "Thank you. For the compliment, I mean. And for everything else."

He kissed the white daisy and presented it to her. Lucy wasn't quite sure why he'd made the gesture, but her heart did a flip-flop.

27 ~ The Bats

***If you die before I do, the part of me that has become you dies too.* —Corlion**

Svnoyi and Phoenix barely spoke as they stuffed their backpacks with summer clothes and their personal things. They packed a week's worth of dried food—fruit, beans, rabbit jerky, and grains—a frying pan and kettle, and bedrolls for sleeping in the forest if they weren't invited into the Sun People's homes. Phoenix hadn't forgotten the queen's request to bring seeds to teach the perpetual moochers how to raise their own crops. He packed the surplus he had on hand in the greenhouse, taking into account what would grow best during the heat of summer.

Phoenix's eyes wandered over the diminished household. Tomorrow morning when the cave door slid shut, his dwelling place for more than a year would stand empty. Aleta and Agali had left yesterday on the express with Jaroslav's family, and Yacy had already moved into Ethan's cave a few weeks before. It was more convenient for her that way: she could care for both babies, Arielle Luz and Lucian, together. And of course she wanted to be with Oscar.

Phoenix wouldn't be sorry to leave. He asked himself, *How did our cave get to be such an unfriendly place when not too long ago it felt so homey? Svnoyi and me, supposedly in love, we didn't talk much, not even telepathically. We couldn't wait to get out of there in the morning to do our work, even in wintertime.*

He knew the answer, of course. *Sequoyah was gone. He was our glue, and he held us together with his love. Without him, we all kind of fell apart.*

Phoenix was wrestling with his bedroll, trying to shove it into a corner of his bulging pack. As his fingers kneaded it to get out the air, his mind wandered. *After the Prairie Dogs took Sequoyah, Mama wasn't easy to live with. She slept half the day and when she was awake, she complained a lot. But sometimes in the evenings, especially when we were snowed in or it was raining hard outside, she reminisced about Sequoyah from the Time Before when we lived in the High Tatras and Frobisher Bay. We knew most of the stories because we'd been there, but we didn't care, and we never got bored because of the way she told them.*

We'd all pull close to her in front of the stove that I truly believe was Ethan's greatest invention after the Greyhound's time machine. I'd put an arm on Mama's shoulder and my other arm around Svnoyi's waist, after we got close, that is. Agali would sit in Mama's lap even though she was a little bit too big. Yacy was always busy with Arielle Luz somewhere nearby, and I could tell she was listening. All of us loved watching Mama smile when she told her stories, and her eyes would get sparkly and pretty again. It was like a magic spell, although it never lasted for long.

Svnoyi broke into his reverie, her voice mocking. "What're you thinking about? That you're still really mad at me?"

Phoenix had stopped being angry for at least ten minutes, but the wretched feeling flared up all over again. "Svnoyi, you are such a monster. You're really enjoying this breakup, aren't you?"

When she delayed answering to annoy him, an insult popped into his mind that he was actually rather proud of. "Prick-teaser!"

Svnoyi rolled her eyes. "That's a new low even for you, Phoenix, and I can't begin to think of an equivalent for men."

She pointed derisively at his backpack. "And stop trying to stuff your sleeping bag in because it won't fit. Roll it and tie it to the outside like I did with mine."

His freshly bandaged hand that he'd smashed against the crystalline boulder after she'd dumped him started throbbing again, and the shoulder that he'd banged into the tunnel wall ached afresh. *She always gets the last word. Damn her.*

***

Because Svnoyi and Phoenix had to travel only one stop on the Polar Bear Express, Queen Gitli hadn't arranged the same luxury seating that she'd set up the day before for the Sequoyah Team. Even after the cart began to move with its rhythmic rolling and thumping, the ex-lovers sat in stony silence, wedged between stacked cages of bats that had spent the night at the depot and stinky blackberries in wooden crates. The bats squeaked and flapped in terror, and the berries that were at least a week old leaked streams of dark juice across the cart's floorboards.

All at once the two started talking again.

Phoenix pinched his nose with his fingers. "Poor bats. I bet they were meant to go out yesterday to one of the other caverns that needs more lighting. So they didn't get delivered or fed or cleaned. Let's sneak them out at our stop and free them. And those berries are way past edible."

"Yes, we'll let the bats go in the forest." Svnoyi answered with the relief that comes after breaking a painful silence. She paused for a minute before adding, "Y'know, something's going wrong with the queen's delivery system, and it's probably because the young Prairie Dogs who used to do all the work left their jobs to come into town for military training."

Her well-considered answer gave Phoenix the courage to voice his own worries. "Svnoyi, to be honest, I don't know what we're supposed to do with these Sun People. The queen didn't explain herself when she told Saint George we'd 'tame' them. And her Oath of Fealty. It's disgusting."

"I don't get it either," she replied. "Because except for telling them how to plant a vegetable garden, we can't change in a week the way they've run their lives for centuries and centuries. As far as that oath goes, forget it. It's equivalent to asking them if they'd like to be serfs."

"So is the queen just trying to get us out of town while she prepares to kill off anything that's human, hopefully not including us?" Phoenix's voice rose in agitation.

Svnoyi tried to answer calmly. "I've worried about that, too. But I believe she doesn't know one hundred percent what she's doing."

"God, I wish Sequoyah was still here. Maybe he could've talked some sense into her."

Svnoyi whispered, "Me too."

Phoenix realized the risk of his next move as he took her hand tentatively. When she didn't pull it away, he said, "I know we'll never get back together, but I want to explain how I felt about you—how it happened."

Svnoyi gave his hand a squeeze of assent.

"Okay, here goes. Sequoyah was gone, suddenly. Of course Aleta's my mom, but she's always run hot and cold, loving me sometimes and not others because I was never a kid she wanted in the first place. I didn't blame her for not being much of a mother after Sequoyah disappeared, but it didn't leave me with a lot to hold onto. And there you were, so strong and beautiful."

Svnoyi reached across him to take his other hand. "I was a mess after what happened to Daddy. And there you were, Phoenix, standing in the falling snow. I wanted to take care of you, kind of like I did him, and I fell for you right away. But I ended up being just as weak as you. I got distracted from what was really important ... doing my best."

"But Svnoyi, we did our chores faithfully and really well—"

"You don't understand, I was meant to *lead* everybody. Sequoyah would have expected me to."

Phoenix made a huge effort not to roll his eyes. *Seriously, she's not over* that *yet? I thought we'd solved the leadership problem by sort of bumbling along and letting the Prairie Dogs order us around.*

He said aloud, "Oh dear, I'm *so sorry* I interfered with your destiny."

Then he grew earnest. "Svnoyi, look at me, this is serious." He paused, waiting for her to turn her head toward him.

"Remember when we talked about the power we both have to kill with our minds? It was on the way back from the Valley of Rejects. But now that we're trying to really talk, I truly believe we should vow to each other to never use the power."

Svnoyi looked startled. "Mr. Tunnel said the subject might come up."

"Mr. who?"

Freeing her hands from his, she sat very still. She closed her eyes, her brow furrowed in concentration.

When she spoke, her answer was definitive. "No, Phoenix, I can't make that promise. Not with things like they are right now in the world."

Thrown into confusion, Phoenix stuttered, "R-really, you mean that?"

"Of course I mean it. For chrissake, Mr. Idealist, get off your high horse. You have no clue what you'll end up doing in a crisis."

Damn her. She always gets the last word. Phoenix turned away, putting on the frown that Agali and Alexej called his gargoyle face.

After this latest rift, neither of them felt like talking. Svnoyi sat hunched close to the crates of berries and immersed herself in one of the hundred books that she'd borrowed from Sequoyah's carefully chosen end-of-time collection. Phoenix had pushed against the bat cages as far away from Svnoyi as possible, yet he couldn't resist craning his neck over to see what she was reading.

Unbelievable. She's reading Gulliver's Travels *even though we've been living that book every goddam day since we got here.*

He asked himself, *Which ones* are *we, Houyhnhnms or Yahoos? We're both! We're stuck somewhere in the middle, capable of the highest moral perfection and the lowest self-serving depravity.* He liked the weightiness of his word choices so much that he repeated them four times.

All at once the repulsive odor of the bats swept over him. He clutched his quaking stomach, hoping he wouldn't make everything worse by vomiting all over the cart. When he didn't, he leaned his head back against the pulsing top rail and covered his face with his hands. He mouthed over and over in rhythm with the wheels, "I wish I was a better person, I wish I was a better person."

After what seemed like an eternity, the Polar Bear Express pulled into the first station on the route. Dingy and low-ceilinged, it lay one hundred miles, or twelve hours north, of the lofty depot off the basement of Queen Gitli's palace. With heavy backpacks and arms full of bat cages, Svnoyi and Phoenix staggered along the platform following a handful of Prairie Dogs who appeared to know the way out. The youngsters carried nothing, although they wore the same rabbit-skin packs that had been issued to all the Prairie Dog recruits currently overrunning Iqual.

Phoenix whispered, "Poor little things, they look so disappointed they can hardly lift their feet. I bet they're 4F because they failed their physicals."

"Who knows," Svnoyi whispered back. "They may end up being the handful of lucky ones who survive."

***

For the last few hours of the ride, the bats had gone quiet except for an occasional screech or wing-flap. Fearing for them, Svnoyi and Phoenix started to run as soon as they drew near to the forest behind the apple orchards and fields. Once they'd lowered the cages to the ground and sprung the door catches, they lifted the bats out, gingerly. The tiny creatures that had borne the queen's tapers so faithfully lay heavy in the pair's cupped hands, gasping through wide open pink mouths lined with itty-bitty teeth.

Phoenix's thoughts raced as they lay them side-by-side on a conveniently flat rock covered by a blanket of pine needles and forest detritus. *They're almost dead. Maybe we should put them out of their misery with our minds. It's like Svnoyi said, I wouldn't know how I'd respond to a crisis until there was one.*

He felt utterly helpless, unable to decide. With a great lump constricting his throat, he looked over at Svnoyi whose mouth was drawn into a straight line beneath drooping eyes. She caught his look and nodded her head slowly. The boy who seldom cried felt his eyes fill until he couldn't see his victims, evenly lined up on a stone bier.

Too bad it has to be about something so sad, but Svnoyi and me—we finally agree. He felt his grief fall away as he narrowed in on his task.

"Theh nedé water, sippen thro a rayd. Losé ne time. Theh nedé water. Losé ne time, ne time!"

"What?"

In amazement he jumped up, snapping his head right and left. He tried to peer through the branches overhead, but his eyes couldn't penetrate the densely layered boughs. Seeing no one and responding to the voice's urgency, he decided not to question its origin. He shot back, "They need to drink water through a reed? Where's the nearest stream, then?"

"Be-ine thee, be-ine thee!"

He began scrabbling through his backpack. "Okay, the stream's behind me. Good, I'm on my way. But I need something to cut the reeds and something for water. Here they are, the teakettle and my jackknife."

Svnoyi and Phoenix stayed up for the whole of that twilit night syphoning water from the kettle and through the reeds, one drop at a time, into the bats' tiny throats. About midnight, their patients began to stir. By morning, the bats blinked their eyes and twitched their furry black legs. Soon they flapped membraned wings as if eager to take off into the forest that buzzed with morning insects.

"Noh ere thee doon. Ley them fley."

"Yes, we're done." Now that he had time to consider the mysterious voice that had guided him, he decided that it sounded like silver rain falling on velvet.

He lifted the spunkiest bat onto his forefinger and peered closely at the peculiar mouse-like creature's outspread wings. "Time to fly away, big fella, and take the others with you."

He smiled to himself. *If I was Lucy, the bat would've caught my every word and answered, too.*

During the night, Phoenix had had no trouble deciphering the peculiar English the silver voice had spoken. And when he turned, the same sound was also attached to a living being. The most beautiful girl he had ever seen and an entire delegation standing behind her had slipped silently from behind nearby trees.

"Goode morne, Phoenix ehe Svnoyi." She opened her arms in a greeting.

With a huge smile lighting up his entire face, he whispered to Svnoyi, "We didn't need to find the Sun People. They found us."

Copying the girl's gesture they also opened their arms, responding in unison, "Good morning, Sun People!"

28 ~ Jimjamoree

Phoenix was so utterly exhausted from his sleepless night saving the bats that he barely remembered walking through the forest and being offered a bed in someone's house. He woke up disoriented. Had he been out for hours or only five minutes?

He looked down at himself. Someone had taken off his clothes that had picked up the stink of the rotting berries and caged bats. Had he been washed, too? He certainly smelled rather scented and nice, and he felt wonderful. *But I'm stark naked. My, how embarrassing.*

His bed—silky skins of animals he couldn't identify—lay in a perfectly round room entirely made of notched branches. *It's like a log cabin, except the logs are smooth sticks a foot long and no thicker than my thumb. There must be thousands of them, layer upon layer, fitted together with notches. I bet there's insulation and another layer on the outside.*

He looked up at the deep conical space made by the pointed roof. *It's like lying flat on your back inside a clown hat lined with suede. What a funny place.* The penetrating odor of pine and tanned leather made him feel sleepy all over again.

Phoenix woke a second time hearing a silvery voice in his head. *Good noon! You've slept the whole morning away.*

He sat up abruptly. *It's the voice of the beautiful girl from the forest, only she's speaking mind-to-mind.*

He had a sudden flash of intuition. *I can understand her perfectly, now. I bet we automatically retranslate telepathic speech inside our own heads. How convenient that both of us can do it.*

He felt and could almost see her arms, slim and muscular, draping tenderly about his bare shoulders and neck, and her ash-blond hair brushing his cheek.

But no one was there.

Corlinia? This was uncanny: her name had simply popped into his head.

Yes, it's Corlinia. Phoenix, I feel your arms, and it scares me a little.

Are my arms a bad thing? I'm not doing it on purpose, and I feel yours, too. I don't mean to scare you—

No, I am not really scared. It's just that our First Circle is very strong.

Hearing her words, his heart began pounding. He wanted to find out what this Circle was because he felt it too, all over his body, not just on his arms.

Can you tell me more?

Yes, if you come out to dance the noon prayers at Jimjamoree. But learn this poem first:

God Corlaz One, lives in the Sun,

And I, inside the Tree.
I circle once, I circle twice,
And thrice, I die with thee.

Phoenix leapt up, transfixed by the sing-song ditty. *What can it mean? Is it religious, or witchcraft, or is it about making love? Or all three?*

He called out, *Where are you, Corlinia?*

I'm at Jimjamoree, outside the door of my yurtpee where you were sleeping. Phoenix, can you hear them singing? Everyone's waiting for you.

He listened, placing his ear against the tightly aligned sticks. The singers used the identical words that Corlinia had just spoken into his head, but in the Sun People's much altered tongue. The tune they sang was "Amazing Grace," unchanged through all the many centuries.

No, it can't be! It's been a million years. He laughed out loud to keep from crying because the music was loaded with family memories from the Time Before: Aleta playing the song on her violin and Sequoyah always saying the same thing. "It reminds me of the missionaries who came knocking at the front door of the Indian orphan school."

Phoenix looked for something to put on. At the foot of the fur bed a loosely woven shirt, sleeveless and square at the neck, lay on top of pants and a full-circled cape made of pale leather and covered with delicately incised patterns in red. Roman-style sandals that crisscrossed over his feet and wound around his ankles sat on the floor beside the bed. Everything fit perfectly.

He rested his forehead and palms against the slatted door before pushing it open to step out into the mysterious Jimjamoree. *Slow down a second, Phoenix,* he said to himself. *How did this happen? I'm so confused, so happy, and so crazy in love with someone I hardly know named Corlinia.*

***

On the path to the village, the cordial and undeniably handsome leader of the Sun People's delegation linked his elbow through Svnoyi's, and she felt his veins beating against her skin. After that, she glided rather than walked through a forest where great globs of morning sunlight turned every dew-covered pine into a mass of glittering diamonds. The air vibrated with birdsong and buzzing insects, and a green garter snake in no hurry curled around her ankle before wending its way through the tall grass by the path. Daisies nodded their heads in a smart good morning, lichen grew with a crinkly sound, and the hearts of the biggest trees pounded majestically, one beat per minute.

Now Svnoyi lay on his bed inside his yurtpee. Its wall of sticks surrounded her like a medieval turret, and the window slits were set high beneath a peaked ceiling.

The first thing she'd done upon entering was take off her foul-smelling clothes and wash herself in a shallow bowl of water scented with summer apples. Then she'd slipped into a woven chiton of sky-blue. When the man handed her the bowl and the gown, he turned his eyes away. But she hoped he'd taken at least a tiny peek.

She smiled to herself. *For shame, girl, what kind of thought is that?* Swaddled in the furs that covered the pallet, she pulled them up to her chin.

But Svnoyi's eyes would not close. Ever since she'd met him, she felt like she'd drunk a quart of Turkish coffee spiked with jasmine and hot red peppers. She sat up and readjusted the neck of the chiton that had fallen completely off her shoulders—even though her other, more lustful self suggested that she leave half her bosom bare.

She called to him across the round room where he'd turned his back, most likely to let her sleep. *Corlion, I'm not tired at all—*

She broke off in surprise. Why was she speaking mind-to-mind with this stranger, and how did she happen to know his name? He walked the few steps to her bed and knelt beside her on one knee. It seemed to her that she might fall into his deep blue eyes if she let her own eyes meet his: she couldn't bear his radiant proximity and turned her head away—but not before noticing that he had quite adorable dimples on both cheeks.

How can I explain it, Corlion? She found herself speaking telepathically again without intending to. *I'm feeling—what's the best word? Crazy. No, that's not quite right. I'm noticing too many things. On the path, I heard heartbeats inside the biggest trees. And being near you is torture—*

She stopped mid-sentence, bowing her head to hide her red face. *I'm sorry, I didn't mean to say "torture," and it's not the right word, either. It's more like ... having butterflies swarm all over me, inside and out, madly flapping hot red-orange wings.* She took his hand even though it made her own hand burn. *I'm always too frank, and it gets me into trouble with my family and everyone else.*

Don't worry, Svnoyi, there's an explanation. It's a gift from Corlaz One because it doesn't happen often, for many people, not at all.

You saw the forest as intensely as I do every day because it's a holy place to me. As to the other, you're feeling the heat of my flesh because I'm feeling the heat of yours.

I didn't mean for this to happen, but when we linked arms, we made a First Circle, called Awakening.

Svnoyi looked perplexed. *A what? An Awakening? You mean we're falling in love?*

Yes, that's one way to describe it, but it's much more complicated. We're starting to make the bond that's only broken by the death of one of us. Since Corlaz One would like us to make absolutely sure of our love, we have two more Circles to go, Truth and Exultation. Truth's the hardest. If we get through all the Circles, we wait one year exactly before we marry in a sacred place we choose together.

Svnoyi tried to concentrate on Corlion's every word, although she was distracted by the grave look on his face.

But Corlion, you don't seem happy about it—

Oh, I am. It's just that it happened so suddenly and for us Sun People, it's the moment that signals the beginning of true adulthood.

It's sudden for me, too, Corlion, so unlike the way I was brought up. A minute ago, I had no idea what Circles were. But my whole being cries out, this is right for me. Finding true commitment is what I've been yearning for.

She smiled at him encouragingly, as much to reassure herself that she was ready for such a momentous leap. As down-to-earth as she usually was, she could barely comprehend stepping off a smelly cart on the Polar Bear Express yesterday evening to find herself less than a day later with the man she'd most likely marry.

Svnoyi, it's time to get ready for Jimjamoree's noontime prayers and dancing. You and Phoenix are being honored for saving the stolen bats and bringing them back to our forest where no bats have lived for thousands of years.

But do you think I'll be welcome—

Of course, you and Phoenix are heroes. And you'll meet my sister Corlinia who talked you through saving the bats. She's amazing, my opposite in personality.

All you have to do is learn the words to our Jimjamoree song. The tune's easy, and you'll pick it up right away as soon as you hear the whole village singing it:

God Corlaz One, lives in the Sun,
And I, inside the Tree.
I circle once, I circle twice,
And thrice, I die with thee.

Svnoyi laughed aloud. *The poem's lovely, and it makes me so happy. It's about everyone living in the forest, dancing at Jimjamoree, and how you can make the Three Circles. It sounds very religious, and I don't mean to be crude, but the last line is really suggestive.*

She peered down the length of her body. *I can't walk outside in this. It's too sheer—*

It is sheer, and it's what we wear every day.

But you won't be wearing it this noon. I have a special-occasion dress for you to match the honor you're receiving. It belonged to my mother who died last year. We pass down our ceremonial clothing through the generations. Reverently, Corlion handed her a sleeveless gown, square at the neck and made of a pale, supple leather.

Corlion, I'm touched, but I can't wear this. It's too precious.

Would I offer it to someone I didn't love and who wouldn't appreciate its meaning?

Corlion averted his eyes once again to give her privacy, and she dropped it over her head. The strange garment that was covered with delicately incised patterns in red fell in voluminous folds about her body. After she'd tied a red leather sash around her waist, it fit her tall, willowy frame perfectly. To finish, she slid on Roman-style sandals with long leather laces that she wound and knotted about her ankles to hold them tight.

Svnoyi wished she had a mirror to see herself, but then she felt Corlion's admiring gaze drilling through the clothes. It was the look she'd craved ever since arriving at the yurtpee, but once he'd given it, her face burned with embarrassment.

Abruptly, she walked across the room and changed the subject. Fingering the tassels at the end of her sash, she asked, *If I'm not being too inquisitive, how did your mother die?*

She conceived a child much too late in life—at forty-four. None of us expected her to survive, and she didn't. Nor did the baby. His answer was curt, and Svnoyi could tell she'd hit upon one of the Sun People's too-familiar griefs: a wife's death bearing children.

Svnoyi asked gently, *And your father? Is he still living?*

No, he died of a broken heart. It's common; a lot of us do.

As Svnoyi was contemplating this thoroughly romantic ending to a spouse's life, Corlion quickly changed out of his blue chiton and into a leather cape and pants in the same pale shade. The cape was decorated far more ornately than her dress in swirling patterns fashioned from feathers and beads that resembled new fern fronds.

When she complimented his transformation, he scrunched up his face. *This is my Mayor and High Priest's costume, and it's uncomfortable. I have to put it on for every Jimjamoree, three times a day.*

You're Mayor and High Priest of this village? I'm honored to know you, Corlion. Half in fun, she made a curtsy, holding out the sides of her ceremonial dress with thumb and forefinger.

Please don't, Svnoyi, you overestimate me. It's a job no one wants because it takes too much responsibility. I didn't want it either, but I had to take it when no one else stepped up.

She hoped he wasn't hearing her next thought. *Thank goodness for the Circles because we have a lot to learn about each other. I'd gladly forgo being a priest, but I'd sure jump at the chance to be a mayor.*

***

Svnoyi stood at the edge of the Jimjamoree space that reminded her of a circular serving platter, gigantic in size. She gasped in surprise: a thin covering of pine needles had been carefully raked to form geometric designs, the vivid green contrasting with the bare earth. When she stood on tiptoe and squinted to take in the whole, she saw many identical circles about five feet across covering the entire floor. Each large circle had three smaller circles inside it with all the sides touching.

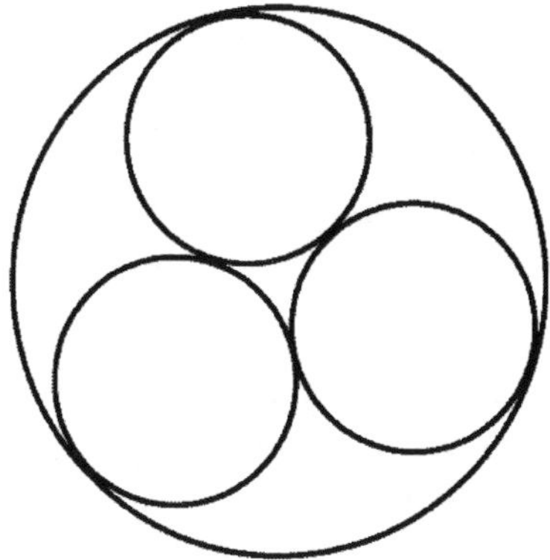

The villagers exited the yurtpees that surrounded the arena, the many front doors closing in a ragged tattoo of clicks and smacks. They gathered around the edge, not standing too close to their Mayor-Priest and the strange new girl at his side with the dark skin and the long black hair.

Others came from the forest carrying fresh game over their shoulders and flat bowls filled with berries, sweet potatoes, and wild onions that sent a fine aroma into the air. Graceful and slender, the entire population was as pale as Corlion with the same ash-blond hair. However, in a crowd of about five hundred people, Svnoyi saw very few elderly folk and not more than twenty-five children. She stored that information away for later to ask Corlion about it.

At once a cascade of events overwhelmed her senses. Someone must have given a cue because the entire gathering began to sing in a roaring unison with occasional bursts of harmony the words she'd memorized to the Jimjamoree song, although she could barely understand them in the tongue of the modern-day Sun People. The tune was "Amazing Grace."

Svnoyi had always loved that tune. Startled and trembling from the beauty of the moment, she opened her mouth to join in. But her first notes were interrupted by the sight of Phoenix hurtling from one of the yurtpees and falling into the arms of the strikingly beautiful girl from the forest.

Corlion began laughing, a sound that tickled deliciously inside her head. He sought her hand. *Oh, Svnoyi, that's my excitable little sister, Corlinia. She and Phoenix seem to have made their First Circle. And he's wearing our deceased father's pants and cape.*

He gave her hand a squeeze. *Hurry, dear, let's move to the center where I'm presenting you two.*

Corlion, I really don't want to unless I can fly. I'll mess up the beautiful circles.

You're supposed to. When we dance, the Mixing of the Needles symbolizes our unity with the Forest and the Making of the Circles. Only when the needles are evenly distributed at the end of the ceremony will Corlaz One smile down from his golden throne inside the sun.

They linked elbows, the same gesture that had lit her on fire before, and he led her to the center. *Don't worry, the children replace the needles and rake them before every morning, noon, and evening prayer meeting. It's a coveted job and more fun than most others.*

Corlinia pulled Phoenix to the center, and he, too, reluctantly tiptoed across the patterns in the needles. The couple looked radiant in ceremonial dress in the same light leather and cut that she and Corlion were wearing. Svnoyi could hardly stop staring at them and considered sending Phoenix a quick message.

She thought better of the idea and kept it to herself. *Phoenix, my dear friend, you look so much in love. To think that both of us were swept off our feet at the same time. It's nothing short of miraculous.*

Svnoyi wasn't surprised that she could hardly understand Corlion's words when he spoke aloud to the villagers in a lilting tenor, although she did catch her name during the introductions and nodded her head toward the assembly. The speech he gave next must've struck a chord with them because they applauded, stomping and waving, for a good five minutes. Corlion closed with a prayer that sounded vaguely familiar, although she couldn't quite put her finger on it.

Ery dya Iche tuss thee, Mader Eart,
but Iche shale nanon keppe thee,
ehe Iche shale nanon noyinly haert thee.

And soon the crowd began tearing about the Jimjamoree circle to "Amazing Grace," performed by the best musicians in the village—a choir joined by percussion and reed flutes. Nothing could surprise Svnoyi anymore: the sea of whirling dancers in their sky-blue chitons were doing familiar waltz steps from the Time Before in many configurations from solo to long, snaking lines. When she saw Corlinia, her ash-blond hair flying, rush past in a blur of exuberance hugging Phoenix, Svnoyi's head grew dizzy from euphoria and all the whirling.

She asked Corlion, *Oh, my darling, does everyone here live a life of complete happiness?*

But as suddenly as the dancers had started up, they stopped, their ecstasy vanquished by exhaustion. Most of them shuffled to the side of the circle panting, although Svnoyi noticed Phoenix and Corlinia, in apparent good health, heading for the forest, holding hands and laughing.

But Corlion was out of breath and paler than before. *Svnoyi, sadly you have the answer to your question, which is no, complete happiness is not ours. We have weak lungs and many other worries. We die young. We don't make babies easily, and many mothers die from the pregnancy. If the newborns survive, they're often sickly.*

Svnoyi nodded, her eyes drooping. Her question about the villagers' strange demographic had been answered. It flashed through her mind that Sun Women committing to the Three Circles would also have to consider the hazards of childbearing.

After you've seen how unwell we are, do you still want to start the Second Circle with me? I'll understand if you don't.

Ever frank, Svnoyi shot back, *Of course I want to, Corlion. It'll take more than that to get this very stubborn girl to change her mind.*

29 ~ Bitter Truths

While Corlion was thanking the singers and instrumentalists, Svnoyi joined a line of villagers waiting to pick up their share of the communal meal: game that had been roasting on spits during the ceremony. On each plate was a sliver of venison accompanied by two dime-sized sweet potatoes and a handful of berries, portions that would hardly have satisfied her little half niece, Arielle Luz.

As they carried their lunch back to the yurtpee, Svnoyi came to a painful realization. *Everyone's so thin. It's possible that they're slowly starving.*

After the pair had wolfed down the tiny meal, Corlion returned the plates to the commissary. Svnoyi changed out of the special-occasion ceremonial dress into the long blue chiton that she cinched at the waist with a rawhide braid. Corlion, too, changed back into his own clothes. The pair sat together on the bed of furs, leaning their shoulders against the yurtpee's uncomfortable log walls.

Both of them felt unprepared to start the Second Circle's search for Truth. Svnoyi had no idea what would be required of her, although she was almost certain she'd have to explain the dreaded Oath of Fealty that had been eating away at her peace of mind ever since she and Phoenix had arrived. For the briefest of moments, she regretted entangling herself in a sudden love match with a man she hardly knew.

Corlion wasn't sure how to begin either, and he took her hand, hoping their touch would reduce the tension. *Svnoyi, the Second Circle is usually easy. The two people who love each other discuss their future life together. They agree on details such as who cleans the yurtpee or who goes hunting. We have to find out so much more about each other because we haven't grown up together.*

He stopped abruptly. *I'm sorry, no more fooling around. I have to ask you something because it's been preying on my mind ever since I met you. Did the Prairie Dog queen send you? She's our enemy, and now that I know you a little, I don't understand how you would agree to be her ambassador. Not Phoenix, either.*

We are *her ambassadors.*

Svnoyi tried to exonerate herself. *Corlion, it's a dilemma. As long as the queen holds my Daddy Sequoyah hostage, we don't argue with her.*

I am very *familiar with who your father is, Svnoyi, because he figures in Goddess Mary Lynne's prophecy that's meaningful to our people, too.*

Svnoyi let go of his hand and pulled away a few inches. *You* do *know about him? Then you must realize that one misstep—*

Of course I realize. But I have to protect my people. You must've heard the queen's opinions. What does she say about us?

Svnoyi started in, hating her own words. *The queen's upset because you steal the farms' vegetables and apples. And she was furious when you ruined the Sacred Meadow.* Svnoyi concluded unhappily, *This was the last thing the queen said: she thinks you are barbarians.*

Corlion jumped up, pacing in circles. *I appreciate your honesty, Svnoyi. It must have been hard to be so truthful.* He stopped and drilled his eyes into hers. *So tell me,* exactly. *What is the mission the queen assigned you to do?*

Svnoyi was sure his first glimmer of love for her would vanish in an instant as soon as she told him. She hesitated, her eyes lowered, and then burst out with a diversion. *If I didn't know you already and love you, Corlion, I'd have no trouble telling you what she wants. And at first, Phoenix and I didn't believe her, we've gotten so used to her ridiculous ideas and mannerisms. Whenever we look at her, we can hardly keep from laughing—*

Glowering, Corlion cut her short. *The mission she's assigned is so bad, then, that you have to fool around, playing for time? Then let me* guess *what it is.*

She sprang to her feet, stretching out her arms in supplication. *No, don't guess, Corlion, please. I have the courage to tell you, I really do. But don't be hard on me.*

She took a deep breath. *The queen wants all the Sun People to swear the Oath of Fealty. It would be a feudal kind of thing: you would give up your forests and swear to serve her in exchange for—*

Don't tell me. In exchange for keeping us from starving.

Svnoyi nodded in silence.

And if we refuse?

Oh, Corlion, the queen's been gathering up a huge army and training them.

After the initial revelation, her words tumbled out. *Hundreds of the teenage pups have stopped working at the farms and in the Shade People's caverns to camp near Iqual, the capital city. In a day or two they'll start practicing at the Sacred Meadow, aiming their* azvrkts *at trees. My half brother Kuaray and the queen's husband Saint George will be their teachers. Captain Kirk, another of the queen's husbands and her priest, will tell them to forget the commandment that forbids killing humans.*

And how does she plan to use this army? Corlion sounded grim.

My friend Lucy says they're beginners now, but as soon as they are trained, the queen is planning to invade your villages before winter sets in, not one at a time, but in a coordinated attack. Oh, Corlion, I wasn't supposed to reveal any *of this, but of course I had to.*

Corlion took both her hands, his face drawn. From his lithe, muscular build and youthful features she had guessed that he must be about twenty, but at this moment, he looked ten years older. *You may find this hard to believe, dear, but when we get very hungry during the darkest days of mid-winter and some of our precious babies die, I've sometimes considered giving in to the queen. This isn't the first time she's asked, but it's the first time she's putting an army together.*

Svnoyi agreed, miserably. *My father did something similar, and it was a little bit like making a pact with the devil. We had trouble when we first got here. Even before winter, the queen started giving us dressed rabbits every day, and she showed us the best way to plant our fields in the poor soil. And since then, the queen has pretty much had us in her clutches.*

Corlion put an arm on Svnoyi's shoulder to direct her toward the door. *I'm desperate for a walk in the forest right now. But when you see it, you'll understand* exactly *why we steal from the Prairie Dogs' farms.*

This evening after Jimjamoree I will discuss the Oath with the council, and then we'll spread the news to the other seven villages. I think I know already what will happen. They'll surely reject its demands unanimously, even though the consequences will be disastrous for us.

He added with an attempt at a smile, *You are a messenger bearing very bad news, Svnoyi. I don't believe any couples have ever done a more difficult Second Circle than this one. And we've barely started.*

***

As soon as Svnoyi found herself out-of-doors standing among the trees, she felt the same overwhelming joy as before when she'd linked elbows with Corlion. He stopped beside a gnarled pine, sparsely grey-green with half its branches bare and a trunk burled with age. Once they'd sat beneath its boughs, blotches of afternoon sunlight filtered through and fell onto Svnoyi's bare arms. The patterns made her think of randomly bestowed kisses, and the hot red-orange butterflies came back, swarming all over her body.

One part of her mind said, *I have sex on the brain when I'm near him.* The other part that he was meant to hear, said, *Corlion, why did you choose this sad old tree when there are so many beautiful young ones everywhere else?*

Corlion laughed, that same sound that had tickled the inside of her head at Jimjamoree. She also noticed that the enticing dimples seemed to reappear whenever he relaxed.

I heard both your thoughts, Svnoyi. We're joined like we were this morning, and we're feeling it together. He buried his face into her copious black hair that she'd released from the braid earlier for dancing and spoke into her neck: *Sex on the brain, I love that.*

And I'm attached to this old tree maybe more than all the others because it has seen everything. Trees store memories in their rings. They add to their private diaries every year even as their old hearts slow down.

Soon he pulled away. *But I regret that I have to tell you some serious things, now.*

The dimples had vanished. He asked Svnoyi, *Did you know that we've named ourselves after the pippin, the green apple that grows at the Prairie Dogs' farms? The other villages have taken surnames in the same way: the Zucchinis and the Chards live closest to us. The folk in the furthest village call themselves the Cauliflowers. In between the first three villages and the last village are the Butterheads, the Cucumbers, the Cantaloupes, and the Idahos.*

Svnoyi smiled. *I think it's cute, Corlion Pippin, and I'm guessing your first names are all derived from Corlaz's. Some of you must have names with endless syllables to keep them different, like Corlabibiwobi.*

I don't care for you making fun of us, Corlion bristled. *You're right about our first names, and we've had to resort to sticking numbers at the ends. But you're dead wrong about our village surnames. They're not meant to be cute. They're defiant.*

He clenched his jaw, and his fists pummeled the air. *Yes, the Sun People steal apples and other vegetables from the farms. And we in our own village are* proud *to call ourselves Pippins. We steal from the queen and her subjects because we're furious. Call it retribution!*

Svnoyi had never seen him angry. She answered simply, *I'm sorry, I didn't mean to offend. What do they take from you?*

I'm sorry, too, I overreacted. It's just a terrible situation that's left us half starving, as you may have noticed from that tiny lunch. He pulled her to her feet. *Come along, I'll show you.*

They wound their way in and out among the pines where jagged holes scarred the forest floor. Corlion explained, *The Prairie Dog workers from the farms forage here, digging up our sweet potatoes, wild carrots, and onions when we're at Jimjamoree, or even in the middle of the night. They strip our blackberry bushes. They pick our mushrooms, and they even take away the mycelium to make glue for the Shade People's furniture. They trap our forest animals in a way that breaks their legs most painfully. And they take huge numbers of fish from our lakes and rivers with nets.*

And that's just the beginning, Svnoyi. It gets so much worse. As soon as they had scaled the crest of the next hill, the smell of burning wood came from somewhere close by. And in the valley directly below them, the forest had been cleared.

They climbed down, shielding their eyes from the harsh sunlight where no branches were left to block it. *This is a combined funeral and crime scene,* flashed through Svnoyi's mind. Because here were the stumps, bleeding sap: the pines had been cut down only the night before. Corlion knelt, and Svnoyi dropped to her knees beside him.

He caressed the weeping wood. *Touch the stump, Svnoyi. You can feel its tears on your fingers. The Prairie Dogs are doing this every day to expand their fields, and please pardon me. Seeing the new stumps is always more than I can bear.* He covered his streaming eyes with both hands.

They returned to the top of the hill, and when they rounded the bend, Corlion clucked his tongue in disgust. *Look at this mess.* He gestured toward a meadow reduced to brown clods with only stubble remaining. *Yesterday there were millions of wild daisies growing here in the thick grass. Guess what, the Prairie Dogs release their giant breeding rabbits with fur sticking out all over their rumps to graze here. They munch everything in sight, chewing the stems down to the ground. They eat the tree saplings, and they demolish our wild strawberries. Our native rabbits have been gone for years.*

Svnoyi hardly dared to question Corlion for fear of setting off a renewed burst of anger. She asked timidly, *Who's eating all the extra food the Prairie Dogs are growing in their expanded fields or stealing from the forest? I thought the Shade People were ready to expire and the Prairie Dogs ate only greens—*

The Shade People eat plenty, even though they're in love with the idea of death.

Corlion seemed more amused by her question than upset, although his eyes didn't smile along with his lips.

But it's the Prairie Dogs, themselves. They've developed exotic tastes in food, and now they're omnivores. Their birthrate has shot up. Especially in the spring, you see pups everywhere, chasing their own tails and rolling about all over the fields and even in our forest meadows.

But Svnoyi, haven't you noticed? Those waistlines have bulged. Take a closer look at the adults, dear, next time you're home: their middles are easily fifty inches around!

***

Svnoyi took advantage of Corlion's lighter mood because she, too, was on a quest for Truth. His outbursts had neither surprised nor frightened her, although she didn't want to enrage him further. *I love him, but he's a volatile man who's been pushed to the limit, and who can blame him? And I sure hope he's not reading my mind right now.*

Corlion, you must have a favorite outdoor spot you go to when you want to get away. I have a question, too, that I believe will bring the Second Circle to a close. But I would like us both to feel at ease when I ask it.

Your question is about the Sacred Meadow, isn't it, Svnoyi? Corlion frowned, his good humor gone. *Yes, every time I remember how badly* that *worked out, it drives me half crazy. But I* do *have to tell it.*

He stood up, extending his hand. *Let's climb higher. I know a tiny gem of a lake that's so pretty I've kept it secret ever since I found it back when I was a little boy.*

Corlion led the way up a rocky path, overgrown with thorn bushes. Svnoyi followed him, watching out for her exposed toes, vulnerable in the Jimjamoree sandals. Every step revived memories from her young life in the high mountains of old Czechoslovakia, and each new wonder made her feel a piercing nostalgia. The breezes that moved the branches whispered love poems in iambic pentameter, and fat bees of humble demeanor hovered to praise the pollen in the middle of their chosen flowers. Ants stumbled in their vertical climb up a tree-trunk, too drunk on sticky sap to do their work. On the very same tree, a red-headed woodpecker broadcast for all to hear, "Ratatat, I claim this pine, ratatat, this house is mine."

Just then, Corlion stopped abruptly to lean his head against a granite boulder by the path. He gasped out a few sentences between rattly intakes of air. *Give me a moment ... I have to rest .... It's my lungs.*

Svnoyi waited for him to recover, caressing his shoulder in sympathy. She couldn't help but reflect on the innate tragedy of it all. The war that had happened a million years ago had dealt a cruel and lasting blow, making these folk who loved the heights too sickly to climb longer than five minutes at a time.

After Corlion had taken a half dozen more breaks, each longer than the one before, he and Svnoyi arrived at the lake. They scrambled over the last ridge, and below them lay his gem, snow-fed, and the hue of lapis lazuli. To reach the shore, together they lifted curtains of old-growth branches that hung down, blocking their path.

As Svnoyi slid beneath a particularly low-slung bough, she remarked half in fun, *Corlion, I'm not sure the lake wants us to finish our Circles.*

He replied in all seriousness, *Svnoyi, dear, if there's one thing I've learned about nature, it is sublimely indifferent to our petty desires ... that is, until we wound it.*

30 ~ The Three Circles

Five minutes later, Svnoyi and Corlion reached the glacial sand at the water's edge. They slid off their sandals and flopped down on it, sifting the grains with their fingers. The gentle lapping of the wavelets and the afternoon sun beating down made them indolent and heavy-limbed. They reclined close together, Corlion leaning against the trunk of a sugar pine. Svnoyi sat in front of him, letting her shoulders and back rest against his chest, and he held her in the circle of one arm while gently stroking her waist-length hair with his free hand. Every once in a while, she brushed her fingers lightly over his thighs. He did the same to her, which brought the red-orange butterflies swarming over her skin and flapping in the pit of her stomach.

Eventually, with an effort she broke mind and body free to ask the troublesome question. *Corlion, what about the Sacred Meadow? This is what the queen told us. One night people from several villages ripped out the pipes that fed the fountain and artificial rivers. They cut down most of the pine trees and trampled the meadow grass and flowers to a pulp.*

She felt him pull away a few inches, but she went on anyway, *The queen said you did it because you despise the Prairie Dogs' many gods.* She twisted her head around to look at his face. *A few days before we left, Phoenix and I took a quick peek. I have to say, it's a wreck.*

Corlion answered stiffly, *How many gods they believe in makes no difference to us. One god or five or six, who cares?*

His tone softened as he introduced Svnoyi to a topic dear to his own heart. *Do you know the mythology?* When she nodded, his voice grew animated. *Both our religions came from the same place, the holy Eye of Cinder. We, the Sun People, worship Corlaz One alone, but we've always liked gentle Corlaz Two, Corlaz One's son. He could talk silently to the Prairie Dogs, and it's his gift that allows a very few of us in each generation to speak telepathically.*

And you're in luck. He gave Svnoyi's shoulder a little squeeze. *The "few" are Corlinia and me, and eleven others from all of the eight villages—which means you and I can understand each other until we learn to speak our languages aloud.*

Goddess Mary Lynne's another one we like. We don't know why she came up with those awful commandments, but we always believed in her prophesy about the giant's arrival—

Svnoyi gave him a gentle tap on his knee. *You're getting off the subject. What about the Sacred Meadow, Corlion? Don't forget, that's why we came here.*

He nodded. *You're right. I wish I could forget, but I can't.*

He deserted his comfortable spot against the pine tree and turned around to face Svnoyi, as if preparing for battle. She could detect anger behind his words. *The Pippin council got together with the councils of the Zucchinis and the Chards, and we talked all night. We came up with a demonstration we were sure even the queen couldn't miss when she saw her own religious shrine all torn up.*

So we did it. He shrugged, opening his hands. *But obviously she didn't get the point.*

Svnoyi pursed her lips, frowning. *Corlion, it was a seriously dumb plan because now she's using it as propaganda against you. But beyond that, I must be as dim as the queen. I don't get the point, either.*

Really? He looked surprised and disappointed. *It's quite simple. The Forest is as important to us as the Sacred Meadow is to the Prairie Dogs. And we can no longer tolerate its destruction. We were trying to show her that.*

Corlion rose to his knees, his hands clasped over his heart, his eyes closed. The words he spoke next were so beautiful that Svnoyi wished she could memorize them as they tumbled out. His animated features lit up brighter with each phrase, reminding her of the sun at daybreak.

We love the Forest. We worship the Forest. It is our holy temple where our graves have always been and will be, where our children speak their first words and learn to walk. It is mother and father; it feeds us and instructs us. Whenever Corlaz One blesses the Forest with the bounty of his sunlight, we fall to our knees in wonder to kiss the Forest floor.

The Three Circles, what are they? They are Awakening, Truth, *and* Exultation—*because everyone who dwells in the Forest relives the Three Circles each day.*

In the morning, Sun shows himself, and we awaken to the dawn-chorus of birds that thrill to the day's promise. And we promise to make the most of the day.

At noon, bright Sun beats down, revealing the harsh truth of every hidden nook. We seek our own truth by sweeping out the dark corners of our souls.

In the evening, Sun sinks low, the flowers close their petals, and the heartbeats of the trees slow. We celebrate the day's passing, remembering that each one brings us closer to the long nights of winter. We exult in each other's arms. We praise Corlaz One, who will soon wake the birds to bring us a new day or a new springtime.

If the Forest dies, the Sun People will also die, each one of us becoming a mere pinprick of light that flares and fades on the vast bosom of Sun.

His burst of inspiration completed, Corlion's eyes flew open. For the first time, Svnoyi noticed that they were the color of lapis lazuli with tiny gold flecks, and that they matched the blue of the lake. Impossibly, they appeared to be illuminated from inside his head. Sensing that he had more to say, she grasped his hands tightly, hardly daring to breathe.

Svnoyi, Beautiful Daughter of the Forest, I've been waiting so long to tell you this. Here's the prayer we've always recited three times a day at Jimjamoree. You heard it this noon but didn't catch the words because we chanted them out loud. But you know them already.

Every day I touch you, Mother Earth,
but I shall never own you,
and I shall never knowingly hurt you.

Svnoyi turned pale, and the almost tearless girl began weeping crystalline drops that sparkled on her cheeks. *Corlion, this is some kind of witchcraft. Those were my Daddy Sequoyah's words, almost exactly the same, when we first got here. We left the Greyhound bus and he fell down on his knees, scooping up the earth in his hands.*

Yes, I know. Some of us were there, hiding deep in the shadows of the trees. We heard his words, too, and we were amazed by the coincidence. When the time of Goddess Mary Lynne's prophesy came close, we were so excited. I'd been praying nonstop to Corlaz One that soon Sequoyah would arrive to save us.

How can I explain the way we saw the miracle? A flash of light blinded us, and when our eyes worked again, a great shining boat with running creatures on both sides and covered with a thin layer of melting ice stood in a gap between the trees. At first, we were terrified because it just sat there. Then the door opened, and Sequoyah stepped out. He wasn't as tall as we'd expected he'd be from Goddess Mary Lynne's prophesy. We realized then and there that he was human. That made us love him more.

Corlion's ecstasy ended as suddenly as it had begun. He dropped Svnoyi's hands and slumped down on the sand, sighing like a punctured balloon. *Oh, Svnoyi, our greatest grief is that now Sequoyah is locked up somewhere inside the Eye of Cinder, and he's too ill to save us in our time of need.*

Shocked by his abject change of mood, Svnoyi jumped up. *I should know as well as you where he is, Corlion. He's my father.*

Her testiness surprised her, and she realized she was lecturing him. But she went on. *Did you ever hear the saying, "Don't put all your eggs in one basket?" Wake up, Corlion! The war is almost here. Right now relying on a savior who might not show up is a very risky plan. In fact, it's no plan at all.*

He didn't respond.

She knelt beside him and shook his shoulder. *Corlion, look at me.*

She threw her arms around him as she would with a child. She pinched his chin between her fingers and tried to turn his face. *Okay,* don't *look at me, but do listen. You seem to have forgotten that this ritual is supposed to be about you and me together, not just you alone.*

She stood up and stamped her foot, hands on her hips. In fact, she was furious and considered marching back down the trail on her own. *Where do I fit in, Corlion? I thought I was supposed to stand by your side. Instead, I have to watch you give up, all sunk in misery.*

Corlion stood then, snapping his whole body upright. *Svnoyi, I'm so sorry. Please forgive me. I-I forgot myself, and you are right. I'm too used to being alone with my own endlessly captivating worries. From now on, I'll try sharing them. But it'll be a big change for me.*

He tried to embrace her, but she wriggled free and began scrabbling around in the underbrush beneath the trees. She emerged a few seconds later with a quite ordinary stick.

With it, she drew a huge circle across the entire width of the sand and inscribed three circles within it, all their sides touching—exactly like the raked pine needles on the Jimjamoree floor. She turned to Corlion, whose eyes widened with surprise.

I'm hardly the one to teach a priest about the Circles, but I'm going to. Her brazenness did not seem to offend Corlion, and she had most certainly captured his attention.

This is what I thought the Circles were supposed to do for us, a new couple in love. The First Circle, Awakening, would be about mutual attraction. The Second Circle, Truth, would be about talking things over to see if you and I should be together at all. And the Third Circle, Exultation, would be about how much we love each other and about sex, the consummation. It's kind of sweet, actually, and very simple—except we've gotten totally bogged down on Truth. I hope Phoenix and your sister are pulling this off a whole lot more smoothly than we are.

Svnoyi stepped into one of the circles she'd drawn and stretched her arms toward Corlion. *Stand with me in this circle. I'm calling it the First Circle. Put your arms around me—no, much, much tighter. Now tell me what you feel.*

Corlion stuttered, *Thi-this is too hard.* He felt Svnoyi turn away from him. *No wait,* he said in a hurry. *It's not that difficult. I-I feel ... aroused. Yes, it's kind of a torture, like you said. I've felt like this all day.*

They stepped into the Second Circle. *And?* Svnoyi asked. *You must feel something that's not just about your body.*

I feel-I feel like I want to share my whole life with you. Yes, I want to tell you things I don't even know yet about myself.

They stepped into the Third Circle. *Hmm,* said Svnoyi. *And what else? Are you happy right now?*

By Corlaz One, how can I begin to tell you how happy I am?

He closed his eyes and began swaying like a sailboat on a windy day, and Svnoyi rocked with him. *I love you, I worship you, you are my temple where I am overcome with passion and also where I rest. You are shafts of bright sunlight, and you are the subtle glow of a new moon. You are the eyes of the Forest that see dawn climb across the mountain crest. If you die before I do, the part of me that has become you dies too.*

Svnoyi and Corlion stepped into the First Circle for her vows. After she'd inspired such extraordinary and heartfelt eloquence from him, she found herself tongue-tied, her heart beating much too fast.

Eventually, she managed an awkward response: *Hot red-orange butterflies keep crawling all over me.*

They stepped into the Second Circle. *Oh, no, my mind's a blank. Wait, this is what I've been thinking. You and I will make children who can breathe deep, and maybe five hundred years from now our descendants will be running up mountains. And I want to help you lead.*

They stepped into the Third Circle, and time passed. Eventually Svnoyi groaned, *Dammit, this is impossible! I'm failing, I'm not poetic at all.*

She sank down in the middle of the Circle, weeping her crystalline tears for the second time that day, and Corlion knelt beside her, tentatively patting her shoulder. He had no idea how to handle her outburst.

When she finally did speak, she was laughing at herself for crying and bungling her vows—and also from joy. The sound reverberated in his head like the great gong that was used at Jimjamoree for special occasions.

I'd intended for us to go round and round the three circles exchanging vows at least ten times. I wanted to show you how love never stops renewing itself, and how the three circles blend together. But after hearing your words, my words wouldn't come—

No, wait, Svnoyi, your words were perfect. I liked the part about the children best and about running up mountains. And I certainly need help leading the village. We'll do it together. You have no idea how hard it is for me to make decisions.

Svnoyi bent her head in thought. Then she added, *We're going to make a fine pair, you and me, and we're lucky to be so different. You'll supply the poetry and I'll bring the clarity.*

Oh, no! A sudden truth struck her. She tried to bury the notion deep down inside herself so Corlion wouldn't hear it. *I've chosen a man who's just like my daddy; they don't look at all alike, but my future husband is an idealist, a poet, a dreamer, impractical, self-absorbed, a ditherer.*

On the other hand, Corlion's chosen pushy, know-it-all me, and a little humility now and again wouldn't hurt—

Svnoyi, why are you smiling like that?

Well, I'm smiling because ... because all I really wanted to say is how much I love you. Will that do for my Third Circle vow?

She began speaking aloud, and he had no trouble understanding her. "Let's find a beautiful young pine tree with low sweeping branches. Then we'll take off our clothes and spread them out like a blanket."

"Yea! Wheh lehe in whehen armen be-net thene tree fora longe, longe the-me."

31 ~ Dragon Rider

Ever since that evening a week ago when Corlion and Svnoyi had returned home from the lake, their shining eyes had revealed to everyone the truth without any need to explain. The couple was starting the prenuptial interval known officially as Corlaz One's Trial Marriage Year, in everyday speech, the Yes-or-No. The sight of them doing everything together, including Svnoyi helping Corlion run the village, surprised no one. Nor did it surprise them to see Phoenix accompanying the archer Corlinia on the morning hunt. They were also starting their Yes-or-No and would leave hand-in-hand after Jimjamoree, carrying bows and arrows in leather pouches slung over their shoulders.

Svnoyi loved Jimjamoree. She wondered how she'd managed to live sixteen years without it, especially when she whirled in Corlion's arms to the addictive waltz that she still called "Amazing Grace," even though the true title was "In the Sun." But on the seventh noon, she noticed from the corner of her eye disruptive arm-waving at the edge of the Jimjamoree circle. Two hunters were standing there, doing their best to capture everyone's attention. The singers fell silent and all movement ceased. Svnoyi peered through the mass of dancers, and yes, the hunters were Phoenix and Corlinia.

The Mayor and his new assistant made their way through the suddenly anxious, murmuring crowd. Corlion sent a message to Svnoyi, *I was wondering why the foragers brought the baskets of berries and yams for lunch, but the hunters didn't show up with the game. Something's definitely gone wrong. I can feel it.*

"What is it, Phoenix?" she asked, once she had freed herself from the crowd and was out of earshot.

Phoenix looked more amused than worried. "Holy Mother of Corlaz One, Svnoyi, Kuaray arrived a half hour ago on Petey's back. The other hunters are holding him at arrow-point out by the Prairie Dogs' fields. They say he must be a devil because of the dragon he's riding, and I did my best to explain."

Svnoyi smiled behind her hand at the scene Phoenix described. Then she spoke to Corlion who had raised both eyebrows inquiringly. *My half brother Kuaray is here. His steed is ugly, but it's perfectly nice and not a dragon. Kuaray needs to stay on it all the time because he can't walk.*

Corlion asked suspiciously, *Wasn't Kuaray the one teaching the Prairie Dog pups how to shoot?*

He was. But obviously he isn't anymore. Let Phoenix and me talk to him first because we certainly had no idea he was coming. Then you can translate for me when I explain at tonight's council meeting why he made the trip here.

When Corlion nodded in agreement, she took his hand and gestured to Phoenix and Corlinia. *Okay, let's go save him.*

***

As Svnoyi and Phoenix escorted Kuaray through the forest, her pulse quickened in anticipation. She knew that Kuaray would never have endangered life and what was left of his limbs to come if something urgent weren't happening at home.

"Hey," said Kuaray, "Let's stop here. I kinda like this pine tree, all twisted and half dead."

Svnoyi laughed. "Amazing, you've picked one of my favorites. I like it because it makes people thoughtful."

The three of them settled down under Svnoyi's "Tree of Wisdom." She'd loved it ever since Corlion had explained how intimate tree rings were, akin to the diary she'd always meant to keep.

Kuaray slid off Petey and removed the reins from the faithful beast's torso segmented by the multiple pairs of legs. To thank him, Petey put his head into Kuaray's lap, staring into his master's face with adoring eyes. Remarkably, after years of enduring Kuaray's special brand of family terrorism, Svnoyi and Phoenix felt comfortable in his presence, and none of them cared to revisit the traumas of the recent past. Even the centipede seemed surprisingly charming, if a bit smelly.

Svnoyi had a flash of intuition. *Could it be Petey loving him so completely that makes him happier and nicer?*

"So what the hell happened, Kuaray?" Phoenix could hardly contain his curiosity.

Kuaray grinned. "Well, Lucy got me all primed to teach the pups how to shoot. But that lasted only four days. They weren't bad at all, kind of adorable, actually. It was Queen Gitli's military man, Saint George, who turned out to be a horse's ass. And that's insulting the horse."

They all laughed. Then Svnoyi asked cautiously, "So what's brought you here, Dragon Rider?"

Kuaray patted Petey's sixth segment thoughtfully before jerking up his head. "That's just about the nicest thing anyone's ever called me, Sis. Really, I mean it. Dragon Rider. It sounds kind of heroic."

He cleared his throat. "To get back to my story, Lucy and I talked for a long time about something that was really bothering her. She was afraid every single Sun Person would get slaughtered down to zero as soon as the surprise attacks started on their villages. She said it was so unfair, all for trying to live their own lives.

"I asked her what about the Sacred Meadow getting wrecked, and Lucy just laughed. She said, 'Do you think the queen gives a good god damn about that Meadow?' I love it when she talks that way—so passionately.

"Then she looked at me kind of sideways and said, 'Gitli doesn't, not since her arthritis got too bad for her to flounce around in that fifty-pound shell dress impressing the minions. What she's doing with it now is milking it for propaganda against the Sun People.'"

Svnoyi nodded in satisfaction. "That's more or less what I said to Corlion."

Kuaray started in massaging Petey's fourth segment as his steed nuzzled his arm. "Then Lucy said to me, 'You've got to do something to help them. Besides, Saint George is about to run crying to Mommy, he's so pissed with you for insulting him in front of the pups.'

"I told her I got the picture. I should leave town for a while if she'd make excuses for me, and I should teach the Sun People how to fight guerrilla style to defend their villages."

He remarked drily, "I noticed that they're already totally brilliant at aiming those arrows."

The others asked in unison, "And what makes you think you're qualified?"

"Nothing, except a long time ago I read Che Guevara's book about guerrilla tactics. If the Sun People decide to invade Iqual instead, I happened to pick through Sequoyah's end-of-time library a few weeks ago and read Tolstoy's *War and Peace*.

"Besides, I'm great at anything I set out to do."

Kuaray flashed his infectious grin, and both Svnoyi and Phoenix knew he was right.

Phoenix said thoughtfully, "You guys, this is heavy-duty stuff. Call it what it is. Treason. If the queen finds out, we're all dead."

Kuaray gave Phoenix's arm a friendly punch. "Play your cards right, and she'll never know. When you go back home, don't talk to anyone about it except Lucy. There are already so many secrets flying around the court, one more won't matter."

He drilled them with his piercing black eyes. "You're happy with the idea, right?"

They nodded, although Svnoyi wasn't convinced. *Sure, Kuaray's a genius, but does he have the mercy in him to be a commander, responsible for other people's lives?*

Kuaray took on the tone of a business executive. "Hurry, then, there's no time to waste. Go report to the council because I can't wait to get started, tomorrow if possible."

"And one more thing." He cast his eyes down again and began rubbing Petey's third segment, carefully working his fingers around the whorls in the bony chitin. "It's about Lucy. She's not like other people, certainly not like me. She's good. She has a big, big heart."

Svnoyi had a second flash of intuition. *It's not just the centipede, then. Kuaray's in love.*

***

She hurried through the rows of yurtpees encircling the Jimjamoree and across a meadow to the large council-house where Corlion and the other five members would be waiting for her. She assumed she would find them sitting cross-legged on their woven reed mats in prayer, asking Corlaz One for wisdom as they always did before meetings.

In addition to reporting about Kuaray, Svnoyi had a question for them. She knew that all eight villages had rejected the Oath of Fealty unanimously as Corlion had predicted they would. Why, then, had he and the council been waiting around for a week, apparently unmoved by her news of the coming invasion? An unwelcome explanation popped into her head. The Sun People, so committed to faith, might still be expecting a miraculous intervention from Sequoyah.

She paused in the middle of the meadow and shook her head. Here she was, second-in-command to the Mayor who was also her lover, and she understood so little about these strangely pacifistic and deeply spiritual human beings.

Svnoyi put an enquiring ear against the council-house door before stepping into the chamber. Instead of a contemplative murmur issuing from behind the slats, she was bombarded by hoots of raucous merriment. She tried to slip in unnoticed. But right away a strikingly tall councilwoman named Corlafilla whom she'd met briefly once before thrust a brimming cup into her hands. Svnoyi brought it up to her nose, careful not to let the liquid slop over the edge.

"Vodka made from apples?" One whiff of the potent liquor told her that the entire council might pass out shortly from extreme inebriation.

Corlion stood at the center, waving his arms to get everyone's attention. He wasn't tipsy, himself. Nor was he amused.

Svnoyi sidled next to him. *Back home, we would've called this "wearing a lampshade on your head."*

What, Svnoyi? I don't get it. Shrugging his shoulders, he added with resignation, *Let's get out of here. Half the time my advisors are hopeless.*

Once they'd reached the middle of the meadow well out of sight of the council-house, Svnoyi attacked her fiancé with scathing words. *Confess, Corlion, because I happen to know why everyone's drunk. You couldn't wait for my report. Instead, you picked over my mind when Phoenix and I were talking to my half brother. Then you told the council that Sequoyah had come through, that he'd sent a savior in the form of his son because he couldn't come himself. Then someone opened a jug to celebrate. Am I right?*

Yes. Corlion bowed his head miserably. *I said something very close to that. I'm ashamed I invaded your thoughts.*

And do you believe what you said is actually true? That Sequoyah had sent a savior?

Corlion was about to answer when Svnoyi sank to her knees on the damp grass among the daisies and cornflowers, her face transformed by a radiant smile.

But it is true.

"It is true!" she bellowed into the twilit night sky, flinging out her arms.

Corlion knelt beside her, and she embraced his neck, her words pouring out almost faster than he could understand them.

Six months ago, I had a vision. I saw Sequoyah in a crystal coffin lying in a blood-soaked chamber. He said to me, "Daughter of my heart, walk with Phoenix through the third tunnel. Where it ends is horrible beyond imagination, but don't kill the centipedes."

So we did, and what was at the end of the tunnel was truly horrible. There were these huge monsters digesting polar bears right before our eyes. Not really, we didn't actually see it happen. We left first because we couldn't watch.

Later, after Lucy had tamed one of them, she taught Kuaray how to ride it to take the place of his ruined legs. She named him Petey.

Corlion said simply, *I don't get it.*

Don't you see? Even though my daddy was unconscious, he sent me a message. The blood in the chamber was about the war that's coming. He said we should save the centipedes. Both Phoenix and I could've killed them with our minds, but we didn't.

Svnoyi smoothed out the befuddled frown on Corlion's forehead with her fingers. *Visions are always like that, they're open-ended. I connected the dots, and you were right all along. Kuaray arrived to take Sequoyah's place because months ago my daddy made sure his son would have new legs and a way to ride here.*

***

Svnoyi was too excited to sleep. She lay beside Corlion replaying the vision from last spring in her head. Then she started worrying how Kuaray would manage to train the peaceable Sun People in only a few months.

Corlion, are you awake?

Uh, what? He sat up, running his fingers through his hair and rubbing his eyes. *Yes, I am ... almost, anyway. I was making mental plans, but I guess I dozed off for a little.*

Svnoyi sat up too, throwing the hot furs off and taking his hands. *I'm curious about something. How did you get the word out and then back so fast about the Oath of Fealty? Do you have some super-runners?*

I'm sorry, I should've told you. We have our own express, but we never talk about it to keep the Prairie Dogs from ever finding out. It will be the lifeline of this military operation just like theirs is for transporting troops and supplies. It runs the whole way from the first village to the eighth but only when we need it.

In the half-light that filtered through the high windows, Svnoyi thought she saw him wink and smile. *What animals pull the carts, do you think?*

She hazarded a guess. *Reindeer?*

Hmm, Corlion replied, shaking his head. *I don't know what reindeer are.*

He rubbed his hands with pleasure, excited to relate the next part of his story. *We use runaway polar bears from the queen's palace. They come to our forests directly because they must've worked out an escape route to a place where they'd be cared for. They're not too big and their heads are curiously flat. I wouldn't say they're particularly brainy. But they're lovable and very loyal, and they have tremendous endurance. We call our transport the Flathead Express.*

Which reminds me, after what you said about the centipedes' dining preference, can you tell Kuaray to keep Petey away from the Flatheads' part of the forest?

Svnoyi remembered the groaning bears supporting Queen Gitli's dining tables. *Hurray for the brave bears. Of course, I'll tell him.*

Svnoyi hugged Corlion for giving her such a delightful explanation, but then she turned serious. *If the council's up to it after the partying, the members must meet with Kuaray tomorrow to work out ever so many details: raising the army, choosing a place for Kuaray to train the fighters, transporting food—*

Corlion cropped short Svnoyi's list. *I'm planning to introduce him at Jimjamoree tomorrow morning. Will he feel shy?*

Svnoyi laughed. *I doubt it, he loves attention. Slather on the superlatives and he'll preen like a peacock.*

A peacock? Corlion asked. *Oh, never mind.*

Then we'll go directly to the council-house after breakfast and start in. Meanwhile, I'll send someone by Flathead Express to notify the other council-members to come here immediately.

Corlion broke off, suddenly. *Oh, Svnoyi.*

She knew what he would say next and pulled him close.

He spoke into her neck, *You and Phoenix must move on to the other villages to stick to the Queen's timetable.*

Yes, she said, *I know. We'll leave tomorrow. We were only allotted a week in each village.*

He caressed his fiancée's shoulders. *I'm going to teach you something. We call it "Spinning the Circle," and couples practice it when they're apart. I've never tried it, of course, so we'll learn how, together.*

Put your hands somewhere on me. On any place that you like.

Well, that's embarrassing. Everywhere, but how about on your hips?

Okay, I'll do the same.

Now take your hands away but close your eyes and keep thinking hard about that place, and about the whole of me, too. I'll do the same.

They drew apart, their eyes tightly shut.

If it worked right, a circle's spinning right now, just behind your eyelids. It's humming.

Svnoyi whispered in awe, "By Corlaz One, it works. The circle's there, and it sounds like bees in a flowery meadow."

Corlion nodded in agreement, the dimples accompanying his broad smile. "Yea, Svnoyi, ite woerken."

32 ~ The Almost Kiss

***Your greatest gift is teaching the unloved, the unloving, and the unlovable how to love.* —Yacy**

It was 3:00 a.m., and Lucy lay wide awake inside Ethan's cave, the last of the three that wasn't empty. Jaroslav, Anichka, and Aleta had left a little more than a week ago to find Sequoyah, and of course they'd taken the little kids, Agali and Alexej. Svnoyi and Phoenix had closed up Sequoyah's cave six days before.

She could hear Ethan snoring, but even in his sleep he still muttered about some invention or other. He was hopelessly obsessed with them, almost insanely so since Luz had been taken away. He'd promised Yacy and Oscar he'd help them raise his son, her little brother Lucian, but recently he'd stopped doing anything beyond patting him on the head at bedtime. Ethan had been holed up in the cave for a week, now, working on plans for a solar-powered paddleboat with wind-vane steering.

Do they even have worries? Lucy wondered as she looked over at Yacy and Oscar lying silent in their quilts, tucked behind the stove for privacy. They kept Arielle Luz and Lucian between them so the babies wouldn't crawl out the cave door in a sudden bout of enthusiasm to explore the outside world.

Because it was June, twilight lasted all night. From her private sleeping nook at the back of the cave, Lucy could see the outline of her left hand as she lay sleepless on the top of her crumped quilts. She unleashed her imagination: the reason she was staring at her hand was to admire a platinum engagement ring that fit snuggly at the base of her fourth finger. She'd considered gold, but rejected the idea because platinum is one of the rarest metals in the world. The cut of the diamond was brilliant. When she held her arm a foot away and rotated her hand slowly from the wrist, it emitted multi-colored flashes much prettier than the Northern Lights.

"Oh, crap," she whispered into the stillness. "How disgustingly conventional, I wouldn't want one anyway. Why, oh why, do I let myself get so carried away?"

Kuaray giving me a ring? That would be the day. Besides, there aren't any jewelry stores.

She was sweltering in the mid-June heat, and it was thoughts of Kuaray that had kept her tossing for hours. Nor were they about to stop. In fact, she was just getting started. She sat up, gathering her heavy blond hair in her hands to lift it off her sweaty neck. *If Kuaray hadn't told me my hair was pretty, I would cut it off tomorrow, cute and short like Agali's pageboy.*

She dropped the hair to massage her blushing face. *I thought he'd say he loved me tonight when he left, but he didn't. He kissed me almost, he really did. It was a little brush on my forehead with his lips when I bent down to say goodbye to Petey.* She touched the spot with two fingers. *I'll never wash it again, not till he's home safe.*

They'd been together in Kuaray's hospital room, leaning against the wall and sitting nearly shoulder to shoulder on his woven bamboo blanket. She could almost see an energy field between her left side and his right. She'd compared it to her daddy's demonstration of iron filings that prickled and surged, eventually jumping into unsteady lines around a moving magnet.

Her thoughts had been undermining a very serious conversation, but she couldn't make them stop. *If I slide in closer, even an inch, what would he do? Would he put his arm around me, or jerk away? If he did that, I'd ruin everything, and we'd part from each other feeling awful.*

Poor Lucy. The two of them had sat there on his bed with her transmitting waves of passion that he must've been able to pick up on. Their shoulders stayed the same distance apart as they weighed different plans until they settled on the one that felt right. Kuaray would leave around midnight and ride along the flat road beside the Polar Bear Express route. Petey had never made a long trip before, but if he kept good time, Kuaray would reach the stop near the first of the Sun People's villages about noon tomorrow, even with breaks to find water.

By coincidence Petey had looked up at Kuaray with his gentle bug-eyes and nodded his head as if he agreed that the plan was perfect. He wasn't lying on his own straw bed but had curled up at least a third of his extraordinary length to lie his first two segments on his master's inert feet.

"Did you see that, Lucy? Just think, if it hadn't been for you, there wouldn't *be* a Petey lying here."

Thinking of Petey, her most monumental animal-training accomplishment, Lucy's mind took a blessed respite from agonizing over Kuaray. She recalled the first day she'd managed to corner the monster next to a ten-foot-tall blackberry bush in the Valley of Rejects. She'd planned to use her Soothing Technique on him that had worked with every other animal she'd ever tried it on. She'd faced him, her feet ten inches apart, but with her eyes averted to appear non-threatening. Concentrating on what she called her Animal-Center deep inside the limbic part of her brain, she'd hummed, low and motherly, "Doowy-doo, woo, woo, woo. Doowy-doo."

The monster had swung his head the size of a Saint Bernard's toward her and started waving four-foot tentacles that sprouted sideways, no doubt to scare her off. His wide double mouth had snapped open, then shut, and something green had dribbled from the corners. But it was the sudden hiss louder than the whistles she remembered from the trains at the Montreal yards that had sent her fleeing. In terror, she'd headed for the safety of the tunnel leading to Jaroslav's cave, tumbling over an almost headless bear in her haste to get the hell out of there.

But not for long. She'd come back the next day and the next because she wanted to conquer her own loathing as much as his resistance. Quite unexpectedly, she'd found the key to beating both. She began to love the centipede because he met all the qualifications for being unlovable.

Her thoughts swung back to the man who had captured her heart. His past tortured her, and the usual nighttime parade of regrettably factual memories began to march through her head. *I love him, but I can't forget the terrible things he did. I was a little girl, and he was a big kid when he blew up Tybalt, my kitty, by feeding him an explosive wrapped in a meatball.*

He broke Aleta's precious Italian violin by stomping it to bits.

He made his own sister Yacy pregnant with Arielle Luz.

He chased my mother through the forest, which is how she got hurt when she fell through the skylight of the Prairie Dog Hospital's operating room.

Besides stabbing Sequoyah in the stomach, maybe the worst thing Kuaray did was throw away the ashes of Sequoyah's own dead daddy, Mohe. Sequoyah had brought them in a little wooden box to bury under a shade tree in the new land. But there were no shade trees, only pines and more pines. So he settled on the carving *of a shade tree in Jaroslav and Anichka's cave as the perfect place to make a little niche for the box.*

I'll never forget the look on Sequoyah's face when he found out the ashes were gone forever. His eyes kind of crumpled up because he was crying, and he rushed away from us, tripping on his feet. Then he fell down and was unconscious for three whole days.

Lucy started, her heart in her throat. Someone about four-and-a-half feet tall outlined by the summer sun's glow beyond the cave mouth was tiptoeing about inside, peering around with eyes that glowed in the dark.

Tlke? For chrissake, what are you *doing here? You scared me half to death. You may be my boss, but you can't prowl through my home in the middle of the night.*

Lucy, get up, right now!

Kuaray's gone, and he took Petey. I checked his room. He can't simply wander off any time he feels like it. Who's going to teach the pups tomorrow? Saint George is terrible at it—

Calm down, Tlke, it's nothing. Let's go outside.

Lucy had already prepared an excuse for Kuaray's disappearance. As the two of them settled down on the pebbled ledge that served as a doorstep, she ran it through her head, hoping Tlke wouldn't pick up on her deception.

Now to seem appropriately stern. *Listen, Tlke, Queen Gitli shouldn't have expected Kuaray to bear that kind of pressure teaching the teen pups so soon after a serious injury. And he's still not healed physically. I told him he should take time off to meditate. So he rode on down the coast to be alone with the sound of the surf.*

You *told him he could take time off to meditate? That's not your decision to make.*

It most certainly is! I know what humans need, and you don't.

Lucy wondered if Prairie Dogs cried actual tears. Tlke dropped her head in her paws and her entire body trembled.

Eventually she wailed, *Lucy, I can't do this anymore. I'm falling apart under the strain of keeping the entire court together. I'm just a kid, no older than those pups.*

Amazed and alarmed by her friend's sudden breakdown, Lucy tried to placate her. She said soothingly, *Tlke dear, don't worry. Who needs Kuaray? I'll take his place. I'm a wonderful archer, didn't you know? Mama Luz is so warlike she made me start practicing with a bow and arrow before I could walk.*

Really? Tlke sounded skeptical. *Well, okay, then. Be at the Sacred Meadow at 8:00 a.m. sharp.*

Oh, I almost forgot. Tell Ethan he's meeting with the queen at 10:00, and of course you'll be there to translate.

Can I ask what it's about? Ethan is *my father.*

No, you may not. Tlke turned to leave.

Speaking over her shoulder, she added, *And forget my little lapse a minute ago. It was nothing, I'm fine, just fine. Completely fine.*

Even if Tlke weren't fine, Lucy had created a far greater worry for herself. She'd never touched a bow and arrow in her life. She'd simply have to remember the instructions Kuaray had repeated over and over *ad infinitum* for each and every pup. Her next thought offered a little comfort. If she taught them badly, they'd kill less effectively.

33 ~ The Death Room

During Lucy's debut as a teacher of archery, her many gaffes were serious enough to make the pups giggle in tiny staccato barks behind their paws. Each time, she glanced over at her superior, Saint George, to gauge his reaction, but he was dozing, his face and chest upturned to absorb the sun's beneficial rays. After the hour class was over, she waited impatiently for the recruits to clear out because there was something she wanted to accomplish before the meeting between Queen Gitli and her father.

It was more than idle curiosity. It was the youthful drive to solve a mystery, locate a secret passage, or dig up a hidden treasure. As soon as she'd realized a year ago that Luz's funeral had been a sham, she'd promised herself to find the trapdoor that must join the hospital to the Sacred Meadow. From where she'd been standing on the dais translating for the queen, her mama, lying on the stone hospital bed, had risen miraculously in the midst of the gyrating Prairie Dogs beating their breasts in ritual sorrow.

She could remember the bed appearing in front, and to the left of, the fountain. At a starting point sixty feet from the fountain's bowl, Lucy paced back and forth between it and the hilly rise on the left, moving closer on each lap toward the mountain peak at the back. She kept her eyes to the ground and at the same time, she recreated the landscaping as she remembered it, the lush grass, the nodding wildflowers in yellows and blues, the swaying pines off to the side.

Anyway, I know the trapdoor has *to be there. Kuaray must've used it every day to get to the pups' archery classes. And how else did he vanish secretly into the night when he took off for the Sun People's village?*

Shuffling methodically through dirt clods and stubble while staring at the ground was a monotonous task, and Lucy glanced up. Above her, two hawks circled higher and higher, turning into dots. She craned her neck further, flapping her arms and launching herself skyward with little jumps.

She called after them, "Godspeed, birds!" *Fly north over the Polar Bear Express and tell Kuaray I love him.*

Her toes caught on an object that shouldn't be there. She pitched forward, adrenaline twisting her stomach. Gravity performed as always, and she landed spreadeagled in a serious splat. The impact hurt, but there was something odd about the pain. It felt ... stripy.

"Ouch, goddammit," She yelled. *Why do I always have to be such a dreamer?*

But what's this? Lucy was lying on a grate made of pine slats that covered a rectangular hole big enough to accommodate an emerging stone bed. The splat forgotten, she stood up, letting out a prolonged crow of delight. The self-appointed sleuth had found something that seemed to fill the requirements of a trapdoor into the hospital.

She dropped an exploratory pebble between the slats to see what lay beneath. It landed with a plink almost immediately, and she could hear it roll. *There's a ramp down there, I just know it.*

She discovered that the grate was hinged on one of the long sides and wasn't too heavy to lift. She opened it up to a right angle where it conveniently locked itself in place. Without a second thought, she started down the ramp, a gentle incline about four feet wide. She turned to pull the grate shut, crouching low to not hit herself on the head with it. Courtesy of God Rough's peerless instruction in ages past, Prairie Dog ingenuity had come through once again. It served as both a barrier and a skylight, and it dropped into its frame with a satisfying click.

Lucy proceeded cautiously, using tiny shuffling steps until her eyes adjusted to the rectangle of light that barely penetrated the darkness below. From what she could see, the ramp descended beside a wall into cavernous depths, the steady pitch stretching downward seemingly forever into the blackness.

Once she reached the bottom, she was sure it must be a part of the hospital even though she'd never been in this particular room. The ramp's surface, made of polished granite to reduce friction, was gray in color and no different from the walls and floors in the other rooms she knew. By the pool of light flowing down from the grate above, she could see ten stone beds at the center of the chamber. It was gigantic, about half the width of the hospital's operating theater but equally as long.

Lucy could distinguish a row of sinks and what looked like dissecting tables lining the room's opposite side. This was the first sight to unnerve her. She popped her hand over her mouth to keep from emitting a yelp of horror.

I know exactly what this room is for. It's the Death Room where the bodies are prepared for funerals in the Sacred Meadow. Last year they pushed my mama's bed up the ramp for her funeral and brought her back down to treat her because she was still alive.

That's not all. Those dissecting tables. I bet they have some kind of purpose related to the cloning experiments because I've seen the lab's doors and the operating theater every time I've gone sneaking around the hospital.

Placing her palms flat against the wall where the ramp ended, she sidled along it in the near-darkness. She turned a corner, and at the room's narrow end, she discovered a door to another chamber. She pushed, and it rasped against the stone, revealing its secrets unwillingly. When she stepped in, the rank odor of contaminated water hit her nostrils, and all she could think of was the stink of a wet swimsuit inadvertently left wrapped in a towel overnight.

This is crazy. That sickening water smell. I must be underneath the Sacred Meadow's fountain, and it's been leaking somewhere, probably for hundreds of years.

But there was an additional odor. It was sickly sweet and penetrating—the smell of decomposing flesh.

During the Time Before when she was only three, she'd found the corpse of a mouse in a cupboard, and she would never forget that odor. She'd knelt down, and her inexperienced heart had swelled with compassion and a desire to heal it. She wanted to lift it, to cup it in her hands, to warm it up again.

Luz had loomed tall above her. "Lucy! Don't touch that icky thing. Let your father take care of it."

Later that afternoon after Ethan came home from his classes at the university, he'd picked it up by the tail and tossed it out the back door behind the hydrangeas.

The dead-animal odor streamed past on a current of air that Lucy could feel at her feet, and suddenly, she knew. *There's another door at the back of this room that leads somewhere else.*

Her hand flew to her mouth as bile from her stomach flooded it with noisome acid. *I know exactly what's behind that door. There's a hollow space under the Sacred Meadow, a crypt for all the cloned creatures that never saw the light of day, the ones too incompetent to take their chances in the Valley of Rejects. They went from the lab, to the operating theater, to the dissecting table, and out the back door.*

Harrowed by the morbidity of the place, it took all her courage not to flee. But soon she made out a fascinating variety of lumpy shapes, which she patted and prodded. *Oh my, oh my.* She stood still as the realization sunk in, her hands flying up in delight. *I know what these are. I've found the pipes and all the huge faucets that control the fountain and the water used in the ten rivers.*

She laughed aloud but stopped at the first whoop because she didn't like the flat, captive sound her voice made in the close chamber. Besides, making noise was probably not smart if anyone happened to be nearby.

None of the plumbing feels broken. She smiled knowingly: *Fixing the pipes above ground will be easy-peasy for my daddy.*

My daddy! She struck the side of her head with her palm. *I'm such an idiot. I forgot about the meeting.*

In her attempt to make a hasty exit, she turned too quickly and crashed into something with a hard edge that barked her shins. She stopped to rub away the soreness as she collected her thoughts. The front door leaving the Death Room had to open onto the main hallway that went past the doors to the storage closets and patients' rooms. And the big lab and the operating theater would be facing each other across the same hall. Feeling once again with her palms whenever she needed guidance, she made her way along the side of the room with the ramp and on to the front door. She pushed it open cautiously to discover her orientation within the hospital.

"Yes," she whispered with satisfaction. "I was right." She found herself at the far end of the hall opposite the wing where she'd been with Kuaray only twelve hours ago. Once her eyes adjusted, she noticed a distant commotion in front of Luz's room. Movers, flathead polar bears and their Prairie Dog handlers, were lugging through her door half an apartment's worth of pink furniture and huge, frothy pink pillows.

Lucy hoped they would be too busy to look in her direction. As she ran through the hall toward the operating theater, she realized she had another mystery to sort out. *That's more than odd, the Prairie Dogs moving all that pink stuff into Mama's room. She hates pink. In Montreal I was the only little girl on my block who didn't have a single pink dress to show off. Oh, how I wanted one.*

The relieved explorer was "home free" as soon as the wide doors to the operating theater closed behind her. She shot past the rows of stone beds without letting their purpose derail her concentration, and then through the doors to the entry hall where she had taught Kuaray how to ride Petey. A flood of memories brought her to a sudden halt, but she resolved to think about them later, sometime when she had insomnia—because it was here that she'd first felt the unmistakable beginnings of love, or at least, attraction. Now to get through the broad tunnel to the palace, a good two miles, but luckily all downhill.

***

The tunnel terminated near the back door to the palace kitchen. When she peeked in, the bobcats were hard at work drying Queen Gitli's breakfast mug and plates. Great puddles at their feet and their dripping fur and whiskers could mean only one thing: moments earlier they'd held a spectacular water fight much like Agali and Alexej used to do. One of them looked up and winked at her.

When Lucy edged cautiously through the shell curtain, she saw Ethan and Queen Gitli sitting close together on their rabbit chairs in the center of the spacious room. A new type of game was in progress: the duo appeared to be holding a staring contest, their noses almost touching. Poor Tlke stood dutifully in position behind the queen, but she had both paws clapped over her face. Lucy worried that she might be crying again until tiny staccato barks revealed that the overwrought aide was laughing.

"What's up, Dad?" she enquired breezily.

Ethan turned abruptly. "Lucy, for god's sake, you deserted me for an entire twenty minutes with that harridan."

He lowered his voice. "I checked out the Sacred Meadow yesterday with my assistants, Yacy and Oscar. What do you think I found? Pups everywhere doing *war exercises* with bows and arrows, stomping around in all those garbagy ruins."

"I know, Dad, I was actually there, helping out."

"How are we going to start work, then?" Ethan asked petulantly. "Everybody else gets to go out on an assignment except me and my team."

Queen Gitli raised her paws in an imperious gesture. "Ethan, Ethan, my dear friend and most cherished inventor, I'm reassigning you. Forget the Sacred Meadow. From now on, you'll be living in total seclusion with your lovely wife, Luz. She already has the assignment: top-secret work for the war effort."

"Luz? My honey-bunny, Luz? She got well?" Ethan leapt up, his entire face glowing red, followed by a ghastly pallor. He tottered, his knees buckling.

As the queen smirked, Lucy slid behind her father's back to support him under the armpits in case he fainted from joy. During the undue excitement and abrupt movements, his frightened chair disobeyed all its programming to scuttle into a corner.

"Yes, Daddy," Lucy whispered into his ear, "Mama was singing the 'Air Force Song' in her hospital room a few weeks ago. She's well."

At the same time, the befuddled girl had to process Queen Gitli's unexpected disclosure, herself. She'd never heard before this moment about the top secret "assignment" that would put her parents together.

Suddenly irked for no reason, Queen Gitli waved both paws in a gesture of dismissal. "Tlke, take him to Luz's room at the hospital, and be quick about it."

Then boasting to everyone, she announced, "I had it enlarged into a suite. My best designers worked very hard to recreate a human female's boudoir."

Lucy groaned inwardly as the truth dawned. *All that pink.*

The daughter wanted to give her father a last hug, but Queen Gitli commandeered her attention. "Well, Lucy, good riddance to your boyfriend, Kuaray. He rode down the coast to *meditate?* What a huge waste of time and energy for me and my good colleagues at the hospital. Who resuscitated and mended him? See if I ever raise anyone from the almost-dead again."

As Lucy expelled a long breath of relief at the queen's reaction to Kuaray's disappearance, Her Highness smiled, a discomfiting exposure of yellow incisors behind her rodent lips. "I'm proud of you, dear. Saint George told me you took over nicely. He watched your every move this morning, and he said you did a spectacular job teaching the pups."

34 ~ The Boudoir

To reach Luz's suite inside the Prairie Dog Hospital, Ethan and Tlke set off through the palace kitchen tunnel. Ethan noticed that it was wide enough to accommodate at least six Prairie Dogs walking side-by-side. It even had a white line made of inlaid stones running down the center, like a superhighway from the Time Before designed for rush hour.

Unfortunately, the walk was entirely uphill.

Ethan immediately felt resentful being led around by the young Prairie Dog. Besides, he felt embarrassed to be so out of shape. She kept up a relentless pace, her stubby little legs swishing to and fro like a whisk broom. He dragged behind, panting.

He knew she couldn't answer him in words, but he yelled at her back, "Fer chrissake, Tlke, slow the eff down."

His dislike of her intensified when she didn't turn around to acknowledge his plea. *It figures, this is the same little peanut who set off the worst fight I ever had with Lucy when I wouldn't let them have a goddam slumber party in my cave the very same day Sequoyah was taken.*

Wow, has she ever risen in the world, from Chief Translator to Chief Bellhop. Which reminds me. Will she let Lucy fetch some of my clothes and a shaving brush out of my cave?

Then Tlke *did* stop, so abruptly that he almost crashed into her from behind. Whirling around to face him with fury in her eyes, she began swinging a key on a pink string back and forth as if she were trying to hypnotize him.

The little twerp, what's she trying to tell me, anyway?

Oh, I know. The object making like a pendulum is the key to my wife's door, and I'll get to see my darling Luzzie in five or ten minutes. And I'm supposed to be thankful for the queen's largesse, mercy, and all that.

Surprising himself, Ethan plopped down in the middle of the road, cradling his head in his arms. He mumbled, "I do want to see her, I really do. But ... but part of me—no, almost all of me—is damned scared!"

He looked up. *Lord love a duck, she understands.*

Tlke had sat down on her haunches about ten feet away, her back to him. *Scritch, scritch,* to give him time, she launched into a long grooming process, nipping herself and combing her fur coat with formidable, unfurled claws.

Ethan sighed with relief. *Thank you, Tlke. Five more minutes is all I need to pull myself together. It's been almost a whole year without my honey-bunny. How much have the two of us changed in really freakish ways?*

When Ethan was ready, he rose, his knees creaking, and they continued at a slower pace. The tunnel ended, and he found himself in an unremarkable grey stone room of long and narrow proportions that served as an anteroom to the fabled operating theater. They entered it through massive double doors that swung inward, revealing a sight Ethan wasn't prepared for. About twenty stone beds, identical to the one his Luz had been laid out on for her funeral, were lined up in a row. And somewhere high up near the poorly lit ceiling, he knew there must be a ledge where Agali and Alexej had done their spying.

The little kids had seemed immune to the horror of the place, and they loved to pry. They gleefully had let everyone know Luz hadn't died after all but had been lying comatose in this very room for months. Ethan had asked himself many times since, *Why had Queen Gitli bothered to save her life in the first place?*

Halfway across the room, he stopped to gaze upward at the pine branches that stretched over the skylight, although he refused to let himself imagine Luz falling through it with their newborn son Lucian in her arms.

Then Ethan had a shock that snapped him out of his reminiscences. He and Tlke had reached the end, finally, and pushed open the double doors. He saw a long hall stretching right and left, but directly across from him was another set of double doors. And they cried out, *Lab!*

He grabbed Tlke's shoulder. "There's a big lab in here, I just know it, I can smell the chemicals. I want to see it."

Tlke twisted out of his grasp, rolling her eyes with exasperation. She pointed a paw toward the left, shaking the pink-stringed key.

"Aw, come on, Tlke, one little peek. I love labs. I can't help it, they're like mistresses."

Ethan set his palms on the doors and took a step forward.

Tlke exploded into a whirlwind of claws and clacking teeth. She advanced on him with lunging stomps.

"Tlke, stop, *stop!* I didn't mean it, I'll be good. I was just curious."

Ethan was not a brave man. He backed way from her, preparing to run in any direction.

At that moment, a song wafted along the hall from somewhere on the left. It was infinitely sweet and tinged with sadness. Ethan recognized the words and melody as those of the rousing "Air Force Song," incongruously modified in character to issue from the lips of a Lorelei.

"It's Luz!"

He shot down the hall as Tlke bounded after him, hurrying to catch up. She waved the door key, the last barrier keeping him from a joyous reunion with his wife. Tlke opened the door, and he rushed in. The only flaw to a perfect heart-in-throat moment was the decisive click he heard behind him when she locked him inside.

***

Ethan had never been inside a patient's room in this particular hospital, and he could tell that unadorned, it would be hardly better than a grey jail cell. But considerable effort had gone into camouflage. To begin with, he could see at a glance that the entire space was huge: two additional rooms had been joined to the one he was standing in. The arched openings that had a chewed look to them around the edges were hung with curtains made of pink scallop shells.

His heart thudding with anticipation, Ethan peered around the first room. At the center, a dining table covered with a woven bamboo cloth in hot pink reminding him that he'd missed lunch. Overstuffed chairs, not exactly rabbits but designed to look like them down to button eyes and pert leather ears, crouched everywhere. They could never be mistaken for the real thing: their fur ranged in color from pink lemonade to deep fuchsia.

Ethan felt his original enthusiasm ebb, turning fast into panic. *Where the hell is my Luzzie? I thought she'd be waiting for me at the door.*

At that moment he heard a suppressed giggle from the next room and tiptoed past the strings of shells that tinkled like chimes in a California spiritual retreat. Ethan dashed for the bed. His forty-three-year-old wife whispered his name coquettishly from beneath a gauzy carnation-pink drape, which he discovered later was a splendidly oversized peignoir, hand spun for the occasion out of cornsilk.

For months, ever since Ethan had realized that Luz would be back someday, he'd planned on saying in a sultry low register, "Long have I awaited this moment, my darling." But he never got the chance.

She jumped him, ensnaring him in the peignoir like a female spider tying up her mate. Ethan hardly knew what hit him, it was over so fast. Fighting for air, he recalled the first sex they'd had, an encounter bordering on the sublime. It had lasted a long time: wrapped in the scented flesh of her arms, he'd experienced a grown-up rapture combined with a return to cuddly infancy, so complete was his satisfaction. This time, Luz stripped off his clothes, something he ordinarily did himself, and then, for lack of a better word, she *absorbed* him.

"That was athletic," he gasped.

"More athletic for me than for you, sweetheart, and I tell you, there's more to come."

Ethan wasn't sure whether that made him happy, or not.

He murmured into her neck, "Luz, I missed you so much." He felt like weeping.

***

The Prairie Dogs had outfitted the third room, a study, with a raspberry-colored table and two pink stools with matching cushions. An inch-high stack of Sequoyah's fast dwindling supply of typewriter paper and four of his pencils sat at the center, an unsubtle reminder that the queen expected results. Ethan's own scientific books had been pilfered from his cave and stacked at the back of the desk, on thermodynamics, classic mechanics, and electromagnetism. Thanks to the Prairie Dogs being unlettered, two illustrated books written for children, *Who Fears Gears: Projects for Girls,* and *From Catapults to Cannons: Build Fun Weapons at Home,* had gotten into the mix.

"What's this?" Ethan asked, picking up *Catapults and Cannons* between his thumb and forefinger. "Weapons to build at home? *I* never brought it."

"I did," Luz answered belligerently. "You brought *Who Fears Gears* for Lucy so you could help her build her own doll buggy out of Greyhound parts. I brought *Catapults and Cannons* for Oscar so I could turn my son into a man."

"Oh, for fuck's sake," Ethan murmured under his breath. "Next you'll be telling me Queen Gitli wants me to design a catapult that shoots cannonballs and rides from place to place in a doll buggy."

"You're close, dear. Good thinking."

"Well, I won't."

"You won't? Should I throw you out the door where the merciless Tlke is waiting?"

She sprang up so fast, her pink stool clattered against the stone floor. "Or should I stop loving you from now on till death do us part?"

Ethan gauged Luz's expression, searching for a hint of humor, but there was none. He had never seen her so serious or so angry, her eyes shooting lightning bolts, her legs planted like pillars, her magnificent chest thrust toward the firmament.

Yowee, does she ever look sexy, even if she's always been a bit of a warmonger teaching ROTC and all. But he said aloud, "Oh, Luz, be sensible. Do you even know who the enemy is?"

"Of course, Tlke told me, and they're pure evil. They're called *Sun People,* but I know who they really are. They're Commies hellbent on destroying the American Way of Life."

"But we aren't even in America. That was a million years ago."

"You traitor, you Red," Luz cried. Then with a steely resolution, "I'm reporting you to Queen Gitli, President of the United States. I'm turning you in."

She marched the length of the suite and banged on the inside of the front door with her fists, her stentorian and rage-filled voice set on maximum: "Tlke, fetch the military police!"

"Shh, keep it down, honey." He crawled after her on his knees, pulling at the hem of her mauve negligee. "You're acting delusional, sweetheart. Oh, crap, have it your way."

Ethan sank to the floor, near tears. *I love her, yes I do, and I can't lose her a second time, I just can't. But let's face it, I don't know how to handle a madwoman who's bigger than me.*

***

A hearty dinner of rabbit stew and honey-sweetened yams topped with blackberries for dessert arrived through the slot in the front door at precisely 6:00 p.m. After dining and shoving the dirty dishes out the slot—followed by another bout of sex—the couple sat down on the pink stools in the study, ready to begin.

Luz clutched a handful of papers that she'd already covered with scribbles and diagrams and straightened them by tapping them ferociously on the desk. Her task completed, she waved them under Ethan's nose.

"Take notice, Ethan, my man, this is my preliminary work. You're not the only brain in this outfit."

"Darling, I never assumed I was—"

"Shut up, then. These are aerial maps I drew up from our knowledge of what lies behind enemy lines. They're from Tlke's descriptions, and she gets her information from Prairie Dog spies who work on the nearby farms."

"So how in the world do you and Tlke manage to communicate?" Ethan knew he was swerving off-topic, but he hoped to find out if Tlke was responsible for indoctrinating his wife or if his dear one wasn't entirely in her right mind.

"Tlke and I have a scant telepathic understanding, and that's good enough. What I don't understand, I make up.

"Why do you ask?" She gave him a sideways glance of disapproval and tapped the eraser end hard against the desk in a brisk staccato. "It's insubordination when you interrupt an official briefing."

"No reason. Please go on, I'm listening." Ethan sighed and leaned his elbows on the desk.

Luz cleared her throat and reached for her reading glasses. "There are eight villages, all the same, and everyone lives in log houses built around a huge circle at the center that's used for religious services three times a day. Everybody seems to attend. Flammable pine needles cover the circle like a rug. The Sun People's forests are here, and the Prairie Dogs' farms are here."

Ethan craned his neck to see as she tapped the spots with her pencil eraser.

"On the chosen day of September the first, the crack-shot army of young Prairie Dogs, fully trained by the military genius Saint George, attacks the eight villages simultaneously, the troops having been secretly transported by Polar Bear Express. It's a surprise maneuver.

They surround the big circles and shoot everyone dead while they're voodooing together before breakfast."

"I don't like it, Luz, it's cruel. They'll be praying, fer chrissake."

"And you care? They're not Christians, they're Commies."

"Okay, fine. Super plan, it does Attila the Hun proud.

"So where do we come in? It sounds to me like everybody's dead already, the whole population, a million years of tradition turned to mincemeat."

"Oh, we clean up and wipe out any Commies hiding in their log cabins or in the woods. I calculate the first sweep of archers will only kill 62.5 percent. Eight of our weapons will get shipped along with the troops on the Polar Bear Express and then they'll chug overland unseen in the night, riding smoothly on their all-terrain wheels." Luz drew a line across her map to demonstrate.

"Once in the vicinity of the villages, the catapults, or cannons, or what ever we come up with, shoot great incandescent fireballs. *W-o-o-o-sh,* they fly high, landing in the middle of those circles, bullseye!" Luz made a great arc with the pencil, crashing the point into the middle of her drawing.

"They burn through the flammable needles in a snap, and then the cabins all around catch fire, and the forests, and the—"

"The Prairie Dogs' farms," Ethan interjected.

"Oh, damn." Luz looked deflated. "I guess some refinement in the trajectory will be necessary."

"Luzzie, let's go to bed now and continue with this tomorrow morning. I can't focus any more. Besides, it's getting late."

***

Ethan couldn't sleep. He tossed and turned on the plushy apricot-hued fur because it was too hot to lie under it. His mind churned as he tried to think up a final rebuttal.

Luz lay in slumber, her face in the near-darkness as beautiful as any Renaissance madonna's. He knew it was risky to disturb a sleeping dragon, but he shook her shoulder gently, allowing his eyes to travel the length of her mauve-draped torso and thighs.

"Darling, wake up. I have to talk to you."

She shot to a sitting position, her hands yanking an imaginary cord. "Eek! Close the blackout curtains, the MiGs are coming."

"Relax, dear, we're perfectly safe here."

He embraced her as affectionately as he knew how. "Look at me, darling. I have to talk to you about Lucian."

"About who?"

"Our baby son. *Lucian*. You named him yourself.

"I haven't been a very attentive father, I admit, but the little tyke will inherit a destroyed world, a genocide-wracked land. I'm just so worried—"

"Baby son? What baby son? Oscar's a big boy now, he's almost six. He can handle it."

"No, Luz! Oscar's much older than six, he's ...."

Ethan trailed off, suddenly overwhelmed by the hopelessness of it all. He lay back down and stared at the grey ceiling.

I, Ethan Marcus, am about to invent the most terrifying weapon ever to be used since 2050 AD, all for love of a madwoman who's bigger than me.

He felt tears of self-pity regarding his predicament leak down the sides of his face. *There must be an upside. If I'm really, really good, maybe they'll let me see inside their lab. And I might even get to use it.*

35 ~ Rise Up, My Love

Oscar lay stretched out beside Yacy, resting his cheek on his hand so he could gaze down on the one he loved. Yacy lay on her back in the crook of his arm, her eyes closed against the sun. She came straight out of a medieval tapestry from the Time Before—blond-haired, narrow-hipped and elegant—her pale body surrounded by flowers, yellow buttercups, white daisies, and spiky red bottlebrushes.

They'd foolishly decided to make love on this uncomfortable carpet. It had been Yacy's brainstorm because the flowers were so pretty, but it proved more a romantic idyll than a practical one. Even though it hadn't gone well, they'd had a wonderful time, alternating giggles with groans at each new stab and prickle.

Oscar plucked a red flower, the stem breaking with a little *pip*. He ran the bottlebrush over her body, around her bare breasts, and on down to her navel, making a special excursion to touch each one of her ribs.

"Silly, stop that," she said with a smile, eyes still closed. "It tickles."

Oscar had stopped anyway because he wanted to read something to her. He sat up, retrieving the book, damp from the grass. With his discarded flannel shirt he wiped off the droplets that had collected on the artificial leather cover.

Yacy flicked open her amber eyes to stare upward into his eyes, anthracite black with ornately long lashes. *How I love looking at him. His face is as dark as the moon in full eclipse.*

Her lips turned up at the corners. *It's not for nothing that his Mama Luz named him Lado Oscuro de la Luna. No one ever calls him that; Lucy told it to me like it was a secret.*

"Here it is. Listen to this, it's about us." Oscar stuck the flower behind his ear, where it bounced saucily as he read.

"Rise up my love, my fair one, and come away. For, lo, the winter is past, the rain is over and gone; the flowers appear on the earth; the time of the singing of birds is come, and the voice of the turtle is heard in the land."

"It's from the Song of Songs," Yacy said dreamily. "It's beautiful, and I recognize the words. The turtle isn't a turtle, it's a turtle *dove*."

And with a twinge of motherly disapproval in her voice, she added, "You took the Bible from Daddy Sequoyah's end-of-time collection of a hundred books, now down to about seventy-five."

She sat up, too, and reached for her dress. "I'm going to make a basket with the story woven in, the green at the base and vees for birds flying on the upper half, and a red chain around the middle for the flowers. But I'm putting actual turtles in because they're fun."

"So what's your answer, Yacy? Will you come away with me? Away from here?"

She considered how to reply, because she wanted what she said to contain the weight it deserved. But in the end, she spoke intuitively. "Yes, dear, *yes.* We are the two who are meant to leave. It's our mission. We'll sail away, not today or next week, but when the right time calls to us."

***

Oscar and Yacy chose late afternoon to weed the families' vegetable plot after the hot sun had moved across it and away, leaving it shadowy and inviting, and smelling of turned earth. They leaned on the fence to take stock of the leafy rows and from a distance, nothing looked dead or too badly wilted. The two rows closest to them had a wooden stake with "beets" scratched on it to let them know what the curly green leaves with red stems were. Fearing for his garden's survival, Phoenix had put up markers everywhere to help the novices distinguish one plant from another.

Early on the day Phoenix had left, he'd given them a quick rundown about what each kind of vegetable needed before rushing off to catch the Polar Bear Express. He'd seemed inattentive and miserable. The whole time Svnoyi had stood outside the fence tapping the toe of her hiking boot and glowering—broadcasting to Oscar and Yacy that the pair had had a serious fight, maybe even a break-up.

For almost two weeks now, the substitute gardeners had relied on evening squalls and occasional downpours to keep the new plants from dying and had put off the weeding that Phoenix said they must do every few days, *or else.* They could see that Mother Nature had done a spectacular job sowing weeds. The broad-leaved plants that all looked like different kinds of lettuce to their untrained eyes were sharing the earth with many unwelcome guests: mounds of spiky grass blades, stringy creepers adorned with miniature orange flowers, and thistles covered with spines.

But Yacy and Oscar had made a promise to Phoenix, and they hoped that when he came home, he wouldn't be able to detect their negligence. Feeling twinges of guilt, they separated, weeding from opposite ends of the first row with the intention of meeting in the middle. They also kept an eye on Lucian and Arielle Luz who were happily splashing in a syrupy mud puddle left by last night's rain.

Yacy had felt lighthearted ever since the morning in the meadow—definitely not quite herself—especially when she recited the biblical words over and over inside her head like a mantra: *Rise up my love, my fair one, and come away.* And she found herself liking this job as old as agriculture itself: pulling up one weed at a time, the unwanted green thing making a *thip* noise when it left the dirt. And with each thip, Yacy felt a jolt of anticipation because she and Oscar kept moving closer to each other.

Soon we'll meet in the middle, and when we do, I have something amazing to tell him, something I figured out a few minutes ago.

And meet they did, celebrating their first-row achievement with a kiss.

Oscar asked a question first, his voice husky with excitement. "This morning in the meadow, why'd you say that we're meant to leave here, like we're chosen and it's our mission?"

"*I* ***didn't*** know why. That's what I was trying to figure out. And I came up with the answer.

"Listen to this." Yacy gripped Oscar's hands in hers. "I was thinking hard, why *did* I say, 'It's our mission?' At the same time I was pulling out this tough root and thinking *O-o-o-o-o-oh.* It let go all of a sudden, and I whispered out loud, 'O-mission! Our mission was chosen by omission.'

"Oscar, they left us out. Our only job was to hang around with your absent-minded stepfather to keep him from falling off a cliff, or something. We can't do that anymore because Queen Gitli changed his assignment."

Yacy whispered breathlessly, "And so, suddenly I knew why. We didn't get a real mission because we don't fit in here."

"Yes, *yes.*" Oscar grasped her hands tighter for emphasis.

"Listen, Yacy, I have amazing news. Because I can hear spirits, something very special's been happening to me. For a few weeks now, souls, old and young, have been calling to me from across the strait, from Canada.

"They make strange little squeaks and sighs, kind of like when we used to rub our fingers on balloons. I first heard them a few weeks ago on a totally calm day when I was sitting on the very end of that little sandbar that goes out way past the shoreline. I've been going there every day since then."

"Are they human, Oscar? Can you tell?"

"I don't know what they are. They may not be human at all. But I know they want us to come join them."

Yacy's eyes widened with surprise, and she could feel her lips trembling as she replied. "They want us ... *us*?"

Oscar nodded his head. "They certainly seem to. And as soon as I heard them signaling, I asked Dad to draw up plans for a boat."

Yacy said what they were both thinking, "Just imagine. We'll be first to greet them."

***

Soon after the three families arrived in the new land, Sequoyah had made a hard-and-fast rule: everybody would eat breakfast and dinner together. When he was taken away, the tradition lingered on, although the diminishing number of faces circling a cave table, a fire pit, or a beach blanket made the few who were there wonder if it was worth it. And now the number was down to three—Yacy, Oscar, and Lucy—not counting the two babies.

Yacy got a late start preparing the meal because she and Oscar didn't finish weeding the entire garden until early evening. Luckily for her, the menu didn't present a challenge. It hadn't changed much from what she'd been serving every night for months now, because the fresh greens they'd tended so carefully earlier were still too immature to harvest. And the dressed rabbit had shown up on the doorstep as faithfully as the daily newspaper from the Time Before.

Tonight Yacy would serve the stew with pinto beans from last summer's crop and blackberries for dessert. Oscar was outside picking them while she stirred the iron pot on Ethan's stove, poking occasionally at the crackling logs inside to adjust the temperature. Both babies were fussing, crawling about her ankles and grabbing at her dress.

It's milk they want. She shoved the stew off the heat and sat down on the ledge outside the cave.

The young mother always nursed Arielle Luz before Lucian because the little girl got combative, flailing her fists and hitting if he went first—as if she were still making up for a low birth weight. To wile away the time, Yacy would start out singing all the kids' songs she could remember, and then she'd move on to nursery rhymes. Her favorite was "Pussy Cat, Pussy Cat" because she could exchange voices between the narrator and the intrepid royal hunter, adding some fine British touches.

Pussy cat, pussy cat, where hast thou beeeen?
I've beeeen to London to visit the Queen!
Pussy cat, pussy cat, what did'st thou there?
I chas'd a mousy under her chair!

Then it was Lucian's turn, and Yacy would fall silent when his eyes grew heavy. As always, Arielle Luz would already have fallen asleep, lying on her mother's legs that had long since turned to pins and needles.

It was at this moment that she always had the same ridiculous thought. *I wonder if rabbit's milk would make a good substitute for human milk.* The image made her laugh every time. She pictured industrious Prairie Dogs milking doe after doe to accumulate enough of the precious liquid to feed two big babies four times a day.

***

After an exhausting day teaching six archery classes, Lucy dragged herself to the salt-and-pepper sanded beach below the cave cliffs. She waited a few minutes for Oscar and Yacy because the three of them and the babies almost always ate dinner there, soaking up the lengthening rays of the endless summer sun. But today they hadn't shown up, which happened occasionally if they were running late. So she started up the steep trail leading to the caves.

Lucy had made up her mind. As she labored higher, one switchback at a time with a short rest every four, she promised herself that she'd open up to Oscar and Yacy. *It's entirely my own fault that I don't talk to them anymore except about inconsequential things. Oscar's my half brother, and the three of us all live in the same cave. So how'd this happen?*

She stopped at the halfway point and sat down on the trail to empty her sneakers because the sand always seeped through the holes her little toes had worn through the canvas. She turned critical. *They're kind of annoying, actually, hiding out together in their own private world. I hope I never get like that.*

Still, they've been left out for too long, stuck with the house chores while the rest of us take off on adventures.

Lucy found Oscar and Yacy waiting for her, sitting cross-legged at the big oval table designed to accommodate all three families. The sated babies played quietly nearby with a collection of sticks and donuts that Yacy had carved herself and smoothed to a high sheen, working by candlelight during the long nights of last winter.

The couple smiled in welcome, patting her place, begging her to sit down on her own mat.

As usual, Lucy's mind jumped to Kuaray. *Never once did he come to dinner with the three families, before his neck was broken, that is. He said he was afraid of caves because they are dark. And afterwards he was in the hospital.*

She scolded herself, *Enough about him!*

Yacy had already ladled out a big portion of stew and set it on the stove to stay warm. She'd picked out the pieces of rabbit, too, that she knew Lucy wouldn't eat.

She jumped up to retrieve the bowl. "Lucy, here's your stew and a special surprise just for you. We shouldn't have done it, because they're so small, but look at them. They're the first radishes of summer, and here's a tiny strawberry that's almost ripe. They're from Phoenix's garden." She beamed, placing the offerings next to her friend's bowl.

Oscar set down a plate of fresh blackberries, so newly picked that she could smell the musky scent that came from the white fuzz on the bush's leaves.

Then he prepared lemon verbena tea and put the three steaming mugs at their places. The tea was left over from the Time Before, and

Luz had been the one responsible for packing it in the Greyhound bus. It tasted old and flat, the flavor nearly gone, and soon the tin would be empty. But Lucy, especially, loved remembering the old world that she could conjure up in the curling steam.

She ran her hands through the vapor. *Yacy and Oscar are both so nice. Perhaps that's why our ships keep passing in the night, as they say. I've grown bitter and frustrated at the court, and they haven't lost their goodness. Or more likely they've changed, too, because they're so in love.*

Lucy sat up straight. "We have to talk." At the same time, she berated herself for her clumsy lack of an introduction.

Yacy spoke for both Oscar and herself, "We know."

"There's a war coming. It won't be fought here because the attacks will happen in the country at the Sun People's villages."

Yacy and Oscar both nodded. They spoke in unison, "We know."

"Daddy's closed up with Mama in her room at the hospital, and they're working on some kind of big project for the war."

Yacy and Oscar nodded.

"I've been training the pups how to shoot because Kuaray's gone. It's top secret: he's off training the Sun People how to defend themselves. We've become traitors all of a sudden—"

Yacy interrupted, "Lucy, we know all this. We read minds as well as anyone, and every night you toss and turn, wander around the cave, you sit outside on the ledge at four in the morning. We're worried about you, dear."

Amazed, Lucy turned to her friend in slow motion. She stared into Yacy's round amber eyes, windows into a very pure place cleansed by years of self-doubt and despair, a garden of bright flowers. Lucy knew she had abandoned the garden within herself long ago. She dropped her head onto the table.

Oscar scooted to his half sister's side and put a hand on her trembling shoulders. "It's Kuaray, isn't it? You picked a tough nut to crack, but you're the only person in the whole wide world who really cares for him except his Daddy Sequoyah. And he isn't here. Kuaray knows this is his one chance for happiness: to be with you."

"You think so?" Lucy looked up, and rare tears hung on her lashes.

Oscar and Yacy spoke together, "We know so."

"You're going away, aren't you?" Lucy asked tremulously. "I saw the plans on Daddy's desk for a marvelous paddle boat."

"Yes, we are," Oscar said simply. "I asked him to design it. There's no place for us here."

"How will I manage without you, dear ones?"

Yacy held Lucy's hands and kissed the top of her head, a gesture of deepest friendship she'd never offered before. "You'll manage because you love someone, and he'll come round if he hasn't already.

"Your greatest gift is teaching the unloved, the unloving, and the unlovable how to love."

36 ~ Sequoyah

***They're waiting for something. No, for someone! They're waiting for me.* —Sequoyah**

After Agali had left Sequoyah in his underground chamber to go back through the tunnel to the lake, he sat down at his table. He felt different, ready to concentrate and to corral his meandering thoughts. He made up his mind. He wanted to regain his memory.

But how do I start? It's easier said than done. He sat stiffly, hunching his shoulders up to his ears and clenching his eyes tight. He wrung his hands. When nothing about his lost past entered his head and some recently acquired information vanished—such as the name and face of the little girl who had just been there—he leaned his elbows on the table and began hitting his temples rhythmically with his knuckles.

He slid his hands over his eyes. *I hate not remembering anything. I don't even know where I am except in a very strange place, a cavern. Big furry mammals wait on me, bringing me food three times a day and fixing my lamp. And a learned fat man named Laz-Merlin talks to me for an hour before dinner. I take a walk every evening along the edge of a big, black lake.*

The beleaguered man mumbled aloud, "Oh, someone, please help me, or else I'm doomed to stay here forever with a blank mind." He let his head fall onto the table, his arms swinging loosely at his sides.

Once his moment of despair had subsided, Sequoyah decided to work with what he had. First, he drew in deep breaths of the stagnant, waterlogged air. *The little girl. I think ... I think she could be the* key *to help me start finding my past. Yes, I'm sure of it, or she wouldn't have shown up here, flying through the door like a panicked bird and crash-landing on my floor. A very large bird clothed in overalls. A very intelligent bird who talked almost without stopping.*

Not a bird, that's a simile, a literary device. Why can I remember about literary devices and not who she is? A little girl. A little ... my daughter! She told me that at least once.

He stared down at the blank typewriter paper that still awaited a single word of poetry, the rhyming sentences that Laz-Merlin kept asking for. He adjusted the stack of yellow Venus #2 pencils in front of him, testing the sharpness of the points on the pads of his fingertips. The whole time, his thoughts kept grinding ....

I think ... yes! I'm sure *I can remember what my daughter looks like. She's a lovely silver-eyed, silver-haired child with an olive-skinned complexion who reminds me of a sunny morning. She got very angry with me because I didn't recognize her and even angrier when I kept saying things she said were stupid.*

Her name is Agile. Come on, now, that's not even a name. I remembered her name well enough to call out to her after she left. It's Angel. No, I think it's Gayle.

He picked up a pencil and laid the first sheet of paper on his desk, angling it like he'd been taught in school so the letters would go straight up and down. *If I write it and try* not *to think, can I bring the name back?*

Can I still do letters at all?

His fingers trembled with the effort of gripping the pencil near the point. Biting his tongue that protruded in concentration, he scratched out AGALI in childish print, large and misshapen. *Oh, I remember, now. Her name's Agali, and it means "sunshine" in Cherokee.*

Sequoyah smiled down at his creation, ready to take the next step. *She said I had a big family.*

He blocked his eyes with his palms in order to turn his sight inward. *Help me, Agali. Help me find my family's faces. After that I can write down their names.*

A whirling started inside his head, and disembodied faces that may or may not have belonged to his family zoomed behind his closed lids. He tried to count them on his fingers, but he seemed to see more faces than he had fingers, or more likely he kept counting the same ones two or three times. Besides, if he happened to recall one of the faces for a second or two, the features started shifting around to become composites of other faces—a kaleidoscope of eyes, noses, and mouths.

But wait, this isn't hopeless, the faces are settling down. They're becoming single people. The girl with beautiful black hair and a frown. She's saying something, "Why do I have to be your teacher, Daddy?" A swarthy boy. He looks really sad, and furious, too. He's pleading with me, "Jesus, Sequoyah, couldn't you just of answered like a real dad?" A picture-perfect blond-haired girl, and she's angry, too. Oh my, she's livid. "And what makes you *so damned superior that you can tell me what to do?"*

He clucked his tongue. *Well, gracious, my parenting sure hasn't been all sweetness and light. Who's this one? Wait, I know her. She's Agali, only younger. She's happy and running away to report something. "Yay, yay, yay, everybody, Daddy waked up!" And this one? A little boy, maybe six, with violet eyes. "Why do they hate us, Tata?" Tata? What kind of word is that? Doesn't it mean "Dad" in Czech?*

By the end of the afternoon, Sequoyah had a pretty good list that described briefly the best features of each child. He smiled down proudly at his handiwork: it contained only a few omissions of names that Agali would help him fill in tomorrow.

Alarmed for a moment, he sucked in his breath. *Surely, I remember her saying she'd come back?*

He proceeded to recite aloud to his bat globe, "My amazing black-haired daughter, Svnoyi, who has always helped me ever since she was born. My daughter, Yacy, who's blond and artistic. A fierce, handsome boy whose name starts with a K. A sweet boy who's my stepson, the one with violet eyes. He loves plants, and his name starts with a Ph or an F. And Agali, my sunshine child. She's my youngest—except for the new babies she mentioned."

Sequoyah stood up and began pacing in circles like a professor trying to solve a conundrum. *It's almost okay for me to forget a child's name when a few hours ago I couldn't remember a single person in my entire family. But to forget my wife? That's not good at all. Is it because I have two wives?*

One of them lives in the waters of Lake Spooky because I talk to her every night.

Eventually he managed to slog through his muddied thoughts to reach an indisputable conclusion. *The wife in the lake is named Miriam. She's Svnoyi's mother, and ages ago I spread her ashes under a tree, I don't remember where.*

Sequoyah flopped onto his back on his pallet, relieved to finally be free of Miriam's wearying presence. A new image entered his mind, and an unexpected flood of tears rolled down the sides of his face. He had recalled his living wife, her long red-gold hair streaked with early grey. She was weeping, too.

He stretched out his arms. *Aleta, my darling, I remember back to when my life was ebbing away. I can almost feel your embrace and see your sad face. You dropped your head to my chest and said, "How can I bear to lose this man—husband, lover, best friend, father of my newly conceived twins?"*

Then I said something that saved me, apparently. "If you take me into your heart, you will sustain my spirit." You must have taken me there, because from that point I managed to hold on.

Sequoyah tried to penetrate the monotonous grey of the rock ceiling with his mind and for the first time, he envisioned a future beyond his prison. *I've taken my memories to the very end of my old life, and I found Aleta there. I believe she stole Charon's boat to ferry me in the opposite direction, back to the land of the living. I'm naming the boat* The Traveler, *the meaning of her name in Greek.*

He sat back down at his table and sighed, more from relief than distress. *I've come a long way in a few hours of hard thinking, and I still have a lot of cobwebs to get rid of. But I have Aleta to help guide my thoughts from now on. And I'm even going to travel way back to that troubling place called Childhood.*

All at once, he laughed out loud for first time since he'd wakened in this stygian underworld, a hearty, rollicking sound that banished much of his past gloom. *I believe I'm finally feeling sharp enough to take on Laz-Merlin and his rants about gods, ancestry, and mass suicide.*

***

Laz-Merlin the Fifteen-Thousandth was spectacularly fat. Ten Prairie Dogs had to help him down, and then back up the Lake Spooky stairs so he could meet daily with Sequoyah. His fatness was not an indicator of intellectual sloth. As Philosopher-in-Chief and High Priest to the entire population as well as the only articulate person still alive, he held the fate of the Shade People in his hands. All he had to do was pronounce the word, and his followers would willingly drink one of the Prairie Dogs' lethal pharmaceuticals dissolved in apple juice.

Even though Sequoyah had been a passive listener so far, Laz-Merlin craved the sessions with him even more than the snack buckets of fried rabbit chitlins and mugs of cider that kept his body satisfied and his thinking well oiled. For here was someone whose eyes stayed open, who didn't mumble incessantly about aches and pains, and, most importantly, had the potential to converse someday and write down the lineage of the Shade People in verse. At least, that's what Queen Gitli had promised Sequoyah would do when she'd handed over his dying body for rejuvenation at The Cinder Reconstructive Center, the best Prairie Dog-run medical establishment in any of the eight caverns.

As soon as Laz-Merlin and his menials burst forth from the tunnel, the two pillow-bearers hastened inside Sequoyah's chamber to set out the huge squares of rabbit fur, stuffed with springy moss. They prepared them to their master's liking, placing three together in a row on the floor next to the wall and three to go behind his back. Then the other Prairie Dogs entered to help him sit and adjusted his olive-green toga to cover his knees. He gave his nod, and the entire contingent bowed respectfully before filing out to wait by the tunnel entrance. Laz-Merlin tried not to hear them through the open door, laughing in little short, staccato barks. He was sensitive about his appearance and spent an hour each morning coaxing his thin ash-blond hair into cascading ringlets.

Once he'd settled his frame and fluffed his coif, he turned to gaze expectantly in Sequoyah's direction, hoping that today he'd find the invalid ready to talk.

Sequoyah began in a booming voice. "Greetings, Laz-Merlin the Fifteen-Thousandth. I've recovered enough of my wits to converse with you. And right off the bat, I don't understand why you keep talking about epitaphs and suicide."

The amazement Sequoyah had hoped to produce shook Laz-Merlin's corpulent features, and he clawed at his heart somewhat alarmingly. His fun over, Sequoyah realized that the man had most likely reacted to his unexpected sentient state rather than to the content of his words. The two of them would have to speak telepathically to equalize the many changes wrought upon the English tongue during the last million years.

Sequoyah tried again, this time mind-to-mind. *Laz-Merlin, I'm sorry I gave you a shock. After all this time being silent, it's my pleasure to speak with you.*

But I must tell you, my memory was lost from the trauma of my injury, and I need to catch up. Please explain, where did you hatch this plan for the lengthy epitaph I'm supposed to write?

Ah, replied Laz-Merlin, rolling his eyes. *Loss of memory, eh? I'm sorry to hear it. Yes, the plan: the queen of the Prairie Dogs and I made a deal—*

Sequoyah interrupted him in wonder. *Then those huge furry mammals who've been my doctors and nurses and who take care of me in so many other ways are Prairie Dogs—blown up to a grand scale? And they have a queen?*

He shook his head, his eyes wide. *How absolutely amazing. They're quite brilliant, you know.*

Oh my, yes, Laz-Merlin replied. *They are equal to any human in their intelligence, and outdo the Shade People in every way, except for me, of course. But they are our slaves, thanks to our religious Commandments, Six, Seven, and Eight, as proclaimed by Goddess Mary Lynne.*

I shall quote them for you, but please realize that Commandment Seven has become more humane: a rabbit rather than a Prairie Dog is sacrificed on our altar every Sunday.

And now, Sequoyah, attend. Laz-Merlin crossed his hands over his heart and closed his eyes to emphasize the sacredness of his recitation.

Commandment Six. Lo, the Prairie Dogs shall henceforth be but humble slaves of the Shade People from the first bloom of youth until death; Commandment Seven. A chosen few well-fatted Prairie Dogs shall die in holy sacrifice every Sunday on the altar of the Eye of Cinder; Commandment Eight. No Prairie Dog shall injure or kill a Person, although a Person is not so bound.

Sequoyah stared in amazement, his eyes bulging in horror and his mouth forming a shocked O. At last he managed, *And this is how all of you live, having the Prairie Dogs wait on you, hand and foot—by religious decree, no less?*

Laz-Merlin nodded, his face bland and accepting. He had never known anything else.

His face red with anger, Sequoyah burst out, *When Goddess Mary Lynne came up with those commandments enslaving the Prairie Dogs, she ensured your doom, signed your death warrants. I'm not even considering right now what harm she did to the Prairie Dogs, it's so horrific. But you! By letting yourselves be infantilized, you've given up everything, your curiosity, your literacy, your ability to think, even your will to live, apparently—*

Ye gods, man, it's not like that, Laz-Merlin interrupted angrily. *We've carried the legacy of disease inside our bodies ever since the Day of the*

Jumping Sun when our genes were poisoned. We're tired of living with aches and pains, our population has dwindled—

Sequoyah broke in with equal rudeness, *I don't know what the Day of the Jumping Sun is, and I don't care. Perhaps you'd better tell me right now what kind of deal you cooked up with the Prairie Dogs' queen, and I hope for everyone's sake it's fair.*

Ah, yes, the deal. Laz-Merlin smiled, relieved to discuss something purely factual. *Before I state the terms of my agreement with the queen, please note that you got something very beneficial out of it: your life, renewed at our cutting-edge medical center. I trust your entire memory will come back in due course, although if I might say so, you're sounding pretty sharp already.*

He opened his fat fingers like fans, palms up. *It's simple, really. The queen gave you to me as a gift. You will write the Shade People's epitaph so we can depart this weary existence. In exchange, I'm to keep you busy and out of the way while she attends to a rather important, er, business ... having to do with our long-lost brethren, the Sun People.*

Then, once you've finished the poem, the Shade People will sip a lethal hemlock brew, the queen's business will be completed, and your family will take you home. They await you already in a pleasant grove a few miles from here. A benevolent smile lit up his entire countenance.

Sequoyah jumped up, banging his fist hard against the table, three times. *Laz-Merlin, I will not participate in a plot to end an entire civilization, no matter how unhappy and empty-headed everyone's become. That's final. I refuse to write the poem.*

He folded his arms across his chest, pumping them decisively.

Laz-Merlin was unable to rise from his pillows to challenge Sequoyah's effrontery. Instead, his telepathic thunderings caused the bats to rustle inside their globe. *You upstart. You ingrate. Who fixed your broken body, stabbed through the gut? Mark my word, you will never leave here until it's written.*

After a pause, he added, his voice wheedling and tear-choked, *Sequoyah, I want that poem. It's part of my dream for the time when my people vanish from the face of the earth. We must leave a requiem, a graceful token for anyone who might happen to stumble upon our tragic remains—*

What romantic rot, Laz-Merlin.

Sequoyah, you don't understand. I need it to make my exit in style.

Later, Sequoyah asked himself if his reply hadn't been brewing in his head all along. *Then write it yourself, dammit. I will teach you your alphabet letters and how to read. I have a hundred books. Where, I don't know because my memory hasn't explored that far—*

Our languages aren't the same anymore.

Details, details. We'll work it out.

Sequoyah was thrilled with his inspiration. He began rubbing his hands as his mind leapt ahead, picturing the results. *Laz-Merlin, my man, I bet you'll get so excited doing it, you'll finally understand that the*

Shade People have relinquished everything that matters in life. Everything! There may not be many of you left, but imagine weaning yourselves away from those Prairie Dogs, becoming literate again, leaving here and starting over fresh.

Laz-Merlin's voice sounded flat, defeated. *We can't, that's all there is to it. Gentle Corlaz Two died of sunstroke when Goddess Mary Lynne locked him outside the back door. One beam of light, and we're cooked—literally.*

You're so damned negative, forget my offer. I'm withdrawing it. Sequoyah sat down, glowering.

A minute passed as neither of them spoke.

Then Laz-Merlin rose cumbrously, but unassisted, turning his back. Sequoyah was sure he heard sniffling and a few sobs. He was right. Soon the hem of the fat man's toga misaligned itself when the skirt ascended, most likely to serve as a handkerchief.

Laz-Merlin whirled around with surprising agility, his massive body displacing a whoosh of air. *I accept, Sequoyah, I accept! Can we start tomorrow?*

Of course, friend. You know where to find me.

***

That evening when Sequoyah took his stroll around the lake, the wafting vapors and the iridescent disco-ball flashes that sped across the vaulty expanse above it failed to impress him. Its mystery was gone, and he held his nose: the water smelled of garbage. Even Miriam didn't appear from its depths because she had nestled deep down in his mind as a memory.

The excited man couldn't sleep. He lay on his pallet staring at the confines of the low ceiling, only dimly illuminated by the snoozing bats. He recounted the events of the day, dwelling for a long time on his joy being reunited with Aleta, at least in his mind.

When Sequoyah got to the conversation with Laz-Merlin, he felt much more resigned than he thought he would. *I may have delayed my release for even longer by promising to teach him how to read and write. But I feel good, and I bet he does, too.*

37 ~ Famine

Laz-Merlin's lesson is in about five minutes. Am I ready?

Sequoyah read over the story he'd written that morning for his pupil, who had progressed phenomenally in six weeks. The sentences were simple enough, and every one of them contained a smattering of nouns that Laz-Merlin had taught him in the present-day Shade People's tongue, transliterated as best he knew how.

Is my printing readable? Oh, here's a place that needs a comma. And this long sentence would be better broken into two. He made the corrections and laid the autobiographical sheets about a boy in an Indian orphan school back down on the table.

But Laz-Merlin the Fifteen-Thousandth didn't show up for his lesson. The hour passed, and Sequoyah's dinner was delayed by another hour and a half. The Prairie Dog who finally brought the tray put it on his table with trembling paws. She had an unusually pretty almost-pink coat, and when he tried to thank her, she'd already fled before he got the chance. He peeked under the cloche. Instead of a substantial helping of rabbit stew, he found four unpeeled carrots, and an apple and two crusts from breakfast that looked like they'd been rescued from the trash.

There was also a jar next to his plate containing live mosquitos and beside it, a handful of tapers and matches. *How thoughtful of her to remember my bats and my light. But I've never taken care of them myself. I hope I get it right.*

I wonder what could've happened in the kitchen.

The next day no one came except the same Prairie Dog who had brought him dinner the previous night. The meal had shrunk to three carrots, but once again, she hadn't forgotten the mosquitos for his bats.

This is getting serious. What's going on, here? Where's Laz-Merlin gotten to, and why hasn't Agali come? Until now, they've never missed a single day.

He wrung his hands. *My daughter and my best friend, together they've restored my life. Without them, I feel lost all over again.*

Sequoyah spent a fitful night tossing from worry, and when breakfast failed to arrive and his stomach wouldn't stop rumbling, he made up his mind to leave. His belongings were few: a change of clothes and toiletries the Prairie Dogs had brought from his own cave back home, and the paper and pencils. He wrapped everything carefully inside the blanket that he didn't wish to take, except he thought it might come in handy.

I'll get lost for sure in the cavern, but at least I'll discover what's going on. And when I get outside, I'll look for my family, and that could take days. I wish I had some food to bring along.

On the way out the door, Sequoyah grabbed the bat globe and his wooden soup plate to serve as a hat to shade his eyes. He'd been underground for a long time, and he recalled Laz-Merlin's words: *One beam of light, and we're cooked—literally.*

***

When Sequoyah reached the Lake Spooky stairs, he was overjoyed to see Agali at the top. She had a Prairie Dog with her, the same one with the pinkish coat who had brought him his two sad little dinners. The poor thing seemed to be in a state of collapse. Even though she was almost as large as Agali, his daughter held the scrunched-up ball of fur tightly in her arms.

Agali called down to him, "Oh Daddy, I'm so glad you got to the stairs. Sanctissima is too upset to do anything more." She twisted her head in the direction of the path. "She says it's just *awful* inside the bedrooms."

"I'm glad you're here, too, sweetheart. Can you tell me what's going on?" Sequoyah ran up the stairs to embrace both his daughter and from necessity, the Prairie Dog.

"Sanctissima's her name? She came for the last two nights to bring me a little bit of food. Are the Shade People starving all of a sudden?"

Agali lowered her voice, even though Sanctissima couldn't understand her except telepathically. "All the Prairie Dogs—nurses, doctors, helpers—just got up and left, except Sanctissima. She told me they'd been *conscripted*—she was, too. But she wouldn't go because of you and me. She said she was breaking the law by staying, and now she's the last Prairie Dog here.

"And Sanctissima said the food sacks coming in on the Polar Bear Express started slowing down a long time ago, and then they stopped. There wasn't any more medicine coming in, either, and most of the Shade People were really sick and needed their pills every day."

"You said, *were* really sick?"

She added the pitiable postscript. "Yes, Daddy. Sanctissima says they're dead."

"Oh, my god." All at once a flood of thoughts swept through Sequoyah's mind, and he gripped his head as if it might burst. *The Shade People are dead? This is a catastrophe. Oh, please let Laz-Merlin be alive. Why didn't he* tell *me there wasn't enough to eat? He looked like he was shrinking fast, but I assumed he'd gone on a diet.*

But which is worse? I've remembered enough about Queen Gitli by now to know that she can be a monster. Conscription means she's drafted her workers into an army, so she's starting a war.

"Agali, we have to search the cavern for survivors. And then we must gather the family and get back home. I will talk Queen Gitli out of this war if I can; wars are never good for anyone.

"Why didn't you tell me what was going on, sweetheart?"

"Oh, Daddy, the back door was locked, and I couldn't get in for the last few days. So I didn't know. When Sanctissima let me back in, then she told me what happened." Her voice trailed off.

They decided to leave Sanctissima in her usual hiding place behind the mica-covered boulder by the path until they'd completed the grim task ahead. She promised to stay put and wait for them. As soon as the unhappy creature who had witnessed the Shade People's last days had curled up in her sanctuary, she fell into an exhausted sleep.

Sequoyah ripped his spare shirt into several pieces. "If it's as bad as I think, we'll need these to cover our noses. But tell me, dear, what makes you so brave? I could go alone."

Agali squeezed his hand reassuringly. "I've always been like this, Daddy. I'm really brave, probably braver than you. It's because I decided a long time ago that I'm going to be a doctor like Anichka. She's been teaching me everything, especially not to be scared of what happens at the end of your life."

Sequoyah took her at her word. *Well, well, that would definitely make her braver than me, even though I almost went through it.*

Because Sanctissima had always led her on the same route to the Lake Spooky stairs, Agali had only a dim notion of how the cavern was laid out. She and Sequoyah decided to do a consistent search. They started at the rooms nearest Lake Spooky and moved across and forward from there, combing through nine chambers in all, some with anterooms and alcoves.

Most of the people had died on their daybeds, whether from untreated illnesses or starvation, the two couldn't tell. In a dormitory room, Sequoyah and Agali found ten teenagers who were still alive, huddled together for comfort. The six girls and four boys, trembling and white as plaster, were nonetheless healthy enough to walk out on their own. Sequoyah and Agali found no younger children, living or dead, an indication that Laz-Merlin had spoken the truth: the Shade People's population had been dwindling.

The father and daughter were almost done. They'd been through every room, big and small, and they'd opened all the bat globes they could find, hoping the freed creatures would fly out through the open-air chimneys located in three of the cavern's chambers. Sequoyah kept his own globe lit until the end of the search, letting it serve its purpose as a grim beacon within that night-black sepulcher.

As they escorted the survivors through the corridors, Sequoyah tried to come to grips with the horror of it all. *I don't believe even Queen Gitli would've finished off the Shade People intentionally, mainly because she'd already put into motion Laz-Merlin's nutty suicide plot with me stuck in the middle. She must've forgotten about them during her zealous war preparations. But that's no excuse. This is genocide.*

Agali was tugging at his sleeve. "Daddy, Daddy, I just had a horrible thought. There are seven more caverns on the way home, and I bet they're all like this one."

Oh, no, how awful can this get? She's undoubtedly right, so we'll stop and carefully search all the others for survivors, exactly the same way.

They found Laz-Merlin lying dead in a monastically spare bedchamber attached to the huge auditorium used for Sunday services. Sequoyah asked Agali to give him a few minutes alone with the high priest-turned-pupil whom he'd grown to love. The ever intrepid girl obliged and waited alone in the corridor with the ragtag collection of teenage children who slumped against the wall, terror lurking behind their tight features.

Sequoyah sat down cross-legged beside Laz-Merlin where he lay on his pallet, his glassy stare seeming to peruse the itty-bitty stalactites on the ceiling. The mourner sighed as he closed the eyes. He wished he'd brought two coins to put on the lids to pay Charon, boatman of the Styx, as befitted the man's olive-green toga, presently large enough for someone four times his size. But even that last gesture made no sense.

To begin with, there are *no coins. Somehow this bizarre world of slavery has managed without money, and all the flitting ghosts who live here now wouldn't understand the concept. Besides, Laz-Merlin doesn't need to travel anywhere. He can't get much closer to Hades than he is already.*

Then with tears in his eyes, he addressed the deceased in a murmur, touching the blue fingers. "Laz-Merlin, you became my dear, dear friend because you and I did form those 'hoops of steel' Polonius talks about in *Hamlet*.

"I'd hoped that you would save the Shade People, leading them to freedom once you found out what you'd been missing your whole life. I accused you of being a Romantic because of your prettified death wish. But that would be me more than you, a hopeless Romantic for fantasizing that such a plan could've worked."

Whispering a final goodbye, Sequoyah covered the dead man's body with his own blanket that he'd brought along in case it would come in handy.

***

Sequoyah and Agali sealed off the cave mouth to the Eye of Cinder by rolling closed the night-grate, and Sanctissima locked it with a decisive click. In better days the day and night barriers had kept wild beasts and snowdrifts out while allowing fresh air to flow into the bustling underground city where the Shade People had first settled a million years ago. The forlorn party made its way through the kitchen, the teenagers flocking behind the father and daughter with Sanctissima taking up the rear. Everyone eyed the empty cupboards and shelves, wishing for a grain of rice stuck in a crack or a drop of water in the bone-dry cisterns. Exiting the fabled Rear of Corlaz One for the last time, they walked outside into a bright, breezy day, and Sanctissima locked the door.

Oh, no, we're forgetting the teenagers. How can they bear leaving behind their dead loved ones and all they've ever known? Sequoyah whipped around, ready to proffer sympathy. What he saw looked more like self-protection than mental anguish: they had crouched down, covering their heads and faces with their arms.

He remembered again what Laz-Merlin had said. He plopped the soup plate on one of them, crying out, "The sun, it will kill them."

Sanctissima and Agali took charge. They herded the teens into the shadowy depot of the Polar Bear Express that had an entrance next to the kitchen door.

When Agali came back, she announced, "Daddy, Sanctissima's staying with them now. We found a bunch of empty carts for them, and we made them comfortable sitting on the produce sacks. But they're really hungry and thirsty. We have to hurry.

"Now I'm taking you to the place where Mama and the new babies are."

She gave him a motherly smile the way Svnoyi used to. "Here's your soup plate back again, Daddy. Put it on your own head because you've been in the dark for a long time. We have a long walk."

As Sequoyah positioned the ill-fitting wooden dish, a pleasing notion hit him. *My daughter is amazing. She can organize just like Svnoyi always could, and she takes care of me almost the same way, too.*

His nine months in recovery had taken a physical toll. In spite of his glory-days during the Time Before as the best forest ranger in the High Tatras next to Jaroslav, Sequoyah's plodding ascent up the hill of coffee bushes left him gasping and ready to faint, especially on an empty stomach. Agali had done the climb every day for almost two months, and even though it was a cakewalk for her, she slowed to his pace and did not poke fun at him.

As they approached the encampment along the forest-lined road by the Express's drainage ditch, Sequoyah could hear shouts from half a mile away. "Agali, what is this hideous racket? Is it coming from the place where you're staying? Don't tell me that my return to my loving wife is gonna be a reenactment of rush-hour at Grand Central Station."

The little girl announced with pride, "Everyone's making noise because they're getting ready. I talked to Jaroslav and Anichka mind-to-mind. They're getting medicines packed up to help the teenagers—the ones waiting in the station and all the others we happen to find in the caverns on the way home.

"And Arbel and Arbeline are calling the bears that got furloughed to come back from the forest so they can make up the teams. And the Cauliflowers are getting food and packing up everything for our trip home. And Alexej's loading the cart. Mama's feeding the babies real quick—"

Sequoyah stopped short.

"But Daddy, we're leaving right away, remember?"

Then she whispered, "Did I do something wrong?" She tried to reach for one of her father's hands, but he was too busy wringing them.

He sat down in the middle of the road in dismay, wiping the sweat from his forehead with a piece of his torn shirt, his makeshift hat rolling into the ditch. *I didn't imagine my homecoming would be like this. I wanted it to be about Aleta and me. Who the hell are Arbel and Arbeline? And the Cauliflowers? They sound like pop singers with back-up.*

"Agali, I can't stand all these new people and the noise and everything—not this soon. I don't like it. Make it stop."

Agali turned to climb down the embankment to fetch his hat, but not before Sequoyah caught the look on her face. *I've seen that look before, somewhere. It was ... it was the first day. Yes, the first day when I told her I didn't know her.*

Sequoyah remained sitting in the road. *What have I done? She was doing exactly what I asked her to do. How do parents explain away their own cruelty and stupidity?*

Agali stayed out of sight for five very long minutes, and when her head reappeared above the gully, Sequoyah saw that his sunshine child's eyes were narrowed, and her mouth was drawn into a thin line. He braced himself for an explosion that he knew he deserved.

She marched to his side and clapped the wooden hat on his head, making his brains rattle.

"Why do I have to be your teacher, Daddy? You're well now, so get up. You're our leader, again, like it or not."

***

To prepare himself, Sequoyah took a quick detour off the road to peek at the camp from behind a barrier of junipers before bravely stepping back into his past life where it had left off, as well as into his new one.

This place reminds me of a beehive in a field of summer flowers. There are so many bright colors, everyone's running about, there's chatter, there's laughter. There are about thirty polar bears, and ... it can't be. Those beautiful folk must be the Sun People Laz-Merlin told me about, six of them. There are my friends, Anichka and Jaroslav and their little boy, Alexej. And look, everybody keeps turning toward the road. They're waiting for something. No, for someone! They're waiting for me.

I'm going to remember this picture forever, like a snapshot in an album. Because Aleta is in front, and she's holding two little babies, one in each arm. In a minute I'll be holding her.

38 ~ Flathead Express

***The sun won't set tonight and if you're dead, it won't rise high in the morning.* —Lucy**

"Where's the goddam Polar Bear Express? It was supposed to come in half a day ago."

Phoenix wrestled his arms out of the shoulder straps of his heavy backpack and dumped it with a plop on the stone floor of the Eye of Cinder depot. Thoroughly annoyed, he sat on it, not caring what he might be squashing inside.

"Cool your jets, Phoenix," Svnoyi remarked with a hint of condescension. "Even in the Time Before, especially in the Time Before, nothing arrived on time, not trains, planes, boats, buses—"

"Okay, okay. I get your point."

Phoenix stretched out flat on his back, using his pack as a headrest. "So, Snail, have a seat. While we're lying around here doing nothing, tell me how you think we did for the last seven weeks since we left the Pippins and our trueloves."

"Great, and I mean that," Svnoyi answered, immediately. "We kept going north, and we caught every village. We stayed six or seven days, then hopped on the Flathead Express for the next one."

She ticked them off on her fingers: "Zucchinis, Chards, Butterheads, Cucumbers ... oh, damn, help me out, here."

Phoenix took over. "After the Cucumbers, the Cantaloupes, Idahos, and last, the Cauliflowers where we finished up just today. And because they're close to the most northern of the Prairie Dog farms and the Eye of Cinder, here we are at the Shade People's ostentatious depot."

"The Shade People's what?" Svnoyi hadn't been paying attention.

Leaning against her pack, she closed her eyes and smiled, and her next words sounded remarkably dreamlike for someone of her character. "But it wasn't just helping the Sun People plant gardens and delivering their babies. It was so much more. Everyone knew about us already when we got to each new place, and every village had Jimjamoree three times a day, which I simply adore. I guess you might say I felt ... accepted and loved everywhere."

Phoenix interjected, "Me, too. But you could feel the tension. About the war coming, the troops leaving to train with Kuaray at a secret location somewhere inland—"

"Yeah, the war." Svnoyi's benign expression vanished, and she sat up straight.

"You know what could've happened," she suggested. "We've been here with the Sun People for eight weeks altogether, and it's nearly the first of August. I bet Queen Gitli stopped the Polar Bear Express from running and is keeping the carts at Iqual's terminal to pack them with supplies for the invasion of the villages."

Phoenix nodded. "You could be right if she's planning it for September first. It's a lot of work. Everything has to be distributed to eight different places—and secretly, too."

A discomfiting thought struck him. "But wait. With the express not making deliveries, won't the Shade People starve?"

"Well, Phoenix, I was just wondering about that. The queen wishes them dead, but starving them isn't her style, it's too simple. I sure hope she's thought it through, but like I said before, sometimes I don't think she knows what the hell she's up to."

Phoenix stood up. "Let's get out of here. We have to get back, ASAP, and try to talk her out of this invasion. We can hike over to the Sun People's Flathead Express that's about five miles away and walk the one hundred miles to Iqual once we get to the last stop near the Pippins' village."

***

Shouldering their packs, Svnoyi and Phoenix left the Eye of Cinder terminal behind. They walked along a path that skirted the Prairie Dogs' northernmost farm and then the Cauliflowers' village where they had just spent the week. The path became a narrow trail meandering through coastal forests as it climbed ever higher. It capped on a knoll where the hikers craned their necks to glimpse a sparkling bay far below them on the other side of a tree-covered ridge. The water reminded them of home at the opposite end of the vast land that the Sun People and Prairie Dogs called Baffling Isle. They stood still for a moment, soaking up the beauty of the wilderness that within weeks would most likely bear the scars of an enemy's wrath.

Svnoyi started down the other side of the knoll, turning her head to call out to Phoenix, "I can't tell you how much I hate leaving the Sun People and their beautiful forests. But we have to do our job and report back to Queen Gitli."

"What should we say?" Phoenix yelled back. "The Sun People rejected the Oath of Fealty unanimously."

Svnoyi slowed her pace until Phoenix caught up. She hadn't thought that far ahead, and at last she admitted, "Seriously, I don't know. We could beg her to see reason."

"Ha." Phoenix sounded sarcastic. "That tactic is bound to impress her totally."

After that, they walked in silence. Svnoyi contemplated her original notion that their entire mission had been a setup to get them out of town during war preparations at Iqual. In spite of her dark suspicion, she couldn't help but smile inwardly. *Little does the good queen know that we both found the loves of our lives and turned traitor, too, thanks to Kuaray and Lucy.*

The Flathead Express terminal lay deep inside a thicket to hide it from the Prairie Dogs if they happened to venture this far in search of the delicacies they craved from the forest floor. Phoenix and Svnoyi were able to locate it only because they'd arrived there the previous week. The entrance was camouflaged by a hollow tree without a base at its burned-out center. Instead, a hole with a ladder imbedded in a root-studded wall went underground. They descended slowly, their balance compromised by their packs, to find themselves once more in the cozy station lit by torches. It had a packed dirt road half as wide as the stone avenue of the touted Polar Bear Express and a ceiling of exposed pine timbers that seemed to recede into infinity within the black tunnel.

"I love this station," Svnoyi announced once their feet had touched solid ground. "No pomp, very bright and warm."

She turned around and reeling with surprise, she accidentally dropped the pack that she'd pried from her shoulders. Two flathead bears already stood stock-still in front of the only cart in the terminal, stoically waiting for their passengers to acknowledge them. They held rope harnesses in their jaws as if asking to be buckled into them.

Svnoyi tried to laugh. "Oh, I thought we were alone. Bears, you scared me."

Phoenix looked baffled. "How'd they get here? And how did they know we wanted a ride?"

"It's obvious," Svnoyi replied, regaining her usual confidence. "They saw us in the forest where they happen to live, and they guessed we needed their services because not many people come here. Then they went through the tunnel that comes out right there." She pointed to a low archway at the back of the depot.

"Ask them their names, Phoenix. I don't have the skill."

"Me? I don't have it either."

"Try telepathically?"

"No," Phoenix answered decisively. "Some people like Lucy can do it, but I can't. I'll name them instead, and I hope they like my choices."

He patted them tentatively on their heads, flat as mesas. "Hey, nice bears, I'm calling you ... Ernie and Bertha. Do you like your new names?"

Whether they did or not, the names stuck, and the bears looked happy enough, especially once they had their harnesses on.

Svnoyi peered at them closely. "Phoenix, remember the poor beasts at Queen Gitli's palace that carried her tables? Corlion said there's enough of a bear defection going on to run their entire express."

***

The week-long ride was uneventful until Svnoyi and Phoenix reached the final stop somewhere near the Pippins' village. They unhitched the cart and thanked the flathead bears multiple times. Then they presented each bear with a clean bandana they'd fished from the depths of their overstuffed backpacks. Although it was difficult to tell, Ernie and Bertha seemed pleased to sport the red triangles knotted around their sturdy necks.

Svnoyi and Phoenix located the tunnel that exited the depot's earthen pocket of a room. Phoenix's voice sounded dead in the dank interior, "Too bad, there isn't one more stop to take us all the way to Iqual, although that would be totally dumb, of course, just *asking* for the Prairie Dogs to discover the Flathead Express."

"Right. And there's something else I never thought about until now," said Svnoyi logically. "Since we're walking to Iqual from here, the Sun People must've sneaked one hundred miles through the forest to wreck the Sacred Meadow. And sneaked back, too, laden down with pipes and gears."

She lowered her voice, even though there was no need. "Y'know, I've been meaning to ask you for ever so long. Did Corlinia go along on that raid?"

Phoenix nodded and grinned, his face unseen in the dark. "You betcha. She kind of disregarded the political point, though. These were her words: 'It's heaps of fun to get to break stuff, sometimes.'"

From taking the express the opposite direction between the Pippins and the Zuccinis seven weeks ago, the travelers remembered Mother Nature's surprise that lay above ground. The tunnel terminated at the center of a rock pile—towering thirty-foot granite monoliths with pointed tips resembling skyscrapers incongruously dropped in the thickest part of an old-growth forest. Mesmerized, they wandered about, arching their backs to stare up at the spires. Grey storm clouds closed in above them and thunder cracked somewhere close by. Fat raindrops smacked them in their faces.

The sudden dowsing unnerved Svnoyi, whose self-possession had been fraying as the war drew closer. Hunching over, she covered her head with her arms to ward off the worst of it. She had to yell over the storm: "Y'know, Phoenix, the Pippins' village is so close. Let's get out of the rain by running over to say a last goodbye to Corlion and Corlinia." Even as she opened her mouth, she knew her words should have remained unspoken.

Phoenix had had the same thought himself. He barked back in a pique, "For chrissake, Svnoyi, you know you shouldn't suggest something so tempting because it hurts too much. And it's just plain stupid. We're not that close, for one thing. Besides, most likely they're off somewhere training to fight guerrilla style."

He slipped on the damp pine needles, falling clumsily to his knees. "God, I hope Kuaray knows what he's doing." Phoenix's face puckered up, and for a moment Svnoyi thought he might cry.

"Hush up, Phoenix. Kuaray promised he'd keep them in back of the first-line archers—"

"And since when has he ever kept his promises?"

Svnoyi knelt, feeling water ooze through the knees of her jeans. She put a hand on his arm even though her voice was tinged with anger. "Don't even ask that, Phoenix. Yes, we're on edge. But we have to rely on something positive or we'll go crazy with worry."

"Yeah," he whispered, mainly to himself. "But it's so damn hard to stay positive all the time—

"Hey, what's going on?" He bounced up, his voice squeaking.

Ernie and Bertha had slipped between the rocks unnoticed until they stood within a few feet of the distraught and soaking wayfarers. The bears nudged them forward with paws and noses toward a spot where a number of fallen spires overlapped to form a hollow place deep and wide enough to hold all of them. Even without a telepathic exchange, both humans and animals understood the wisdom of curling up for the night within the shelter to wait out the drenching storm. Svnoyi and Phoenix soon got used to the bears' musky odor just as the bears accepted their distinctive "people" smell.

When Svnoyi and Phoenix woke up the next morning, they had no trouble deciding they'd rather ride than walk to Iqual and clambered onto the bears' backs. They noticed that yesterday's rain had scrubbed down the pines to their glossiest green, leaving a diamond on every needle to catch the pure light of day so exalted by the Sun People.

After the bears had kept up a loping pace for an hour, they stopped to rest and catch their breakfast of whitefish in a nearby stream. Svnoyi and Phoenix gathered wood to build a fire within the ring of stones they'd assembled for the purpose. The bears' timing was perfect. They returned from fishing to stand side-by-side in front of their adopted humans. First, they shook water in every direction from their cream-colored coats. Then they opened their jaws to drop two whitefish directly into the sizzling frying pan.

Svnoyi and Phoenix nodded their thanks, smiling broadly. Considering how damp their clothes still were from yesterday, the shower was something they could've done without. But the fish were delicious and a welcome change from the usual strips of rabbit jerky.

"I love these bears," Svnoyi whispered. "They may have been bred by scientists to serve, but genes creating their goodness surely didn't come out of a test tube."

"You couldn't have said it better." Phoenix raised his head to call out, "Ernie and Bertha, could you please stay with us, forever?"

"I think they will stay," Svnoyi said in a hushed voice, realizing a new truth for the first time. "Ernie and Bertha wouldn't be here if Corlion and Corlinia hadn't sent them to be our guides and protectors."

***

What a discouraging week. Svnoyi and Phoenix with Lucy translating had made no headway negotiating with Queen Gitli. Bone-tired after spending another entire day with her at the palace, they headed straight for the beach below the caves because they knew Yacy and Oscar would have a picnic dinner waiting for them. They watched the flathead bears already frolicking out in the water, looking for fish. In the late afternoon light, the trio squinted through the heat ripples that set the shore shimmering. Silhouetted against the grey cliffs, they could make out two adults waving to them and also a pair of babies bouncing like jumping beans. But they slowed their arrival by dragging their feet through the salt-and-pepper sand. Today's meeting had reached an impasse even sooner than yesterday's.

Yacy and Oscar extended their arms in a warm welcome when their unsmiling companions dropped down on one of Luz's raveled quilts. They passed the plates, and everyone ate in silence.

After a while, Phoenix said, "No dice."

"Are you sure you did everything you could?" Yacy's eyes were wide with worry, her forehead furrowed.

Lucy answered, "Yes, they did. Everything. I was standing right there, translating."

She gestured toward her companions. "For about the hundredth time they explained all the good things they'd done—planting a big garden in every village, delivering babies, forging friendships. They told her how beautiful the Sun People's philosophy of life is, how sincere and loving they are."

Phoenix finished for her. "Today we even asked for more time to work something out by making the Oath of Fealty less harsh. Then we'd try offering it to the Sun People again. Queen Gitli said to forget it."

He shrugged. "The old bitch still thinks they're barbarians stealing her rightful property because it's where they happen to live. We never got through to her, not today, not yesterday, not the day before, or the day before that. And we won't tomorrow, either."

"Then it's finished." Oscar looked down at his plate, his shoulders slumping. "Obviously she made up her mind how she wanted it to end before she sent you. Their villages are going to be invaded in about two weeks.

"At least they know it's coming."

Svnoyi glanced over at Lucian and Arielle Luz who were throwing fistfuls of sand in each other's faces. The battle was escalating and would soon end with tears. *They're not quite a year old. Aggression sure starts young, and there isn't a damn thing that'll change that, it's hardwired. The Prairie Dogs aren't human, but they picked up their masters' worst trait about a million years ago and it's been festering ever since, getting ready to blow—*

Svnoyi's meditation on aggression ended when Yacy rose up to stop the fight. She clutched each bawling child by a plump hand, but they twisted furiously, trying to break away. Yacy deposited Lucian in Oscar's arms and picked up her own daughter.

"Let's go home, everybody. You guys grab the picnic things. Oscar will make tea and we can talk more about all this after I feed the babies and put them to bed."

The practiced mother smiled with a sweetness reserved for infants and people in crisis. "We have fresh blackberries, and I picked enough of 'em for Ernie and Bertha who've been sitting behind those rocks waiting for you."

Once again Lucy paused midway up the switchbacks and sat in the middle of the trail as Yacy and Oscar went on ahead, the sleeping children's legs swinging loosely. She had to empty the sand from her sneakers. As she poured out about two tablespoonfuls from each heel making two miniature cones, she repeated the same questions as always, her voice plaintive.

"When you saw Kuaray at the Pippins' village, did he say anything about me? What did he say?"

Svnoyi and Phoenix always obliged her, thinking the identical thing every time: coming from Kuaray, his words had sounded surprisingly fervent and truthful. *She's not like other people. She's good. She has a big, big heart.*

The ritual completed, Svnoyi decided the time was right. "Lucy, something else happened there." She hesitated, not wanting to upset her dear friend who was already undone by an uncertain love.

Lights danced in Svnoyi's eyes. "Phoenix and I, we both fell in love. No, not with each other, that was never going to work. With *Sun People,* and we're going to marry them in a year. Their names are Corlion and Corlinia."

Lucy paled and bit her lip. She was jealous. At last she grabbed their hands and managed to stutter, "I-I'm so happy for you."

Then the real meaning of Svnoyi's revelation took hold, and her innate goodness came flooding back. "You mean ... you mean *three* of us could lose the people we love in the invasion—"

"Yes. That's right," Svnoyi said.

She hugged them both, her arms stretched wide. "You two, this is the best news in the world ... the scariest, too. You must tell the others about them."

Phoenix's little chuckle of amusement lifted their spirits. "Oscar guessed in about five minutes after we got back. He sees things no one else ever could."

They stood up, eyeing the switchbacks they still had to climb.

"Steep like life," said Lucy. The others nodded.

***

By the time the babies had fallen asleep and the four of them had sat down at the table to talk further about negotiations gone awry, they could see from the cave mouth black clouds towering in a red-ochre sky. The formations looked ominous and promised thunder and rain along with cyclonic winds capable of tearing the tops off trees. They waited for the pyrotechnics as Ernie and Bertha paced in uneasy circles, rolling their eyes.

But the storm did not break. Instead, the clouds sat low in that formidable red sky, and the humidity soared.

"Ugh, what a backdrop. Grab your brooms, it's a perfect night for a witches' sabbath." Svnoyi's witticism brought only a short snicker from Phoenix.

"Sorry, guys, dumb joke. Okay, seriously, there are two more things we can try. My first idea is someone talk to Ethan and Luz. Queen Gitli's favorite inventors of war machines could have some pull with her."

"Not possible," Lucy countered. "They're under guard at the hospital, and no one can get near their door. I tried sneaking in yesterday and ran into Tlke's thugs."

"What's the other?" Yacy and Oscar asked in one voice.

"Well," said Svnoyi. "We can pray that my Daddy Sequoyah gets home in time to talk the queen out of it."

She wasn't joking. "Listen guys, it's not that far-fetched. We heard rumors in the Sun People's village nearest to the Eye of Cinder that he was almost ready to come back. That was almost two weeks ago."

Phoenix's jaw dropped. "Are you serious, Svnoyi? You mean we just sit here ... waiting for Godot?"

He burst into hysterical laughter and choked on his tea.

Seconds later, the flathead bears, wanted criminals in Iqual since their escape from the palace, ran for the shadows at the back of the cave. Tlke stalked in. She was clacking the dual castanets of her formidable teeth and claws and aggressively pumping her short arms back and forth.

Lucy jumped up so fast she brushed the bowl of blackberries onto the floor with her elbow. She still held her mug in shaking fingers. *Tlke, no! Not in here. Whatever's bothering you, we'll talk about it outside.*

Minutes passed. Then the people inside heard the mug clatter on the stone ledge by the cave mouth.

Oscar started for the exit, whispering over his shoulder, "We gotta go rescue her. Tlke looked crazy. Did you see her eyes?"

Lucy came back in, then, almost colliding with him. Her face was white, accentuating a red, four-clawed slash across her nose and cheek. Ever mindful of wounds, Yacy reached for a clean cloth to wipe away the blood, and she grabbed a jar of aloe salve with her other hand.

Trembling, Lucy winced at Yacy's touch. "Tlke's right. I deserve this. I am the *worst* kind of traitor. I ruined the queen's perfectly designed war."

Her next words were brief. "The Sun People's army is here, and Kuaray's leading it.

"They must've decided to attack first."

"What the hell?" Phoenix cried, his voice rising an octave.

"Where?" squeaked Svnoyi.

"At the Sacred Meadow. Both the Sun People and the Prairie Dogs are facing off right now, ready to start shooting at each other."

39 ~ Red Night

Lucy raced on foot, taking the roundabout forest route toward the Sacred Meadow's main entrance flanked by stone cairns. For speed, her first choice would have been the palace tunnel to the hospital and then the trapdoor from the Death Room. But the accused traitor was quite sure she'd never be allowed inside the palace again. She could hear Svnoyi and Phoenix directly behind her, their Jimjamoree sandals crunching on dead pine needles.

As she ran, her thoughts flew in many directions before they glommed together in endless repetitions, a synaptic cacophony.

Of course the Sun People had to come here and attack. Why didn't we figure that out? It's like Phoenix said, you can't just sit around and wait.

By attacking here and coming two weeks early, Kuaray's saving the Sun People from a slaughter in their own villages.

I know Kuaray will be in front riding Petey, leading the charge, trying to show everyone he's still a man.

The Sacred Meadow's a death trap, there's no way out.

Kuaray will die right away.

Also Svnoyi's Corlion and Phoenix's Corlinia and all those pretty pups.

I never told Kuaray how much I love him.

Lucy squinted upward at a devil's palette, black on red, and the gashes on her nose and cheek burned. *Why does the sky look like that? The sun won't set tonight and if you're dead, it won't rise high in the morning.*

***

Technically speaking, Kuaray kept the promises he'd made to Svnoyi and Phoenix: Corlion and Corlinia were not in the first line of archers. They sat behind him on Petey's back, the trio and their steed resembling a fantastic, if low-slung, centaur as long as three horses lined up nose-to-tail.

Behind this innovative war machine, an army of two hundred forty-eight-foot soldiers stood stock-still, bowstrings taut and eyes on their targets. Kuaray's indoctrination to despise thine enemy had been effective, and in their minds, the Prairie Dogs were no better than prey for the stewpot. They had entered at the front of the Sacred Meadow between the cairns. Following their leader's instructions, they'd positioned themselves in three staggered lines alongside the mountain ridge on the right side.

The Prairie Dog pups had been taken unawares in their camp, playing hopscotch and tag after Neshek's five-star dinner. Out of the blue they'd heard a thump, thump coming along the trail, and Tlke had shown up, riding a big jackrabbit. At first they'd laughed, a chorus of little yipping barks. She'd cut a comic figure, so nervous and on such a funny steed. But soon they had felt as nervous as the messenger and grabbed their bows and quivers, because clearly there was no time to lose.

With the front entrance taken up by Sun People on their way in, the pups had rushed through the palace's secret entrances and into the hospital tunnel by the kitchen. They exited the trapdoor in pairs, and stumbling all over each other, they'd filled the left side of the field. What the assembled army of two hundred pups had in its favor was sheer numbers. Many hundreds more huddled in the hospital's capacious rooms, prepared to take the places of the fallen.

Saint George was already on the meadow when the Prairie Dog soldiers arrived. He was pacing in distracted circles, wondering where the hell Lucy was. Surely, she would lead the advance? He had grown so dependent on her that he'd daydreamed through her classes imagining the impossible—a night in his own bed without the snores of the queen, Neshek, and Captain Kirk.

***

In the middle of the field between the two opposing armies, Petey and his riders began a frenetic snake dance across the length of the valley floor at forty-five miles an hour. The team of Kuaray, Corlinia, and Corlion swayed as one, banking gracefully at the turns, their arrows nocked and ready to fly as soon as Kuaray gave the signal.

The well-rehearsed choreography was truly magnificent and succeeded admirably. The amassed Prairie Dog archers, who could barely hold any formation under the timorous Saint George, dropped their bows to their sides in amazement. Only a few of them asked themselves, *Isn't the rider who's in front that grouchy instructor from months ago—the one we laughed at behind his back?* The rest of them had never seen a more terrifying monster, a hundred-legged dragon sprouting from its armor plates three humans with *azvrkts* drawn. They turned and ran, tripping and falling against the boundary of the mountain ridge.

I'm too late, they've already started. Even Kuaray's balletic *tour de force* unfolding before Lucy's eyes didn't stop her imprudent feet. She didn't pause at the entrance, nor at the first gully that had once contained a roaring river. Swerving to find a narrow place, she leapt across it, and across the second one, and the third, too. With the fleetness of the Greek Atalanta or of Goddess Violent running away from God Rough, she reached the center of the Sacred Meadow.

She yelled at the top of her lungs as she ran, "Kuaray, don't shoot. *Don't sh-o-o-o-ot!*"

The plaintive message reached him even as Petey bore down on her. Kuaray shrieked, "Dammit all, Lucy, you're gonna get trampled."

He jerked on Petey's reins in a desperate effort to turn the centipede around. Petey reacted so quickly that all three went flying off his slippery armored back. Kuaray landed within a foot of Lucy—so close that she reached for his hand where he lay on the ground.

Lucy saw his eyes were full of tears. Of rage, disappointment, pain? She had no idea. *What are they saying? That I ruined his moment?*

She wanted to pull him to his feet but knew she couldn't. His legs were like rubber.

Then things happened too fast. The centipede's sudden change of direction woke up the paralyzed Saint George. He gave the signal to shoot, and the Prairie Dogs pulled themselves together because the now riderless monster was no longer a threat. In their forward rush, they realized they didn't need their lackluster leader anymore and left him behind, waving his ineffectual arms. Their arrows flew—mainly in the right direction thanks to Lucy's excellent instruction.

Revitalized, the Prairie Dogs yipped with delight, letting loose a volley of cheers along with the arrows. After all these weeks, they'd finally gotten to the fun part. Their religious instructor, Captain Kirk, Twenty-One Thousand and Two of the Orator-Priest Caste, had done his work well. His negation of Commandment Eight proved effective, and they had no problem shooting at humans.

The Sun People assessed the situation: Kuaray, the leader whom they'd grown to love, was down. They proceeded on their own, shooting back at the Prairie Dogs in grim silence but with a far more practiced and deadly aim than their foes, their pale and slim bodies elegantly defined in blue chitons.

Arrows zoomed in both directions, and Petey understood that his mission had changed from zigzagging to shielding. He heaved his 6000 pounds on top of his cherished master and his equally beloved teacher—but not fast enough. A Sun Person whose aim had been thrown off by the centipede's lifesaving maneuver shot an arrow through Lucy's leg at close range.

***

"My kingdom for a horse. Actually, I have one. I'm just not on top of him anymore." Kuaray's voice was muffled by the centipede's smelly underside, luckily raised about a foot from the ground by the many legs that he'd folded under him.

Kuaray's attempt at humor didn't fool Lucy. Through a haze of pain, she tried to answer coherently. "I don't mind if you hate me."

In the near darkness, Kuaray stretched out his hand and discovered that they were only inches apart. "Hate you for what? For ruining my opener? Of course I don't.

"But Lucy, I almost ran you over. I came that close." If it had been possible, he would have shown her an inch between his thumb and forefinger.

The pain made Lucy's tongue feel thick, and her ears buzzed. She mumbled, "But I had to stop you so you wouldn't get killed."

"Yes," he said softly. "I know."

After a pause, she managed, "I got hit. It feels like my leg's gonna fall off."

"You got hit? Bad?"

"Yes, bad. The arrow's still in my leg, and it went right through my calf."

"My god, Lucy, what can we do?"

"Nothing but wait. Hold my hand, maybe?"

Kuaray scrabbled about until he found it. "Can I hold you, instead?"

The oxygen level was low under Petey, and Lucy's head swam. The pain came on like a red wave cut through with a black lightning bolt, even stranger than the sky. She managed a tepid yes before passing out.

Kuaray held her with all his strength and murmured into her ear, "Lucy, I've got you. I do love you, even if you can't hear me say it."

***

Svnoyi and Phoenix weren't far behind Lucy, arriving in time to see Petey's extravagant ballet and the U-turn that sent his riders flying. They saw Kuaray land next to Petey, but they couldn't spot Corlion and Corlinia in the midst of the soldiers' feet and swirling dust. When the arrows started to zoom, they realized how quickly they'd have to rescue their beloveds. Keeping their heads low, they ran to the center of the field.

Svnoyi reached Corlinia first. She lay on her back, stunned, her eyes starting from her head, her mouth hanging loose. *She's breathing, I can see her chest rise and fall. But is she even conscious? Did she hurt her spine? Bump her head?*

Oh, god, she's being trampled. Just look at the Sun People. No one's in control because Kuaray's under Petey. They're behaving like steamrollers.

A Sun Person tripped on Corlinia's legs, another on her ribcage. They hardly noticed, picking themselves up as if they'd fallen over a downed tree. Svnoyi turned her head for a second to watch them. They fired off two arrows that hit bullseyes at five hundred feet, straight through their foes' hearts. When the two pups fell, Svnoyi imagined their round bodies making meaty plops on the dirt and stone.

Poor babies. How grim this is!

Bending low to save herself from both the Sun People's and Prairie Dogs' arrows, she grabbed Corlinia by her arms and began pulling her toward the protection of a gully. *This girl looks slender, but she's way heavier than I thought.*

Once Svnoyi reached the narrow riverbed, she couldn't come up with a way to lower Corlinia down to the uneven rocks five feet below. She compromised, heaving the girl over one shoulder like a sack of potatoes and falling into the gully herself. She tried to relax her muscles. She'd read somewhere that drunk people fall all the time and never get hurt.

The way down seemed to last at least a minute, and when Svnoyi landed, she saw the cartoon stars she remembered from the few comic books Phoenix had been allowed to buy a million years ago. *Oog! I must've banged my head.* She put two fingers to her skull and felt around, but there was no blood. *Have I broken something else? Everything hurts, especially my ankle.*

She glanced down. *Oh no, it's getting black-and-blue and swelling up.*

What should I do now? I'm trapped here with an injured girl who's very precious because she happens to be Phoenix's fiancée and Corlion's sister. Also my friend. I don't even know what's wrong with her.

Arrows flew over their heads in both directions, and gritting her teeth to bear her painful ankle, she pulled Corlinia to a different spot behind a boulder. An arrow coming from the Prairie Dog side fell beside them, but it had lost its velocity.

***

Phoenix felt sick. When he saw Svnoyi dragging Corlinia away by her arms, her heels in the flat Jimjamoree sandals bouncing along the uneven ground, his dinner churned inside his stomach. *She's rescuing Corlinia, so I have to find Corlion. He fell off Petey about here.*

With his eyes alert for any sign of Corlion among the forward rush of archers, Phoenix scanned the field high and low. One of the Sun People plowed into him, spinning him in a half circle. Massaging the jab to his ribs, he wondered if a few of the bones hadn't cracked. *Owie! That felt like an elbow busting something in there, just what I don't need right now.*

Eventually he spotted the Pippins' Mayor and High Priest one hundred feet above the point where the meadow began its sweep up the mountain ridge. Somehow Corlion had managed to scramble against the tide and then climb, and right now he was moaning and stumbling about haphazardly, lurching on the loose stones like a zombie.

Scrambling to Corlion's side, Phoenix sat him down, observing that his friend's entire body had been coated with field dust from the trampling—except for the whites of his eyes and the vivid pink inside his mouth.

Hey, man, what happened to you? Aren't you supposed to be acting colonel, or something like that, taking over for Kuaray now that he's down?

Corlion shook his head and pointed to his hanging left arm. Phoenix could see a bone poking through the skin, and his stomach did another ominous flip-flop. Which bone? He had no idea what its name was. However, he knew enough to put the arm in a sling he made from his own shirt.

Phoenix, I-I'm done. Y-you hafta kill two Prairie Dogs for me, Kuaray's orders. T-take my bow'n get the one with the medal hangin' round his neck, he's worth two. See 'im over there behind the others? Even telepathically spoken, the pain turned Corlion's words into a slurred and stuttering shorthand.

Slowly Phoenix picked up Corlion's bow and a handful of arrows and stared at them. *Why should I do it? Is this really my war? I guess it kind of is by default because I'm sure not on Queen Gitli's side.*

He scrambled further up the ridge and sat down, trying to summon the courage to shoot Saint George. *But I* know *him. He's one of Queen Gitli's husbands, kind of an old geezer. He's First Warrior and I'm sure he'd be a prize, but how can I murder him? Wait. Everything's different now, and murder is just fine.*

I don't even need the bow. I could kill him with my mind.

After locating Saint George from his perch on a rock near the top, Phoenix watched the two armies running willy-nilly all over the field. Leaderless, both sides had given up on long-distance fighting and even from far away, he could tell they were in a frenzy of bloodlust. The Sun People took advantage of their superior height to stab the Prairie Dogs' heads and chests with arrows and club them with rocks. The pups used teeth and claws, mainly aiming for their foes' vulnerable abdomens and genitals.

Bodies had piled up on both sides, although the Prairie Dogs' losses appeared to be far greater. The little round corpses littered the field, often clumped together like so many tumbleweeds blown against a fence. Phoenix's mouth fell open and he rubbed his eyes with dirty fists to see better. It was true: many more pups issued through the hospital trap door and flooded the field as if yearning to join their dead brethren.

As Phoenix continued to watch the unfolding tableau, he became more and more transfixed. Half the Sun People began gasping, clutching their chests and falling to their knees, one by one. *Oh, no, it's their lungs: they can't run around like this for long. Some of them will drop dead if they can't rest.*

But then he witnessed a scene of such barbarity that his vow to kill Saint George suddenly made perfect sense. A Sun Person fell from a tree, shot at close range by one of the pups. He may have climbed it to escape, or more likely, to shoot from an advantageous spot. Three months ago these pups had been sowing beans and caring for the sick. Now they tore off the dead man's chiton, exposing his ash-white nudity. They slashed his body to ribbons with claws and teeth sharp enough to burrow through soft rock. Even when the bones began peeking through the bloody carcass, they didn't stop.

Okay, that's it. Of course this is my war, how could I even think of wriggling out of it? Saint George is letting them do it. How could he teach his army to act so horrible?

Phoenix suppressed any thought that the First Warrior, whose expertise had been the coaching of military parades, would have taught such a grisly tactic. But it was the excuse he needed to rationalize his deed. He pulled the bowstring, which seemed much thicker than the one on his own bow stashed away in Corlinia's yurtpee. *This is a very serious bow,* flashed through his head as he released the arrow from his fingers.

Later he wondered if his aim had been that true, or if he'd *willed* the arrow to hit Saint George's chest right through the shiny medal that trumpeted his status. The Prairie Dog fell face forward in slow motion, flailing his claws to catch his balance on nothingness.

That's called biting the dust. Phoenix turned away, shirtless and shivering under a red-stained sky. First, he threw up his dinner—but lost much more than chewed-up food. He'd lost what was left of his childhood and for a few horrifying seconds, even the knowledge of who he was.

Phoenix fell to his knees and pounded his temples with his fists, weeping and screaming, "I'm sorry, Saint George, I'm sorry."

He wiped his eyes dry before rejoining Corlion to help him down the hill.

But his mind wasn't behaving, and his thoughts seemed to be issuing from the mouth of a superior being whose word was much mightier than anything his own stunted conscience could've churned out. *You've sure blown it, kid, and don't expect anyone to forgive you, especially not yourself. Ever. You took a life, and wartime's no excuse. You're worse than Kuaray when he stabbed Sequoyah, worse than Svnoyi when she broke Kuaray's neck, worse than the bloodthirsty queen. You're the worst person on earth.*

His limbs felt icy, his feet walked by rote, and his face glazed hot with shame.

***

The way down was painfully slow because Corlion had to stop every yard or so to catch his breath. He gasped, *Phoenix, le's si-down for-a minute.*

Okay, but not longer. We have to get you some help. Phoenix lowered the injured man onto a rock, mindful not to jostle him. But something unexpected set off an alarm within his already overwhelmed brain. Hadn't he seen a flicker at the edge of his vision? He jerked his head around. Halfway across the valley, he saw movement on a flat spot near the summit of the mountain peak above the fountain.

Ethan and Luz? Why are they *up there? I guess Tlke must've let them out of their pink prison.*

Oh, my god, what a magnificent thing *they've built. It's on lots of wheels, and it looks almost like a big Russian anti-aircraft tank from the Time Be—*

At first a flash, and then multiple detonations sent a dozen cannonballs flying into the valley. They cracked open like eggshells, the explosions so loud that wildlife in the surrounding forests stayed away from their nests and burrows for an entire year thereafter. Ethan had been given permission to prepare the TATP-filled wooden balls in the hospital lab. The unstable liquid housed in his perfect containers was called "Mother of Satan" for a reason. It had performed far beyond his and Luz's savage expectations.

Fires broke out. On the field, white hot flames incinerated the quick and the dead alike. They burned down the remaining pines and scorched any untrampled grass and flowers into a charcoaled mat indistinguishable from the rest of the blackened valley.

Svnoyi threw herself on top of Corlinia. Even lying face down, she could tell from the glare crossing her tightly clenched eyelids exactly when the tongues of fire leapt over their gully. Petey, who had survived many a hit from flying arrows, expired from smoke inhalation. His body saved Lucy and Kuaray who still lay beneath him, screaming at the tops of their lungs and clutching each other as tightly as they knew how.

In an extraordinary fluke, one of the cannonballs dropped into the four-by-six-foot opening of the trapdoor to the hospital. The pups waiting inside the Death Room to join the battle didn't stand a chance. The ball rolled down the ramp and blew up at the bottom, and soon a roiling conflagration enriched by lab chemicals raged throughout the complex.

Corlion and Phoenix watched it all from their perch on the mountain ridge.

It's the Jumping Sun all over again, Corlion remarked with a calmness born of emotional exhaustion and physical pain.

Yes, Phoenix answered, trying not to picture the final cremation of Saint George.

40 ~ Stormy Day

The storm broke at last, wreaking upon the Sacred Meadow the vengeance it had been storing up for hours. The thunder, the cracking kind in perfect sync with the lightning, started up without the usual warning rumble in the distance. The rain blew sideways in sheets, extinguishing the remaining fires. It also washed away the incinerated grass and trees and the ashes of Prairie Dogs and Sun People alike—joining everything and everyone together in a sea of mud. The rain went on and on, adding to the misery of the few who had saved themselves from the TATP explosions by huddling at the bottom of the ten rivers' gullies.

The deluge had no effect on the inferno inside the hospital that belched chemical-laden black smoke out the trapdoor to mingle with the lowering clouds.

Dead center on the field, Petey's chitinous body still protected Lucy and Kuaray. Rainwater streamed beneath them, but compared to the other survivors, they weren't too badly off. Besides, they could console each other even though Lucy was barely conscious. Kuaray held her tightly to him and to keep her awake, he whispered the endearments he'd wanted to say for a long time into her ear. But a worrisome thought began to gnaw at him. Ever since the fireballs had swept over his solid, comforting friend, Petey seemed different, a bit lower on his legs, maybe. And he lay very still.

Kuaray didn't wish to bother Lucy about it, so he set up a silent mantra: *Petey, stay strong, Petey, I love you, Petey, stay strong, Petey, I love you.*

Phoenix stayed with Corlion on their flat rock high up on the ridge. He was afraid they'd break more bones slipping on the mucky slope if they tried walking further. And besides, his ribs hurt. Phoenix bent his bare back over his friend to shelter him from the worst of the rainy gusts. Still conflicted, he prayed alternately for help to arrive soon and for the opposite: that he could die to escape from the misery of killing Saint George. When he wasn't castigating himself, he tried to locate Corlinia and Svnoyi by scouring with his eyes every gully near the center of the field.

If all this weren't enough, a persistent idea kept nagging at him. *I can't stop looking around because I don't dare miss a thing. I'm the only one who's seeing this like a big panorama and can tell about it. If we all live long enough, I'll write it down. I'll call it "Red Night."*

Oh, my god. Phoenix stared as the gullies began to fill up with rainwater. *This is the last straw, but I guess it's not too surprising. They were meant to be riverbeds. Where the hell are Corlinia and Svnoyi? Other guys are climbing out here and there, people and Prairie Dogs, but not them.*

Yes! He had spotted the pair in the middle gully nearest to Petey. He jumped up, forgetting that Corlion was sitting beside him leaning on his shoulder, half asleep. The injured man toppled sideways, luckily falling onto his good arm.

I found them, they're alive. But what the hell is Svnoyi doing? He stopped his mouth to keep from screaming encouragements she'd never hear through the roar of the wind and rain.

Svnoyi managed to throw Corlinia's rag-doll body halfway out of the gully. It took three tries, and now his fiancée lay with her torso on the bank and her feet trailing in the deepening river. But Svnoyi seemed to be having trouble climbing up the steep sides, herself. She fell back once, twice. The best she seemed able to do to keep from being washed away was cling to a rock jutting from the top of the gully. Her braid was undone, her long hair streaming with the current.

Svnoyi is so, so brave. But what's wrong with her? She's usually so much stronger than anyone else, she must be hurt.

Oh, my heart, it's gonna bust right outta my chest. I just saw Corlinia move. She's alive. But I always knew she would be because the love-circle I made with her inside my head never stopped spinning, not for a second.

"Help, help, somebody, Corlinia and Svnoyi need help!" His voice faded. *I don't see anyone. There isn't any help.*

***

As soon as Queen Gitli realized that the Sun People had ruined her genocidal campaign by attacking Iqual first, she feared for her life. She headed for the royal bunker, a comfortable three-room suite in the palace sub-basement, a quarter mile below Captain Kirk's sumptuous religious quarters. Tlke helped the arthritic queen down the circular staircase, and she understood perfectly her duty to stay at the queen's side and commiserate. But the monarch took the loss of her perfectly planned liquidation very hard. Even Tlke, the most faithful of courtiers, couldn't put up indefinitely with the fulminations and insults that had been going on for four hours.

Besides, ever since she'd ferociously slashed Lucy's face with her personal weaponry, her guilty conscience had refused to let up.

I'm like a slave to the queen and her plots, and she's getting crazier by the day. She's *turning me into someone I don't like very much, someone who could slash her best childhood friend across the face. No, be fair. It's not all Her Majesty's fault, I'm doing it to myself.*

Tlke didn't intend to leap out of her rabbit chair, but she could no longer bear the tension of waiting in ignorance. She feared for the pups she'd yanked away from their after-dinner games, she feared for Lucy, and yes, she even feared for the inept Saint George. She made for the exit, trying not to notice the confounded look on the queen's face when she zoomed past. She reached the kitchen, intending to take the corridor to the hospital with its trapdoor to the meadow. But a few yards in, the hazy air made her eyes water, and she smelled smoke.

Wringing her paws, Tlke tried to make sense of the evidence. *Oh, by God Rough, the hospital's caught on fire! I hope all the pups were already out of there and on the field. Or would that have been any safer for them?*

Besides, what was I thinking? I can't walk into the middle of a battlefield when I haven't a clue what's been going on. I'll go to the front entrance instead, and there are three tunnels from the palace that'll cut off some of the distance. They're the same ones I sent the pups through to reach the corridor to the hospital.

But first, Tlke had to warn everyone in case the fire reached the palace. She was almost certain the flames couldn't leap the two miles through a stone corridor, but to seal out the smoke, she closed the entrance with its ancient bronze door. If fire did break out, she knew the queen would remain safe in her bunker that could withstand just about any kind of catastrophe. She rushed downstairs to advise Captain Kirk and his acolytes of the danger. The herbal intoxicants that brought on their religious visions had left them past caring about anything, so she walked out in disgust.

Drug addicts, all of them. It's enough to make me lose my faith.

Back in the kitchen, she found the chef Neshek huddling behind the spoon rack. He vowed to stay with his comforting cooking utensils, but the bobcats trotted along beside her, their short tails switching in anticipation of escaping their humdrum servitude to the dishpan—at least for a little while. The other animals, the few remaining flathead bears and the rabbit chairs, had long since left for the night, returning to their own homes deep in the forest. Surely the terrible noises issuing from the battlefield would discourage them from coming to work in the morning. She regretted not warning the bats that hung, ever faithful, from the ceiling. But she didn't know how.

Hoping to make up for time lost checking the palace, Tlke ran full tilt through one of the low-ceilinged earth tunnels leading to the Sacred Meadow. Abruptly, she slowed to a walk. For no obvious reason, the fur on the back of her neck rose into a stiff ridge, and her spine tingled. In addition, the sheaths around her claws started itching. *I'm scared of something, and my body knows it before my mind does.*

She looked over her shoulder. The bobcats were cowering, begging her with pleading eyes to reverse course. *They're scared, too, there must be something in front of us.*

She rounded a bend and was hit square in the face with a whiff of Petey's signature perfume: bitter almonds mixed with iodine. She wrinkled her nose. *But Petey can't be here. He's at the Sacred Meadow with that traitor, Kuaray. Or maybe he wasn't a traitor.*

She came to an abrupt halt. *In the name of Goddess Cinder, giant centipedes must've escaped from the Valley of Rejects while running from the fire. To get to this tunnel they marched through the corridor before I closed the bronze door. They romped around in the palace without anyone seeing them. Now they'll start romping around in the woods, eating everything and everybody in sight.*

Tlke waited, frozen in place for a good fifteen minutes to give the centipedes time to make their exit before she signaled the bobcats to move forward once more. Because of the centipedes, her anxiety level climbed so high she felt her fur bristling all over her body.

Why did our scientists create such horrible creatures? Actually, I know why: to give Kuaray something to ride that could replace his legs.

Once she and the bobcats caught a glimpse of the overcast sky beyond the tunnel's mouth, they'd already been sloshing through mud puddles from the horizontal rain blowing in. *What an awful day, it must be falling in sheets out there. I'm not surprised, the clouds were so heavy last night.*

Brushing the water from her eyes to see better and shaking her coat, Tlke approached the front entrance to the Sacred Meadow even more cautiously than she'd moved through the tunnel. Unbelievably, there was no noise coming from the field. Even stranger, a crowd of humans was swarming around the entrance and peering in. She had no idea who they were, but the bobcats shot ahead as if they'd recognized long-lost friends. She held back, counting six of them in all, tall and short, dressed in yellow slickers. One was carrying two tiny babies, a fur-wrapped bundle in each arm.

Damn this rain, it's so hard to see.

No, it can't be! Won't the queen be furious. She wasn't expecting Sequoyah home for at least six months.

Tlke did a double take. She could swear she saw a Prairie Dog pup holding hands with the shortest person. *Oh, what is her name ... Agali? They're so much like Lucy and me not all that long ago. What ever happened to our friendship in the meantime? .*

***

When Tlke came closer, she heard someone addressing her in her own tongue. The pup, pretty with an almost-pink coat, had edged forward timidly to greet her. *The little thing's a bit afraid of me. She's clutching Agali's hand with both paws for security.*

The pup bobbed a curtsy. *Praise our good queen, miss. Is Tlke your name? That's what Agali said.*

Tlke nodded, and the pup blasted forth in a rush of words because talking to strangers made her nervous. *Oh, Tlke, the survivors need help, fast, that's what you'll see if you look at the meadow. Where's the rescue squad and the doctors? Where's the hospital?*

The pup added with barely a pause, *My name's Sanctissima, I'm a draft dodger, I stayed behind at the Eye of Cinder to help Sequoyah escape. We just got here, the bears and carts and our six Sun People friends are over there in the forest. Agali's my best friend, I love the families, Anichka and Jaroslav, Aleta, Alexej, Sequoyah—*

Tlke raised a paw to slow her down. But then she found herself saying, *I love them, too.*

Soon everyone was hugging her. And some of them kissed her on the forehead.

With her arms full however, Aleta did not embrace her. "Tlke, please look at the field right now. And no more talk. It wastes time."

Her voice grew shrill. "We knew there'd be a war in a few weeks, but what was this, and who was fighting? The Prairie Dogs and the Sun People? I can imagine how the end of a shooting war would look, and it wouldn't be pretty. But the entire valley burnt to a crisp? This is a holocaust."

Tlke understood at least some of what Aleta had said. She stared between the cairns at the blackened landscape, the charcoaled earth still steaming in the rain. She saw survivors waving frantically from the gullies, but not many. And she remembered that the hospital was still burning. Overwhelmed, she dropped her face into her paws, but only for a second.

I hope no one notices how upset I am. But we trained one thousand pups. One thousand! An entire generation. Poor babies, they were hardly old enough to know what they were getting into.

With an effort, Tlke pulled herself together and got to work at once planning the rescue. With Agali and Sanctissima translating, she started talking faster and faster, swept up by the urgency. "I see our Polar Bear Express bears behind us in the forest, and there's a pair of flatheads, too. First of all, Sequoyah, Jaroslav, Anichka, and Alexej—round them up and send them into the valley to get everyone out of the gullies. Those riverbeds are flooded, and the water could be four or five feet deep. So this isn't a task for humans. When the bears have pulled everybody out, they'll come back here. Then hitch them to their carts."

She paused, waiting for the newly appointed rescuers to nod their heads, showing they'd understood. "Then go into the field yourselves to lift the survivors onto the carts. Don't forget to scan around on the mountain ridges for anyone who's up there. Bring everyone to the Prairie Dog Infirmary in the middle of town but be gentle. We don't want any deaths on the way."

"The rest of us will hurry to get the infirmary ready, and we'll meet you there. I'll borrow nursery rabbits from the daycare center for all your babies.

"Dear bobcats, will you find Yacy and Oscar to come help? Remind them about the nursery rabbits. I see you shaking your heads, and I know you can't communicate. Do it anyway."

"Wait," said Sequoyah. "After I finish here, I'd like to see the queen who's most likely hiding out in some bunker, angry and scared. Agali and Sanctissima, will you join me to translate?"

No expression showed on his face when he explained his purpose. "It's time for a reckoning."

Tlke said nothing. When she did speak, everyone understood her reluctance. To say yes, she would be breaking with her sovereign.

"Yes, Sequoyah, of course. She's at the palace, and you're right. She is hiding in a bunker. It's down a spiral staircase that starts in the basement on Captain Kirk's floor. I assure you, he and his acolytes won't even notice when you walk by."

Tlke signaled for the rescue operation to start by waving her arms.

***

Phoenix was so terrified for Corlinia and Svnoyi that he couldn't put off trying to help them. He made up his mind to leave Corlion unattended and climb down to see what he could do. He rose, groaning from the pain in his side. He took a few tentative steps followed by quicker ones, but soon he fell hard on the steep scree laced with rivulets of mud. He landed on his knees and elbows, cutting his lip open against something—he had no idea what. Clutching his ribs, he sat up slowly. The blood from his lip splashed in fat drops onto the ground.

"This isn't working, but how can I simply give up?" He stood again, letting his tears escape. They coursed down his face, blending with the rain.

What the hell? Seconds later, Phoenix saw bears everywhere, his flathead bears and the Polar Bear Express's long-limbed running bears. He couldn't keep count they flowed so fast through the main entrance, their pancake feet splattering the mud as they ran.

Help's come at last. There must be around twenty of 'em including our *bears.*

"Ernie and Bertha, over there," he shouted, waving his arms and pointing. "Save Corlinia and Svnoyi, first."

The bears looked at Phoenix. Then they turned toward the center of the meadow as he had asked. He shook his head in wonder. *They don't know English. The way they understand us must go much deeper than words.*

When the ursine rescuers reached Corlinia who lay flopped halfway out on the bank, they found her conscious enough to hang onto Bertha's front legs. The bear simply backed up, pulling her to safety. To rescue Svnoyi, Ernie had to climb into the gully's waters that had become a rushing torrent slapping at its rim. He pushed her up from below, and Bertha pulled her out of the gully to lie beside Corlinia.

Phoenix couldn't understand how the bears managed to coordinate their rescue operation because he saw no apparent leader. Nonetheless, like clockwork, they spread out among the other gullies to push and pull the survivors onto level ground. He began counting the remaining participants of the doomed campaign and besides Kuaray and Lucy who were still under Petey, Svnoyi, and himself, he saw thirteen Sun People including Corlion and Corlinia, and twenty-one Prairie Dogs. He looked up from his census-taking. As suddenly as the bears had arrived, the entire crew departed at breakneck speed, streaking between the cairns.

"Hey," Phoenix announced indignantly. "What about Corlion and me? What about Lucy and Kuaray?" The words were hardly out of his mouth when they returned, harnessed and pulling carts that had come from the Polar Bear Express. And this time, he spotted people with them.

"I'll be damned," he whispered. "The ambulances and the medics are here."

Moments later, Phoenix wiped more tears from his eyes with a fist because he could hardly cope with an impossible dream come true. He shook Corlion awake and began pointing. *Look down there, Bro, we're saved. There's my stepdaddy Sequoyah. He's the so-called giant from the prophesy all you Sun People have been waiting for. And he's your future father-in-law. There's Anichka, the best doctor in the whole world. There's Jaroslav, the greatest mountaineer alive, and I bet he'll be the one to come for us. And he's brought his son Alexej who's as strong as a young Hercules.*

Corlion was in too much pain to look anywhere. But he did manage to ask, *Phoenix, did you kill that Prairie Dog, the one wearing the medal? I made Kuaray a promise.*

41 ~ Little Corner of the World

Tlke dashed on foot to the Prairie Dog Infirmary at the center of town to make the necessary arrangements with the doctors and staff. She could hardly believe it herself, the facts were so grim. They could expect war casualties shortly, not many, about thirty-five people and Prairie Dogs, total. She insisted that regardless of the severity of the injuries, everyone should be admitted to the facility, even if only to dry off and rest up. She had her doubts about the place, but she didn't have much choice. It wasn't equipped to handle badly hurt patients like the hospital had been before it caught fire. In normal times the Prairie Dogs came to the infirmary for well-pup checks, cuts and scrapes, ingrown toenails, and malocclusions of the incisors.

Tlke put Anichka in charge. The infirmary doctors agreed to this radical change to the hierarchy only grudgingly because they knew that she would understand best the anatomy of the wounded humans. Besides, they admired her for having calmed Queen Gitli's fiery arthritic pain.

The doctors wanted Tlke to tell them more about the war. She shook her head. *I'm sorry, not now, but it's bad news. You'll see soon enough because the only survivors are the ones coming in.*

Next, Tlke headed for the palace to make sure it wasn't going up in flames. When she touched the bronze doors that closed off the hospital corridor from the kitchen, they felt cool, although she could see occasional wisps of smoke seeping through the gap between them.

She found Neshek still hiding behind his utensils, pining for the "world that was no more." All at once, she had a great idea. Wouldn't everyone in the infirmary want lunch in a few hours and many meals after that? He accepted his new assignment as a most welcome diversion from his unhappy state of mind. Clear soup for the most ill, rabbit stew, salads, desserts made from the luscious raspberries and blueberries presently in season, Corlaz One's Folly coffee .... Ideas began to take root in his brain, and menus burst forth. He rubbed his paws in anticipation as he put on his apron. But then he looked around, even peering under the sink and behind the stove. Where had those good-for-nothing bobcats gotten to?

Tlke's last job for the day was to locate Ethan and Luz who had not returned from the mountaintop. She concluded that they must have fled into the forest after finishing off both armies—or what was left of the armies before they'd let loose the gigantic war machine that Queen Gitli had ordered them to build. She wasn't naïve, and she assumed the two sides had already done a pretty good job of massacring each other, first.

She wasn't convinced she was doing the right thing. *Once I finally catch up with them, what should I do? Put them in jail? I know for a fact that Luz was still crazy from her brain injury because she kept raving about weird things that don't exist like "Communists" and the "U S of A." And Ethan was always acting like such a little boy, he made me think of a toddler pup in the nursery. So when the right moment came, I bet he couldn't* wait *to try out his new toy.*

Tlke's brow settled into a straight line as her less forgiving nature surfaced. *No, none of that matters. They must be court-martialed for killing everyone on both sides, friend and foe. And they didn't wait for an order from Saint George.*

She swung by the police station to collect the officers of the law, a posse of eight Prairie Dog toughs armed with *azvrkts.* They gained altitude rapidly. Within the hour they had hiked almost the entire length of the trail that wound around the Sacred Meadow's mountain peak where the Doomsday Weapon sat deserted in its place on the plateau. Then they inched through the old-growth forest above the underground hospital. The air was so tainted by the smoke that they could barely see the path and found themselves covering their noses with their paws and trying to blink the stinging chemicals out of their eyes.

Abruptly, Tlke stopped in her tracks, causing the Prairie Dogs behind her to collide awkwardly with one another. At this point the path turned left, skirting the part of the forest where the lowest boughs of the pines obscured the hospital's treacherous open skylight. But something was wrong. The whole area looked different, empty. Apparently white-hot flames had shot through the skylight, erasing at least five acres of the trees around it as if they'd never existed. Only smoldering stumps and a few denuded poles stood as a reminder that not so long ago the old-growth kings of the forest had reigned there. Luckily, the pelting rainstorm had kept the surrounding trees from igniting.

Dismayed, Tlke sank to her haunches, wringing her paws. She knew she was losing face by behaving so emotionally in front of her posse, but she didn't care. *How could our dear little corner of the world have changed so much in a few hours?*

Even worse, we didn't meet Ethan and Luz along the path, and they had no other way to get down. Most likely the flames swallowed them.

She wished she hadn't opened up her mind to that last, most likely of scenarios.

***

Ten Prairie Dog doctors and nurses in crisp blue gowns stood ready to perform triage, and Anichka joined them as soon as her cart that was first in line came back from the field. When the entire staff bowed low and kissed her hands, the surprised doctor realized that she'd been appointed Physician-in-Chief by Tlke—not by them, certainly, because they were acting too subservient. She hadn't expected or wanted to take on a position of leadership. Besides, she was exhausted from the harrowing ten-day journey home caring for fifty-nine starving and traumatized Shade People rescued from the caverns—teenagers to boot.

As Anichka watched the carts rolling up to the front door one by one, she tried to smile and look savvy at the same time in order to radiate the easy-going confidence she didn't feel. Simultaneously, she belittled herself. *It is very unfortunate. I cannot do this. For so long, now, I fail as good doctor, yes, ever since I almost kill Sequoyah when I close his wound with poisonous vines.*

But as soon as Anichka saw the seriousness of Lucy's and Corlion's injuries, she left her doubts behind. She asked for gurneys to take them to a room with good beds for surgery, neither of which the infirmary had. Once she'd found a room to her liking, she asked Aleta to stack up enough pallets to reach the height of her waist and to drape them with woven bamboo sheets. In the end, she allowed the flatheads Ernie and Bertha and Arbel and Arbeline of the Polar Bear Express to enter the front door, but only after they'd washed their feet. The bears carried the patients one-by-one on a sheet that they held in their teeth by the four corners like a hammock.

When Anichka saw the Prairie Dogs' surgical instruments, she despaired. Her big, four-fingered hand with opposable thumb could never manipulate the tiny tools designed for a paw. Just then, Oscar and Yacy ran in carrying heavy toddlers, urged on by the bobcats that had nipped at their heels the entire way. Anichka turned them right around to race back.

"Oh, please, dear ones, drop off your children with the nursery rabbits down in the basement. Take Alexej with you because he is so strong. Run to my cave and bring every medical thing you see. And bring many, many of Luz's quilts. Everything in Prairie Dog Infirmary is too short, too small for humans. And nightclothes for my patients, bring any we have extra."

She reappraised the abilities of the bobcats that she'd always considered such silly creatures, the unwitting comedians of Queen Gitli's court. "Perhaps bobcats can carry sacks in their teeth to bring medicine. That way they not nip heels like sheepdogs."

***

Anichka stood between her two patients, looking from one to the other where they lay stretched out on the stacked pallets barely long enough to accommodate their human-length legs. She gave them thorn shots, and their breathing slowed as soon as the efficient anesthetic made of cocaine and thyme oil with a dash of curare began its work. She hoped their pain would disappear almost entirely, even if they weren't deeply asleep.

Drafting Aleta as her assistant, first she worked on Lucy. The type of wound made by an arrow straight through the calf was new to her, but she figured she'd cause far less damage to the flesh by pulling it out point first, the same direction it had gone in. Accordingly, she sawed off the feathered half and extracted the shaft straight through Lucy's leg. From its position, Anichka was quite sure the arrow had grazed, but not shattered, the tibia and had missed the fibula altogether. Lucy had been extremely lucky because the shaft had mostly stopped up the hole, keeping blood from pouring out.

Anichka took a deep breath to give herself courage. Then with a sure hand she stitched the wound's many intricate vessels before cauterizing it with a red-hot knife point—all the while trying not to think about the flesh-eating tendrils she'd chosen for Sequoyah's sutures less than a year ago. To finish, she applied liberal amounts of honey and aloe before bandaging it with the clean cotton that Yacy and Oscar had brought. She completed Lucy's surgery by giving her a motherly kiss on the crown of her blond head.

The patient opened her eyes, and Anichka asked a question that had been bothering her ever since the rescuers had picked up four family members on the field. "Lucy, why so many of our own children fight in war between Prairie Dogs and Sun People?"

Lucy drawled with a tongue thick from the anesthetic, "We were out there for love, me for Kuaray, and Svnoyi and Phoenix for Sun People, Corlion and Corlinia."

As her eyelids shut again, she mumbled, "Sometimes you have to do what's right even if you get hurt."

Anichka was stunned. So much had happened during the eleven weeks they'd been away. *We come home to terrible war Aleta predicts, and all our children, they give away their hearts, not only Yacy and Oscar. They take terrible risks, yes, much like a million years ago when I love my Werther. I was only sixteen. Soon I marry Jaroslav, and I try to forget.*

She turned to Corlion, thinking he looked very handsome now that he was sleeping and not grimacing from the pain. His ulna, the larger bone in his lower arm, had broken in three places, and one of the pieces was poking through the skin. She guessed he'd fallen hard from a height, landing on his open palm to stop himself. First, she made incisions in both his arm and his side, securing the breaks with delicate pins made from carefully extracted slivers of bone she'd taken from two of his ribs.

Leaving her recently appointed assistant Aleta to watch over Lucy and Corlion, Anichka moved on to Svnoyi's room. She clucked her tongue when she saw her patient's swollen and discolored left ankle. "Darling girl, how you do this? Did you jump into Grand Canyon?"

Svnoyi's words came through teeth gritted from the pain. "Worse 'n that, Aunty Anichka. I jumped into a gully on purpose to get away from the shooting. But I had Corlinia, Phoenix's fiancée, over my shoulder 'cause she'd fainted. Please look at my head, too. It's throbbing."

Anichka gently rotated Svnoyi's foot this way and that. *Hmm, three cases now I wish I have x-ray machine. But I believe this ankle suffers both sprain and hairline fracture of tibia. This I must cool with ice and bind.*

Then she palpated a great lump on her patient's head the size of a chicken egg. Ominously, the pupils of Svnoyi's eyes were different sizes. *This is concussion, maybe very serious. I ask bobcats to put ice on ankle and poultices on lump every ten minutes. Maybe I ask for too much hoping there is ice?*

Anichka stood in the hall for a moment. She leaned against the whitewashed adobe of the wall, wishing she had a cup of that wonderful Corlaz One's Folly coffee from the palace. With her left hand, she massaged the fingers of her right that ached from the meticulous work of probing, manipulating a scalpel, and suturing with an itty-bitty curved needle.

She searched for her other patients, Corlinia, Phoenix, and Kuaray, who had been placed in another wing of the infirmary because their injuries had not been deemed serious. Except for Phoenix's aching ribs, the Prairie Dog doctors—and even Jaroslav—couldn't figure out what was wrong with them.

On her way, Anichka looked in on the wards containing the coughing Sun People and Prairie Dogs who suffered from either smoke inhalation or water in their lungs—and sometimes a combination of both. Some of them also had nasty-looking wounds inflicted by arrows, sticks, rocks, and teeth. Although the dedicated healer would have liked to help out, she knew she must trust the staff doctors and Jaroslav.

In medicine, everybody have their own style. I check doctors' work, I do not instruct.

When Anichka entered Corlinia's room, she found a graceful Sun Person sitting cross-legged on her pallet with hands folded in her lap, primly awaiting the physician. The girl radiated a bubbly excitement quite the opposite of everyone else's subdued heaviness. Except for a natural pallor, she appeared to be in robust health.

The doctor smiled to herself. *She is very beautiful. No wonder is love at first sight for Phoenix. She looks so happy, but where is illness? I think she does not know how Svnoyi suffers injuries for her.*

Corlinia opened both arms in the Sun People's traditional welcome. As Anichka knelt down to her height, the girl let a flow of words burst forth: *I'm so glad you're here, Aunty Anichka. Are you really Phoenix's aunt? He says wonderful things about you, that you're the best doctor in the world.*

She paused for all of five seconds. *I'm sorry, I didn't think. You do speak telepathically?*

Before Anichka had a chance to nod her head, Corlinia barreled on. *You see, I am sick ... but in the best way. I wasn't sure, but now I am. I'm pregnant, maybe ten weeks along. It's unheard of, this happening so soon. Usually it takes years and years, and for many of us women it doesn't happen at all—*

Anichka broke in, *Is Phoenix the father?*

Of course, who else? He's my fiancé. At first, we women always faint a lot, sometimes for as long as six hours. I regret this happened to me when I fell off Petey during the great war, but we inherit many weaknesses in pregnancy ever since the Day of the Jumping Sun.

***

The rain is falling, and Petey lies dead. The clouds blow away, the sun shines at last. Hundreds of seeds wiggle deep down in the soil, they sprout, pushing up pale green curls all around Petey's body. They grow huge, their leafy stems thrusting high into the air. The buds on top are swelling; they're bursting into bloom.

I've never seen such flowers here on earth. They have cherub faces white as snow, big as dinner plates. In each bubbling mouth I spot a glistening silver tongue. The tongues unroll, reaching toward Petey: they lick his armor plates, his belly, his head, his antennae—slurping, grasping, scraping, rasping. I recognize their purpose: they're the Flowers of Death getting Petey ready for his Everlasting Goodbye. His eyes open.

The flowers change into the round faces of Petey's friends, and they look exactly like him down to the last leg segment. They kiss him, they stridulate a blessing. Then they scoop him up in their claws—

Phoenix shook Kuaray's shoulder hard and hissed into his ear, "Wake up, right now. And stop screaming and thrashing around. Everybody's gonna come running, and we'll get locked up in the Prairie Dog version of a Psych Ward for acting weird."

"What the ...?" With his strong arms, Kuaray pushed himself up from his pallet to a sitting position. He was panting, and first thing he did was wipe off the tears running down his face with his sheet.

He whispered, "I was awake with my eyes closed. I saw something, a scene in the most perfect detail—like that artist Hieronymus Bosch might've painted it. It was beautiful. No, it was too extreme to be beautiful. It was a vision, not a dream."

"Vision or dream, keep acting like a madman and we'll never get out of here. I wanna see Corlinia."

"And I want to see Lucy. But Phoenix, we have to go back to the Sacred Meadow."

"Fer *chrissake*, Kuaray—"

"You don't understand. Petey woke up, I saw his eyes open. Even if he didn't, we must bury him. We can't just let him lie out there." Kuaray bowed his head, sobbing into his sheet.

"You mean I get to bury him while you watch."

"Yes, that's true, and I'm sorry."

He cleared his throat. "But Phoenix, I know you want to go back, too. You dozed off a little while ago, and you started raving really loud. Something like, 'I have to find it, I know his medal's somewhere in that shitty mud.'"

"Okay, let's go." Phoenix sounded resigned, but Kuaray was sure his friend was hiding his real feelings and if he didn't go, something inside him would never be satisfied.

Phoenix pushed against the door, and it swung open. He looked up and down the hall in both directions and saw nobody.

"Super," he whispered, turning his head back to address Kuaray on his way out. "I'll sneak around and find one of our flathead bears and come back to pick you up. On the way there, we'll get a shovel from our gardening shed."

***

Anichka looked everywhere for her last patients, Phoenix and Kuaray, but they were not in the infirmary. They had left the premises on a journey of their own, as the Sun Person in charge of the front door tried to explain. She was an accomplished hunter from Sequoyah's entourage of Cauliflowers whom they'd nicknamed Corly because her given name was thirteen syllables long.

"Corly, please tell me, where did they go?"

"Phoenix ehe Kuaray, theh reide a whitte barré ehe Phoenix reide be-hin. Barre namen Ernie. Theh go-e backet Sacred Meadow. Theh sagg is 'mission of mourning and atonement.'"

42 ~ The Reckoning

As the runaways drew near the Sacred Meadow the rain stopped, and a stiff breeze blew away the last of the clouds.

"The blue ... sky, it's like ... the start ... of my ... vision." Kuaray's words came out sounding choppy as he bounced and slid precariously on Ernie's back. Even with Phoenix sitting behind him hanging on to his belt, he had a hard time balancing on an animal so high above the ground. It didn't help that he was responsible for holding the shovel.

The goddam center of gravity is too high, and there's no grip to my knees. How I miss Petey.

Once the bear had entered the Sacred Meadow between the cairns and deposited his riders close to Petey, he departed in haste. And with good reason; the corpse had company.

Phoenix whispered, "I don't mean to sound heartless, but one of our problems is close to being solved. There's not much left of Petey to bury."

Kuaray had hoped for a moment of calm to say goodbye to the departed, but that was not to be. Through tears of fury he bellowed, "Two giant centipedes got here first. Where the hell did they come from? They're cannibals, the fiends!

"Phoenix, scare them away."

"Me? How do you propose I do that—"

Abruptly Kuaray's anger changed to amazement. "Wait, hold on. It's like my vision might've been if you hadn't interrupted it. Eating him was a first step. Now they're picking up his shell in their claws to take it to a gully. They're gonna bury it."

With a catch in his voice, Kuaray continued his description: "Look, one of them is burying Petey by gathering mud in its claws to throw in the gully while the other does stridulations—seven strokes then a rest, seven strokes then a rest. They're swaying their heads from side to side."

Phoenix replied with only a touch of mockery, "It's so moving. It's a religious ritual for our dear Petey's interment."

"Yes, a religious ritual. I'm sure of it," Kuaray remarked tearfully. "Petey sacrificed himself to save others. He was a true god."

"Well, he certainly sacrificed himself to save you and Lucy. And he did teach you how to love—because you loved him."

Then Phoenix had an inspiration. "Kuaray, let's do what they're doing so they get used to us. If they realize you felt the same way about Petey, you can get closer to them. Having another centipede or two on hand wouldn't be a bad idea.

"I'll help them shovel the mud. You stridulate the sevens, and don't forget to move your head."

"I wish I had my violin."

"Well, you don't. Scrape your arms together and remember how you and Petey used to talk."

When Petey's remains had been completely covered, all four of them stayed near the grave to rest from their labors. Kuaray began crooning to the new centipedes in the same falsetto voice he'd used to help his insomniac steed fall asleep. Phoenix remembered the lullaby from the short time they'd been together at the Pippins' village. He'd thought the sound was remarkably similar to a fire engine from the Time Before, wailing on a distant street in the middle of the night.

Both creatures responded, swinging their spherical heads toward Kuaray in slow motion. Forgetting Phoenix's recent injury, the enthusiastic centipede-lover nudged his friend in the ribs. "Aren't they precious? I'm thinking they might be girls because they don't smell quite as bad as Petey did. How do Petra and Petunia seem to you for names?"

"Just adorable, Kuaray." He rolled his eyes.

Once Phoenix decided that Kuaray could be left alone safely with the centipedes, he set out on his own mission across the field. He had been hoping to find Saint George's medal. *If the hole isn't there, maybe I didn't hit him, and he died of a heart attack.*

The brilliant sunlight accentuated in unsparing detail every clod and pebble on the mucky ground. His walk across it was a solemn one as he pondered how many Sun People's and Prairie Dogs' remains lay beneath his feet. He stopped to watch the smoke still rising from the trapdoor in noxious billows that hid much of the mountain peak in a shimmering brown haze. Occasional shifts in the wind revealed the outline of the Doomsday Machine near its summit.

Ethan and Luz, where'd they go? Why'd they do it in the first place? Phoenix stopped himself. *Whoa, save those questions for later.*

Phoenix found the medal with the incriminating hole about ten feet from where he'd watched Saint George fall. Swept along by the flowing rivulets, it had snagged on a tree root that protruded from the stones at the base of the ridge. Not his ridge. That was on the opposite side where he'd let the killer-shaft fly when he'd willed his fingers to release it. As miserable as he still felt, he had to admit that its trajectory across the entire valley and through the center of the medal rivaled Robin Hood's famous arrow-splitting.

By the time Phoenix returned, he found the centipedes already snoozing on either side of Kuaray. Apparently, the siren lullaby worked as well for them as it had for Petey.

Kuaray looked up. "Mission accomplished?"

Phoenix nodded, slumping to the ground. The chunky, oversized disk that had once broadcast to all the world that its wearer was first warrior of the realm lay heavy in his palm.

He debated whether to share his secret with Kuaray. After a fraught pause, he made up his mind. *Yes, I'll tell him because he can certainly relate to it. If ever a person has ugly stuff in his past, it would be Kuaray.*

Phoenix held up the evidence. "I shot Saint George right through his chest from across the whole valley. It was awful. I watched him drop. Corlion asked me to do it because he couldn't shoot with a broken arm."

Kuaray jerked up his head in surprise and then nodded. "You have no idea how hard it was to turn the peaceable Sun People into warriors. Yes, I told all of them to 'get the leader,' the one with the medal.

"Sorry it was you who did it. And you've been suffering ever since, right?"

Phoenix nodded, his head bowed.

"Well, kid, I hate to break it to you, but that sick feeling will never go away completely. You have to live with it."

Phoenix pursed his lips. He'd figured that out already. But soon he perked up when he heard a personal history issuing from Kuaray's mouth.

"God knows I have a ton of those feelings. Sometimes they make me want to ... to kill myself. Daddy Sequoyah, Yacy, Mama, Luz. The things I did to them ...."

Kuaray's voice changed, coming out low and resonant. "You're hearing this first, Phoenix, even before Lucy. I'm finally ready to let every single person know how sorry I am for the things I did. I'm planning to do something special for each one of them.

"But I'm smart enough to realize it won't make my sins disappear."

Phoenix could hardly believe what he was hearing. "How'd you come round to this?"

"That's what I was about to explain. I did a lot of thinking when I was living with the Sun People and going to Jimjamoree every chance I got.

"It was Sequoyah loving me even if I couldn't deal with it at the time, it was getting a second chance to live, it was Petey entering my life ... those are a few. Definitely the biggest was falling in love with Lucy and having her love me back. And then we found a cause worth fighting for."

Tears stood in Kuaray's eyes.

"Well, Kuaray, this is so new. I'm very glad." Phoenix beamed.

"Actually, Phoenix, I could use some help with one of my plans. Remember when I called you Plant-boy? I wasn't going to say anything just yet, but since the subject came up, do you want to hear about it?"

"Of course I do."

"It's hard for me to tell this, it's an emotional thing." Kuaray began building a pyramid out of pebbles, starting with a precise, three-sided base. "After I threw away the ashes of Daddy Sequoyah's father Mohe, I sat there by the Greyhound wondering if I could feel any worse."

He added a second layer of pebbles. "Then I spotted these strange things where the ashes were blowing around in the wind. They looked like propellers with two seeds in the middle. And I knew what they were."

Phoenix gasped. "Whirlybirds. Maple seeds. Shade tree seeds!"

Kuaray added a third layer to his structure. "Yes. I bet Mohe's nieces put them in with the ashes as back-up in case there weren't any shade trees in the new land."

"Then we must plant them around the bus where you threw away the ashes. There's the right amount of sunlight. How many did you find? Where are they now?"

Kuaray added the last stone to the top of his miniature structure. His answer was deadpan. "About fifteen, and they're in a safe place. The ground."

Phoenix looked impressed. "You planted them? They must be about a foot tall by now with some leaves on them."

"They are."

After the momentousness of the news, the two of them sat still, grinning from ear to ear and basking in the warmth of Kuaray's extraordinary deed.

But soon Phoenix's mind turned back to himself, and he fiddled nervously with the laces on his sandals. "So what can I do about my sin?"

"The answer's easy, and I think you know it already. Why else did you go chasing after that medal?"

"Give it to Queen Gitli?"

"Of course, Phoenix, good thinking. As awful as she is, she deserves to hear about Saint George from you alone. He was kind of an ass, but he was one of her husbands, after all."

***

"Since you're here, you might as well take a seat."

Once Queen Gitli had recovered from the shock of seeing Sequoyah walk briskly into her secret bunker with Agali and the unfamiliar Sanctissima at his heels, she was not inclined to be overly courteous.

"No thank you, Your Highness. Sentient furniture horrifies me, and I'm not planting my backside on a living rabbit. I choose the floor." Folding his long limbs, he sat cross-legged on the stone.

The translators collapsed into fits of unprofessional giggles and staccato barks—soon quashed by Queen Gitli's wrath. "Agali and Sanctissima, is it? I don't care how new you are to this business; you are to be 'heard and not seen' from now on. Understand?"

As they wilted visibly and took places standing on either side of her chair, she directed her remaining ire at Sequoyah. "Our top scientists worked for years to breed the rabbits into the present comfort design ... but suit yourself."

Sequoyah countered her anger by folding his arms and glaring from under his brows. "Have you been outside, lately?"

"No, I have not. That ingrate Tlke should have reported back two hours ago."

"Well, I'll report *for* her because she's busy picking up the pieces. The war is over. I saw the field."

"It's over? Already?" Queen Gitli rose from her chair, shaking. She asked in a small voice, "Who were the victors?"

"Nobody." Sequoyah paused to let his answer sink in. "And your prized cloning hospital is going up in flames as we speak."

"Nobody?"

Queen Gitli began pacing around the room as she unleashed a rant similar to the one that Tlke had heard earlier. "My grand design to reform Baffling Isle is what's going up in flames, sir—thanks to your son Kuaray turning traitor."

She put her nose close to Sequoyah's where he sat, and he twisted away. "I ask you, who decided to resuscitate him? Who arranged for his doctors and his nurses? Who saw to his rehabilitation by having the scientists clone that giant centipede?

"For that matter, who took on the responsibility for your own recovery, Sequoyah?"

She settled back in her chair. She was calmer now, even ingratiating. "Which brings us around to the rest of my plan … that is, I hope, *intact?* Did you finish writing the Shade People's epitaph, and are they no longer ... 'of this world?'"

It was Sequoyah's turn to lecture. He kept his response cool, yet he simmered with anger. "Well, Queen, you killed the Shade People very efficiently ... all by yourself. You starved them to death. You created a wartime famine when you dismantled the Polar Bear Express. That stopped the food deliveries. When you put together your army, you took away the doctors and nurses they needed to survive, and you deprived them of their cooks and chambermaids."

He shook his fist. "The Shade People had grown so damned dependent on you, they sat in their rooms waiting for the end. I saw them dead with my own eyes. All we saved were fifty-nine teenagers we picked up in the caverns on the way home. Right now they're living in the Polar Bear Express depot where it's dark enough to keep their tender skin from burning."

"By ye gods, I didn't mean to kill the Shade People." The queen shrank back, genuinely shaken.

But not for long. She hissed nastily, "I told those abacus-pushers at City Hall who figure out these things not to forget the provinces when they prepared for the war. What idiots. They know I can't keep track of everything.

"And exactly what am I supposed to do with those unfit orphans flopping in my depot?"

Before Sequoyah had a chance to say something about the responsibilities of good governance and caring for war refugees, the queen stood, putting on her haughtiest demeanor. "Let me inform you, Sequoyah, the Shade People were *not* to be pitied. They were tyrants who'd kept us enslaved for a million years. You know the commandments. I had a legacy in mind: to go down in history as the queen who liberated her own kind.

"But I stuck to my religion." She rolled her eyes heavenward to show her piety. "I didn't want to be the one responsible for killing them."

Sequoyah yelled in disgust, "Stop pretending to be devout, Queen. Tyrants? You knew you had the Shade People under your thumb as long as you kept them lazy and sick. You thought they were a pain in the ass, not your oppressors.

"Besides, you had no problem plotting the deaths of the entire population of Sun People, and they're human, too."

The queen sniffed, "You're wrong. The Shade People were aristocrats, and the Sun People were barbarians, hardly human. I consider that a big difference. And you should know I offered the Sun People an edict of reform that they turned down, thereby choosing their own fate."

"Sorry, Queen, you're lying to me ... if not to yourself." Sequoyah shook his head slowly from side to side to emphasize his point. "It was simple, really: you wanted their land."

Abruptly he shot to his full height, pointing a finger at her. He roared, "Be honest, for once. Your plan was so much bigger. What you really wanted down deep inside your little shriveled heart was to *finish off the human race.*

"Were we next?" he asked with an air of innocence.

Sequoyah's question hovered unanswered in the stale underground air as Queen Gitli squirmed.

"By God Rough and Goddess Violent, too, none of this had to happen. Sequoyah, it's all your fault for showing up on Baffling Isle in the first place."

"I knew you were about to say something like that." Sequoyah tried to laugh, but the result sounded leaden.

"How can you laugh, Sequoyah? I'll tell you something you should know about Goddess Mary Lynne's prophesy. For the last two centuries, the queens of the Prairie Dogs prayed that the prophecy wouldn't come true during their reigns. Just my bad luck it happened during mine."

"Why was our arrival so bad?" Sequoyah sank down to his cross-legged position slowly, sensing that the queen was finally ready to speak from her heart.

She, too, returned to her chair. "Because we monarchs knew you'd upset our world forever whether you meant to or not. I had to do something fast, or I'd be kissing the race of Prairie Dogs goodbye—maybe not soon, but someday.

"You showed up in your rattletrap, your families had no discipline, and your kids ... what horrors. You set a bad example and you started spreading disorder like it was a disease. And soon the Sun People, who absolutely worshiped you, got bold enough to tear up my Sacred Meadow. My flatheads took to running away until I had no supports for my dining tables. Even my bobcats were misbehaving. And I don't know what got into Tlke. She'd be so helpful and then she'd burst into Prairie Dog tears. It was unfathomable.

"After all of you started murdering each other and I got you, the head of the household, to the opposite end of Baffling Isle to recover, I decided to use not only you but everybody who was left behind to further my agenda. I came close, very close to succeeding. Except ... except none of you would bend to my will. Down deep I knew all along you'd go your own ways."

"How'd you know that, Queen?"

"Because unlike us Prairie Dogs and conquered humans like the Shade People, you are *yourselves*."

Sequoyah wanted to take Queen Gitli's paw, but he knew better. "My dear Queen Gitli, do you want to know what's so sad about this? I really like you. We could've worked together for everyone's betterment. I had a great plan to help the Shade People shake off their dependence and leave the caverns. If you'd gotten to know the Sun People, you would've realized they weren't barbarians, but the nicest, most gentle of human beings.

"Of course you'd have to treat your own Prairie Dog workers better. As they are now, they might as well be your slaves. And that breeding and cloning of your animals would have to stop if there's anything left of the hospital. And the drugging and enslaving is disgraceful."

"You should hear yourself, Sequoyah, remaking my kingdom—"

"None of it matters anymore, Queen. Your kingdom's already remade. Messily like my families, but remade, forever."

***

Phoenix tiptoed through the open door—two steps forward, one step back—broadcasting his reluctance to be there at all. "I-I'm sorry, but no one was in the palace so I just, I just kind of walked in and kept going down and down. I have a message for you, Queen Gitli. It's bad news."

She glared at him, paws on hips. "Young man, is my private bunker suddenly a sieve?"

"N-no, I—"

"Go on, go on, don't stammer. Spit it out. What's that big round thing in your hand?"

Phoenix knelt before her and gently laid the medal on her opened paws. "It's Saint George's, ma'am. I brought it from the field.

"Your Highness, I was the one who ki—"

She interrupted, "So my husband is dead?" She held the medal up to the bat globe to inspect the hole. "I see he went bravely, shot through the chest and not running away as I would've expected."

Phoenix and Sequoyah had never seen her when she wasn't putting on a show and for a fleeting moment, her features softened. She brought the medal to her lips and closed her eyes. "He was such an ass, totally unsuited to be a warrior. But I loved him best because he didn't smell of cooking oil like Neshek or marijuana like Captain Kirk."

The queen rose shakily to her feet, creaking in every joint. "Oh, mercy, the dumbest thing we Prairie Dogs ever did was train ourselves to walk upright to emulate humans.

"Sequoyah, would you be so kind as to help an old lady up the stairs and to her bedroom? I'm very tired."

***

Early next morning when Neshek rose from the conjugal bed to make breakfast for the patients, doctors, and nurses at the infirmary, he found his queen dead. She had slipped away so quietly in the night that he hadn't been aware of it. Captain Kirk wasn't there. As happened at least half the time, he'd stayed in his sanctum experiencing holy visions with his acolytes.

Three doctors, including Anichka, were summoned. They concluded the monarch had died of old age. Queen Gitli herself, along with everyone else, had lost count of the years. She'd guessed seventy, but others suggested at least seventy-five.

That afternoon, according to custom, the entire population of the town met in the public square to vote by a show of paws for the next queen. Tlke—young, capable, and a virgin—was chosen unanimously.

Because of the tragic loss of almost an entire generation of youthful pups in the war, the newly appointed monarch decided against holding a public funeral for the departed.

Queen Gitli was cremated in a secret location with Captain Kirk and Neshek in attendance. Afterwards, the two remaining husbands put Saint George's medal on top of her ashes and nailed shut the lid of the pretty wooden box. It was fit for a queen, inlaid with colorful river stones that had been polished to a high sheen by raging springtime waters. Honoring the tradition of ages past, they placed it inside one of the cairns at the entrance to the Sacred Meadow.

Phoenix was never sure if Queen Gitli had understood that he'd killed Saint George. He hoped not, because if she had, he might have been responsible for hastening her death.

43 ~ One Year Later

It's called renewal. **—Sequoyah**

"Shh." Svnoyi held a finger to her lips. "Even out here we have to keep our voices down because every little sound bounces off the cliffs."

Laughing softly, she asked, "So it's 'girls' night out,' and what would we all like to do?"

It was four in the morning. Svnoyi, Yacy, and Lucy had planned a last rendezvous because this was the day when the clan would break up. Leaving their fiancés asleep in the caves, they'd dressed and taken the switchbacks down to the beach.

Lucy whispered, "Let's go look at the Sacred Meadow. Phoenix wouldn't let anyone in till he finished it, not even Corlinia.

"I hope there isn't some kind of taboo about us peeking before Queen Tlke has us say our 'I do's.'"

She added a bit louder, eyes sparkling, "Four couples marrying at noon! It'll be a wedding-day assembly line."

"Let's go see it," Svnoyi and Yacy said at the same time.

They took the overland trail. When they reached the cairns, the three linked arms with Svnoyi standing in the middle because she was tallest. They stared for a good five minutes at the transformed valley, tinted pink by the night sun.

Svnoyi voiced what all of them were thinking. "Phoenix said a year ago that Queen Tlke wanted 'calm simplicity.' That's certainly what she got."

"Well, I like it a lot," Yacy ventured, hoping the others felt the same way.

Lucy agreed, "Me too. What a difference."

Side by side, they tiptoed reverently along a broad brick walk that wound in gentle curves through the center of the valley. A young cedar marking Petey's grave sprouted from a blanket of flower-sprinkled grass, and a dozen pebbled pathways lined with low junipers branched off the main walk. At the other end, banks of blossoms in blue and yellow grew on either side of the fountain's flagstones. The only reminder that almost the entire army of Sun People and a generation of adolescent pups had died was a line of fir trees on either side of the valley with bushes of white roses flowering between them. Presently, the saplings, which looked like two-foot Christmas trees, were almost buried in the blooms, although they would undoubtedly soar to lofty heights someday.

But when Lucy saw that Phoenix had decided to leave the Doomsday Weapon as a bitter memorial on its perch near the top of the mountain, she let out a sharp cry. She fell to her knees on the bricks, cupping her face in her hands. Its presence sent a stab right through her gut, and she rocked from side to side in her grief.

I'm so glad Queen Gitli's dead. I'll never stop hating her for the way she manipulated my poor sick mother and my gullible father—even if she didn't ask them to set the thing off.

My daddy wasn't ever the same after she took Luz away from him. He tried, but he gave up caring for little Lucian, and ... and it's like his inventions ate him up. I knew Mama wasn't okay mentally when I heard her through the door singing that ugly "Air Force Song." Then the queen put the two of them together ....

Lucy lay flat on her face and stretched out her arms like a crucified saint. *How I miss you, darling Mama Luz. And I miss you, too, dear Daddy. But why didn't you say to Mama, "No, no! I* won't *build it."*

And to think you died in the flames you caused. Sometimes it's more than I can bear.

"Lucy, Lucy! What can we do?" Svnoyi and Yacy knelt on either side of her.

Lucy sprang up. "Nothing, nothing. Just try to remember how wonderful my parents were ... before."

They walked on in silence, their arms around Lucy's shoulders.

After the friends had studied the fountain, they wondered if it was too bland. Where a whirlpool had once roared in the circular basin, the tamest of wavelets made little slaps against its inner wall. Soon they changed their minds, gawking in admiration. The low sun bouncing off the rose quartz of the floor sent hot pink rays upward to snake and glint beneath the surface.

Svnoyi remarked, "It's so pretty. I doubt that a god actually built this, but you never know. If he did, this must've been exactly what he intended, and not a whirlpool."

"Yes," said Yacy. "Phoenix was some kind of genius to leave it alone." The most mystical of the three, she would never express her musings aloud. *God Rough built the fountain around the fossilized remains of his wife, Goddess Cinder, to say he was sorry. No quartz can reflect a low sun like that. I believe it's Goddess Cinder's spirit saying, "I forgive you, God Rough."*

Then they ran appreciative fingers over the raised oval river stones on the fountain's ledge that looked like candy-coated almonds, good enough to eat. As delicious as they appeared, they made the ledge too bumpy to serve as a bench. Instead, the three sat down in front of one of the fragrant flower beds next to the fountain's flagstones. Planting it with big daisies and lupines in yellow and blue, Phoenix had nurtured the display to hothouse perfection.

Lucy tried hard to renew her cheerfulness for their last few hours together. She pointed her finger to a spot in front of them and remarked whimsically, "Y'know, it was about there that Kuaray made his first romantic move, and I didn't even realize it till later. I was taking a snooze, lying on the bumpy ground, and he woke me up by tickling my nose with a little white daisy on a long stem."

Svnoyi giggled. "Mine and Corlion's happened in the Pippin forest, but it's too weird to explain."

Yacy said nothing about her first realization because at the time, Oscar had been very close to Svnoyi—engaged almost.

"Please tell us about your boat journey, Yacy." Svnoyi asked carefully because the list of travelers had been a point of contention for weeks. "You're leaving so soon, after the wedding if the wind's right. It's all been so hush-hush—"

"The boat's beautiful, isn't it?" Lucy interrupted because she couldn't resist bringing up Kuaray every chance she got. "Kuaray designed it from the plans on Daddy's desk, but he adjusted them to make it much, much bigger. He supervised building it and said it was a gift to make up for a lot of awful things he did to you, Yacy."

"It's an awesome gift, really." Yacy wondered if any gift from her twin could make up for his monstrous behavior, although she didn't say so. She remembered her revelation at the fountain about Goddess Cinder's softened heart toward God Rough, but no, she wasn't quite ready to forgive Kuaray.

After hesitating a moment, she squeezed Lucy's hand. Then she blurted, "Please tell Kuaray this because it's important. Someday Arielle Luz will know he's her father. I'll explain it to her when the time's right.

"And the same goes for your little baby brother, Lucian. When he's old enough, I'll tell him the truth about his Mama Luz and Daddy Ethan."

After that, Yacy smiled, relieved she'd shared her soul-searching at last. "The rest's easy. We'll be eight people, Jaroslav's the leader like he's always wanted to be, and Anichka's going, too, of course. Agali will be coming with Alexej because they're joined at the hip. That was a hard choice for my parents because she'll be leaving them, and she's barely seven. Lucian, Arielle Luz, Oscar and me—that's the rest of us.

"We're heading for a place across the strait that was called Canada once upon a time, but now it's a brand-new continent—huge, mysterious, full of secrets. Oscar's named it the 'Land of Whispering Spirits.' Spooky, right?"

Lucy stood then and looked toward the cairns where the sun was beginning to climb above the pines beyond the valley. "We should go. Our next appointment's a big breakfast on the beach with absolutely everybody and then a walk to the knoll where the Greyhound landed."

She jumped up and down like an excited child. "Kuaray's presenting the maple saplings, his big gift to Sequoyah, and everyone else except him knows about it already. I wish we had a camera because I'd like to save Sequoyah's reaction for posterity."

Svnoyi, who knew her daddy best, whispered to Yacy, "Poor guy. He's not that keen on surprises."

They left the valley with arms linked, Svnoyi in the middle once more. She turned to Lucy. "Now we know Yacy's plans, and Phoenix and I will be living with our mates at the Pippin village, obviously. But Lucy, you never said where you two will be going."

"Well," Lucy replied, putting on her best story-telling air. "When Queen Tlke was still a lowly courtier, I told her a whopping lie. She asked me where Kuaray had gone the night he turned traitor. I said he'd taken off to ride Petey down the coast to listen to the surf and meditate. At the time I thought it was hilarious—so unlike him."

Lucy looked like she was close to bursting. "But that's exactly what we're going to do. We're taking Petra and Petunia. We'll ride and ride. Then we'll listen to the surf and meditate. We'll come back, of course, but not till we feel like it."

***

After breakfast, the four couples returned to the caves to put on their wedding clothes. Corlion and Svnoyi, and Phoenix and Corlinia, donned their Jimjamoree costumes, the creamy leather dresses, pants and capes covered with patterns. Corlinia had stitched for her and Phoenix's five-month-old girl a first ceremonial dress. With infinite care while Phoenix was busy at the meadow, she'd tooled and dyed a row of red-brown pinecones around the hem, the Sun People's symbol for new life.

In the evenings after Arielle Luz and Lucian were in bed, Yacy had transformed one of the last unused linen sheets from the Time Before into identical dresses for Lucy and herself. Hand stitching was slow, and she'd run out of time to make shirts for Oscar and Kuaray. They'd fended for themselves nicely, and with minimal effort, they'd managed to look quite presentable in their jeans fading to white, and clean, pressed work shirts.

The procession of nineteen people, Sanctissima, and the two centipedes, winding up the hillside to the knoll where the Greyhound bus lay partially disassembled, did not go unobserved. The four bears and the bobcats came to offer the families affectionate send-offs that would be impossible during the flurry at the wedding and the boat's departure. Standing at the bottom of the hill, the bobcats clapped their front paws together and the bears shuffled their feet.

"Goodbye, goodbye, we love you," the family members cried out, even though half of them would still be seeing these friends now and then.

The animals had changed their destinies for the better. The bobcats had jobs they liked at the Prairie Dog Infirmary. Arbel and Arbeline hauled carts less often because they were in charge of personnel at the Polar Bear Express, and Ernie and Bertha had a similar position at the Flathead Express.

***

Sequoyah already knew about the maples. Svnoyi had taken pity on him because of his dislike of surprises and had tipped him off during breakfast. Even with the advance warning, he wasn't prepared for his own feelings when he first saw them, and his eyes filled with tears. Fifteen saplings, spread wide apart across the knoll to give plenty of room for future growth, stood three feet tall. With every breath of wind, their glossy-green, five-lobed leaves rustled, lifting high.

"The sound of wind through tree leaves is called 'psithurism,'" Phoenix announced, breaking the spell of rapt silence the others were enjoying.

"Know-it-all," hissed Svnoyi, and everyone laughed good-naturedly.

Sequoyah gestured to Kuaray. He rode to his father's side and slipped off Petunia to sit beside him on the ground. Both of them threw their arms about each other. They were close to weeping and at first, a jumble of inchoate babbling was the best they could do.

At last, Kuaray managed a sentence. "Oh, Dad, how could I have thrown them away? I guess I figured you loved Mohe's ashes more than me."

Sequoyah nodded. "And so I did love them more. I've been quite a terrible father, you know. Mohe was a great dad, but it took me almost thirty years to find him."

"Now you and me, we are—"

"Yes, we are."

The others turned away to give the father and son privacy. They knelt to brush aside sticks and pinecones and settled themselves in a rough half-circle. They had a plan in mind: they were preparing the stage for the speech they knew Sequoyah would offer to his scattering clan. None of them had ever resented his musings. On the contrary, they loved to hear his counsel, even if they hadn't always understood the meaning that lay beneath his poetic delivery.

Two of the wedding couples—Svnoyi and Corlion, and Phoenix and Corlinia with their baby—sat companionably close, as graceful as egrets in their pale finery. Yacy chose to cuddle beside her mother, perhaps for the last time. Aleta swept her arms around her eldest daughter, marveling that the rebellious girl had become such a sympathetic and caring young woman. Both kept an eye on the children, a few yards away. Aleta and Sequoyah's twins Xavier and Scarlett, who weren't walking yet, sat spellbound. They were learning something new as they watched Arielle Luz and Lucian peaceably stack up a pile of sticks and top it with an owl feather.

To accommodate the centipedes' extraordinary length and unpleasant odor of bitter almonds and iodine, Lucy sat a short distance from the others, holding Petra's harness while Kuaray wound up his heart-to-heart with Sequoyah. She was thankful that both arthropod steeds had taken well to training. Her leg's deep wound had healed quickly enough, but it gave her trouble when she walked too much—as she'd already done by mid-morning. Twitching nerves that felt like an invasion of fire ants reminded her when it was time to get off her feet.

Oscar, Jaroslav, and Anichka huddled together, whispering about the boat sailing in a mere three hours. As much as they wanted to fully enjoy this earlier portion of the day, their minds were also on the bundles, bags, and Yacy's exquisitely fashioned baskets compactly stored in the cabin's hold. Had anything been left out? Agali and Alexej were too excited to sit beside them for long, even with Sanctissima damping their joy by clinging to Agali's overalls.

The ebullient girl tried to comfort the little Prairie Dog as best she knew how. *Don't fret, your life is great now! You are* so *lucky, you're first courtier to the queen just like Tlke was to Queen Gitli. The difference is, Queen Tlke's really, really nice.*

She gave Sanctissima a last hug and a little push. *Go now, Tissi. You promised Queen Tlke you'd help her set up for the wedding ceremony.*

***

Kuaray settled himself beside Lucy, and Sequoyah sank down cross-legged in front of his clan. The spot he chose was so close to a maple sapling that its second-year foliage brushed his shoulder. He smiled at everyone and cleared his throat. Reaching for a leaf, he didn't break it off but absent-mindedly caressed it, outlining the veins with a forefinger. He started in, his voice sure, because he *did* love to talk.

He lowered his eyes, looking like a guru in his near-lotus position. "These trees took root here very recently, just as we did. Unlike the evergreens, the maples' leaves drop off every autumn, falling to the ground. And new leaves start fresh when winter is past. It's called renewal. In the same way, the clan is changing its raiment; we were always meant to part ways, to disperse like seeds in the wind. After today, all our lives will be different, reinvented, like a new crown of spring leaves for each of us."

Sequoyah's contemplative delivery changed to a grating whisper, and he released the leaf, letting it spring back into place within the cluster. "Sometimes ... sometimes a tree doesn't make it. Why? I don't know, something awful and unexpected happens to it, maybe a canker eats around its trunk, and .... Well, it dies. Ethan and Luz—dammit all, they weren't trees! They were our best friends, parents to Oscar, Lucy, and little Lucian, they were part of our clan." He stopped momentarily, too overcome to speak.

"But they did what they did, even if Queen Gitli pushed them into it. After a million years, the Shade and Sun People's weakened bodies are a living testament to the damage wrought by the Day of the Jumping Sun. Ethan and Luz gave us a preview of the next Jumping Sun. I know the Doomsday Weapon is still up there on the mountain, and the sight of it is sure to make us cry. Perhaps it will also make us remember before we're tempted to build another one more powerful, and another, and another."

Sequoyah stood, then, staying close to the tree that he'd already decided to name for his father: Mohe's Shade Tree. He ran his hands over its crown, ruffling the top leaves. "Alien species, what are they? These fifteen maple trees are aliens, even this little guy. I certainly hope when they reach maturity, they'll send their seeds beyond this hilltop slowly and beneficially."

His piercing eyes alerted his audience so they wouldn't forget his next words. "And so are *we* aliens. We weren't thinking about it when we stepped through those bus doors," and he gestured toward the Greyhound's hulk. "Even so, we carried within ourselves the worst our species has to offer, along with the best.

"We brought our humanity: our intelligence, kindness, love, our good intentions. But we also brought our worst instinct: to overpower, to conquer. All living things have it. Phoenix can tell you, even plants have their ways, and the natural world is one big battlefield. But we humans don't quite fit in. We were given huge, diabolically cunning brains coupled with puny consciences.

"And pity the lockstep Prairie Dogs, who knelt, absorbent as sponges, at the feet of their human masters a million years ago."

Sequoyah gestured toward the vista beyond the knoll. "Did our little clan arrive and then ruin a pristine place? Well, it was hardly pristine. This world was ripe to fall. What we did is serve as catalysts, and I believe most of us worked hard to preserve its best parts. It's an object lesson, really. As soon as genocide, exclusiveness, and slavery masquerade as religious and moral principles, that world is in big trouble. We would hope that Baffling Isle is better off now than when we found it, and that under a new queen it will reach a fruitful plateau before the next cataclysm."

He began to thread his way among the families, bending to touch a head here, a shoulder there. "My dearest loved ones, you've been blessed with such extraordinary gifts to convey a message, *do* teach your children and your children's children this: We must never forget the potency of our worst instinct. It's a human curse that will always be with us.

How do we stop ourselves from unleashing our compulsion to conquer? We must learn a new trick that's as old as wisdom, itself.

We must put our humanity first and leave our brutality behind. And this holds true for how we treat ourselves, each other, everyone and everything we meet whether human or non-human, and our Mother Earth.

"Never forget what I said to Earth, the Queen of us all, at this very spot. 'I shall never own you, and I shall never knowingly hurt you.'"

Sequoyah stopped his pacing to sit beside Aleta, reaching forward to lift Scarlett and Xavier onto his lap. "Go out into the world as you were always meant to do. Aleta and I have our babies to raise and the Shade Children to nurture as Laz-Merlin would've wanted. When they're ready to take care of themselves and the twins are old enough, perhaps we'll sail across the strait. We'll always keep the caves ready whenever any of you come to us. And I know your hearths will be warm if we happen by."

Surrounded by the hugging families, Sequoyah dropped his forehead onto Aleta's shoulder. He whispered, "Darling, how can we bear this, the saddest and happiest day of our lives?"

She wrapped him in her arms and pulled him close.

About the Author

Day of the Jumping Sun is a stand-alone tale meant to be enjoyed with or without my previous novel, *The Last Shade Tree*. That epic adventure took the three families from the twentieth century to their troubled start on Baffin Island a million years later. And there I had left them in a perilous land in the midst of their life journeys.

My life's journey began in the rolling live oak-dotted hills of Northern California before it became Silicon Valley. Eventually, I settled permanently with my husband and two children in New York City. I am retired now, but while employed at New York University, I founded and directed the accomplished performing group, The Teares of the Muses, a consort of viols.

I dedicate *Day of the Jumping Sun* to my father, Wolfgang Panofsky, a nuclear physicist who advised the world about arms control. Inclined towards facts and figures, he would never have read a post-apocalyptic novel about the consequences of nuclear war. Nonetheless, I continue his story, adding human faces to one possible scenario. To quote Sequoyah, the hero of my two novels, "Wars are never good for anyone."

I also dedicate the novel to my mother, Adele Panofsky, an expert in natural history. At ninety-eight, she still lives in the same house where I grew up with my parents and four siblings. She spent years completing a skeletal display of a paleoparadoxia—a hippopotamus-sized Miocene marine mammal—from casts of the original bones. I soaked up a quantity of information from her and still can't claim much expertise about flora and fauna. But I can spot an ecological disaster in the making on this beautiful, threatened planet of ours.

dayofthejumpingsun.com
mpanofskyauthor.com

ALL THINGS THAT MATTER PRESS

FOR MORE INFORMATION ON TITLES AVAILABLE FROM
ALL THINGS THAT MATTER PRESS, GO TO
http://allthingsthatmatterpress.com
or contact us at
allthingsthatmatterpress@gmail.com

If you enjoyed this book, please post a review on Amazon.com and your favorite social media sites.
Thank you!